KT-421-925

LOUISE VOSS AND MARK EDWARDS

Forward Slash

HARPER

This novel is entirely a work of fiction.
The names, characters and incidents portrayed in it are
the work of the author's imagination. Any resemblance to
actual persons, living or dead, events or localities is
entirely coincidental.

Harper
An imprint of HarperCollins*Publishers*
77–85 Fulham Palace Road,
Hammersmith, London W6 8JB

www.harpercollins.co.uk

A Paperback Original 2013
1

Copyright © Mark Edwards and Louise Voss 2013

Mark Edwards and Louise Voss assert the moral right to
be identified as the author of this work

A catalogue record for this book
is available from the British Library

ISBN: 978-0-00-746074-8

Set i

London Borough of Southwark		
B		
SK 2355492 4		
Askews & Holts	23-Jul-2013	
AF FIC	£7.99	

A
re
i
ph

Thi
by
oth
in a
is p
c

FSC
www.fsc.org

Paper from
responsible sources
FSC™ C007454

FSC™ is a non-profit international organisation established to promote
the responsible management of the world's forests. Products carrying the
FSC label are independently certified to assure consumers that they come
from forests that are managed to meet the social, economic and
ecological needs of present and future generations,
and other controlled sources.

Find out more about HarperCollins and the environment at
www.harpercollins.co.uk/green

Acknowledgements

Thanks to Dr Terence Bartlett and Dr Wera Schmerer at the University of Wolverhampton for help with forensics and the tour of their excellent CSI suite; and to Nik Waites and the mysterious 'Detective Nick' for answering all those annoying questions about police work.

Several characters in this book were named after real people who volunteered their services via a number of online competitions, including Bob Clewley and Melinda Moore. Thanks to Carmel Adams for putting forward her late husband's name, Declan Adams, and letting us use it.

For being a great editor, thanks to Kate Bradley, who helped make this book better, and love and gratitude to Sara Baugh for her excellent suggestions. Thanks too to Sam Copeland for keeping the faith and Hannah Gamon for all her support and efforts.

Finally, the biggest thanks of all go to all those lovely people on Facebook and Twitter who make it all worthwhile. Thanks for all your comments, likes, shares and retweets. This book is for you.

For Margaret Cutting and
Veronika Jackson

Prologue

Him

She looked nothing like her profile picture. I mean, it was definitely the same woman but in the flesh she was seven or eight years older, her hair duller, skin pale and wrinkly, with saggy bags under her eyes, bags in which she appeared to be carrying half the world's woes. When I saw her and realized this was Karen, my date, I almost fled. She so clearly wasn't The One that there was no point even talking to her. But she had already seen me. Because, although I may be dishonest about everything else, including my name, on my dating profiles, I look as good in the flesh as I do on the screen.

'I thought you were blonde,' I said, after enduring a preliminary round of chitchat.

She pinkened. 'Yes, I know, that photo is a couple of years old.'

And the rest.

'I prefer to go natural now.'

She had ordered pasta with cheese sauce. As she talked, I could see strings of yellow saliva threaded in her mouth, making my own food inedible. She kept asking me stupid questions about my made-up job. She thought I was a professor of sociology, a subject in which she had a GCSE. She looked at me through her lashes as she went on, putting on that ridiculous sub-Diana coyness that many women believe drives men crazy but just makes me mad.

'You're a nurse,' I said.

She nodded and shovelled more pasta into her cakehole. No wonder she was overweight. She had put on at least a stone since the sunny holiday photo she'd posted on the dating website. This was the big problem with Internet dating. You couldn't trust anyone.

'Any interesting accidents at the hospital recently?' I asked.

'Accidents?'

'Yes. Like, I don't know, I was reading about a woman who fell out of a window and was impaled on railings.'

Her eyes widened. 'Nothing like that, no. Just people bitten by dogs and chopping their fingers off when they're cooking.'

I yawned.

'Am I boring you?' she said, putting down her fork.

'Yes.'

'Oh.'

I leaned closer so the diners around us wouldn't hear and beckoned for her to come closer, giving me a better view of her jowls.

'Not only are you boring me, but you disgust me. You eat like a pig and you're not so much "mutton dressed as lamb" as "tripe dressed as mutton".'

Her expression made the date worthwhile. For a second I thought she was going to slap me, which would have made the evening lead to more interesting places, but instead she burst into tears.

2

'You're the pig,' she said, voice wobbling. She'll probably make a complaint about me to the site, but who cares? It's a rubbish site and I'm removing my profile later anyway, if this is typical of the calibre of women on it. Plenty more to choose from.

I pushed the tip of my nose to form a snout.

Karen stood up and, after groping around in her brain for a few seconds to find an adequate word, spat, 'Bastard!' at me. Pathetic.

I watched her go. She will never know what a lucky escape she had.

After Karen had stormed off into the night, I felt coiled and dissatisfied. My blood itched in my veins. Not wanting to go home, I headed to the bar next door to the restaurant. It was a cool place, all blue lights and shadowy corners, but crowded. That suited me. Nobody would notice me standing alone, watching.

I paid for a bottle of beer and stood against a pillar, phone in hand, and tapped to open the Girls Near Me app. The app works just like Google Maps or the GPS in your car. Geo-location, they call it. After a few seconds it found my location on the South Bank.

Then came the clever part, the feature that makes Girls Near Me such a handy tool. It showed me women who were also in the area by scanning the Facebook, Twitter and Foursquare profiles of women who had 'checked in' using their phones to let those and other social networks know they were in the area. Very soon, I was looking at a list of women who had checked in within a hundred yards of where I stood. There were two, in fact, in this very bar. Tara and Charlotte.

A glance told me Tara wasn't right. Too ugly. Wrong hair

colour. Nothing like The One. But Charlotte looked very promising indeed. Long, honey-coloured hair, gorgeous eyes, pretty smile. I clicked on her name and was shown links to her Twitter profile and Facebook page.

I glanced around the bar but couldn't see her. No matter. According to her Twitter feed she was still in the bar – she had tweeted just five minutes ago about how she and her friend Lucy were drinking cocktails here. I clicked through to her Facebook page for a look through her photos. Jackpot. She hadn't protected them and there were two dozen pictures of her on holiday on the beach, in a bikini. Great little body. Skinny, boobs not too big and, most importantly, not fake. I can't bear breast implants. I messed up once and took home a girl with implants. I had to cut them out.

I went back and had a proper look through her tweets, discovering that she went to see Foo Fighters in concert the day before and loved it, but on the way home some woman trod on her foot on the Tube. Lucy also tweeted that she needed to lose weight, that she was sick of her job at Topshop, that she was going to a school reunion soon in Wimbledon. She usually drank white wine spritzers and she had an ancient Siamese cat called Milky.

She also tweeted that she was sick of guys her age and wanted her next boyfriend to be someone older, more sophisticated, more grown-up.

I love technology.

I nudged my way through the crowd, looking for Charlotte. This was where the density of the crowd became irritating. I spilled some shaven-haired moron's drink accidentally and he started grunting at me so I pressed a tenner into his fat hand to shut him up. But then, as I emerged from a thick knot of bodies, I saw her.

4

She was sitting on a tall chair by the bar with a girl with curly dark hair. Lucy. Lucy was a serious problem for me, and I directed spears of hatred towards her back. The two of them were huddled together, drinking Sea Breezes, their shoulders shaking with laughter. Best mates, according to Twitter. She would remember me, be able to describe me.

I clenched my fists. There were things I could do to the friend. I could take them both, but that would cause complications, make everything more liable to get messy. I could slip something into her drink, render her sick or unconscious, but the chances were that Charlotte would feel the need to help her get home, and my prey would slip away. Fuck. I might have to accept that Charlotte was a no-go, that fate was telling me she wasn't right.

Still, no harm in watching the beautiful creature as she drank and chatted and ran her hand through her hair. I nursed my drink and reminisced about a more fortunate encounter, a lone girl I'd met, with the help of my app, in a bar in Soho. After reading up on her interests – scuba diving, *Mad Men*, reality TV – I had gone up to her and started laying on the charm.

Her name was Jennifer. Jenny. Call me Jen, she had said. I bought her a few drinks then asked her back to my place. That's one of my rules: never go back to theirs. At my place, I can control everything. Plus, there I have all my props. All my tools.

Call-me-Jen had hesitated for a moment – just a moment – then accepted my invitation.

I was so excited all the way home. Rather overexcited, in fact. I wasn't careful enough. I think it's because I've been feeling frustrated recently. I've been searching for so long now. My patience is running thin, and Jen bore the brunt of that frustration, my loss of control. It was messy. I used my best set of knives. Very expensive and very sharp.

I can picture her now, lying back on the bed, quite drunk. Irritatingly drunk. Her eyes were rolling and she had a sheen of sweat on her body. There were pink marks on her skin where her underwear was too tight. I knew the instant I saw her body I'd made a mistake, that yet again this was the wrong girl. I had to eliminate her.

There was so much blood. I must have hit an artery or something. It was everywhere. Even my hair was soaked with it. I suppose I was in something of a frenzy.

She screamed like crazy. It was incredibly annoying. When I stuck the knife in her mouth she made this horrible gagging sound and spat blood all over my face. She didn't last long after that. I slashed her throat. She was already dead when I made love to her. It took her a little while to go so cold that I couldn't bear to touch her any more. It's called the *algor mortis* phase – did you know that? The death chill.

I reminisced about all of this as I watched Charlotte; I was churning with frustration and thinking that I was going to have to go to some sleazy pick-up joint, or find some cheap prostitute, a woman no one would miss. But then a stroke of luck, or *kismet*. I had noticed, absentmindedly, that Lucy kept looking at her watch. Now she stood up and slipped on her jacket. Charlotte flapped a slender hand at her drink. Lucy left – leaving Charlotte alone.

An hour later, after employing the methods I had learned from studying the techniques of the world's most successful pick-up artists, Charlotte was sitting beside me in my car, heading back to mine. She was sozzled, to an almost irritating degree, but her eyes blazed with lust and she squirmed against my hand as it rested on her thigh between gear changes. She was 23, younger than I usually like them, but she had the look, the attitude, the vivacity. Exactly the right bust size and the perfect colour and length of hair. Her eyes were the most beautiful thing about her. They sparkled like a tropical sea. She had the fresh, open demeanour and easy smile of a girl who had never been through bad shit, whose greatest tragedy had been the death of a decrepit grandparent, who had never suffered or felt pain.

Those are the girls who excite me the most.

As soon as we got inside, she tried to kiss me. A bit forward, but she was young and excited so I could let that go, though others have paid the price for being so sluttish. I sat her down and started asking her about herself, mentally noting her answers, all of which pleased me, enjoying the way she smiled through it. There was that thrumming in my blood. *Could* she be The One? There was one final test.

I led her through into my special room. Of course, looking back now, I realize it was too soon. She wasn't ready. She hadn't been prepared. Her mouth dropped open and she stared at me, then around her, then back at me. And she giggled.

'What the fuck?' she said.

'Do you like it?'

'Are you all right? You look . . . strange.'

'I'm great, Charlotte. Are you?'

'I think I want to go home.'

I shook my head emphatically, before ducking through the doorway and bringing out the item I wanted her to wear.

'Put this on,' I said.

She goggled at it. 'You're joking. Right? Oh, my days.'

And I realized with a cold shudder that she was not the woman I was looking for. I gritted my teeth, felt my jaw muscles expand and contract. Again. I had wasted my time again. Why can't any of these stupid sluts be the woman I want them to be? What is wrong with them all?

As I pictured myself ripping her throat out with my teeth, she continued to look around the room. She had gone very pale. Then her eye fell upon an object that made her stagger, as if she were about to faint.

'What . . . is that?' she said, her voice trembling.

'Oh, that? I must have forgotten to put it away. I was playing with it earlier.'

The look of utter horror in her eyes was delicious – I would get something from tonight after all, especially when she realized that, while she was staring at my plaything, I had taken a knife from the sideboard. When Charlotte saw it she started screaming, ran to the door, tried to yank it open before realizing it was locked. I walked over to her, holding up the knife. She scrambled in her pocket for her phone. Her hand was shaking so much she could barely get it out of her pocket. I smelled something unpleasant and looked down. Liquid ran down the inside of her leg. She had pissed herself. Finally, she produced the phone.

'There's no signal in here,' I said and stepped towards her.

She swung the phone at my head. It was one of those huge beasts, a Samsung, and because I wasn't expecting this, I failed to block the attack. The phone connected with my head, just above my eyebrow, sending me staggering. It really hurt.

'You little bitch,' I spat. I could feel blood trickling

down towards my left eye. I was so stunned that I didn't anticipate the kick, which missed my erection by an inch, sending me staggering backwards. Charlotte lunged for the knife, but as she did I recovered my wits. A flaming ball of anger whooshed through me and, as her hand reached for the knife, I sliced it, the skin of her palm gaping open and blood gushing, making a terrible mess that I was going to have to clear up later. That made me even more furious. As she clutched her bleeding hand I punched her in the face, twice, knocking her to the floor.

I fell on top of her, straddling her and holding her throat with one hand, pointing the knife between her eyes with the other.

'Please,' she begged, her voice rasping, barely able to escape from her squeezed throat. 'Please . . . my mum . . .'

I banged her head against the floor until she passed out.

I carried her through to the bedroom and stripped her, bagging her clothes for disposal later. Her body really was something special. It was such a shame. I handcuffed her to the bed and gagged her, then waited for her to wake up. I needed to get some information out of her before she died.

I was furious with myself. The whole night had been a disaster. I had acted impetuously and dangerously. Looking at it rationally, I could see it was a result of my growing frustration. I needed to be more careful, plan things better. I had let things slip.

I took out my anger on Charlotte. Made her suffer more, stay alive longer, than I would normally. So in the end, I suppose the day wasn't a total waste. It provided me with a sharp reminder that I needed to raise my game, and provided me with a couple of hours of pleasure at the end.

I also got a pair of new souvenirs to add to my collection. Those beautiful eyes.

Before going to bed, I checked my emails and had a pleasant surprise. A little fish I had my eye on had nibbled at the bait.

The One may be closer than I thought.

1

Amy

Amy did not notice her sister's email straight away. As
the Mail program, loaded she was idly listening to the
soft *drip-drip* of coffee through the filter in her mug, and
trying to organize her thoughts into a prioritized list for
the day ahead. No matter that it was a Sunday – being
this busy meant that having the weekend off wasn't an
option.

It was going to be a scorching hot day again. Seven
thirty a.m. was the best time to be out in the tiny garden,
her laptop resting at an angle on the wobbly, rusting
table, dew still clutching the tips of the grass stalks and
a blessed silence from houses of the neighbours, sleeping
off their Saturday night excesses. The new intake of email
scrolled up in bold in the mailbox, one by one,
four screens' worth.

Amy scanned a couple of the subject headings:
Wool Enquiry – Pattern doesn't state Gauge!
Painless Quilting; Idea for Article

11

She was going to have to employ someone soon. Upcycle.com – her baby, her passion – had boomed in popularity over recent months and the orders and enquiries kept her busy from dawn till midnight, seven days a week. As someone she had once worked with would have said, it was a quality problem. The site had expanded from a few magazine-type articles about crafts and hobbies to a full-blown 'vertical portal', or 'vortal', with everything from video clips on different knitting stitches or how to mosaic a garden table, to guest blogs from craft experts, an online shop and a lively forum to which women from around the world contributed.

Then she saw Becky's email address on the list in her Inbox. There was no subject heading. Her stomach gave a small flip. Becky had not spoken to her in weeks, after the blazing argument they'd had about their parents – whose turn it was to visit them in Spain, why Amy always had to have them staying at her place when they came over, why Becky never paid back any of the loans she got from them when Amy had to . . . She'd spent years trying to ignore all the little slights but on this occasion had failed, and out they had all come. She and Becky were usually so close. They had always bickered, ever since they were small girls – not uncommon with such a small age gap, not quite two years – but the trouble was, this one had been a full-blown row, so bad that Amy had wondered if her little sister would ever speak to her again. She opened the email, feeling a rush of relief that Becky had contacted her.

Dear Amy
I'm going away, and I'm not coming back. Don't try to find me. I'm going to Asia, probably. I've always

wanted to visit Vietnam and Cambodia. Sorry about our row. It's not your fault. Tell Mum and Dad not to worry. Look after yourself.
Love
B

Amy's relief immediately turned to puzzlement as she tried to make sense of it. Going away to Asia? Becky had always been more prone to tantrums. She remembered her shouting, 'I'm running away!' at their parents, stuffing her make-up and a four-pack of Mars bars into a bag and storming off, but she never made it much further than the end of the village.

She read the email again. *Don't try to find me.* That was the line that sent a little shiver up Amy's spine. And there was something else about the email too, a little niggle that she couldn't quite put her finger on.

The time on the email was 11.27 p.m. the previous night, a Saturday. So it had probably been written and sent while drunk. She pictured Becky lying on her sofa with an almost-empty bottle of Merlot on the floor, tapping away at her phone, the TV chattering unwatched in the background. Well, she thought, hangover or not, you can't expect to send an email like that and not get an early morning call from your sister.

Amy rang Becky's mobile, which went straight to voice-mail, then her landline, which rang out, then her mobile again, this time leaving a message:

'Rebecca Ann Coltman, you are a pain in the arse. What the fuck is all this about going to Vietnam, eh? Call me as soon as you get this.' She paused. *Don't try to find me.* 'I love you, though. And I'm sorry about the row too. Call me, OK?'

She put the phone on the table and returned to her emails.

An hour later, Becky hadn't rung or texted back, and Amy couldn't concentrate on her work at all. She made herself another cup of coffee and, while she waited, checked Becky's Facebook page on her phone. It hadn't been updated for a few days. She checked Twitter too. Ditto. No tweets since Wednesday. 'End of term. Whoo-hoo! Seven weeks of freedom. #schoolsoutforsummer'

She tried to call both of Becky's numbers again. Still no reply. She was 90 per cent sure that her sister was enjoying lie-ins for the first week of the school summer holidays, as most childless teachers in the country were probably also doing. But there was still that 10 per cent niggle . . .

Sod it, she was going to have to go round there. Just to set her mind at rest.

Becky's flat was in a small boxy fifties block built in the space left by a German bomb, incongruous in a road of Edwardian semis in Denmark Hill, a stone's throw from Ruskin Park. It took Amy seven minutes to get there on her Triumph when the traffic lights weren't against her. This morning they were all green, and Amy arrived with the taste of coffee still in her mouth, and the day's 'To Do' list scrolling through her head. This was To Do number one: get her sister out of bed, find out why she'd sent such a crazy email, smooth things over between them.

She parked the bike, dragged off her helmet and buzzed Flat Nine. No answer. After a moment's hesitation, she tried Flat Eight instead. While she waited she ruffled her hair wildly to make the curls spring back into place – helmet hair was the bane of her life. It was such an automatic reaction now that she wasn't even aware of doing it. Thirty seconds later, a sleepy male voice came over the intercom: 'Yerrghello?'

'Hi, Gary, it's Amy, Becky's sister. Sorry it's early. Can you buzz me in, please?'

The door clicked open in response, and Amy heard another door opening upstairs, the sound bouncing down the concrete stairwell. She strode up to the second floor, taking the stairs two at a time. Gary stood waiting for her, bare-chested in stripy cotton pyjama pants. He wasn't bad looking, Amy thought. He and Becky were good friends, although Amy suspected this was mostly because Gary was nifty with a screwdriver and willing to unblock Becky's U-bend at any hour of the day or night. She remembered Becky confessing this to her in a mock-suggestive comedy accent, and grinned. For the first time she felt a real pang of worry about where Becky was.

'Sorry,' she repeated, taking in his bed-head hair and sleepy eyes. He smelled of morning breath and slight BO.

'S'OK,' he replied, scratching his chest. 'Becky all right?'

'Probably. Just had a weird email from her last night, and now she's not answering her—'

'Phone,' interrupted Gary, and Amy instantly remembered the most annoying thing about him was his habit of trying to finish people's sentences. She wondered if he was aware he was doing it.

'Her mobile *or* her landline,' she corrected. 'Yeah. Anyway. Do you have a key? Just want to check she hasn't had an accident.'

'Accident,' he agreed, ushering her into his living room and rooting around in a drawer under a black-ash coffee table. 'I think I've still got her keys, they should be in here somewhere.'

While Gary went into his bedroom to fetch a T-shirt,

Amy put down her helmet and bike keys on the smoked-glass dining table. Gary was in his bedroom for a good minute, and Amy tapped her foot impatiently. When he came back he didn't say anything apart from, 'OK, let's go.'

They walked from Gary's flat to Becky's. He put the Yale key in the top lock and the door swung open.

Amy stared at it, then at Gary. 'It wasn't double-locked. She always double-locks the door, even if she's just going to bloody Sainsbury's.'

Amy realized she was holding her breath as they stepped inside. The flat was dark and silent, blinds drawn.

'It looks tidy,' she said. 'Well – as tidy as Becky's flat ever is. Becky?' she called out, feeling foolish and strangely light-headed. She went straight to her sister's bedroom, dreading the sight of her spread-eagled face down on the bed. But all was in order. The bed had been made, in a perfunctory sort of way, with a few items – a bra, a T-shirt – hanging from the bedpost. She opened the wardrobe. Clothes were crammed inside, so tightly that Amy wondered how Becky ever found anything to wear. There was no sign that she had packed a suitcase, although it was difficult to tell. Amy kept her own suitcases under her bed, but Becky's bed was too low to the ground to fit much underneath it.

In the kitchen, a mug stood in the sink, rinsed but unwashed, with no other washing-up in sight. Amy opened the fridge. It was empty apart from a jar of pickles that looked as if they would survive a nuclear holocaust. The freezer was empty too and appeared to have been recently defrosted. Both signs that she had planned to go away. But the boiler, attached to the wall beside the sink, had been left on.

Gary stood in the doorway of the kitchen, watching her and scratching his belly.

16

'When did you last see her?' Amy asked.

He pondered a moment. 'Haven't seen her for a while. She came over to ask me if I could help her set up her new computer, but that was a couple of weeks ago. What's going on? What was this weird email all about?'

Amy walked into the living room, Gary following. Everything appeared to be in place in here. The TV wasn't on standby but a copy of *Heat* was open on the armchair. 'She told me she was going away, to Vietnam and Cambodia, and said she might not come back.'

Gary frowned. 'I'm sure she wouldn't have gone without telling me.'

Amy picked up a framed photo from the bookcase, her face creasing with nostalgia at the sight of it. The photo was of her and Becky at Becky's graduation, ten years ago. Their faces were close to the camera, smiling into the sun, so fresh-faced. They looked so alike in that photo that they could easily have passed for identical twins.

'She'll probably walk in the door at any moment and ask what the hell we're doing—'

'Here.'

Amy felt cold inside. If Becky really had gone away without discussing it with her beforehand, that would hurt. And what was wrong in Becky's life that made her feel the need to do such a thing?

'When did *you* last talk to her?' Gary asked.

'I haven't seen her for about a month. We had a fight.'

Gary was clearly too English to ask what the fight had been about.

'I'm really worried,' she said, pulling out her phone and checking both her texts and emails, just in case something had come in from Becky. But there was nothing – just a load more emails from customers.

With all the contradictory signs in the flat, Amy didn't know what to think. But it was the email from Becky that jarred the most. Something about it was *off*, something she couldn't quite put her finger on. Either the way it was written or . . . something else. What was it? Despite the recent row, she and Becky were close. They emailed and texted each other all the time, and left comments on each other's Facebook updates, so she was familiar with Becky's written 'voice'.

She hurried across to the desk where Becky's new iMac sat. It looked as though Becky had been splashing the cash, she thought. She switched it on and waited for it to boot up.

'She never told me she'd got a new computer.'

Gary shrugged. 'But you said you weren't talking . . .'

'Nothing's password-protected.'

'She told me she'd do it herself when she could think of a suitably good password. Maybe that was just an excuse, though. I told her she must make sure she did it.'

'I was always nagging her about that too.'

Amy went straight into her sister's Mail program, where she checked the sent items. Because of the way the iMac synced with Becky's phone, emails sent from either would show in the sent items of both.

There was the email. She read it again: *Don't try to find me*. It was the last email Becky had sent. She scanned the list of emails sent over previous days. There didn't seem to be anything else very interesting.

She turned away from the screen, all the energy that had propelled her since receiving Becky's message ebbing away. At that moment, as if in sympathy, the room dimmed as a cloud passed over the sun. She was out of ideas. She looked up at Gary and was about to tell him that she was going to go home when the computer made a pinging sound.

A new email had arrived. The sender was CupidsWeb. She recognized the name – they were always advertising on TV. How did it go? *True love is just a click away.*

The subject line read: 'You have a new message!'

'What's this?' she said. Gary came closer to take a look as Amy opened the short email that was simply informing Becky that she had received a private message and that she needed to log in to read it. Amy clicked the link and CupidsWeb popped up, asking her for a username and password.

Amy clicked back to the email program and did a quick search for CupidsWeb. There were no emails from them other than the one that had just arrived.

'That's really weird,' she said. 'How long has she had this iMac?' Without waiting for him to answer, she added, 'Do you know what she did with her other one? Her laptop?'

Gary shook his head. 'Sold it, probably. She's into eBay and Gumtree and all that, isn't she? In fact, I'm sure she did mention that's what she was going to do.'

It was true, there were a few emails from various online marketplaces saying that Becky had won or sold different items. Amy had coached her on it a couple of years back and since then her sister had made quite a bit of extra cash from flogging her unwanted items.

Amy got up and started roaming around the flat, looking for Becky's distinctive stripy laptop case. No sign of it on the bookshelves, in the cupboard, on Becky's desk . . .

'Thinking about it, though, if she's gone away, she probably took it with her,' Gary said, pushing his hair off his forehead. 'Want me to look at those eBay emails for you?'

'Sure,' Amy called, walking into Becky's bedroom and looking around. It was so dusty it looked as though Becky had been gone for months, not a day or two. She wasn't even sure that her sister possessed a vacuum cleaner. All the pictures on the walls were very slightly crooked, too, and Amy shuddered. She had to straighten them all before she did anything else. No wonder she and Becky never thought of sharing a flat – they'd kill each other.

Amy leaned down and peered into the narrow space under the bed frame. Through all the dust bunnies she spotted a corner of the laptop case. 'Wait, no need – I've found it!' she said, sliding her hand under and dragging it out. She brought it back into the living room and switched it on.

'Nice one,' Gary commented. 'But it's not going to have anything on it that's not on the new one, is it? I mean, she hasn't changed her email address, has she?'

'No . . . but . . .' Amy sat on the sofa with the laptop open on her knee, logged in and scanned the numerous folders still on Becky's desktop. 'Look – she was very good at backing stuff up. Not good at filing anything – in her flat or on her computer – but I bet it's all here. She used to get really paranoid that the computer would crash and she'd lose all her school reports and lesson plans.'

'Good thought,' Gary said as she clicked on a folder called 'Old Emails Back-Up'. There they all were, with a sub-folder entitled 'Personal'. Dozens of messages from CupidsWeb dating back two months.

'I had no idea Becky was into Internet dating,' Amy said.

'Didn't you? Well, everyone does it these days, don't they? Every unattached person, anyway.' Gary snorted. 'Quite a lot of married ones too.'

'I don't.'

'Yeah, well, maybe you don't need to.' He looked her up and down and she resisted telling him that her own love life was so nonexistent that she doubted even Internet dating could help her.

She turned back to the screen. 'Internet dating. I wonder what other secrets she was keeping from me?'

2

Becky

Once I'd given Shaun my mobile number, we texted continuously. His texts were dry and funny, and I felt increasingly excited as the day of the date wore on, checking my phone after each lesson period – and sometimes during, too. I managed to resist the temptation during assembly, thankfully.

The home bell finally rang and I did the minimum amount of tidying up in my classroom before bombing out to the car, to go and get ready. But then, of course, I had to bloody run into Simon Pinto in the staff car park. I literally bumped into him – I just didn't see him, I was so busy reading Shaun's latest. Poor little Simon, his home life is appalling and he's got the sort of face that cries out, 'Bully me!' I think I'm the only one he talks to. I've tried to get him to tell me who is behind the campaign that finds him curled up, crying, behind the bins every day, but he's too scared. He's been crying now, and so I take him back into school and sit him down with a Coke and a stale digestive from the staff room. After half an hour, I know all about his nan's Alzheimer's and his dad's drink problem, but nothing about who gave him the long scratch on his face. I give him a lift home, making a mental note to talk to the head about him tomorrow, and trying not to look at my watch to ascertain whether I've still got time to wash my hair before the date.

I do have time to wash my hair, just about, and I straighten it into a sheet of blonde that I then immediately worry looks too artificial. I wish I had naturally curly hair like Amy does. Our hair is the exact same shade of blonde, but she can get away with towel-drying and leaving it to dry into perfect curls, whereas mine is neither one nor the other and has to be coaxed in either direction. It's a source of continual irritation to me.

Shaun and I meet later in a nice riverside pub I have chosen, a short bus ride from my flat. I wonder if I will recognize him – the clearest of his photographs on the website featured a very large black Labrador, with him cuddled up to it in the background. I'd probably be able to pick the Labrador out of a line-up, but Shaun himself looked distinctly blurry. I could see from the picture, though, that he appeared to have a strong jaw, and he described himself as in the six to six foot four category. Bald, but most of them are. How bad can it be, I thought?

I do recognize him, as soon as I walk into the bar, but mostly because he is the only man there alone, and he is sitting on a bar stool staring fixedly at the door. He jumps up when he sees me, bears down on me and shakes my hand vigorously. He doesn't look anything like six foot tall, let alone six foot four.

'Becky! You must be Becky. Lovely to meet you.' He pauses and gazes into my eyes, dropping his voice by about an octave. 'You look even more beautiful in the flesh than your picture.'

I am pleased and surprised – unless of course he's just trying to flatter me. But I think he means it. The photo I've got up on the website is, even by my standards, not bad. I look almost sexy, and it's not often that I'll admit to that. It was taken by my ex, Harry, when we were on a weekend away in Bournemouth, and right before he clicked the shutter, he told me what he was planning to do to me in bed later, so I have a sort of 'cat who's about to get the cream' grin.

Shaun isn't too bad himself. Despite our flirty texts, I don't feel any spark of attraction, but I tell myself not to be too hasty. I scrutinize him while he's pouring the wine. I hadn't planned to drink wine tonight, because I have a tendency to guzzle it when I'm nervous – but never mind. He has a good profile, but a slightly petulant mouth. He keeps his lips tight when he talks, and I wonder if it's because he's embarrassed about the gap between his front teeth, which I've had flashes of. He probably is quite a good-looking man, but even though I'm trying to keep an open mind, I can't help my heart sinking.

He hands me a glass of wine, steers me onto a bar stool and starts to tell me all about himself.

Two hours later, he's still telling me all about himself, his motorbike, his planned trip around Canada with 'the lads', how many followers he's got on Twitter. He hasn't asked me a single question, apart from what I do for a living, which was on my profile, so he ought to have remembered anyway. When I tell him I'm a French teacher, his face lights up:

'Oh, yes! I was going to be a teacher, I'm great with kids. But then I realized that my skills really lay in business, so I did an MBA . . .' blah blah blah.

I switch off, and study the collection of pottery jugs hanging on hooks around the top of the bar. I'm bored, but I don't want to go home just yet. I've had three glasses of wine and soon the bottle is empty. I hope I have more fun than this on Saturday, with my next date. Shaun is doing me a favour by being so completely tedious. Onwards and upwards, I think. There are always more.

'I'm just going to the little boys' room,' says Shaun, standing up. I notice that the top half of his body is a lot longer than the bottom half, and his hips are quite wide. I bet he looks stupid on a motorbike. 'Can I leave you to order another bottle; the same as we just had? Do you think you can manage that?'

I look sharply at him to see if he's joking, but no, it appears that he isn't.

'Yes, I think I'm quite capable of ordering a bottle of wine, thank you.' But my sarcasm appears to be lost on him.

'Blimey, is he always that patronizing?' asks the woman next to me at the bar, applying a thick layer of lip gloss.

'I don't know,' I say. 'I've never met him before. But I would imagine so.'

We watch him walking away towards the men's toilet. 'And he's got a big arse,' she says and, although I know it's mean, we both laugh.

'Good luck, anyway,' says the woman, after she's paid for her drinks.

'Thanks. I'll need it,' I reply, and she fights her way out of sight through the crush around the bar.

The pub is very full now, and I'm being jostled and bumped by people trying to squeeze around my stool to get to the bar, and Shaun has to speak even louder to be heard. I don't want to suggest that we go and sit at a table,

25

because that implies more commitment than I'm willing to offer. Plus, if I catch the woman's eye, I'll get the giggles. So I allow myself to be jogged and cramped and yammered on at. I notice myself withdraw, like a tortoise, closing down, just nodding occasionally and punctuating his monologue with the odd 'Really?' and 'Oh, right.'

Just when I think I might actually weep with boredom, my mobile phone beeps in my bag. I fish it out and retrieve the text message, while Shaun continues unabated with his life history. I don't bother to apologize for looking at the message. I get the feeling that he'd continue talking to the empty bar stool if I wasn't there. The message is from my friend Katherine, and reads:

Hhello iis tthiis tthhe oownnerr off the sshhopp tthatt ssolldd meee tthee vvibrattor? Hhow ddo uu tturn tthhe ffuccckkinngg thingh oofff?

I snort into my wine, accidentally spitting some out. It lands on the leg of Shaun's beige chinos, leaving a wet splatter mark, and – finally! – halting him in the middle of a diatribe about his appalling neighbours, who apparently play very loud music until two in the morning every night. Probably to drown out the sound of his voice, I think, and it makes me giggle even more. I can feel something give inside me, like snow melting and shifting, the beginnings of an avalanche of pent-up hysteria.

'Sorry.'

He doesn't look amused, and I half expect him to say, 'If it's all that funny, Becky Coltman, would you care to share it with the class?' He almost does: 'What's so funny?'

'Um . . . Just a silly text from my mate.' I swallow the laughter hard, and it feels as if my nose is going red from the effort of suppressing it.

'Let's see?'

Mutely, my shoulders beginning to shake, I hold out the little screen for him to inspect. He looks at it without expression. 'Very droll,' he says in a flat voice. Then something changes in his face, and a lascivious glint pops into his eyes. Ewww, I think, he must be thinking about me with a vibrator.

He leans closer, and whispers into my hair. 'Have you got one of those?' he murmurs.

'One of what?' I ask brightly, feigning innocence. As a matter of fact, I don't possess a vibrator; I don't like them. An ex bought me one once in the last gasp of our relationship, but I was never sure whether it was meant to be for us to use together, to try to rejuvenate our sex lives, or whether it was an acknowledgement that things had got so dire between us in that department that I'd be better off going it alone. I gave it a try, because Kath swears by hers, but I didn't like it at all. I wrapped it in a Tesco carrier bag and threw it in the outside bin.

'You know what I mean,' Shaun replies, his lips brushing my ear. 'You certainly won't need one of those when we're—'

I can't hold it in any more. I burst out laughing, too loudly, but I can't help myself. I laugh so hard that I almost fall off the bar stool. The crush at the bar has thinned out a bit, and I see the woman who spoke to me earlier looking over at me and laughing too, with me. I can tell she's guessed that I've reached my limit with Mr Dull, and it makes me even worse. I can't speak for laughing. I wish that woman were a bloke; she and I would get on like a house on fire. Why can't I meet a man I'm on the same wavelength with?

'It's not that bloody funny,' says Shaun, looking offended. He waves at the barman, who brings over a bill on a silver tray. 'Well, I'd better be going. I've had a great time, it's been lovely to meet you. Let's split this, shall we? Thirty-eight pounds each should do it.'

He must have ordered one of the priciest wines on the menu, knowing he was going to make me pay half, the bastard, I think, tears of mirth streaming down my face. I hadn't even touched any of the second bottle – I was driving, so I changed to tap water.

I'd never normally do this, but for some reason I just don't care. I stand up, make a show of peering in my bag and say, 'Gosh, Shaun, I'm terribly sorry, but I seem to have forgotten my purse. Can I leave you to sort this one out? It'll be on me next time, honest. Give me a call sometime?'

I peck him on the cheek, grab my coat and rush out before he can say anything, waving at my new friend on the way, still heaving and gulping with hysterics.

The text comes when I'm halfway home, so I pull over and open it. It says, 'You are an insane bitch and I've totally wasted my evening and my money on you.'

What happened to, 'I had a great time, it was lovely to meet you?' I wonder, roaring with fresh laughter. I pull out my phone to ring my sister and tell her about it – but then remember that I don't want her to know I'm Internet dating; she's so paranoid about it after what happened with her and that freak, even though it was years ago. She'll get too involved and start insisting that she vets all the guys, even though I keep telling her that she was just unlucky. She wouldn't understand that although I do want a relationship, I also just want some good old uncomplicated sex . . . I might tell her, at some point. Just not yet.

3

Amy

Sunday, 21 July

'Do you think I should call the police?' Amy asked Gary.

He pulled a face. 'I don't know. Maybe it's a bit early? I mean, assuming the email was a wind-up, she could walk in at any moment. She probably *will* walk in at any moment.'

'I'm not worried about looking foolish. I think I should—'

'Call them. Yeah, well, maybe.'

She was seated on Becky's desk chair, with Gary perched on the edge of the sofa, one leg bouncing back and forth, one of the most pronounced cases of restless leg syndrome she'd ever seen.

'You can go now,' she said. His expression made her realize she'd sounded dismissive. 'I mean, if you need to.'

He checked his watch. 'I suppose I really ought to get going – I'm playing five-a-side this morning . . . Will you be all right?'

'Yes, don't worry, I'll be fine.'

'If you hear anything, let me know, OK?' He wrote down

his mobile number for her on the back of a copy of *Heat* magazine, ripped it off and handed it to her.

'Of course. Can you leave me the spare key?'

He gave her the key, went to leave, hesitated in the doorway as though he was about to say something else, then changed his mind. He was an all-right guy, Amy thought, despite his annoying little habits. It was a truism that people in London didn't get to know their neighbours, and Amy's main interaction with the people next door to her had been listening to passive-aggressive comments about her noisy bike, so Becky was lucky to have a friend living next door.

So, the police. This would only be the second time in her life she'd called them. In a flash, she was transported back to that moment – the bleak loneliness underpinning the utter panic and disbelief at what had just happened to her at the hands of someone she loved. She hugged herself for comfort and shook the memory away, as she had so many times before.

She was about to look up the number of the local station on the iMac when it struck her that the police might need to examine the computer, and any more activity she did on it could muddy the trail more than she had already. So she looked it up on her phone, then called them.

'Camberwell Police.'

She took a deep breath. 'I want to report a missing person.'

She waited while she was put through to somebody who identified himself as Police Constable Ian Norris.

'How can I help?'

She cleared her throat to unstick the words. 'I want to report my sister as missing.'

'Can I take your name please?'

'Amy Coltman.'

He asked for her address and phone number, which she gave him.

'And your sister's name?'

'Becky . . . Rebecca Coltman,' she said, and gave him her sister's full address and date of birth.

'How long has your sister been missing?'

'Well . . . I haven't seen her for a couple of weeks, but I got an email from her last night.'

She heard an intake of breath at the other end of the line. 'Last night?'

'Yes.'

'And what did the email say?'

'I know this sounds silly, and that it was only last night, but she said she was going away – going abroad – and that I shouldn't try to find her.'

His tone changed entirely. 'Right.'

Before he could say anything else, Amy said, 'It's completely out of character. I can't believe she would go away like that and ask not to be found.'

'She's never done anything like this before?'

'No. She went backpacking around Asia for her gap year but it was all pre-arranged.'

'What about work? Have you checked with them?'

'She's a teacher. The school broke up for the summer holidays last Wednesday.'

'Last Wednesday. Right . . .' He paused, and she imagined him tapping details into his computer. She imagined him as the kind of bloke who typed with one finger, seeking out each letter as if for the first time.

'What about friends? Family?'

'Our parents live in Spain. I haven't checked to see if they've heard from her yet. And I haven't spoken to any of her friends yet.' Despite what she'd said to Gary, she felt embarrassed now.

'And have you been to her address?' Norris asked.

'I'm there now.' Pre-empting his questions, she said, 'It's hard to tell if she's packed up and gone away. But the door wasn't double-locked. I can't believe she'd go away without doing that.'

'You'd be amazed, miss. Some people might as well hang a sign on their front door: "Burglars welcome". What about her passport?'

'Oh. I don't know where she keeps it. Please, Officer Norris, I need you to take this seriously. There's something . . . not right about the email. I'm sure something has happened to her.'

'We take all reports of missing persons seriously, miss, I can assure you. Was there anything in the email that suggested that she planned to harm herself, or that she was being threatened?'

'No. Let me read it to you.'

Before he could stop her, she read out the email, in a rush.

Norris didn't respond immediately. Eventually, he said, 'Here's what I suggest, Miss Coltman. Why don't you speak to your mum and dad, call some of your sister's friends, and have a look for her passport? It sounds very much like Rebecca has gone away of her own volition. People do things that are out of character all the time, believe me.'

'I know, but—'

'I expect you'll get another email in a day or two, or a postcard, saying she's having a lovely time in Vietnam, wish you were here.'

She could feel him closing down the call, and she tried to hang on. 'So you're not going to do anything?'

'I'm sorry, miss, but if she hadn't sent the email it would be a different story. The fact is, though, that she did. She has clearly told you where she's going and what she's doing.'

'But what if someone else wrote the email? Or forced her to write it?'

'There's no evidence of that, is there?'

'No, but . . .'

She hung up, feeling utterly deflated.

As the call had gone on, her conviction that something had happened to Becky had become increasingly weaker. Norris was probably right. Becky had decided to go away. Her wheelie suitcase wasn't anywhere to be seen. Maybe what she should be worried about was *why* Becky would do something so uncharacteristic. What had driven her to it?

She rubbed her face, feeling totally confused. More than that, though, she was sick with worry. Had Becky had some kind of breakdown?

She read over the email for the tenth time. And then it struck her. How could she not have seen it before – or maybe that was what had been niggling at her?

I've always wanted to visit Vietnam and Cambodia.

When Becky had returned from her gap-year travels, she had made Amy sit through all of her printed photos. Thailand, India, Indonesia, Malaysia, the Philippines – and Cambodia. She had bemoaned the fact she hadn't got to visit Vietnam – for some complicated reason Amy couldn't recall, involving trains and visas and a boy from Oxford – but she had definitely been to Cambodia. She had visited the Killing Fields near – what was it called? – Phnom something. The visit had affected Becky badly. She told Amy she'd had nightmares about it for weeks afterwards, about the families who had been brutally murdered. The children.

33

In fact, it had disturbed her so much that she refused to talk about it further, said she wanted to forget she'd ever been. Now, when she talked about her time in Asia, she would list all the places she'd been, and she would miss out Cambodia.

But she had definitely been there. And even though she didn't talk about it, or want to remember it, she herself would remember she'd been there. So why would she write, *I've always wanted to visit Cambodia?*

She picked up the phone, ready to call Officer Norris back. But she hesitated. She could hear his exasperated sigh in her head. There were a couple of things she needed to do first.

She went into Becky's bedroom and looked around. The blinds were open and sunlight poured into the room. She heard a car pull up outside and rushed to the window to look out, hope flaring. It might be Becky coming home in a taxi. But it was a Royal Mail van, parking up behind Amy's motorbike.

Where would Becky keep her passport? She opened her bedside drawer and found condoms, assorted jewellery, Vaseline, old keys – but no passport. She checked every drawer in the flat, along with the bookshelves, various boxes and chests, every place she could think of where her sister might keep her important documents. There was no sign of it.

Everything she did made her feel conflicted. Half of her wanted evidence that her sister had indeed gone away through her own free will. The other half wanted confirmation that her instincts were correct.

She sat back down at the computer and brought up Becky's address-book program. She knew a couple of Becky's friends from work, had met them at a party last year, here at Becky's flat. Becky's best friend from work was called Katherine, and Amy had spoken to her at some length about jewellery-making, Katherine's hobby. Amy had been trying to get her to write a piece for the website. She was the obvious first port of call.

Amy dialled Katherine's number, hoping she hadn't gone away on holiday.

She answered after just a few rings. 'Hello?'

'Hi – is that Katherine?'

The other woman paused before answering. 'Yes?'

'This is Amy – Becky's sister.'

Katherine's tone changed. 'Oh, hello. Is everything all right?'

'I just wondered if you'd heard from Becky recently?'

'No, I haven't spoken to her since Wednesday, when we broke up. You're making me worry. What's happened?'

Amy was about to launch into it when she realized it would be much easier face to face, so she could show Katherine the email. Besides, she wanted to get out of the flat. It was making her feel even more antsy than she would otherwise, with every noise in the hallway making her jump; the hope that it was Becky coming back and then the return of the dread and disappointment when it wasn't.

'Can I come and see you?'

Katherine agreed, though Amy detected a hint of hesitation in her voice. Tough, she thought, leaving the flat and taking the spare keys with her. As she walked down the stairs, pressing down the helmet on her head en route, a door opened on the ground floor. 'Er – hello!' called a man's voice. 'Miss Coltman! Could I have a word?'

Amy stopped, surprised, her helmet as far down as her eyebrows. The man was in his forties, and very square – she could clearly see the vest through his blue nylon short-sleeved shirt. His thick brown hairline grew unattractively low on his forehead.

'Yes?'

'Yes. I need to talk to you again about the complaints we've had about noise levels coming from your . . . oh! I'm so sorry. I thought you were Miss Coltman.'

He squinted myopically at her and she lifted the helmet clear of her ears again so she could hear him better.

'I *am* Miss Coltman – but I'm Amy, not Becky. Becky's my sister.'

The man laughed in an embarrassed sort of way. 'I do beg your pardon! You look so alike!' He thrust out his hand. 'I'm Damian Fenton, head of the Residents' Association.'

'Hi,' Amy said, shaking it. It was clammy and felt like uncooked dough. 'People do say we look similar, although I can't see it, beyond the blonde hair. Have you seen Becky lately? I can't get hold of her.'

Damian pondered. 'No, I'm afraid I haven't. Not since . . . ooh . . . must have been last Tuesday? Yes, Tuesday, because that's bin day, and I had to have a word with her about the fact that she always leaves the tops on when she puts milk containers in her recycling, and they don't like that. And she has a bit of a naughty habit of putting plastic trays in too, and they *really* don't like that, they're supposed to go in—'

Amy looked at her watch. 'I'm so sorry, Damian, I don't mean to cut you off, but I'm late for seeing someone and I really need to get going, otherwise . . .' She grimaced conspiratorially at him, having the feeling that unless she said something, he'd be in full flow for hours.

'Right! No, no, I understand, I could talk till the cows come home, me. I do apologize. When you track your sister down, could you please ask her to pop down and have a word? Many thanks.'

He shot abruptly back into his flat before Amy could say anything else. She made a note of his flat number, thinking that a busybody like him might come in handy at some point.

Five minutes later, she was back on her bike, heading away from Becky's flat down Herne Hill towards Brockwell Park. Katherine lived at the cheaper end of Norwood Road, the only end where a teacher could afford to buy. When Amy moved to London after leaving university, to take her first lowly job as a marketing executive at a publishing house, Becky had spent several weekends with her sister that included a riotous night out in Brixton and a hungover day at the Lambeth Country Show, the only low point being when she got whiplash on the waltzer. After finishing her PGCE, Becky had managed to get a job in the same part of London. Now she lived in Denmark Hill while Amy was in East Dulwich, off Lordship Lane. Amy couldn't imagine living anywhere else.

As she waited at the traffic lights on Herne Hill, her mind hopped frantically from the subject of Becky's whereabouts – the word 'disappearance' kept trying to creep in but she was holding it at bay for now – to her To Do list. Site updates, customer emails, talking to a supplier, some pay-per-click ads, an interview with a local magazine . . .

Even on a normal day it would have been enough to send her spiralling into a mild panic, and she couldn't help but curse Becky for putting her through this. *If you're happily browsing duty free at this moment while I'm chasing around London looking for you . . .* She didn't finish the thought. Because, really, that's what she hoped Becky was doing. What was the alternative?

A white Audi cut her up as the lights changed and she raised her middle finger. *Dickhead.* She had a theory about people who drove expensive white cars. This theory didn't stretch much further than thinking they were all dickheads, but they proved her hypothesis again and again.

She rode past the row of shops where, last year, somebody had beaten a woman half to death for no reason. To the right lay the beautiful park with views towards central London, the Gherkin and the Shard glinting in the sunshine. But she didn't give any of that a thought today. She concentrated on the road ahead.

Katherine's cottage was easy to find. Amy parked the bike outside and unzipped her leather jacket, expecting to see steam coming off her like a baked potato removed from a microwave.

Katherine opened the door and stepped forward to give Amy a kiss.

'Would you like a cold drink?' she asked, wiping her cheek. 'I was sitting out in the garden. Come through.'

Amy followed her through the cottage, surprised by how messy it was: clothes spilling out of an open hall cupboard, dishes stacked in the sink, a layer of grime on every surface.

She stood on the small, square lawn and waited while Katherine searched for a clean glass. A Kindle lay face down on a metal table beside a packet of cigarettes. Katherine came out and made a big show of dragging a chair, filthy with cobwebs, out of the shed.

Amy sat down. 'How are you?'

Katherine did not look great. Her auburn hair hung in greasy clumps and she was considerably thinner than Amy remembered from their previous meeting. She seemed nervous, picking up the pack of cigarettes and lighting one, taking a hungry drag. Amy didn't remember her being a smoker either, though it was a detail she could easily have missed.

'Yeah, I'm OK,' Katherine said. 'So happy school's out at last. By June every year, I think if I have to mark one more piece of shitty Art homework I'm going to go berserk.' She smiled with one corner of her mouth.

'How's the jewellery-making going? I still want you to write that article, if you get time.'

'Oh. I haven't made any new pieces for months. I've been too busy.'

'That's a shame. How's your man? Clive, isn't it? Is he here?'

Katherine's expression didn't change. 'We broke up.'

'Oh. I'm sorry.'

'Don't be. He was a nightmare.'

If she'd known this woman better, Amy would have asked more, but thought it was best to move the conversation on. Especially as Katherine was acting like a junkie who couldn't wait to get her next fix.

'This was the email I got from Becky.'

Amy handed Katherine her phone and watched her read it, her brow furrowing.

'That's nuts,' Katherine said.

'I'm glad I'm not the only one who thinks so. She never said anything to you about going away?'

'No. Definitely not.'

'She was OK on Wednesday at school?'

Katherine stubbed out her cigarette and immediately lit another. She stared into the garden and Amy turned to see what she was looking at. But she was staring into space, a peculiar smile on her lips.

'Katherine?'

'Huh?'

'Are you all right?' Amy asked.

Katherine blinked. 'What? Yeah, I'm cool.'

She still had that look on her face, as if she found the whole thing amusing – or at least intriguing. She was swinging her leg in the same way Gary had been and Amy noticed that she had bruises around her ankles. 'You were saying about Wednesday.'

'Oh, yeah. We went for a drink after work – most of the younger teachers – to celebrate the end of term. Becky was there.'

'For the whole night?'

'Yeah. Well, we both left quite early.' Katherine looked over Amy's shoulder again and this time a black-and-white cat appeared, running past Amy and disappearing into the house. Katherine watched it go.

'And how did she seem?' Amy asked.

'Normal. Fine. In fact, she was all excited.'

'Excited? What about?'

Katherine crushed out her cigarette beneath a flip-flop. As she raised her leg, Amy spotted a fading yellow bruise on the inside of Katherine's thigh. It looked like a bite mark. She looked Amy in the eye. 'She had a hot date lined up for Thursday night. She was really looking forward to it.'

4

Becky

Wednesday, 15 May

Kath and I are having a great laugh round at mine, going through the profiles on CupidsWeb.com. I have enlisted her help after the date with Tedious Shaun, which, incidentally, pretty much sums up the inherent flaw in Internet dating: no matter how flirty your texts are before you meet, or how attractive their photo is, or how much you have in common on paper, there is still every chance that you won't like each other when you do meet; that the most important ingredient of all – sexual chemistry – will be missing.

Kath keeps telling me to do speed dating instead, but I can't handle the idea of it. It does make sense, first impressions and all that, but I'm rubbish at making small talk at the best of times, and the thought of some geek asking if I was an item of food what would I be . . . no thanks.

'I'll do it if you do it with me,' I said, making a face at her.

'OK, you're on,' she replied, a glint in her eye, clicking back to the main menu and scrolling down a list of

41

thumbnail pictures of men that I can tell, even from a photo one-inch square, I'd rather stick needles in my eyes than date.

'What? *You* can't do speed dating! What would Clive say?'

'Between you and me, Clive isn't going to be for ever.'

'What do you mean?' She and Clive have a mortgage on a tiny cottage that backs onto a railway line. I've been to their house for dinner. They have a cat and photomontages in clip frames of themselves on skiing holidays. It's not exactly a casual relationship. 'I thought you two were fine. Does he know?'

She looks shifty. 'No. I'm not ready to tell him yet either, so don't mention anything. I'm just window-shopping for now.'

I feel a bit sad at this. Clive is OK, as far as I can tell. I mean, I wouldn't date him myself, he's always apologizing for things, and tells Kath so often that he's really lucky to have her that I don't blame her for feeling superior to him. And he *is* lucky to have her. She's gorgeous – long curly red hair, the right number of freckles, and so curvy in all the right places that she makes me look like an ironing board standing next to her.

'The grass isn't necessarily greener, you know,' I say, gesturing to the computer screen.

Kath snorts. 'It couldn't be any *less* green,' she retorts. 'Right now, it's already a bleeding drought situation. Hosepipe ban and everything.'

We giggle at the innuendo and I pour us each a large glass of wine.

'Poor Clive,' I say. 'I'll make a deal with you – I won't tell Clive, if you promise not to tell my sister.'

Kath pauses, the glass halfway to her mouth. 'Why not?'

I don't answer immediately because I'm distracted by a picture of a guy on CupidsWeb who looks so ridiculously sexy and handsome that I can't believe he doesn't have women camping outside his front door. 'Ooh, look at HIM! He's gorgeous.' I click on his profile. 'SolsticeLover – thirty-five, divorced, a two-year-old who's the love of his life, five foot nine. A film editor . . . and he only lives in Streatham!'

Kath tuts. 'A two-year-old who's the apple of her dad's eye? Don't go there, Becks, just think of the baggage he'll have. Do you really want to be spending every other weekend with a needy, whining small person?' She pauses for comic effect. 'And that's just the dad!'

We laugh, although I sometimes wonder why on earth Katherine became a teacher when she seems so anti-kids. 'But he is lovely, though, isn't he?' I stroke his stubbly cheek on the monitor and make a mock lovey-dovey face at it.

'I wouldn't kick him out of bed for eating crisps,' Kath said. 'You haven't told me why you don't want Amy to know?'

I was hoping she'd forgotten. I take a minute to choose my words, although I know they will be severely edited when I do – I swore to Amy I'd never tell anybody what happened with her and that arsehole, and it feels disloyal to even hint at it.

'Oh. She's just a bit old-fashioned. Wants me to get married and have hordes of kids, so that she doesn't have to.'

Kath frowns. 'Why would she object to you finding someone online?'

'She assumes they're all weirdos and nutters. A . . . er . . . friend of hers had a really bad time with a guy she was living with . . .' I trail off, being deliberately vague.

'Fair enough. Well, it can be our secret then.' She taps

the side of her nose and pulls a cigarette out of the pack in her handbag. 'Just going for a fag and a wee, back in a mo.'

When she squeezes out onto my tiny balcony, I click back to SolsticeLover and read his personal statement. He sounds amazing – until the part where he says, *I think I should probably state upfront that I'm a Druid, and my spirituality means everything to me. I want someone to share my beliefs with.*

I wonder where a Druid living in Streatham goes to practise his rituals? However gorgeous he is, I can't quite see myself donning white robes and joining him and his cronies to perform blood rites on a squirrel on Wandsworth Common . . .

Kath comes back into the room, the smell of cigarettes following her like an acrid cloud, and she has this familiar look on her face, the kind of look that gives me a little tingle of excitement in the same way I used to feel excited at school when my best friend suggested we do something naughty.

'I've decided,' she proclaims.

'On what?'

'That I'm going to do it. Join you in the wonderful world of Internet dating.'

I look at her, sitting there on the arm of my armchair, her nipples clearly visible through her thin T-shirt, her tongue stained black with wine. Her eyes are shining with mischief and the flesh of her throat is flushed pink.

'But, really – what about Clive?' I ask.

'Oh, he doesn't have to know. You won't tell him, will you? I just need a bit of fun, Becks. While I'm young and hot.' She winks and pads over to the computer.

'You're a nightmare,' I say, but I have to admit, it's exciting. And God knows, after some of the dreary dates

I've been on recently, and with my seeming inability to find the kind of man I fantasize about, I could do with some help.

Kath grabs the keyboard and pulls it towards her, biting her lower lip, waves of sexual energy pouring off her.

'Come on,' she says. 'Let's find ourselves a couple of real men.'

I have a flicker of hesitation – what am I letting myself in for? I had it all under control; sedate drinks with men whom I then let down gently when they ask for a second date, back to the drawing board, find another one, ad infinitum until I – hopefully – find one I want to see again and who likes me too . . . Somehow, I feel that Kath's involvement might change my little routine. She's a loose cannon, on the prowl. Then I think, sod it, and giggle to myself at the mental image of a cannon on the prowl. A couple of real men. That sounds good.

No. It sounds great.

'Bring it on, girlfriend!' I crow, in my best fake-Harlem accent.

5

Amy

Amy let herself into her flat and smiled for the first time that day.

'Hello, gorgeous,' she said. 'What do you fancy for lunch?'

He raised an ear and licked her face.

Boris was her greyhound, adopted from a rescue centre two years ago, a great, lazy, affectionate mass of skin and bone and, as she often joked, the only man in her life. She had even started letting him sleep on the end of her bed, although she would never tell anyone that. If found out, she would say it was for security. Boris was her guard, growling at strange noises, though she suspected that an intruder would get nothing worse than a big lick on the nose.

The dog followed her into the kitchen and watched her pour dried food into a bowl.

'I'm worried about her, Boris,' she said. 'Her nutty friend said she'd been on a hot date on Thursday night. But she didn't know the guy's name, where he lives, what he does, or anything useful except that Becks met this bloke on a dating site and had met up with him a couple of times before.'

On her way out of Katherine's, Amy had noticed a framed photograph of Katherine and her ex, Clive, hanging on the wall in the hallway. The glass had been smashed, a jagged pattern of cracks spreading out from a centre point directly above Clive's mouth. How strange that Katherine would leave a broken frame on the wall – but then, the girl was strange, full stop, and it had pissed her off how Katherine had seemed to find the whole thing so amusing. She made a mental note not to push for that article on jewellery-making any more. Dealing with unpleasant people, whether in her business or personal life, was something she had vowed to avoid at all costs.

'So this is what I know so far,' she said, flicking the kettle on as Boris scoffed his lunch. 'Wednesday, Becky went to work as normal and went out that evening with a bunch of teachers. Katherine says they left early but that was the last time anyone saw her. Thursday, she had her hot date, apparently, and Saturday night, she sent me the email.

'No sign of her passport at the flat – but it could be somewhere I didn't look. Ditto her suitcase, though I can't think where it could be hidden. The fridge was empty. All signs that she's done what she said in the email and gone away.'

She took an individual coffee filter out of the box and ripped open its plastic packet. Her eyes felt scratchy and her body yearned for caffeine as she plonked the filter into the top of her mug and poured boiling water in, inhaling its delicious scent.

'But the boiler was on and the front door wasn't double-locked. She hadn't said anything to her neighbour about going away, either. And then there was the thing about Cambodia in the email. She's definitely been there before, so why say that she's always wanted to go there?'

She went out into the sunny garden and sat down, sipping the steaming coffee. Boris stayed in the kitchen, unhurriedly eating his food.

Contradictory evidence. Her mind leapt from fact to fact and inserted a big fat *but* between each one. The door was unlocked *but* I can't find her passport *but* the fridge was empty *but* . . .

The biggest *but* of all was the feeling in her gut: that cold, sick feeling that had been there since she'd read the email. That instinct, along with her knowledge of her sister – because this really was so unlike Becky – convinced her that something was very wrong. And she knew that sick feeling wouldn't go away until she spoke to her sister and found out exactly what was going on.

Boris trotted into the garden, nails clicking against the paving, and sat at her feet. She stroked his smooth head.

'I need to make a new To Do list,' she said.

She opened the Notes app on her phone and thought for a moment. What did she need to do?

Call airports, she tapped on the tiny keyboard.

Call mum and dad. She knew she ought to do that now, but she was reluctant. The worst thing she could imagine – no, not the worst thing by far, but something annoying and upsetting – would be her mum coming over and getting involved. Her parents caused enough problems from Spain as it was.

Find the hot date.

That had to be the most important item on the list. She chewed the inside of her cheek, worriedly. Why hadn't she brought the laptop home with her last time? She was going to have to go back to Becky's flat to get it.

She tackled Item One first, starting with Heathrow, but they told her she would need to speak to the individual airlines, so she looked up which ones flew to Vietnam and Cambodia. She called Emirates, then Malaysia Airlines and Cathay Pacific. They all told her the same thing: nothing.

'Our passenger lists are completely confidential,' a bored-sounding Australian woman said. 'We'd only be able to give that kind of information to the police.'

Amy thought about calling the police again. But her instinct was that she would need more information to go back to them with before they would take her seriously.

She pulled up outside Becky's flat and went inside, carrying her crash helmet. She had been riding now for four years. The leather felt like a protective shell, the wheels made her swift and hard to catch. Half-cheetah half-tortoise, she thought, and suppressed a smile.

As she passed Gary's door, he came out. 'I heard your bike,' he said. 'Any news? I only got back about an hour ago – pub lunch with the footie lads.'

'Nothing,' she said.

'Maybe she's back home now. Shall we go and have a look?'

The flat was still empty.

Amy checked her watch. It was 6 p.m. 'Nice day?' she asked.

'Yeah, not bad. To be honest, I lost us the match because I was worried about Becky. Kept looking at my phone to see if I'd had a missed call from you.'

Amy scrutinized him. 'That's sweet of you.'

He smiled his lopsided smile and ran a hand through his thick hair. His shirt, she noticed, was slightly too small for him and rose up to expose an inch of belly. She remembered his body from earlier. He had that thing going on – what was it called? A V cut. Those lines of muscle that ran in two diagonals from his abs down towards his groin.

She told Gary about her visit to Katherine and the hot date. 'I came back here so I could take another look at Becky's—'

'Computer,' he finished.

She was grateful to him for reminding her of his annoying habit and taking her mind off his abs.

'Do you want a coffee?' he asked. 'I'll make one in my flat and bring it through.' He slunk off and she sat down with Becky's laptop, pressing a button on the keyboard to bring it back to life.

She went straight to the 'Old Emails Back-Up' folder and scrolled through it, looking for interesting messages – particularly, anything connected to Internet dating.

It was an unknown world to Amy, something she had never tried, although she had been tempted a few times on cold nights in her flat when it was dark outside and the thought of having someone to watch TV with, to share her bed with other than Boris, filled her with yearning. But she was happy with her dog, for now, and too busy with her fast-growing business. That's what she told herself.

'You need to move on,' she heard Becky say. 'There are good men out there, Amy.'

It had been four years since 'that thing', as she called it in her head, on the very rare occasions it pushed its way into her conscious mind, and she knew in her stronger moments that Becky was right. For a while, she would start idly thinking about how she was going to find one of these good men. Since she had left her office job to work for herself from her kitchen table, working in a world peopled almost exclusively by women, there was little opportunity to meet any men, good, bad or ugly.

Then an advert for a dating site would come on TV and she'd think, 'Should I?'

But she had heard so many horror stories about Internet dates. All her friends who had tried dating sites came back with funny or depressing stories about lack of chemistry, dull conversations and people who were almost always balder, fatter or shorter than their profile pictures suggested. Or worse, creepier. Her friend, Sally, the graphic designer who helped her with her site, had recounted how she had once pulled out a couple of hairs and left them on the carpet of a date's flat while he was in the loo, just in case he murdered her and the police needed evidence she'd been there.

Someone had told her that 30 per cent of relationships start online these days, but she didn't know any couples that had met through a dating site, let alone Facebook or Twitter. Nearly everyone she knew had met at work, or through a mutual friend.

There were numerous identical emails in Becky's folder from CupidsWeb, with the subject line: 'You have a new message!'

She clicked on a link in one of these emails and was taken to the Login page of the dating site. She didn't know Becky's password but, as she had access to her email, getting in was easy. She clicked on 'Forgot Password?', entered Becky's email address and was sent an email with instructions on how to generate a new one. Seconds later, she was in, with full access to her sister's sent and received CupidsWeb messages.

She soon became absorbed by the long list on the screen, dating back to May that year. She created a new Word document and copied and pasted any interesting messages into it, her pulse quickening as she concentrated on the task. Gary came back into the room and put the coffee down in front of her, a splash spilling over the lip of the mug, then stood behind her shoulder and watched. She could see his reflection in the screen but tried to ignore it. She didn't like having a man standing behind her, watching what she was doing, but right now, she found Gary's company more comforting than disturbing.

After ten minutes of copying and pasting, she sat back. There were messages from fifteen men. She started to read through them, making sure that Gary wasn't able to see. It was Becky's private correspondence, after all, and she felt uncomfortable enough about reading it, without the added betrayal of Gary being privy to it too.

'*You look gorgeous in your profile pic. Is that really you, LOL?*'

'*You're a teacher! I used to fancy the pants off one of mine. I've had a thing about teachers ever since.*'

Amy shook her head. She could collect together some of these emails and compile them into a guide: 'How to Blow Your Chances of a Date.' Rule 1: Use LOL, ROFL and LMAO at all opportunities. Rule 2: Be as creepy as fuck.

If she saw that the exchange of messages had not resulted in a date – usually when Becky had sent them a message at the end of the flirtation to say she was too busy to meet up with them, sorry – Amy cut and pasted these into another document. These made up the majority, but there were a few exchanges that ended with the promise of a meeting. Amy wrote down their user names, real names (if indeed they were) and the dates of the correspondence.

'I'd very much like to meet up. Where's good for you? I work in Soho so we'd be spoilt for choice but there's a very nice wine bar on Dean Street. How does that sound?'

All of the men with whom Becky had arranged a date appeared sane and, well, normal. But Amy knew from bitter experience that men who appeared pleasant and ordinary at first could be anything but.

She turned to Gary, who was checking his watch. 'Take a look.'

He leaned forward and read the list of names aloud. 'Ross – Rosski20; Shaun – Notthesheep; Daniel – DannyBoy? He gave her a puzzled look. 'What exactly are we looking for?'

'Becky had a date on Thursday night. I'm trying to find out who it was with.'

'Well, all of these messages are from ages ago. There's nothing about a date last weekend.'

'I know. But if she'd already been on a date with this guy – starting back with one of these messages – they probably would have switched to arranging things by phone or text.'

'Oh, yeah.' He slapped his own forehead. 'I'm an idiot. But you're good at this.'

'What?'

'Investigating.'

'I don't think so.'

He smiled at her. 'Yeah, you are. You're clever. Becky's lucky to have someone so smart watching out for her.'

She flicked her eyes up to his and couldn't help but enjoy the praise, feeling it like warm sunshine on her face. But a moment later, the dark cloud returned along with a stab of guilt. What was she doing flirting – was it flirting? – with Gary, when Becky was missing?

She stared at the list and tapped the desk, thinking, wondering. Becky hadn't been seen since Wednesday, and trawling through Becky's computer was making Amy even more convinced that something awful had happened to her. There was nothing on there to suggest Becky had been unhappy or having problems. No weird emails. No gloomy Facebook status updates. Both Gary and Katherine said that Becky had seemed fine when they'd last seen her. Happy, in fact, according to Katherine. Excited.

Amy went over to Becky's new iMac, opened the web browser and went on to Google, which showed a list of Becky's recent searches. All of the searches were completely innocuous: *Kate Middleton dress*; *Chinese takeaway SE21*; *Made in Chelsea*. Nothing to suggest she was depressed or had any worries. Neither were there any searches about flights to Asia or accommodation over there.

No evidence at all that she had been planning to flee the country, nor that there was any reason for her to do so.

She needed to track down the hot date urgently. Because she could only think of two scenarios:

One: Becky had been in love with this guy but he had let her down, broken her heart and sent her into a wild tailspin, making her leave the country in a desperate bid to get away from him and forget him. Amy would have hoped that Becky might have confided in her, had this been the case – but she supposed that she never told Becky anything about Nathan, not until it was too late.

Two: He had done something much worse than break her heart.

'What are you going to do next?' Gary asked.

She shook her head, stood up and crossed over to the

bookshelf, picking up the framed photo of her and Becky, hugging it against her chest. The flat seemed to be mourning its owner, the sunlight that washed the room felt cold, the sofa looked sad and empty. A peace lily drooped its head on the windowsill, and Amy went into the kitchen and filled a small jug, returning to water the plant.

'I don't know,' she said. 'What do you think I should do?'

He flexed his shoulders and she could almost hear the muscles pop. 'The obvious thing, I guess, would be to call the blokes she emailed.'

'But I can't do that. I can't just call them.'

'Why not?'

'Because . . . for one thing, I don't have their numbers, and for another . . . what if one of them has done something to her?'

Gary's eyes widened. 'You don't think Becky's been *murdered*?'

Hearing the word out loud made Amy's eyes fill with tears and for a moment she was unable to reply. 'I don't know. But there has to be a chance. Someone sent that email, didn't they?' She told him about Cambodia.

Amy liked the way Gary's eyebrows scrunched when he was thinking. 'Maybe she's blocked the Cambodia thing from her mind so much that she's actually forgotten she went. Or she just made a mistake. It wouldn't be hard to do.'

She stroked the leaves of the lily between forefinger and thumb. 'I know that. But don't you understand? I have to find out. If something awful has happened to her, even if the chances are really slim, I'm the only person who will look for her.'

'You can see why the police aren't being that keen, though, can't you? They're obviously just waiting for her to email

55

you from Thailand or wherever. Probably happens all the time – people take off, and the police get brought in for nothing. Don't you think you should give it a few more days? Otherwise, what are you going to do? Sneak around spying on all the dates she's been on?'

She looked at him.

'Amy. You can't do that.'

'But like you said, the police don't want to know. They've made that clear already.'

Gary sat down on the sofa and rubbed his face with the palm of his hand.

'OK. I understand. If it's what you think you need to do.'

'I'm going to try the police one more time, though. Just so it's on record.'

Gary paused. 'Fair enough. And if they won't help you, I will. It's not safe for you to do it on your own.'

'But . . .'

'Don't argue, all right? I want to help you. I really like Becky. She's a . . . mate. I'm not taking no for an answer.'

She noted his eyes had misted over as he'd delivered these words. 'Thanks, Gary.'

His mobile rang.

He muttered an apology before answering it. 'Hi. Yeah, sorry . . . I'll be there in ten.'

Amy looked at him quizzically

'Sorry, I'm meant to be meeting my mate for a drink. I'm already late. But call me if you need anything. And let me know what the police say. Are you going to stay here?'

'Not for long. I ought to get back. Boris needs feeding.'

'Is that your bloke?'

She laughed. 'My dog.'

'Oh. And do you, um, have a bloke?'

'No.' Amy spoke a little more curtly than she'd intended. Surely, he wasn't trying to hit on her? That was the last thing she needed.

Gary walked over to the door, then hesitated and turned back.

'I know what else you could do. You could put an appeal out, see if anyone's seen her.'

'What, like a poster?'

He grinned. 'For someone who runs a website, you can be surprisingly old-fashioned.'

'I guess I'm an old-fashioned kind of girl.'

'I was thinking you could use social media. You do use Facebook and Twitter, right?'

'I use them a bit. Facebook, of course, for keeping up with friends, and everyone keeps telling me I need to use Twitter for my business, but I don't really have time.'

'Well, I've got a friend who's an expert at all that stuff. Social networking. Maybe he could advise you of the best way to go about it. I'll give him a call, see what he says.'

Gary left and Amy went back over to the desk, tapping the names of the three men who had sent Becky messages into the Notes app on her phone. She called the police station and, after being passed around, was told someone would call her back.

She intended to go home but got drawn into surfing through Becky's web history, trying to find some clue. She logged into CupidsWeb again and trawled through profiles, read through Becky's Inbox repeatedly. The room grew darker around her and she felt sleep tugging at her.

Soon, she was dreaming – that Becky was back, with a golden tan, telling Amy about the wonderful time she'd had in Cambodia. 'I went to the Killing Fields,' she said. 'Lovely place. You should go sometime . . .'

She jerked awake, lifting her head from the desk. The room was almost dark, her neck throbbed and it took her a second to recall where she was, to remember that Becky was missing and to realize what the noise that had woken her was.

Somebody was unlocking the front door.

6

Becky

'Wait for me, Kath, what's the matter?'

How Kath can run so fast is beyond me, considering the amount of fags she smokes, but she seems annoyed about something and is doggedly jogging much harder than me. We're on our third lap of Dulwich Park and I'm too knackered to speak. I stop, and bend over to put my hands on my knees, panting. A man riding one of those reclining cycles almost crashes into me. Katherine stops too, but continues to jog on the spot. She scowls at me.

When I get my breath back enough to speak, I straighten up, trying to rub a stitch out of my side. '*What?*'

Her shoulders slump a little.

'Nothing – well, nothing that's your fault anyway. Shit date the other night – he took me out to dinner, and I must have eaten a dodgy prawn. When I got home I spent the whole night puking my guts out. Still feeling a bit rough today.'

'Oh, no! Poor you. Can't believe you can feel that rough

59

and run so bloody fast, though . . . Who was he? And what did you tell Clive?'

I walk over to a nearby bench and sit down on it. Katherine looks disapproving, but joins me, looking at her watch. 'Might do another lap in a minute, but let's have a rest anyway.'

She takes a big suck on her water bottle and hands it to me – as usual, I've forgotten mine. I feel dehydrated; crusty, like an empty hull.

'So?'

'Oh, yeah . . . It was just really disappointing. He'd seemed like such a laugh in his profile, and then on the phone – you know, one of those really confident, quirky guys who say outrageous things. Sexy.'

I wipe my dripping face with my sleeve, and feel spikes of damp hair plaster themselves to my forehead. I remembered back to my first date, Big-Bum Shaun. 'And then they turn out to be the opposite of sexy.'

'Tell me about it. When I got to the restaurant I didn't even recognize him at first, he looked so embarrassed – and embarrassing. He was quite a lot fatter than I thought he'd be and he had these awful smokers' teeth, really yellow and crumbly and disgusting. I realized that he hadn't been smiling in any of his profile photos.

'Good on the phone, rubbish in the flesh.'

We watch a sparrow land on the topmost, flimsiest branch of the bush opposite. The branch bows, taking the bird with it, until both are horizontal, and the sparrow flies off, looking confused.

'It was such a bloody waste of an evening. I only agreed to stay for dinner because I was starving, and I'd told Clive I was going out for a meal with the girls and he'd think it was weird if I came home so early having *not* eaten.'

I stand up, mostly to try to quash the impulse to say, *Well that's what happens when you start lying . . .* 'Come on, tell me the rest as we walk – let's just have a cool-down for a lap. But honestly, Kath, it doesn't sound that bad! One dull evening with one dull guy?'

'It really pissed me off. I mean, this guy honestly thought that we were starting a relationship! I thought most men were just interested in sex. They're supposed to think about it every fifteen seconds or something, aren't they? Surely, it can't be that hard to find men who just want some uncomplicated naughty *fun*? It's so difficult for me to get away from Clive for an evening without having to tell a ton of lies, so I don't want to waste it sitting in a BORING restaurant with a BORING man who is waffling on about the hamster called Chips he had when he was eight years old!'

I sort of see her point. I remember the only one-night stand I've ever had – a night of smooth skin, words, admiration and sex, which was all the better for its lack of intimacy and the knowledge that it would never come with all the dull constraints and conditions of coupledom. A man I'd never want to be in a relationship with, but who was just perfect for one night. I wouldn't mind a few more nights like that, with other men like him.

'There's an obvious answer though, Kath – if it's so hard to get away, and you don't want to be with Clive, why don't you finish it? Then you'd be free to go on dates every night!'

She scowls again. In fact, I think I see her lip wobble, which is very unlike her.

'It would be really hard for me to leave him.'

'Why? Your cat? The mortgage?'

We walk on around the track in silence for a couple of minutes, as the serious runners whiz past us, giving us an exaggeratedly wide berth to express their annoyance at us cluttering up their track.

'Come on, you can tell me, I'm a doctor,' I joke, although I'm starting to feel a little worried.

There are actual tears in her eyes now, so we stop again. I put my arm around her and she looks at me.

'Yes, the cat, yes, the mortgage – but it's worse than that. Thing is, Becks, I owe him money.' Her voice is flat and resigned.

'A lot of money?'

She nods. 'He's been lending me cash for years – for my car, and that kiln I bought so I can make those silver pendants of baby footprints, you know. My laptop, holidays we've had together. The mortgage. It's thousands, on top of what I already owe on my maxed-out credit cards. And when I said I wanted us to split up, he said, "There's no way you're leaving me till you pay me back." Arsehole. He knows I've got no money. He told me if I ever leave him he'll shop me to the Inland Revenue about not declaring my income from my jewellery sideline, and he'll tell the school that I'm sleeping with the sixth-formers.'

I put my hands on my hips. 'That's ridiculous!' A thought occurs. 'You're *not* sleeping with the sixth-formers, are you?'

She shrugs. 'I did once give Jonty Pendleton a blowjob, but he left years ago. It's fine.'

A jogger runs past at that moment and does a comic double take over his shoulder at the word 'blowjob'. 'Oh, Kath! You're outrageous. But you can't let him blackmail you into staying.'

She wipes her eyes. 'No. You're right. I can't. I'm going to have to risk it, let him do his worst. But in the meantime, don't give me a hard time about wanting a little fun in my life too?'

62

'I can't believe Clive would ever be that horrible,' I say.

She catches my eye for a split second, then stares at the ground, watching a ladybird crawl across the path. 'It's why I don't feel guilty about what I'm doing – or intending to do. You have no idea what he's like behind closed doors.'

I wondered if Kath was exaggerating, as she had a tendency to do. Clive always seemed pretty innocuous to me. But then I remembered Amy's experience with Mr Lover-Lover man, and what hidden murky depths people are able to conceal from the outside world, when they want to . . .

'I'm sorry, darling,' I say. 'What a nightmare for you. Let me know if there's anything I can do to help, won't you?'

She smiles, a trace of the old wickedness returning. 'How about joining me in having some fun?'

7

Amy

'Becky?'

Amy yelled her sister's name then jumped up from the desk chair and ran into the hallway, almost falling over her boots, which she'd taken off hours before. The front door was open an inch, but as she reached it she heard footsteps pounding in the opposite direction.

'Becky!'

She yanked open the door and ran out of the flat. Someone was hurtling down the stairs. She chased after them, down one flight, skidding and almost tripping in her socked feet, grabbing hold of the rail to steady herself, her heart leaping into her throat. As she reached the first floor and started to run down the next flight of stairs, the outside door slammed below her.

She raced out and stood in the street, looking left and right. There was no one in sight. Her heart hammered in her chest. She called Becky's name again, but with less conviction. She ran along the road to the left, wishing she'd never taken her boots off, but there was nobody to be seen apart from an elderly black woman who eyed her suspiciously.

'Did you see anyone run this way?' Amy asked.

The woman scowled and hurried on.

Thanks a lot, Amy thought. It was no good. Whoever had opened the door to the flat was long gone. But who had it been? Becky? If it had been her, why had she sprinted away upon hearing Amy's voice? And if it wasn't Becky, then who was it?

She shivered.

She headed back inside after a final look around, and knocked on Gary's door. No answer. She pressed her ear against the wooden panel but couldn't hear anything. Pulling out her phone, she pressed Becky's name in the 'Favourites' folder of her address book, but nothing had changed. The call still went straight to voicemail. After a moment's hesitation, she called Gary instead.

He answered on the fourth ring.

'Hello?'

'Gary, it's Amy. Are you in?'

'Eh? Oh – no. I'm still at the pub. Everything all right? Has Becky turned up?'

'Somebody just walked into her flat. They had a key, Gary. When I called out they ran off.'

'Are you still there?'

'Yeah – well, I'm in the hallway, outside your place. Just been knocking at your door.'

'Right, well, get back into Becky's, lock the door, and I'll come straight back.'

'You don't have—'

But he had disconnected.

She wandered back to Becky's place, shaking with

adrenaline and unable to stand still. She paced around the living room, frequently looking out the window. She felt sick. If it hadn't been Becky, then did that mean it was whoever had sent the email? Oh, God . . . What if they came back? She went into the kitchen and slid a knife from the block.

Five minutes later, someone knocked on the door. Her stomach lurched.

'Who is it?' she called, holding the knife with a trembling hand.

'It's me, Gary.'

She went to open the door but had second thoughts. 'How do I know it's really you?'

'Er – don't you recognize my voice? OK. This morning, when you knocked on my door, I wasn't wearing a shirt. I just spoke to you on the phone and told you I was in the pub.'

She opened the door. Gary looked as if he'd had a few drinks.

'Are you OK?' he asked, sending a blast of beery breath in her direction.

She nodded. 'I've calmed down a bit now.'

'I got back as quickly as I could. You look like you could use a drink. Why don't you come to mine?'

She was relieved to get out of Becky's flat. Moments later, she sat on Gary's leather sofa, gripping a glass of whisky.

'My dad bought me that whisky,' Gary said. 'Can't stand the stuff myself.'

It felt good going down, spreading warmth through her throat and chest. Gary sat down in the armchair opposite. He was more sure of himself on his own territory. A strong smell of fresh sweat came off him, mingling with the beer. Masculine smells. Not unpleasant.

She told him what had happened.

'That's fucking scary,' he said. 'What did the footsteps sound like?'

'Um . . . they sounded like footsteps!'

'No, I mean, did they sound slower and heavy, like a big man's, or fast and lighter, like a woman's – like Becky's would be?'

'Good point.' Amy tried to remember. 'But I don't know. I'd say somewhere in the middle – heavy but fast. That's not very helpful, is it?'

Gary smiled faintly at her. 'Did you call the police?'

'I called them earlier but they said they'd call me back. That was hours ago.'

Gary took out his phone. 'Let's do it now.'

'I really need to get back. Boris has probably chewed the leg off the dining-room table by—'

'Now. Why are you so reluctant to keep calling them?'

'I'm not.'

He looked at her sceptically. 'You could have fooled me.'

Irritated, she stood up, almost spilling the remains of the whisky, and grabbed the phone out of his hand. 'The only reason I might have reservations is because they're useless and won't listen to me.'

'Well, your decision, I guess.'

'Oh, all right, I'll call them.'

She ignored Gary's smirk and crossed to the window to call the police station for the third time. It had been a really long day and she ached with exhaustion, the adrenaline deserting her body, leaving her feeling cold and depleted.

'Well?' Gary asked.

'They're sending someone round. Finally.'

The police officers stood in Gary's living room, filling it with their alien presence, a scene she had watched many times on TV but had never experienced until now. Amy was always astonished when she saw people being rude or confrontational to the police. She had been conditioned as a child to be respectful, even fearful, of the police and, even though she had little respect for them now, her own experiences brutally reversing that conditioning, she couldn't relax in their presence. She felt awkward, under suspicion. But also desperate for their help. They introduced themselves as PC Jay Sewell and WPC Minnie Whitaker.

'So,' said PC Sewell, who must have been six foot four – he had to duck as he came into the flat. 'You fell asleep in your sister's flat and woke to find someone opening the door.'

'That's right.'

WPC Whitaker, who reminded Amy of the hockey captain from her school, said, 'Who else has a key? Did she have a cleaner, or a lover who might have had one?'

'Just me,' said Gary. Two pairs of eyes lasered in on him, and he hurriedly added, 'We had copies of each other's keys in case we ever locked ourselves out. But Amy has my key.'

'And he was at the pub,' Amy added.

WPC Whitaker wrote something in her notebook.

'Maybe you could take fingerprints from the door?' Amy suggested.

The police officers exchanged a look. She had seen mechanics exchange similar looks when she took her bike in to be serviced and suggested what she thought was wrong with it.

'The issue we have,' said Sewell, 'is that no crime has been committed. We have nothing to make us think that something suspicious has happened to your sister, apart from your feelings and this . . . fact about Cambodia. And nobody tried to break into the flat. They opened it with a key.'

Amy looked at Gary. *I told you so.*

'Don't you think it's strange, though?' Gary said.

'Whether or not I think it's strange is irrelevant, sir. We have no evidence of a crime. There's nothing we can do.'

Amy awoke the next morning in her own flat, with sunlight in a warm shaft across her cheek and the dawn chorus in her ears. She had fallen into bed in a punch-drunk daze, leaving the curtains open, still wearing her clothes. Boris was in his usual position at the foot of the bed and, as he heard her stir, came round to lick the side of her face.

'Oh, lovely . . . Thanks, Boris. How—'

Suddenly, all the events of yesterday whooshed into her head and she grabbed her phone to check her texts and emails. *Please let there be something from Becky.* But there was nothing. Instead, there were dozens more emails from customers and suppliers that had come in overnight, filling her Inbox on top of all the messages she'd failed to respond to yesterday. She felt a lurch of panic. It was only four a.m. but she knew she would never get back to sleep. She stank; her mouth was dry. She needed to do some work. She needed to find Becky. But she needed to catch up with her work, Becky, work . . .

She remembered what the therapist had taught her about dealing with panic attacks. She swung her legs around and sat on the edge of the bed, put one hand on her abdomen and the other just above her breasts, breathed in slowly through her nose, held it, then exhaled through her mouth. Repeat. She felt her mind emptying. She would deal with what she needed to do calmly, one thing at a time.

After a minute or two, she relaxed, opened her eyes. The

dog gazed up at her, his serious expression making her smile.

She went into the kitchen and gave Boris a bowl of Weetabix, let him out into the garden then headed into the shower. The water usually spat torrents of hot water then cold, but this morning it was behaving, and the warm water cascading over her body soothed her, allowed her to compose in her head an ordered list of what she needed to do. The first item on the list was to outsource her customer-service enquiries to a third party – and a quick Google search brought up half a dozen options. She would arrange that later. The second was to concentrate on finding the men Becky had dated.

By five a.m., she was dressed and finally felt fully awake, ready to sit down at her computer. She'd already emailed herself the new CupidsWeb password for Becky's account, so she checked it and logged in, clicking straight into the message Inbox. There were two new messages from men saying they liked the look of Becky's profile. There were lots of messages like this received over recent weeks and Becky didn't appear to have answered any of them. That was odd. Had she stopped using the site?

She found the messages from the three men she knew Becky had arranged dates with: Rosski20, Notthesheep and DannyBoy. Naff usernames or what? she thought, curling her lip.

She clicked onto Notthesheep's profile, which proclaimed: *Cheeky Chappy Seeks fun lady 4 Adventure!*

'Oh, Becks, really? He's a twat!' Amy said disgustedly, looking through his profile pictures, many of which featured him taking sharp corners on a large, ugly motorbike or raising a pint with a load of other identical-looking fat bald blokes in a pub. The only close-up was a blurry shot of him looking as though he was strangling a big black Labrador.

Amy thought that she personally wouldn't touch him with a twenty-foot bargepole, but she could sort of see why Becky was attracted to him. Becks had always had a penchant for 'fun' blokes, especially ones with fast bikes. And Shaun Notthesheep had come on pretty strong to Becky in his CupidsWeb emails, raving on and on about her beauty, her hair, her sense of humour. That was the other thing about Becky: she could never resist flattery.

Amy read his About Me section: 'I love to travel to those far-flung places; equally I enjoy a weekend getaway to places closer to home that I've never been to. I often go for long rides on my beloved BMW bike, taking that fork in the road you always wondered where it leads.'

Aah, bless, thought Amy, he fancies himself as a bit of a philosopher. She went to the last message, dated from May, and noted that Becky had helpfully demanded to know his surname as well as his mobile number before they met – undoubtedly, so that she could Facebook-stalk him.

'Good girl,' she murmured, noting both down. His full name was Shaun Blackman. Not too common – that should help.

Next, she went to Rosski20's profile. He was quite nice-looking, in a clean-cut, slightly boring way, dark hair slicked back and a goofy smile. Very boy-next-door, Amy thought.

'Hi! I'm Ross. I've got my own company providing motivational speakers for events – which I also do myself, so if you date me, I'll always be able to help you think positive! I'm also a Reiki practitioner, and author of the book *Help Yourself to a Better Life Experience*. I lived abroad for some years and love to travel. I'd love to find someone who would like to explore new places. My last big trip was to Vietnam and Cambodia and I can't wait to get back there.'

Vietnam and Cambodia! Amy sat up. That was a bit of a coincidence, wasn't it? Although of course it didn't mean that they were there together. If Becky had recently read his profile, perhaps that was where she had come up with the idea.

He seemed pleasant, and his private messages to Becky were polite and funny. Amy could see why Becky had picked him. She Googled 'Ross' plus 'book' and *Help Yourself to a Better Life Experience* and immediately discovered that his last name was Malone. Becky must have done the same, since she hadn't asked him for his surname in any of their messages.

The last man on the list, DannyBoy, had a short profile in which he said he was a property investor, never married, no kids. He was the most attractive of the trio – or, at least, the one Amy thought was the best looking: he still had a thick head of hair, and oozed Alpha maleness. His About Me section claimed: 'Me . . . Just an ordinary guy, looking for a lovely lady, who might be prepared to put up with me and my sometimes difficult ways . . . I'm not very difficult, just a bit demanding, impractical, romantic and spontaneous! I don't have a long list of likes and dislikes or wants and needs . . . I'm prepared to see how things go with the right someone. I want to love and be loved – not too much to ask, is it? :-)

Amy read through their Inbox exchanges. His name was Daniel Bentick, and he liked scuba diving, reading, his beloved vintage Jaguar, and experimental theatre. She noted that Becky had claimed to love theatre too, which made her smile. Becky *hated* theatre, unless it was the most commercial of West End musicals. After a few increasingly flirty emails back and forth, Becky had given him her mobile number – but he hadn't given out his. Amy cursed. The messages stopped after that, their communications having obviously transferred to the phone. He could definitely be the hot date, she thought.

She went back to Google and carried on reading the search results for Ross Malone. There were literally millions of results, though she knew she would only need the first couple of pages. It would have been more problematic if he was called John Smith, but she knew what he looked like and she knew his profession. There were several men with that name on Facebook, but she quickly spotted him from his profile picture. Unfortunately, he had all his security settings switched on, so she couldn't find out any more useful details. But he had a page on LinkedIn, the site for professional networking, as she thought he would, and this gave her all the details she needed.

He did indeed run his own business, providing motivational speakers for events, and on LinkedIn, she found the address of his website, which provided his office address. He also kept a blog, which he updated regularly. Most of it was stuff like *17 Ways to Take Control of Your Life*, but there was some useful personal information in there too. He blogged about his dog, Wiggins, a cocker spaniel: 'This afternoon when I was taking Wiggins for his daily walk in the park opposite my office . . .'

Easy. Thank you, Google. She looked up his office address on a map and immediately found the name of the park – it was called Marble Hill Park, in a place in southwest London called St Margarets.

'Right, Boris. If Becky hasn't shown up by the end of today, you and I are going for a walk in a different park tomorrow,' she told him. 'Let's see if you can make friends with a dog called Wiggins, eh?' Boris's ears pricked up at the word 'walk', but when he realized none was forthcoming, he slumped his nose back down onto crossed front paws and sighed.

Amy moved on to Shaun Blackman. He was harder to track down, but she found him on Twitter and identified him from his avatar. He tweeted several times a day, mostly about his bike adventures. But as she read through his tweets, her heart sank.

He had been in Canada for the last three weeks, on a trip with his 'buddies', fishing and riding motorbikes. He'd got a nice bike for the trip, a Harley, much nicer than the Tupperware BMW he drove at home, and she paused for a few moments to admire it. He'd uploaded dozens of photos of his trip: 'Me with a large fish, me in front of Niagara.' 'Me drinking beer in Vancouver.' 'Me and some sexy Canadian girls.'

She found him on LinkedIn, too, revealing the company he worked for. She picked up her phone and called the direct number listed for him on their site, which – unsurprisingly at 5.12 a.m. – went straight through to voicemail: *'Hi, this is Shaun Blackman, leave me a message, but please be aware that I'm away on annual leave until July the thirtieth so won't be able to—'* Amy hung up.

So she had to rule out Shaun Notthesheep. He couldn't be the hot date. He'd been tweeting from Toronto all weekend, where he'd met 'an awesome babe'.

Still, at least that was one less guy to worry about.

Finally, she Googled Daniel Bentick. There were lots of results, as always, but none of them actually seemed to relate to the man she was looking for. She checked Facebook and looked through the profile pictures. He wasn't on there. Just her luck to be trying to track one of the few people on the planet without a Facebook account. He wasn't on Twitter either, nor LinkedIn. She scoured a few other social-networking sites but there was no trace of him.

She spent ten minutes clicking through Google's search results, but it was as if Daniel Bentick didn't exist – except on CupidsWeb.

She got up and paced the room, patting Boris as he trotted up to her.

'What to do?' she said, looking out at the garden, thinking the lawn needed mowing, adding it to yet another list in her head, filing it away for later. She felt calm, almost able to ignore the unease gnawing at her gut. Every few seconds, when she wasn't absorbed in something else, she felt the urge to check her phone for a message from Becky.

An idea came to her. Sitting back at the laptop, she logged on to CupidsWeb again, checked when DannyBoy had last been online (last week – good, so his membership was probably still current) and spent the next thirty minutes setting up a profile for herself and paying for the minimum membership package – one month. Annoyingly, although you could browse profiles and see when potential matches had emailed you, you couldn't read the message or send your own message without taking out membership. She felt butterflies as she did it. She needed to use her real picture just in case she had to meet up with Daniel Bentick. But she used a fake name: Sarah Jones. A hard name to check up on. She wrote a description of herself, mixing up real things that she liked, such as dogs and indie music, plus some stuff she thought might appeal to Daniel – the same things he had listed as liking: theatre and scuba diving. She even found a photo of herself on a dive she and Nathan once went on in Kefalonia, cropped Nathan out, and added it to her profile pictures.

Then she clicked on to DannyBoy's profile. She hit Private Message and pondered for a short while before typing:

Hi
I've just been checking out your profile. I love diving and theatre too. My diving photo was taken in Greece – my first ever. Didn't see many fish, though, but I definitely got the diving bug! Where's the best place you've been diving?

You look really hot in your pic. Seems like we live quite near each other too. Send me a message if you want to connect.
Sarah x

She hesitated for just a moment – was she doing the right thing? – then hit Send.

8

Him

Thinking about Katherine gives me a strange taste in my mouth – metallic, like blood, and my head throbs when I picture her. She makes me want to defile someone.

She thought she was so special but she was ordinary in every way, from her shoulder-length hair to her size-twelve body, from her average wage to her median IQ. True, her appetites were stronger than most women's – to an unseemly degree. Cock-hungry, mum would have said. A slut. I've trawled the profiles of so many just like her.

All of which made it infuriating when I realized she was going to be a problem. That she could spoil things by poking her pointy nose in where it wasn't wanted and asking for it to be bitten off.

I decided I had to remove the risk and deal with her.

I kept an eye on her Twitter feed in order to see what she was up to. She was quiet for most of the day, then *bingo. Got a big date tonight. V excited. Soho here I come!*

It was 19.29. According to the geo-location of the update, she was at Herne Hill station when she updated her status, so I wouldn't have time to intercept her. But that was fine.

I could wait. Patience is a virtue. Another thing Mum used to say.

Who was the date? That's what I wanted to know. I didn't know her password to the dating site she used, and had no quick way of finding it. That meant I was going to have to go to Soho and find out for myself.

I took the train, sat in first class so I didn't have to mingle with any of the scum who frequent the normal carriages: fat-arsed mums with buggies, maggots scoffing fast food with a stench like greased death, slack-trousered teenagers speaking in that fake *patois* they all use – a noise that makes me wish the knife-crime problem was far, far worse.

Soho was buzzing. I walked past the Admiral Nelson and smiled to myself, imagining nails piercing soft flesh, and grimaced at the sight of men walking hand in hand, at all the bitches with loose morals strutting about, drinking in the street and screeching. I had a wonderful fantasy in which I drove down the street in a limo with blackened windows, a machine-gun protruding through the window, pumping bullets into the skulls of passers-by. I sometimes think that if I'm ever diagnosed with something fatal, like cancer, I'll do just that. Take as many of the happy, smiling maggots with me as I can.

Maybe I should do it anyway.

Seeing all the pond life, all the girls with their tits on show and the couples eating each other's faces in broad daylight between puffs on their cigarettes, made me wonder if anyone – anyone but me – has ever really understood love, about the magic of two pure souls uniting as one, a person and another person coming together to create the perfect union, driven by an all-consuming desire for each other, willing to do anything for the one they love.

Anything.

Like some of the great couples in history.

Romeo and Juliet. They died for one another, so consumed by love they would rather swallow poison than spend another day apart. *The fearful passage of their death-marked love.* Beautiful.

Fred and Rose. Another couple devoted to one another. I love to picture the tender scenes of them torturing and killing girls together, perhaps making love with the young, fresh blood still on their skin. Like Romeo, poor Fred was unable to take the prospect of a life spent apart from his beloved. I wonder if he whispered her name as he hanged himself in his cell?

He was stronger than her though. More devoted. Because she's still alive. Do you think Fred would see that as a betrayal? I would. I'd see it as proof that she didn't love me as much as I loved her.

Armin Meiwes and Bernd Juergen Brandes understood love too. About utter devotion and sacrifice, even though they only knew one another for a short time.

Meiwes advertised on a website called the Cannibal Café for someone willing to be 'slaughtered and consumed'. Yes, yes, this is all true. It's a touching tale. Meiwes found Brandes and the two quickly discovered they were a perfect match. They attempted to eat Brandes's severed penis for dinner. Then Brandes gave up his life to his new-found love, and after Brandes was dead, Meiwes gobbled him up.

Of course, most people don't understand. Most people go through their lives never knowing that wonderful, painful, all-consuming emotion. They don't know what it's like to love and be loved. So they punish people like Meiwes and Fred West.

It's why I do everything possible to ensure I never get caught.

I methodically made my way through Soho's grid of streets, looking into each bar I came to, checking to see if the Slut was in there. I didn't bother with pubs – I didn't think she would go to a scummy, crowded pub on a hot Sunday night. If she had a date, it would be somewhere a little more upmarket, though not too upmarket, unless she was punching considerably above her weight.

Unable to stop myself, I popped into Agent Provocateur and picked up a few pieces. The girls in there are so different to the tramps walking around outside. Classy, educated. They are always welcoming, and whenever I go in there, I think I must look one or two of them up online. There is a young lady in there called Coco, who I at one point thought could be the love of my life, but she doesn't appear to be on any social networks. I bought some double cuffs, a patent-leather paddle, some nipple pasties, a lovely Fifi slip and a white corset from the bridal range that gave me a hard-on just looking at it. I think Coco noticed. Her eyes were full of admiration.

I found Katherine in a cocktail bar. I went in and sat with my back to her, watching her and her date in a mirror. He looked like a money man, a City idiot. He was loud, pawing at her, buying champagne and tipping it down his thick neck like there was no tomorrow. She kept throwing back her head and laughing, running her hands through her hair. I wondered if she genuinely liked him or was making these gestures because she knew that's what men expect women to do.

Between glasses of bubbly, the two of them also kept going off to the toilets and coming back sniffing and rubbing their noses, as subtle as two dogs fucking in the street. After I'd watched them do this a couple of times, I got up and went into the Gents', and was washing my hands as City Boy was coming out of a cubicle.

'Got a little powder showing,' I said, touching the skin below my nose.

He scowled at me and I thought how nice it would feel to smash his chubby face against the mirror. He had a scar cutting through his eyebrow and I wondered how he'd like a whole map of scars on his face. I said, 'Don't suppose you've got any spare?'

He looked me up and down.

'Don't worry, I'm not a cop.'

His lip curled. 'Sorry, mate, only got my personal supply, you know what I mean? But come back tomorrow night and maybe I can sort you out.'

'OK, thanks,' I said, all smiles. 'Who should I ask for?'

'Fuck off,' he replied.

So he was a dealer. That was interesting, and useful.

I finished my drink and went out. The disgusting party was still raging in the street. A girl was being sick in a shop doorway. I walked to Leicester Square and got a cab to visit an old acquaintance – let's call him Joe – who deals coke. I told him I wanted the best stuff he had and he was happy to oblige.

Joe had a flat in Chelsea. Nice pad, overlooking the river. He and I did some business together once. He's an idiot but he had a reputation for being able to get hold of any drug ever snorted or injected by man, woman or beast.

'I'm looking for some china white, too,' I said.

He gave me a surprised look. 'What do you want that shit for?' he asked.

'It's for a friend,' I said. 'A girlfriend.'

'You know china white is, like, really fucking strong?' he said. 'I don't sell that shit.'

'But I bet you know a man who does, right? I'll give you a referral fee, of course.'

That persuaded him. He made a couple of calls, and next thing I knew it was being delivered like a takeaway pizza. Fentanyl. It's like a synthetic form of heroin, a hundred times as potent. Joe looked at me like I was a cockroach as I left, but I was buzzing so much I forgave him.

Then I booked into a hotel and watched porn for a few hours. I took the bridal corset out of the pretty Agent Provocateur bag and masturbated over it. The porn wasn't as strong as my usual tastes but it had to do. I pictured her – not slutty Katherine, of course, I mean my new Number One girl, wearing the corset on our big night, bending over and telling me I was a good boy, the best boy, all grown-up and so big . . .

Part of me wants to take her now. Grab her and carry her home, across the threshold and into the darkness. Knowing she's out there now, living her life, unaware of my plans for us to be together, is a kind of delicious torture. But the time is not quite right. For now, I will have to continue to keep an eye on her. Everything about her ticks my boxes. She has the blonde hair, the blue eyes, the right proportions. As important as that, is the way she carries herself, the words she chooses to use. She is not coarse or tacky or trivial. She is intelligent and sensitive. She feels things strongly. I also sense that she has been wounded in the past, although by whom or what I don't know. I picture her lying on my bed, happily secured, gazing up at me with respect and love, telling me all her secrets. I can't wait to share my secrets with her too.

To whisper in her ear as she exhales her final breath, to bathe in her blood and kiss her silent mouth.

Sitting in the hotel room, aroused by this lovely fantasy that will soon be reality, I reminisced about my first Internet date, turning the corset over to its clean side and imagining it splashed with blood along with my come.

I started using the Internet in the mid-nineties. Online dating already existed then but it was primitive and there was hardly anybody using it. There were very slim pickings. But I met a beautiful girl through one of those early sites.

Her name was Diane. She was a northerner living in London in a pathetic bedsit. Lonely. Trying to make it as an actress. Extraordinarily pretty. Incredible tits – the ideal shape and size. In the perfect woman, her nipples should sit at 45 degrees from the top and point skywards. Plus, she should have a curvy hip-to-waist ratio of 0.7 and the distance between her eyes and mouth should be 36 per cent of the overall length of her face.

Luckily, I'm not quite so fussy. I only want the perfect woman for *me*. But Diane could have been put in a museum as an example of physical perfection.

She had a lovely vagina too. I still have it somewhere.

I was Diane's first Internet date, she said. I told her we were pioneers. She liked that. She had this chiming laugh that I've read can be highly appealing, so I ticked that off as a positive even though the sound made my brain throb.

I took her out on a couple of dates. Traditional. I wined and dined her. I dazzled her with treats. She was a poor actress, living off Cup-a-Soup and thin white bread. Over dinner, I could tell she really liked me. She ticked all the boxes. She played with her hair, twirling it between her fingers, stroked the rim of her glass with her fingertips, pushed items on the table towards me, fiddled with the cheap necklace she was wearing. She looked at me then looked away before returning her gaze to me.

Yes, she definitely liked me.

She wanted to sleep with me on the second date. I was

disappointed. The perfect woman waits until the third date. She was too easy. I was almost willing to give her another chance, as she was clearly overpowered by my masculinity, but I refuse to settle for anything less than perfection.

It was a shame.

But we were never meant to be. Every time I eliminate a girl, I see it as progress. One fewer possibility. Another step closer to The One.

At first light, I checked out of the hotel and went in search of a minicab. I'd been checking Katherine's Twitter feed and Facebook page through the night, taking a little bump or two of coke to keep me awake, not that I really needed it as the adrenaline was keeping my heart pounding, even after my second orgasm. She hadn't updated it, so I didn't know if she had stayed over with City Boy or whether he'd chucked her out once he'd finished having his fun with her. But it didn't matter too much.

I found a minicab office, said I wanted a cab to Herne Hill and was accompanied outside by the weary Middle Eastern driver to a heap of junk on four wheels.

'Where in Herne Hill?' he asked. When he got in, I held open his driver door and leaned down to him through the gap.

'How would you like to earn a hundred pounds?'

He looked up at me with disgust.

'No, no – not that. I'm not a fucking homo. I want you to deliver something for me.' I showed him the slim box with the Agent Provocateur logo scripted across its pink lid. 'This needs to go to a young lady in SE24. If she's not in, please put it through the letter box.'

'You pay up front,' he said.

'Sure, of course. Here's the address. And if I hear it didn't get there, I'll be back looking for you.' I smiled, man to man. 'This is for a very special lady. It's very important.'

I winked.

'OK, no problem,' he said. And with that, he drove off, audibly crunching into second gear as he turned the corner and disappeared.

Katherine was going to be thrilled to pieces with her gift. I just wish I could be there to see it.

Bang bang bang.

Katherine had been dreaming about her ex again – though not Clive. Funnily enough, she didn't miss Clive at all; the early times, back when it was all so thrilling and the bed – and the carpet and the sofa and the toilets on the 22.37 out of London Bridge – drew them like magnets. Sexy magnets. She giggled in the dream, her laughter drowned out by loud banging. She pulled the pillow over her head, but the banging was insistent. Someone was knocking at the door.

She opened one eye and lifted her phone from the bedside table. Eight a.m. She'd only been asleep for ninety minutes. She'd made a sharp exit just before dawn when Fraser started pawing at her bum and asking her if she liked anal sex, and got back just as the birds were waking up in Brockwell Park.

Ordinarily, she would have ignored the banging and gone back to sleep, but she was expecting a delivery from Asos and she didn't want to miss it. Knowing she could come straight back to bed – God bless the summer holidays – she got up, pulled on a long T-shirt and made her way to the front door.

The man on her doorstep didn't look like a delivery man. He held up a little pink box. His eyes widened when he saw her and she realized what she must look like, with her hair sticking up like a fright wig and mascara all round her eyes.

'It won't fit through the letter box,' he said.

She took it, perplexed. 'What is it?'

'A man asked me to deliver it to you. He said it was very important.' He turned to go.

She scrutinized the box. Agent Provocateur. Much too expensive for her with her teacher's wages. She'd tried to get something in the sale once but everything sold out within seconds. 'Who's it from?'

He shrugged. 'He didn't tell me his name.'

After he'd gone, she went inside and sat on the bed. She opened the box and gasped. Inside was a lovely pink-and-black slip, in a size 12, just right, and a couple of naughty little items: some black discs with little tassels, which she realized were meant for her nipples, and a small black patent-leather paddle. And beneath the slip, a special little present. A bag of coke.

She squealed with delight and grabbed her phone, finding Fraser in her contacts.

Hi Fraser – I just got your gift. Thanks so much! You naughty boy ;) See you soon – if you're lucky . . . xxxxxxxx

She stripped and held the slip against her. It was beautiful, but she didn't want to make it dirty by putting it on her smelly body. The tassels looked fun, though, and after working out how to attach them, she stuck them over her nipples and admired them in the mirror, laughing. What silly things. She peeled them off and put them back into the box.

She was wide awake now – well, not wide awake. She could do with a lift. Her eyes fell on the bag of coke on the bed. It was a ridiculous hour to snort coke, but it wasn't like she had any plans for the day. She felt like taking a couple of bumps and having a bath.

She went into the bathroom – it needed redecorating, but she couldn't be bothered with such mundane things these days, not with Clive gone. He used to take care of all that boring stuff. She turned on the taps and sat on the closed toilet, grabbing a hand mirror, which she balanced on her lap. She shook a couple of lines out of the bag. Then shook out a little more to make two fat lines.

What a star Fraser was. Maybe she'd go back and shag him again.

9

Amy

Monday, 22 July

Amy's phone pinged at just after nine a.m. It was a text from Gary:

My friend, Lewis, the social networking expert, said he can meet you for lunch today to give you some advise. Is that OK? x

She smiled at the spelling mistake and texted back: *Sure. Thanks. Can you send me the where and when?*

His reply came back immediately: *His name's Lewis Vine. He said he can meet you at Azzurro outside Waterloo at 12.30. Good luck x*

She wondered briefly how she was supposed to recognize him but decided she'd figure it out when she got there. She wasn't keen on going to meet someone she didn't know in order to talk about Twitter, but if there was any likelihood at all that it would help her find Becky, she had to do it.

As it was, she figured out who Lewis Vine was the moment she walked into the pizza restaurant. She had been here before, with Nathan, when they had just started seeing each other. In the evenings, the upstairs area was dark and quiet, making it a favourite haunt for couples who wanted to kiss more than they wanted to eat. Gary's friend was sitting downstairs by the entrance, a copy of *Wired* magazine on the table in front of him, an iPhone in his hand. He had dark brown hair that touched the collar of his expensive-looking white shirt and when she opened the door he looked up and gave her a quizzical look.

'Lewis?' she said.

He stood up and shook her hand formally. His grip was dry and warm, his wedding ring pressing against her finger. She guessed he was in his late thirties, but with boyish looks and a manner about him that she recognized well from working in digital media. London was heaving with men like him – Internet experts, consultants and freelancers who made a living advising others on how to do their jobs. He probably had a couple of kids at home and a wife who worked in publishing or TV. From his clothes and flashy watch, she guessed he was doing very well.

After buying a mineral water at the bar, she sat down and they exchanged small talk about the journey, the weather, the magazine he was reading, which had a photo of Mark Zuckerberg, the Facebook founder, on the cover. This led naturally to the topic she had come here to discuss.

'So, Gary told me about your sister.' He pulled a face.

'Yes, and he said you might be able to give me some advice about how to use social networks to find her?'

Lewis nodded eagerly. 'Yes. The power of crowds – that's what it's all about. You have to get the word out there, spread it as wide as possible, so everyone is keeping an eye out for her.'

'Uh-huh.' She had a horrible feeling that at the end of this he was going to invoice her for his advice.

'Have you got a recent picture of, um . . .'

'Becky.'

'Yes, sorry. Becky.'

'I've got one that was taken a month or so ago. Plus, I could always get one off Facebook.'

'Good idea. It's actually quite straightforward – the trick is that you have to create something that people want to share. It's marketing, basically.' His eyes shone with excitement and Amy tried not to take offence that he was talking about her finding her beloved missing sister as a marketing campaign.

He went on: 'What job do you do, Amy?'

'I run my own business. A website called Upcycle.com.'

'Oh, what's that? Sounds interesting.'

'It's a website for people who are interested in crafts. Women, mostly, who want a platform for selling items they've made, plus there's a big community where my users exchange tips, advice, that kind of thing.' I'm using his kind of language, she realized.

'That's cool,' he said, in a slightly patronizing way. She was sure he was about to ask her how much traffic she got. But instead, he said, 'So you probably know a lot of this stuff anyway.'

She shrugged. 'I don't use social networking as much as everyone says I should.'

'A familiar story. Well, like I'm saying, you need to make your appeal have some kind of "wow" factor, a hook. I see a lot of tweets about missing people but I rarely take any notice of them unless they grab my attention. Missing kids, obviously, that always makes one pause. You have to appeal to people's basic human emotions. Women – you have to make them feel sympathy. Men . . . um, is Becky pretty?'

'Very.'

90

'That will make things easier. Make sure you use the best picture you can – she needs to look pretty but not tarty. The girl-next-door type, the sort you'd see advertising yoghurt rather than perfume. And your story needs a hook. Not just, "Have you seen this woman?" but something like . . . What's her job?'

'She's a secondary-school French teacher.'

He nodded deeply. '*Perf*ect. Couldn't be much better. "My schoolteacher sister has mysteriously disappeared. Please help me find her." You need something like that. Hey, maybe you could get some of her schoolkids involved. No, you're right, that's too much.'

He carried on, explaining how to go about setting up a campaign, the best time to tweet, how often she should do it. He told her that her aim needed to be to get as many people to share it or retweet it as she could, so it spread as far as possible. 'That's the power of social networks,' he said. 'If you've only got, I don't know, five hundred followers, that's not going to get you anywhere – unless a good number of them share it, and then their friends and followers share it, and it goes viral. That's the trick. If you can get a celebrity or two to retweet it, then you'll really be in business.'

As Lewis gave her more details, Amy scribbled notes in a pad. Every five minutes, his phone would go off and he'd apologize but answer it, leaving her sipping her water as he talked business. It wasn't that she was ungrateful – she very much appreciated his help and it was good advice – but she wished he wouldn't talk about Becky as if she were a product they were trying to sell.

Finally, he looked at his Rolex and said, 'Right, I've got a meeting to get to. Was that helpful?'

She told him that indeed it was.

'Give my best to Gary,' he said, as she left, handing her his business card. 'And if you need any more help, don't hesitate to give me a ring. Especially if you need any help with Recycle. Hope you find your sister.'

He strode away. *Recycle.* She tutted. But on the way back to where her bike was parked, she paused and logged into Twitter on her phone. No harm starting now, she thought.

Boris sat on the floor of the bus, his body pressed close to Amy's calves. Holding him on a tight leash, she put her other hand on his warm back, feeling the way that he rocked in rhythm with the motion of the bus.

Amy pulled out her iPhone and checked TweetDeck, the app on her phone that she used to check Twitter. It had only been two hours since she'd posted the first appeal for information about Becky's whereabouts on Twitter, following Lewis's advice, and she'd done the same on Facebook as soon as she'd got home.

'MY SISTER BECKY COLTMAN IS MISSING – HAVE YOU SEEN HER SINCE FRI? SO WORRIED. PLS.RT'

Along with the message, she'd added a link to a gorgeous photo of Becky laughing at a party, but Amy saw that thirty-seven people had already retweeted it to their followers too, and it had had dozens of shares on Facebook so far.

She herself only had just over a thousand Twitter followers, most of them members of the crafting community. When she got home, she thought, she would send the appeal directly to some famous tweeters – Jonathan Ross, Caitlin Moran – people with many thousands of followers, just as Lewis had told her to.

Amy and Boris got out at Waterloo – it was a pain having to go to Waterloo, then go home, then back again, but she needed Boris with her now – and boarded a South West train heading out of town. Twenty-five minutes later the train pulled into St Margarets station and Amy led Boris up the steps to the street. She turned right and headed purposefully towards the park – she had already memorized the directions.

'Very chi-chi, Boris, isn't it?' she said, taking in the flower shops and artisan delis.

She reached the mini-roundabout she'd seen on the map, and nerves clumped in a tight ball in her stomach – that meant that Ross's office should be . . . just . . . *here*. She looked along the row of shops and at the brass plates on the doors between them. There it was: Malone Associates.

She and Boris hurried over a zebra crossing and, trying not to look anxiously around her, she wondered what time exactly Ross took Wiggins for his afternoon walk. She had assumed a vague 'after lunch' sort of time, but that could be completely wrong.

The park was extremely pretty – a vast sweep of lawns with the backdrop of an imposing white Palladian villa. She looked around. The only dogs she could see nearby were a fat placid black Labrador, and an excitable Lakeland terrier racing after sticks.

Boris whined and strained at the lead, so she jogged with him along the path. The Lakeland terrier ran up to them and sniffed Boris, then its owner, a kind-looking ruddy-faced man in a Barbour, smiled apologetically at Amy. Then, in a flash of black and white, a cocker spaniel streaked over and joined in. Amy's heart jumped. There was no sign of his owner. He was a nice dog, glossy and enthusiastic, smiling gleefully in the way that spaniels did. He and the Lakeland ran in delighted circles for a few minutes, and Amy and the ruddy-faced man stood watching, like parents at the school gates.

'Haven't seen him before,' said the man, nodding down at Boris. 'What's his name?'

'Boris,' Amy said. 'No, we don't live here – we're just, um, visiting. So you know all the regulars, do you?'

'You get to know their names, yes,' the man said, turning his foot over to rub a small clod of mud off the side of his shoe. He sounded extraordinarily posh. 'That's Wiggins.'

Amy tried to contain her excitement.

'Oh, and there's his owner,' said the man, pointing with a chubby finger towards the path. Amy followed his gaze.

The man on the path looked absolutely nothing like his photograph on CupidsWeb. Amy thought she'd never have recognized him had it not been for the help of the ruddy-faced man. Ross's profile had said he was five foot eleven, but this man was no more than five foot eight. His web presence – photos on both his own website and CupidsWeb – had depicted him looking healthy, clean-shaven and well coiffed, but the person walking towards her now was anything but. He was a physical wreck – greyish stubble, bowed shoulders flecked with dandruff, vast puffy bags under his eyes.

'Lovely day, isn't it?' Ruddy-Faced Man called out to him, and he nodded back. 'Right, must get on with it. Come here, Jimi! After Jimi Hendrix,' he explained to Amy as the terrier bounded over. 'Nice to have met you.' He smiled over his shoulder as he headed towards the park gates.

Ross ignored Amy, even though they were only standing a few feet apart. Blimey, she thought, he doesn't look as if he could motivate anyone. She wandered as casually as she could up to him, grateful to the ruddy-faced man for having effected an introduction

'So, Wiggins is yours, is he? That man over there just told me his name. He's lovely. Have you had him long?'

Ross met her gaze, and for the first time she recognized

him from his photos. 'Two years,' he said, appearing slightly more animated. 'What's yours called?' He reached down and gave Boris a half-hearted pat.

'This is Boris. He's a rescue dog – been with me for four years now.' She pretended to do a double-take. 'Oh, my goodness, I'm sure I know you from somewhere!'

Ross pushed back his shoulders and looked pleased. 'Have you been to one of my talks?'

Amy pretended to consider. 'I don't think it's that . . . Forgive me if I'm wrong, but are you by any chance on CupidsWeb?'

Ross blinked at her. 'Er, yes, I am, actually.'

Amy clicked her fingers. 'That's it! So am I. I remember now – I was looking at your profile yesterday. You're a writer, aren't you? What a weird coincidence! I don't even live around here, I was just staying with an old schoolfriend last night who lives up the road.' The words gushed out and she wondered if he could tell how nervous she felt – it sounded so implausible. She had to keep reminding herself that this man could have something to do with Becky's disappearance. He might be dangerous.

Ross looked properly at her and held out his hand for Amy to shake.

'I'm Amy,' she said, taking his hand.

'Ross. Very nice to meet you, Amy, and yes – what a coincidence. I'm not a writer as such, although I've written a book on self-help techniques. I'm a motivational speaker.'

'Oh, yes, that was it, sorry. I remembered something about a book.' She lowered her eyelashes and pretended to look coy. Her heart pounded and she felt a fluttering sensation in her stomach. She was aware that if how she felt was visible, Ross would mistake her nervousness for desire.

'I added you into my Favourites, actually.'

'Did you now?' he said, putting his head to one side and regarding her flirtatiously. It was incredible how different he looked to the miserable-looking man who had shuffled into the park not five minutes earlier.

He looked at his watch, pushing his arm forward in an exaggerated manner. As his sleeve shot up, Amy caught a glimpse of what looked like either a hospital bracelet or a festival wrist pass. 'I don't suppose you've got time for a coffee, have you? Strike while the iron's hot, as they say?'

He grinned hopefully at her, and Amy smiled back.

'I could murder a latte,' she said, and he gestured towards the little café behind them.

'Let's go!' He whistled to Wiggins and they set off together, Amy marvelling at how easy it had been. Now all she had to do was work out what to say to Ross to find out what, if anything, he knew about Becky's vanishing act.

Ross hooked Wiggins's lead over the fence outside the little café, picking up an empty stainless-steel dog bowl on the ground by the gate. 'Can we sit out here so I can smoke?' he asked. 'I'll go and get the hounds a drink. Latte for you?'

Amy nodded, and sat down at the picnic table inside the little picket fence. Boris sat next to her, regarding Wiggins with curiosity. She took out her phone again and checked Twitter. Four new retweets of her appeal – that was good. Then something caught her eye, in her Mentions folder: BColtman . . .

Amy's hand flew to her mouth. A tweet from Becky! All it said was:

@Amyjo stop looking for me. I'm in Thailand. I'm fine.

Amy felt as though she had been winded, all the breath left her lungs in a weird squeeze of suction. So Becky really was in Asia? But even after an argument, surely she'd never write something as cold as that, knowing from the appeal how worried Amy had been.

96

She typed a reply immediately, as a direct message: *WTF? Why didn't you tell me?* She paused, thinking that it sounded a little aggressive, then sent another message: *I love you. Been so worried.*

As she hit Send, Ross emerged carrying a tray containing two coffees and a bowl of water, which he put down for the dogs. He handed Amy her latte and, as she took it, he saw her face. 'Hey, are you OK?'

He climbed over the fixed seat of the bench and sat opposite her, pulling out a pack of Silk Cut. 'Want one?'

'No, thanks, I don't smoke,' she said. Her hands were suddenly shaking so much that she could hardly pick up the cardboard cup.

'Has something just happened?' Ross looked concerned, but slightly wary, as if the last thing he needed was to listen to a strange woman's troubles.

Amy hesitated, then decided. She would just have to go for it – not least because she did not believe herself to be nearly a good enough actress to be able to pull off a convincing flirting act.

'I'm sorry,' she said. 'I haven't been straight with you. I did see you on CupidsWeb, but I came here today to try to find you, after you put on your blog that you walk Wiggins here every afternoon. I need to talk to you.'

Alarm was printed all over his face, almost comically. Amy wondered what he'd do if she leaned forward and said, 'You're going to be a daddy!' just to freak him out, but she was in no mood for levity. The expression he didn't wear, though, was guilt, or any sort of fear.

'My sister's gone missing,' she blurted. 'And I think you went on a date with her recently. Becky. Becky Coltman. Do you remember her?'

He raised his eyebrows and, if anything, seemed relieved.

'God. Sorry to hear that. How awful. A teacher? Yes, I remember her. Lovely girl. I really liked her and wanted to see her again, but she emailed me afterwards and said she only wanted to be friends, that she didn't think there was any chemistry between us. I left it at that – I've got enough girls who are mates, I'm after a girlfriend.' He looked momentarily sad, and Amy felt sorry for him. 'How long has she been missing for?'

'She was last seen on Wednesday. Then on Sunday, I had this weird email from her saying she was going away. Did she mention going travelling to you?'

Ross thought for a moment then shook his head. 'Definitely not. I specifically remember asking her if she had any plans for the summer holidays, and she said, no, that she was skint and had already had a holiday this year – let me think . . . yeah, hadn't she been to Spain, or Portugal or somewhere at Easter?'

Amy had forgotten that, because she herself had been away then, at a big craft expo in Manchester. Becky had gone on a week's tennis holiday in Portugal in April. There was no way she could afford another holiday this year.

'You need to go to the police,' he said, stubbing out his cigarette beneath his shoe.

Amy looked at him. He certainly seemed utterly transparent, and genuinely concerned – but some people were expert liars, weren't they? 'Can I ask you a question? What's that on your wrist?' She pointed at his sleeve, and he blushed slightly.

'Couldn't find any scissors at home,' he said, showing her that it was a hospital wristband. 'I just got out of hospital last night. I was in for three nights. Kidney stones. Awful. That's why I look so shit, in case you were wondering. It really took it out of me.'

'Sorry to hear that,' Amy said. 'Which hospital were you in?'

'West Mid— Hey, are you going to check up on my alibi?' He sounded offended, but Amy smiled wryly. 'The police will want to know, if I can ever get them to take this seriously.'

He shrugged. 'Well, it's certainly a solid alibi.'

'It sure is,' said Amy. She paused, then added, 'I'm glad it couldn't have been anything to do with you.' It was her turn to blush, hoping he wasn't going to ask her out. He was a really nice guy, but, like Becky, she didn't fancy him at all.

'Look at this,' she said, getting out her phone again. 'You asked if something had just happened, and it has – I've just had a tweet from her account. I sent out an appeal last night, asking if anyone had seen her, and she – or someone – has replied from her account. But I still don't believe it's her. I'll show you.'

She scrolled through the icons to TweetDeck, and opened it on the same column the first tweet had arrived in.

The tweet had been deleted.

After saying goodbye to Ross, Amy walked back along the path with Boris, deep in thought and barely concentrating on where she was going. She walked with her phone in her hand, gazing at the screen, obsessively refreshing Twitter every few seconds to see if the phantom tweet would return. It didn't.

'Mind where you're going!'

She had been so focused on her phone that she had almost bumped into a jogger.

She looked around her. Absent-mindedly, she had wandered into a quiet area of the park, where the trees were dense and there were few people around. No other people, in fact, except the jogger who was now retreating into the distance.

'Where the hell are we?' she said aloud.

As she turned around, to retrace her footsteps, she saw and heard something move in the trees, about twenty feet away. The foliage was so thick that she couldn't see through it. But the hairs stood up on the back of her neck. If it hadn't been for everything else that was going on, she might not have thought anything of it, but now she was convinced she was being watched.

'Hello?' she called. 'Is someone there?'

Silence.

She took a step towards where the sound had come from – and a pine cone fell from a branch and landed at her feet, making her jump and catch her breath. She laughed to herself and was about to make a comment to Boris about how she was being stupidly paranoid, when she heard a phone chirrup – from the spot where she had heard the noise. There *was* someone there.

'Who is that?' she called.

At her feet, Boris growled.

She stooped and picked up the largest stick she could find, and ventured into the trees, the dog straining against his leash, his lip curled, baring his teeth.

'I've got a dog,' she said. 'He bites.'

She reached the point where she was certain the noise had come from. There was no one there – just trampled grass on the path that led back into the heart of the park.

10

Declan

A body.

They had found a body, smack bang in the middle of nowhere. Detective Inspector Declan Adams leaned forward in his car seat, shifting his hips, unable to sit still. His lower back, which had seemingly got fed up with his shoulder getting all the attention, ached like hell. Ever since 'the incident', his body had developed a pain zone that roamed around his body like one of those wandering wombs from ancient medicine.

'This sat nav is shit.'

He turned his head to look at the man who had spoken, DS Bob Clewley, who was looking at the TomTom rather than the road.

'I know we're in the countryside, but that doesn't mean there aren't any other cars on the road, Bob.'

'Hmm? Oh, but this thing is crap. How do you turn the fucking volume down?'

Calmly, Declan pressed a few buttons on the sat nav and

101

the – admittedly irritating – voice of the navigator fell from a bellow to a murmur.

'Better?'

'Yeah. Thanks.' Bob was five years younger than Declan, just starting to lose his hair, a fact that made Declan feel blessed, as his black hair was as thick as it had been when he was a teenager, back in the days when he used to back-comb his hair in an attempt to look like Robert Smith from the Cure. Declan knew that if any of his colleagues ever got hold of any photos from his Goth days, he would never hear the end of it. He still loved listening to his old Cure records, though. That and the Sisters of Mercy and the Fields of the Nephilim. Those were the bloody days.

'What's got into you this afternoon?' he asked Bob, who was in a right mood.

Bob rubbed the bridge of his nose. 'Sorry, I'm knackered.'

'Freddie still keeping you up?' Freddie was the sergeant's one-year-old son.

He sighed. 'Freddie. Jessica, the world's only four-year-old Nazi. The dog. The bloody cat.'

'Everyone but Isobel, eh?'

They laughed. The countryside sped by. Sheep, trees, boring stuff. It was a glorious day, though, the sky so blue it made Declan want to hum that old ELO song, which would have got him thrown out of the Cure fan club years ago.

'Well, look on the bright side. Only, what, seventeen years to go before you have a nice empty nest. Then what are you going to do?'

'Fucking celebrate.'

'You won't, I bet you. Because then you won't have anything to bitch and moan about. And let's face it, Bob, you're never happier than when you've got something to moan about.'

Bob looked at him sideways. 'And you're never happier than when you have a real ball-acher of a case to work on.'

'If anyone else but you said that to me, Detective Sergeant Clewley, they'd be the one with the ball-ache. How is Isobel, by the way?'

'Still lovely,' Bob said, smiling at the thought of his wife.

They drove on for a while. They were based with the Surrey and Sussex Major Crime Team in Eastbourne but were heading for a tiny village called Stonegate, roughly halfway between Tunbridge Wells and Hastings. More accurately, they were heading to a farm several miles outside the village. It was beautiful around here, if you liked that kind of thing. Declan, who had grown up in a place similar to this, associated rolling hills and sheep with his stultifying teen years. He had fled to London the moment he could, ditched the black drainpipes, joined the Met, found noise and fumes and crowds far more to his liking than silence and fresh air and flocks, before circumstances had driven him back out of the city. But at least he lived and worked in a large town. This place wasn't even a hamlet.

'Watch *Serial Killers* last night?' Bob asked.

Declan rolled his eyes. 'You and your bloody crime documentaries. Don't you get enough of that at work?'

'It's research,' he said. 'The one last night was awesome. You heard of BTK?'

'A kind of burger, isn't it?'

'Lol.'

Declan looked at his partner. 'Did you actually just say "lol"?'

'Yeah. It's what all the kids are saying these days. Sir.'

Declan sighed. 'There really ought to be a law against it.'

'Rofl.' While Declan banged his forehead with the flat of his palm, Bob went on. 'Anyway, BTK was this mild-mannered bloke who murdered at least ten people in Kansas. "Bind torture kill" – that's what it stands for. That's how he signed off his letters to the police.'

'Oh, he was one of them, was he? A letter writer.'

'Wouldn't you love to work a serial-killer case?'

'I worry about you sometimes. Actually, I worry about you quite a lot.'

'Arriving at destination on left', said the sat nav. It had instructed them to turn off the A-road and they had soon found themselves on winding country lanes framed by tall trees and strewn with roadkill, before emerging again into open countryside.

'What, here?' said Bob. 'It's just a field.'

'Over there.' Declan pointed. In the near distance, they could see a small cluster of farm buildings. They drove towards them down a dirt track, baked hard by the sun. As they grew closer, Declan got a better view of the farmhouse, which appeared to be held up by scaffolding, its thatched roof full of gaping holes, the red brickwork crumbling. Close by was a barn that was in an even worse state of repair. Yellow-and-black crime-scene tape had been strung up around an area between the house and the barn.

'This reminds me of one of those places where teens in horror movies get butchered by psycho hillbillies,' Bob said. *'The East Sussex Chainsaw Massacre.'*

They pulled up beside a parked police car, a sergeant from the local constabulary, sweating in his uniform, leaning against it. He looked up at them as they got out of their car. 'Sergeant Alexander,' he said, mopping his brow with a handkerchief.

Declan introduced himself and Bob, then said, 'So what have we got?'

Alexander led them towards the farmhouse. Declan looked up as something fluttered above them. 'Was that a bat?'

'Not at this time of day,' said the sergeant. 'More likely a swallow. Bats come out later. You're not wrong though – apparently, the old farmhouse is full of them. The project manager was telling me they've been having a nightmare with the conservation people.'

Declan stopped and waited for him to continue.

'This place is called Robertson Farm, after the family who farmed the land last century. But it's been standing empty for years. Empty and forgotten until a couple from London decided to do a "grand designs" and bought it. They're in the process of restoring it and converting the barn into a studio or something.'

The three of them approached the crime-scene tape. A couple of uniformed officers in short sleeves stood a few metres away on the other side of the taped-off area, chatting to a middle-aged woman wearing jeans and a vest-top, her shoulders pink with sunburn. 'Go on.'

Alexander cleared his throat. 'That's the project manager over there. She's a friend of the couple who've bought the place. She was down here this morning, supervising the builders—'

'And they found a body,' Bob interjected.

'I don't know if "body" is the word I'd use,' said Alexander.

'And what word would you use, Sergeant?' Declan asked.

'Remains. Whoever was down there looked like they'd been there a bloody long time.'

'What do you mean "down there"?'

Alexander pointed to a hole in the ground, about the same size as a manhole in the street. The top of a ladder protruded from it. Declan suddenly had a horrible feeling, like a shadow passing over him, despite the warmth of the sun and the brilliant, cloudless sky.

'In the cesspit,' he said.

Declan's grandad, who'd lived in a little cottage on the outskirts of Hastings, had a cesspit under his house because it was not connected to the main sewage system. He remembered how once, on a childhood visit, a truck had arrived to empty it. The smell was unbelievable. Years later, he'd been to the Glastonbury Festival and, looking down into the pit beneath the toilets, the smell of twenty thousand digested veggie burgers wafting up towards him, he'd been reminded of his grandad's cesspit. Declan also remembered him warning Declan and his sister never to try to open it lest they fall in. 'Nobody wants to drown in shit,' he said. He was very down-to-earth, his grandad. He missed him.

As Declan approached the hole, Bob a step behind him, the project manager came over, rearranging her long ponytail as she walked.

She stuck out her hand. 'Fiona Phillips,' she said. 'Bloody nuisance this.'

Bob eyed her. 'Was it you who found the body?'

She shook her head. 'No. One of the builders. We've only been on site for a few days and thought we should take a better look at the cesspit. We put a ladder down and he squeezed in. He came back up so fast it was almost comical. Like one of the moles in that whackamole game.'

'Where are the builders now?'

'I sent them home for the day. No point paying them if they're just going to be standing around drinking tea.' She laughed ironically.

'We'll need their names and addresses,' said Declan. He turned to Bob. 'We'd better take a look.'

Bob blanched. 'I don't think I'd fit through that hole.'

'It's all right. I'll do it. Is it dry in there, Ms Phillips?'

'Oh, yes. It must be twenty years since it was last used. So all the liquid will have evaporated and the excrement solidified long ago.'

Declan ignored the face Bob was pulling. 'OK, good. Have you got a torch?'

Fiona fetched a Maglite and handed it to Declan. He got down on all fours and climbed backwards onto the ladder, treading carefully until he was fully underground.

'Careful,' Bob said, as Declan disappeared from view.

Twisting his body, Declan shone the torch downwards but couldn't see the bottom. The air inside the cesspit was as fetid as he'd imagined, but at least all of the effluent had become almost fossilized. If the body had been found in an active cesspit, he wouldn't be volunteering to go inside. But he imagined he was descending into a cave. A nice clean cave. As a former Goth, he wasn't afraid of bats.

Declan descended another couple of rungs, then one more, sweeping the torch beneath him.

And there it was, lying on top of a solidified layer of waste.

Declan dropped a little closer. The skeleton stared at him from empty sockets and the bones were twisted at odd, jagged angles, one arm bent over its chest. The left leg at first looked cut off at the knee, until Declan realized the lower leg was folded beneath the femur.

He descended further into the darkness to get a closer look.

The skeleton didn't make him feel scared or repulsed, just sad. Imagine ending up in a place like this. But stronger even than the feelings of sympathy were questions, bubbling up so fast that he couldn't keep up with them. Had this person died in here? Who were they? How long had they been here? What had happened to them?

Did they fall or were they dumped? All his training and experience told him this had not been an accident.

Murder scenes were usually fresh, bullets or knives, ripped-open wounds or crushed throats, thickening pools of blood and the creeping stench of death. The buzzing of flies come to feast. This was very different. In this sealed chamber, years after death, the scene was curiously peaceful. Declan wasn't a religious man but he had an image of this person's soul being trapped down here, escaping when the cesspit cover had been removed, leaving behind a quiet calm.

He swept his torch around the area surrounding the human remains. There was no sign of any other objects. No jewellery glinted in the torchlight. No sign of a murder weapon. Just the body, alone in its tomb.

Shivering, he ascended the ladder and clambered onto solid ground, the skeletal face of the man or woman beneath fixed in his mind, staring at him – and asking him to find out what had happened to them.

11

Amy

Monday, 22 July

'Hang on, tell me again?'

'The message from Becky wasn't there when I went back to re-read it.'

They were in Gary's kitchen, talking loudly to be heard over the top of a washing machine on the spin cycle, whose drum was banging as if it was in a marching band. The window was open because the day was growing hotter, the thermostat edging towards 30 degrees. Gary was wearing shorts, flip-flops and a *Star Wars* T-shirt. He handed Amy a beer, so cold it gave her a shock as she tipped and swallowed. But it tasted good. She noticed Gary watching her as she licked her lips.

'Weren't copies of the messages emailed to you?' he asked. 'When I get replies or messages on Twitter, they're usually emailed to me.'

'No. I have too many emails to deal with as it is. I turned that setting—'

'Off.'

She smiled to herself. His annoying habit was becoming more endearing. Clearly, she'd been out in the sun too much.

'And what about this guy, the one you sent the message to on CupidsWeb?'

'Daniel.'

'Yeah. Has he got back to you yet?'

She shook her head and took another sip of the beer. She watched Gary lift his bottle and found herself thinking what nice arms he had. He must work out. She wondered what gym he . . . She stopped herself. She had definitely had too much sun.

'So . . . if he does contact you, what are you going to do? Go on a date with him?'

She shrugged. 'That's the idea. Find out what he knows about Becky. If anything. Probably clutching at straws, but—'

From nowhere, she was hit by a wave of emotion that rolled up from inside her. Tears sprung into her eyes and she felt herself wobble, having to put a hand on the worktop to hold herself up.

'Are you OK?' Gary said, stepping towards her.

His soothing voice opened something inside her and suddenly she was sobbing, her body shaking, unable to stop, the emotions of the last two days seizing control of her body. What if Becky was dead, or hurt? Her beautiful, stroppy, vivacious sister. She was the only person Amy really had in the world. She thought, 'Don't cry, don't cry,' but she couldn't stop. She dropped the beer bottle and heard, as if from a great distance, the shattering glass, and then Gary's arms were around her, pulling her face against his solid shoulder, stroking her back.

He made hushing noises until the sobs subsided. It had only been a minute but she felt exhausted. Gary continued to hold her and they stayed like that for a short while longer until Amy started to wriggle, feeling uncomfortable.

Gary stepped back and smiled at her. There was a damp patch on the shoulder of his T-shirt and he was standing in a puddle of beer and glass.

'I'm so sorry,' she said. 'I'll clean up the mess.'

She expected him to tell her not to worry, that he would do it, but instead, he said, 'I'll get you the mop . . . Actually, I don't have a mop. I think there's a dustpan and brush. Somewhere.'

She laughed, and sniffed. 'I'll get one from Becky's.'

After she'd cleaned up the beer and glass, Gary said, 'You need a break from all this worry. Let's go out for a drink.'

'I don't—'

'Come on. It will do you good, honestly. You can't do anything right now to help Becky, can you? Let's go to the pub, have a drink, just try to forget about it for a little while.'

'I can't forget about it, Gary.'

'I didn't mean it like that. I meant, stop thinking about it. And yeah, I know you're going to say you can't – but you really do need a break. OK?'

She sighed and smiled at the same time. 'OK. I give in.'

'Cool. But you'd better sort your face out first.' He grinned. 'You've got mascara *all* over it.'

'Busy in here tonight, for a Monday.'

Gary looked around for an empty table outside the Crown, but they were all full, crowded with smokers enjoying the evening sunshine. Inside, the queue at the bar was two bodies deep. 'I think there's a gig on tonight. Do you want to try somewhere else?'

'It's OK. Everywhere's going to be rammed on a night like this.'

It was one of the things she loved about London – in the summer, when the pubs and the pavements outside would fill up with drinkers, the city buzzing with pheromones, the smells of sex and money in the air, the promise that something, anything could happen. Becky loved nights like this too . . . Amy stamped on the thought before it took hold and made her cry again.

'Do you want to find a spot while I get the drinks in?'

Fortunately, just as she went outside, two guys stood up and left, so she nabbed the table, swabbing ineffectually at the spilled lager on its top with the flat of her palm. Her meeting with Ross earlier was still fresh in her mind – but, more than that, the disappearing tweet. She wiped her hand on the side of her skirt, dug out her phone and checked TweetDeck for the fiftieth time. More retweets of her appeal, but no useful replies, and no more messages from Becky. She checked her email. Nothing from Daniel either.

Why had Becky deleted the message? It made no sense.

Since receiving the original email from Becky, Amy had been vacillating between two possible explanations. The first was that the email was genuinely from Becky, but that something awful had happened to make her act so out of character. This was bad enough, but the second possibility was far worse – that someone else was *pretending* to be Becky.

If this second awful scenario was true, that meant the Twitter message was from the impostor too. And if *that* was right, that meant this person was watching her tweets, probably stalking her on Facebook, too.

And who knew how else they were watching her . . .

Her hands began to tremble and her phone shot out of

her grip like a fish leaping from a net, landing face down on the hard pavement.

'Oh, fuck.'

'What is it?' Gary stood over her, holding two pints. She liked the fact that he'd bought her a pint unasked.

She held up her phone to show him. The screen was shattered, cracks zigzagging across its fragile surface.

'Oops,' he said. 'Don't worry, you can get a kit off eBay to fix it. I'll do it for you, if you like.'

'You're so nice, Gary,' Amy said, half serious, half wistful, as she accepted one of the pints. 'I wish I had a neighbour like you. My neighbours are horrible. I went away for two days once and they complained to the council because I forgot to turn off my clock alarm. It only beeps for ten minutes! What's it like, having Becky as a neighbour?'

Gary frowned and sat down opposite her. 'Becky's a great girl,' he said carefully. 'Plays her music too loud at times, but doesn't freak when I tell her to turn it down – which I've done a few times. This one time she was decorating her bedroom, and she played that Lana Del Ray album at full volume, on repeat, the whole frigging day, and by the evening I was ready to weep. I banged on the door and said, "For the love of God, Becky, PLEASE stop playing that album," and she just laughed. She did turn it down though. It's not all her fault – we share a living-room wall, and they're pretty thin. She has a lot of—' He stopped abruptly.

'A lot of what?'

'Visitors,' he said, and his lips set in a hard line.

Amy affected misunderstanding. 'What – parties, and people over for lunch, that sort of thing? She's always had a really good social life, much better than mine.'

'Yeah, that sort of thing . . .'

Amy hesitated, before deciding to park that particular piece of information. It was worth pursuing, definitely, but she didn't feel robust enough to go there just now. Not with two beers inside her, the evening sun rosy on her sunglasses, music floating out from inside the pub, and too much else to extrapolate first.

'How do you and Becky get along?' Gary asked. He stretched his feet out under the table, and accidentally banged Amy's ankle. She pulled her leg out of the way, and they both apologized, then laughed.

'We're really close,' Amy said. 'At least, I thought we were. We've always argued, usually about stupid stuff, almost always started by her – I love her to bits, but she can be so *confrontational*! Especially if she's hormonal. She just can't let anything lie; she nags and grumbles and makes snide digs about things that she perceives as having upset her. She definitely gets that from our mum. Goads me into a big row. Then we scream at each other, one of us storms off, then someone – almost always me – holds out an olive branch, and we kiss and—'

Gary grinned. 'Make up. Well, if it's any consolation, I don't think it was just you that she acted like that with. I heard more tantrums coming through the walls than I thought strictly necessary from anyone out of their teens. I heard her argue with lots of people. Slamming doors, insults, tears . . . it could be a bit like living next door to—'

'Naomi Campbell?' Amy suggested, at the same time as he said, 'John McEnroe,' and they both laughed.

Then Gary looked worried. 'I hope you don't think I'm slagging her off or anything. I really like her, she's such a laugh, and, you know – really kind.'

Tears pressed behind Amy's eyes again. It had been easier when they'd been discussing her shortcomings.

Gary nudged her gently. 'So, tell me to mind my own business, but when you came over the other day, you said you and her had fallen out, and you hadn't seen her for a while . . . Was it a bad one?'

Amy twirled her pint glass round and round, watching its amber contents swish up the sides. 'Hmm. Yeah. It was a pretty bad one, for us. It was one of those rows that just escalated, you know, like: *And another thing . . .*'

'Thing . . .' Gary agreed softly.

'It started because my folks were over from Spain and wanted to take us out to dinner, but Becky said she couldn't make it because she was going to a party, so she couldn't have them to stay either – and she's the one with the spare room. I always seem to get lumbered with them when they come over, even though they have to sleep in my bed and relegate me to the sofa bed 'cos I don't have a second bedroom . . . Anyway, I think I just resented her ability to put her foot down – she never does anything she doesn't want to do, whereas I'm such a bloody pushover, it's not even funny – and we ended up in this big fight. I remember I told her that if she didn't turn up at Carluccio's by 9 p.m., I'd never speak to her again. And she wouldn't tell me about where the party was, or whose party, or why it was so important – I started to think she was making it up. We were screaming at each other.'

'Most people would think that being taken out to dinner by your parents would be a treat, not an ordeal,' Gary said.

'You clearly haven't met our parents, then, have you? No, of course you haven't – because they're always staying at my place, that's why. Not that they come over much any more.' Amy waved her now-empty glass at him. 'Another pint?'

115

'Don't mind if I do, thank you very much. And a packet of cheese-and-onion?'

'Coming up,' Amy said, noticing the way his stubble darkened in his dimples when he smiled.

As she waited at the bar, being jostled on all sides, she thought back to that evening, the horrendous row followed by the grim dinner with their mum and dad. Her parents had seemed to hold her entirely responsible for Becky's absence that night, and the meal had seemed to drag on for hours, her mother moaning at her about why Becky wasn't there – you'd have thought they would be happy that she, Amy, *was* there – and how Becky never kept in touch or returned her calls, and her dad banging endlessly on about the new filtration system in their pool at the villa in Ronda.

Amy had ended the night in a fury, tossing and turning on the thin foam mattress of the sofa bed with the metal struts underneath sticking into her whichever way she rolled. But it was herself she was most furious with, not her folks, or even Becky. Why did she do this to herself? She too could have said she had a prior arrangement. They could have stayed in a hotel, they had plenty of money – they were only in the UK to attend a friend's seventieth the next day. She had decided that she'd had enough of people taking advantage of her. She was going to stick to her guns, and not contact Becky. Let Becky come crawling back to *her*, for once!

Only she hadn't, had she? And now she was missing.

Amy finally got served and headed back outside, a pint in each hand and a bag of crisps held between her teeth. Gary shamelessly eyed her up as she sat down.

'Can I ask you something? How come you don't have a boyfriend? You're so pretty.'

She shrugged her shoulders, trying to make her voice light, but fumbled as she opened the crisps. They spilled out onto the table.

'Been there, done that, got the—'

'T-shirt,' Gary said, staring intently at her face, then frowning as he noticed the way her hands had suddenly started to shake. 'Are you going to tell me about it?'

Amy looked back at him. She never told people about Nathan. Perhaps it was because she felt so vulnerable at that moment, or perhaps even just to take her mind off Becky's disappearance, she didn't know – but either way, she realized for the first time that she did want to talk about it. It was oddly liberating.

'Yes,' she said. 'I am.'

12

Six years earlier

When Amy walked into the conference room at APW that
day and saw Nathan sitting at the table ready for the weekly
briefing, she understood the literal meaning of the word
'swoon'. Her vision gave a wobble, her knees went weak
and she felt a blush wash over her from top to toe. She
had never seen a sexier man.

'Everyone,' announced Martin, the MD, when they had
all taken their coffees off the tray in the centre of the
boardroom table, 'this is our new recruit, Nathan Stott.
He'll be heading up the business development team and
taking over the Randsome account.'

Nathan nodded politely at everyone present as Martin
introduced them all, but when it was her turn, Amy saw
his pupils dilate and the corners of his lips curl up into
a wide smile. He held her gaze for so long that she had
to drop hers first, and reach for a sachet of sugar for
her coffee, even though she never took sugar, just for
something to do to break the sexual tension. She thought

118

afterwards that she never had been brilliant at spotting when someone fancied her, but there was nothing ambivalent about the immediate lightning bolt she and Nathan experienced when they first met. So it was no surprise at all when he emailed her from across the office right after the meeting, and asked her out for a drink that night.

Amy couldn't get anything done that day for thinking about his sensual mouth and incredible hazel eyes. She counted down the hours, and had this fizzing, roiling feeling in her stomach at the thought of being able to stare at him unhindered across a pub table.

The date did not disappoint. She scrutinized him so much that she could straight away have told you how many little dark freckles he had scattered on his cheeks and down his neck (eleven), the length of his artful stubble (about three millimetres), the five silver hairs sprinkled around the crown of his thick silky black hair, the sort of hair that would have been described as 'floppy' in a Richard Curtis movie. He had Celtic patterns tattooed around his taut right bicep, which he showed her by unbuttoning and pushing his checked shirt off his shoulder, and peeling away the sleeve of the tight khaki T-shirt he was wearing underneath. Amy pointed out to him the flowery letters around her ankle, A&B, and he laughed.

'Get us, showing each other our tats on the first date. I love a girl with tattoos, though. So who's B, an ex?'

'My sister Becky,' she said. 'We're really close. You'll meet her soon. She'll love you.'

Then she blushed – how much presumption had been in those last two sentences? Nathan saw her embarrassment, reached across the table and grasped her forearm, gazing into her face with those amazingly long-lashed eyes.

'This is it, isn't it?' he said, and the intensity in his voice was visceral. 'You're the one.'

All Amy could do was nod, and gaze back.

As it turned out, the first of her two presumptuous sentences was correct: Nathan and Becky did meet soon. Amy moved in with him in less than a month, and Becky came over to see her flash new apartment in a gated development on the Kingston riverfront. Nathan cooked Pad Thai in a stripy chef's apron tied firmly over a faded Nirvana T-shirt, and boasted about the surround sound he'd recently had installed in the living room.

Amy thought the evening had been a great success. Nathan was lively and inquisitive, asking them both about their childhoods, their likes and dislikes.

'What are your worst fears then?' he'd asked them both, so casually.

'Spiders,' Becks had said with a shudder. 'And Amy's is enclosed spaces. I've never known such a wuss.'

'I'm not a wuss, I'm just claustrophobic,' she had protested.

'Are you now?' Nathan had said pensively, before turning back to stir the Pad Thai.

'What about you, Nathan?' Becky asked. 'What are you scared of?'

He laughed. 'I've got one of those weird irrational fears – velvet, believe it or not. It makes me puke with terror, don't ask me why. Luckily, Amy doesn't have any velvet dresses, otherwise I wouldn't have let her move in.'

Amy draped an arm around his neck. 'I'd have burned it for you, sweetie. Even if Stella McCartney had personally designed and sewn it for me.'

'Ahh, you're so adorable . . .'

Nathan kissed her, and Amy saw Becky look away, out of the window at a group of rowers sliding along the smooth evening river.

Amy hoped Becky wasn't feeling jealous. She kept trying to see him through her sister's eyes, and thought that Becky couldn't fail to fancy him – in fact, she even felt slightly worried that Becky would fall in love with him, too, and her overactive imagination started conjuring nightmare scenarios in which he left her for Becky, creating a rift that would never be healed . . .

She need not have worried. The second of her presumptuous sentences had not been true at all.

'How can you not like him?' Amy asked incredulously when they met for breakfast the next day. 'He's lovely, and he adores me.'

Becky shrugged and stared into her coffee.

'Becks?'

'I didn't say I didn't *like* him,' she said. 'He's cute and all. There's just something . . . I dunno . . . a bit *cold* about him.'

Amy made a face at her. 'Cold? He's not cold. He asked you all about yourself, about us as kids, our lives so far. I mean, he even asked us what our biggest fears are! He's interested, Becky, not cold. I don't see how you can possibly think that.'

Becky checked the pocket of her handbag for her Oyster card. 'Sorry, Amy, I didn't hate him or anything, I just got a bit of a weird vibe off him. It was almost like he was asking me stuff about us because he wanted ammunition, rather than to get to know us better. Anyway, I'm probably imagining it. As long as you're happy, what does it matter what I think? I've got to go, otherwise I'll be late for the register.'

121

Nathan was already at his desk when Amy got into work that day. She sneaked up behind him and put her arms around him, burying her nose into his thick clean hair.

'Oh, you guys,' said Martin, passing by Nathan's workstation. 'Get a room!'

'We already have,' Nathan replied, reaching his hands behind him to squeeze her bottom. 'And soon we'll get a whole house, and then some kids to fill it with, and eventually grandchildren . . .'

Martin laughed and made puking noises as he walked into his office. 'Just don't shag on the photocopier. It's against company policy,' he said, closing the door behind him.

Amy hugged Nathan more tightly, her heart swelling with happiness. 'I love you,' she whispered into his ear.

'I love you, too, angel,' he whispered back.

Three weeks later, they had their first argument. Nathan had always been morbidly curious about Amy's past relationships, even though Amy had repeatedly told him that there had never been anyone who even came close to Nathan's position as the love of her life. Then one night they had been out, drunk, in one of Kingston's many noisy bars, a dark neon-flashing cellar full of men on the pull and girls in micro-skirts and fake nails.

'Amy!' bellowed a voice in her ear as Nathan was paying at the bar for their designer beers. They both turned around, and Amy squealed with delight at the sight of someone she hadn't seen since her schooldays.

'Chris!' She hugged him tightly. 'It's been years, how are you? What are you doing these days? Do you live in Kingston? This is my boyfriend, Nathan.'

Chris stuck out his hand and Nathan shook it, but in as

122

perfunctory way as he could, without a smile. Chris raised his eyebrows, then turned back to Amy, answering all her questions. Amy tried to take Nathan's hand, not wanting him to feel left out of the conversation, but he picked up his beer instead.

'Sweetie, Chris and I did our A levels together. We sat next to each other in Economics.'

'Right,' said Nathan flatly.

Amy and Chris chatted for a few more minutes, and then Chris pulled out his phone. 'Give me your number and let's have a proper catch-up soon, yeah? Lunch or something. I've got to go – I'm with a bunch of college mates and we're about to head over to Oceana.'

Amy dictated her mobile number. 'Text me later so I'll have yours too,' she said, giving him a kiss on the cheek before he walked back to his friends. 'Great to see you!'

She turned back to Nathan. 'I can't believe it! I haven't seen him for about ten years, and I was always gutted we lost touch after school, he was such a laugh. I looked him up on Facebook a couple of years ago but—'

She stopped at the expression on Nathan's face. 'What's the matter?'

He carefully placed his beer bottle back on the bar and leaned close to her so that his mouth was right by her ear. Anybody looking would think that he was whispering endearments.

'You are not to see that guy ever again. If he texts you, you ignore it. If you save his number in your phone I will chuck it into the Thames. Do you understand me?'

His voice was loud and harsh above the noise of the bar, and it hurt the inside of her ear. She recoiled, but he grasped the back of her head and dragged her closer again.

'What's the problem, Nathan?' She struggled to move

so that he could hear her. 'Do you know Chris? Has he done something to upset you? He didn't seem to know who you are.'

'Never seen him before in my life, and don't want to either. He's a cocky little twat and he clearly fancies you.'

Amy laughed. 'Chris doesn't fancy me! He's gay!'

'Don't you dare contradict me! I saw the way he looked at you.'

Amy pulled away from him. 'That's insane.'

Nathan snatched the beer bottle out of her hand and slammed it and his own onto the bar, causing a group of girls to look over and giggle nervously at witnessing a domestic. 'We're going.' He grabbed her hand and marched out of the bar. Amy tried to protest but he would not let go. Chris waved at her as they left, undisguised concern on his face, and Amy blushed with mortification.

Once they were outside on the pavement, out of sight of the bar, she shook herself free and planted her hands on her hips. 'Nathan. You can't talk to me like that, it's completely out of order! Chris is *gay*. And even if he wasn't, he's an old friend and I'm perfectly entitled to talk to an old friend. What's more, I fully intend to go out to lunch with him. Come along if you want, as long as you're not going to be as rude as you were just then, but— *Hey!*'

He had shoved her hard up against the wall and put his face close to hers so that she was inches away from his wild, furious eyes. Amy pressed her palms against his chest to push him away from her, but it was like trying to move a rhino, and she felt pressure and pain in her wrists. She stared at him in shock and disbelief as he yelled at her, flecks of his spittle decorating her cheeks. She couldn't even fully take in what he was saying: an incoherent diatribe about her being a whore and a slut.

This was not the man she loved.

'Oi, twat, that's uncool,' said an Asian teenaged boy, passing with a group of friends. 'You don't shout at your bird like that.'

Nathan released Amy and turned to lunge at the group, flailing wildly and screaming abuse, and they scattered, laughing. Amy ran, as fast as her spindly stilettos would allow her. She ran all the way down the pedestrianized precinct until she stumbled and fell, not caring that all the weaving revellers were staring at her with concern, or amusement. Someone tried to help her up, but she shook them off. All she could think about was getting home and pulling the duvet over her head. She ripped off the shoes and ran the rest of the way home barefooted.

Once back in the flat, she went into the spare room and climbed straight into bed there, fully dressed, her feet bleeding and dirty and her heart pounding out of her chest. A text bleeped on her phone, and she got out again to retrieve it from her handbag on the floor.

HERE'S MY NUMBER BABE. LET'S MEET SOON. GREAT TO SEE YOU. HOPE ALL IS OK. CHRIS XXX

Amy deleted it.

'I'm so sorry,' said Nathan the next morning. He appeared in his boxers in the doorway of the spare room, carrying a tray with a mug of tea, a single rose in a vase, and two croissants on a plate. 'Forgive me? I feel terrible. I know it's no excuse, but you know how work is at the moment, how stressed the Randsome account's making me. I just had too much to drink. It won't happen again, I promise. I love you, Amy.'

13

Amy

Monday, 22 July

'Sorry,' Gary said sheepishly. 'I didn't mean to touch a nerve. I'm a nosy git, that's all. It's none of my business. Let's talk about something safer – tell me about your job? Becky told me you're, like, an Internet entrepreneur.'

Amy managed to laugh, even though she felt like crying again. She found herself gabbling: 'That's flattering – I like being called an entrepreneur.'

'Your sister is very proud of you.'

Tears pricked Amy's eyes. 'Don't . . . you'll get me started again.'

'Sorry.'

'It's OK. So . . . I'm not sure about being an entrepreneur but I'm self-employed – I get to go to work in my pyjamas. I started up this craft website about three years ago, you know, an online community for people – women, mostly – who are into making things to save money: knitting, sewing, making your own jam, that sort of thing. Generally, it's about recycling household stuff. Upcycle.com, it's called. My

126

background's in marketing so I knew about how to build up mailing lists and stuff, and now it's taken off so much that I've got thirty thousand members, and proper advertising revenue . . . I'm outsourcing most of the content now – I've run out of recipes for rosehip syrup and instructions on how to crochet hot-water-bottle covers . . .'

Amy felt better, now she was on safer ground. Upcycle.com was her baby, her only real success story in life. She sometimes sat and scrolled through the membership lists, marvelling at the number of strangers who had signed up to read her articles and tips. She didn't say so because it would sound ridiculous, but privately she thought of herself as a sort of Internet pop star – albeit an anonymous one – with fans and the odd hater, people out there commenting and complimenting her on her creative ideas.

'You don't look like a knitter to me,' Gary said, tilting his head.

Amy leaned towards him, aware that she was flirting. 'I'm a *demon* with a pair of knitting needles,' she whispered, and he laughed.

'Doesn't it get a bit lonely, sitting at home all day, knitting?'

'No, not usually. I take Boris out twice a day – in fact, that reminds me, I can't be too late home tonight, he'll be crossing his legs – and meet people, other dog walkers. And I'm constantly talking to people about the site – advertisers, copywriters, suppliers. I go to craft fairs, too, to promote it. No, I'm fine.'

There was a slightly awkward pause, in which Amy dreaded Gary was about to get back on to the topic of relationships. The distorted sound of the bar band floated out through the pub doors.

'Want to go and watch the band for a bit before they finish?' she asked hastily, to head him off.

'Sure – they sound pretty—'

'Wicked?' Amy grinned and, after looking confused for a second, Gary smiled back.

'All right, all right. I know it's a bad habit. But I would never use the word "wicked". Not since I was fourteen anyway.'

'How about awesome?'

'Yeah, I'd say that. As in, "I think you're awesome, Amy."' Then, hurriedly, 'That was just an example. Obviously.'

Drunken flirting, that was all it was, she reasoned, as much as her beer-lubricated brain could reason. He wasn't really interested in her . . . Did she want him to be interested? It certainly felt exciting, having a hot man say things like that, look at her the way he did. She felt an unfamiliar tugging feeling, a fizz of excitement – but even though she was drunk, another part of her fought it. She was scared, and being forced back into memories of Nathan had definitely not helped.

She didn't know what expression – or mixture of expressions – showed on her face, but now Gary looked embarrassed. He looked as if he was going to say something, was searching in his head for something flippant or funny to say, but before he could find it, she said, 'Come on, I love this song.'

She grabbed his hand, not caring at that moment what this would signal to him, and pulled him into the pub, where they were hit by a blast of noise and heat. In the back room behind the bar, a crowd of people stood around the stage, a few of them dancing, most of them nodding their heads or singing along. The band were playing an Oasis song that reminded Amy of being at school, of discos and snogging and cans of cheap cider.

She guided Gary into the throng until they hit a wall of

bodies. The Oasis song ended and a slower song came on, another cover version, and a shiver went through Amy's blood when she realized what it was: that Everything But the Girl song, the one about a loved one going missing. *Now you've disappeared somewhere . . .*

It was horribly apposite and she almost fled, but Gary was in the way and, as she turned back to the stage, the line in front of her shifted so she got a good view of the band. The singer was less attractive than his voice, but the guitarist was nice – and then a shock of realization hit her.

She grabbed Gary's shoulder and pulled his ear towards her lips.

'I know that guy,' she shouted.

'Who?' Gary mouthed back.

'The guitarist. That's Clive, Katherine's ex. You know, Becky's best friend.'

Gary lifted his chin, not sure what he was supposed to do with this information. He shrugged.

They continued watching the band, who ran through a couple of their own songs and then climaxed with another couple of covers. The crowd clapped and cheered as if Oasis themselves were playing a reunion gig in front of them. Then people began to disperse, drifting back to the bar. A space cleared between her and the stage, and Amy watched Clive put away his equipment, laughing and chatting with the other members of the band.

'Another drink?' Gary asked.

'Go on then. One more.'

She approached the stage and waited till she caught Clive's eye. He was bending down, unplugging a cable from his guitar.

'Hi,' she said.

He didn't recognize her. Probably thought she was one of those 'I'm with the band' types.

She leaned closer. 'You don't remember me, do you?'

From the panicked look on his face, he probably thought she was some girl he'd had a one-night stand with. She put him out of his misery. 'I'm Amy – I know Katherine.'

His expression switched. All light left his face and his mouth turned down at the edges. 'Oh.'

'Yeah, I was sorry to hear about you guys breaking up.'

'Hmm.'

'I saw Katherine the other day,' she said, deciding to plough on, even though she wasn't exactly sure where she was heading. She was riding along on a wave of alcohol. 'She seemed different. Was acting really weird, I thought.'

He looked at her properly, his expression serious. 'How do you know her?'

'I'm her friend's sister. Becky's sister.'

Immediately, his eyes narrowed and his lip curled. It was, Amy realized with shock, a look of absolute hatred.

'Becky,' he spat. He stood up, and Amy saw that the other band members were watching, their concerned glances moving between Clive and her. 'I'm sorry, but I don't want to talk about that bitch.'

All of a sudden, Amy was sober. 'But . . . why?'

Clive stared at her, his lip curled, eyes ablaze with hatred. Without saying any more, he turned away.

14

Becky

Tuesday, 11 June

'Clive's found out what we've been doing.'

We're sitting outside the café we often go to after school, two cups of frothy coffee steaming before us, the day damp and cold. Katherine lights a fag, seemingly unbothered by the horror on my face.

'What we've been doing?' I say. 'Don't you mean, what you've been doing?'

She shrugs, exhales. A pair of Year Twelve boys walk past and Katherine follows them with her eyes. 'Tyler Clarke. Fucking little shit. Thinks he's so clever. Well, I've got news—'

'Kath! Please.'

She sniffs. She's so infuriating sometimes, the way she withholds important information because she loves the drama and the power it gives her. I lean forward and stare at her.

'When Clive and I had that massive row the other day, it was because he looked at my emails.'

'No! Nightmare,' I say, waving away her smoke.

'He saw what you and me have been up to.'

'Ri-ight . . .? You mean . . .' The cold air seemed to penetrate my body and I shivered. 'He knows about the Internet dating?'

She pulls a face.

'Oh, no – Kath! What . . . he knows all of it?'

She sucks on her fag, her cheeks hollowing. 'Yeah, and . . . I'm sorry, Becks, but I copped out. I should've told him that it was because I just don't want to be with him any more, but instead I . . . I—'

'*What?*'

'I told him it was all your idea.' She says it in a rush, without looking me in the face.

'Kath! That's like the opposite of how it happened – it was *your* idea.'

'I know, I'm sorry. But I thought it would be less hurtful to him and his male ego if he thought I was coerced into it.'

'*Coerced?*'

'Um . . . persuaded, anyway. I don't want to hurt him, you know. I'm not a complete bitch.'

I don't say anything to that.

'Plus, he might be less likely to shop me to the Inland Revenue . . . Sorry, Becks,' she adds.

'So what's going on now?' I ask. 'Are you still together?'

She lights another cigarette, not caring that there are more kids from the school around and that she's setting a bad example. If the principal walked past now, he'd be spitting blood.

'Just about. We had one of those nights – you know, where you're up all night, talking and crying – well, he was crying – and then you have really intense sex, the best sex we've had for years, actually. Shame it's not always like that. And he's said he's going to change, be more spontaneous, spend less time rehearsing with his stupid band. And that I can pay him back in instalments, no rush.'

'So you're going to give it a go?'

She smirks. 'That's what he thinks.'

I make an exasperated sound. 'Kath, you *are* a bitch.'

She shrugs. 'I'm just looking out for number one. And yeah, it's gonna hurt him. But it's not like what we're doing is hurting anyone else, is it? Well, not really.' She grins dirtily. 'I'd keep away from Clive, if I were you, though. He's really mad with you. He was threatening all sorts.'

I'm horrified all over again. 'What do you mean, threatening?'

She waves a hand. 'Oh, don't worry. He won't do anything. He's a pussy cat.'

15
Amy

Tuesday, 23 July

Amy rang Katherine's doorbell and waited. When no reply came, she knocked, then knocked louder. Arms folded, she stood back, looked up at the windows, hoping for a sign of life. She had to know why Clive had called Becky a bitch so vehemently.

Clive had refused to speak to her, his bandmates forming a protective circle around him. What had Becky done? He'd said she was a bitch – not a thief, or a liar, or any of the other accusations he could have made against her. Calling her a bitch might imply that Clive somehow blamed Becky for his break-up with his girlfriend. But why? And in the answer, was there a clue that would lead her closer to Becky? By dissecting her sister's life in the weeks before her disappearance, Amy hoped to think herself into Becky's head, to walk in her shoes. Discovering why the mild-mannered Clive loathed her so much was, it seemed to Amy, an important part of the puzzle.

Katherine didn't appear to be at home. Amy walked over

to the solid wooden gate, just over six feet high, that blocked the passageway running down the side of the cottage to the garden. She put one foot on the low wall that edged the front garden and pulled herself up on it so she could just peek over the top.

'Katherine! Kath!' she called.

Fuck. She was assuming she'd just have to come back later, but then she thought she heard a noise in the garden. She called out again and heard another odd noise. A murmuring voice.

Before she could chicken out, she hauled herself up onto the gate, so it pressed hard against her belly, and leaned over so she could reach the bolt. She slid it back then dropped back onto the balls of her feet. *I really shouldn't be doing this*, she thought, but it was too late now. She went through the gate into the garden.

'Who the hell are you?' A man's voice.

An old man in a stained tank top gawped at her over the low garden fence. He was leaning over, holding a piece of cooked meat in his hand, and it took Amy a couple of seconds to realize he was trying to coax Katherine's cat out from behind a tree. The cat eyed the meat hungrily but appeared equally wary of the old man, who reminded Amy of a taller version of Gollum. She half expected him to hiss 'My precioussssr' at the cat and, thinking this, she giggled to herself.

'Who are you and what's so bloody funny? Do you want me to call the police?'

'No, I'm sorry.' She felt slightly hysterical. 'I'm a friend of Katherine's. The gate was open. Have you seen her? Mister, um—'

'Williams.' The old man threw the scrap of ham to the cat, who pounced on it and began eating. 'I haven't

135

seen her since Sunday night. This poor little flower is starving – look at her.'

It was Tuesday now. Three days since she'd woken up to find Becky gone.

'Do you normally see her every day?' Amy asked. It occurred to her that she too had last seen Katherine on Sunday.

Mr Williams nodded. 'See her – and hear her.' He licked his lips, somehow conveying both disgust and hunger, and Amy took a step back, repulsed. 'Hear her late at night getting up to all sorts with her visitors.'

That was exactly what Gary had said about Becky last night. Two women who had, it seemed, a lot of sex. Becky had never mentioned this, and had recently been so vague when Amy had asked her if she had any men in her life that she'd assumed that, like her, Becky wasn't getting any. Were these men Becky had met Internet dating? From the paltry number of dates Becky had arranged through CupidsWeb, this seemed unlikely. So who were they? What were she and Katherine up to?

Amy felt uneasy discussing Katherine's sex life with this guy. But she could tell he was starved of company and was a potential goldmine of information about his young, sexy neighbour. 'So . . . you saw her on Sunday?'

'Yeah. Saw her heading out around, hmm, six o'clock, I think. She was all dolled up, looked like she was going to meet someone. Nothing unusual there, though. She goes out like that most nights. I never knew it was possible for a woman to have so many different clothes. My Mary, God rest her soul, liked clothes, but she was happy with the few outfits she could afford.'

Amy felt a stab of pity, nodding for Mr Williams to carry on.

136

'I usually hear her come home, either late at night – usually with company, if you know what I mean – or the next morning, on her own. But I haven't seen her.' He looked down at the cat, which was staring at him, hoping for more meat. 'I've gotta tell you, I'm worried about this little 'un. She's been meowing at the back door for the last two days.'

Mr Williams fixed his gaze on Amy, and an expression of genuine concern creased his face. 'I've never known her not come home to feed the cat before. I hope nothing's happened to her.'

Amy rode her bike straight to the police station in Camberwell. She found a space to park, turned off the engine and kicked down the stand, but remained straddling the bike, needing to gather her thoughts for a moment. She took off her helmet, and noticed that her leathers were attracting admiring and disapproving glances from pedestrians walking past. A pair of businessmen gave her a lustful once-over, before the filthy look she shot at them made them avert their gaze. She felt like sticking her foot out towards them and saying, 'See these? They're not fuck-me boots. They're fuck-*off* boots.'

Becky would have said that. She wasn't frightened of what people thought of her. Amy remembered Becky's face when she had bought the bike and the leathers and the boots, turning up outside Becky's flat and trying to act nonchalant. It was in the first days after Nathan, and Becky had looked her up and down and said, 'You got yourself a suit of armour. Nice.'

Amy took her phone out and opened the Facebook app, navigating her way to Katherine's page.

The most recent status update was on Sunday, at 19.29: *Got a big date tonight. V excited. Soho here I come!*

137

A number of Katherine's friends had left comments, asking for more details, or saying things like: *Don't do anything I wouldn't do ;)*

But Katherine hadn't responded or left any other updates – furthermore, there were a number of posts on her wall from friends saying they'd tried to contact her and was she OK? Looking back through Kath's Timeline, Amy could see that Kath was one of those people who updated their status at least two or three times a day, compelled to tell everyone even her most mundane thoughts and actions. But since her announcement of her date, Katherine hadn't updated her status at all.

Amy had seen enough. She swung her leg over the bike and marched straight up to the front desk of the police station, crash helmet in hand. A drunk woman with greasy blonde hair sat on a bench by the door, fumes coming off her that made Amy's stomach churn.

'How can I help you?' said the constable behind the desk.

'I want to talk to somebody who deals with missing persons.' As she spoke, a small part of her brain noted how she had been trained by the media to say 'persons' not 'people'.

'You can talk to me.'

She took a deep breath and leaned forward, determined to make this police officer take her seriously.

'A few days ago, I called you to report that my sister was missing. No one took me seriously. But now her best friend has gone missing too.'

The PC opened a notepad and started to ask her questions, the same ones she'd been asked the first time she'd called about Becky. The names and addresses of everyone involved, details of what she knew, was there any sign that either of the young women involved intended to do themselves harm? The facts.

'So what are you going to do?' she asked.

There was a queue building up behind her, a woman shouting that someone had stolen her son's bike, the teenage boy standing beside her looking mortified at both his mother's behaviour and having to deal with the 'Feds'. The PC at the desk kept looking over Amy's shoulder at the shouting woman, who was by now issuing a litany of threats about what she was going to do if the police didn't arrest the bike thieves.

'Sorry?' The PC looked back at Amy as if he'd forgotten she was there.

'I said, "What are you going to do?"'

'Did you say someone has already been out to see you about your sister, Miss . . . Coltman?'

'Yes. But now Katherine's missing too. The neighbour told me she'd never failed to come home to feed her cat before.'

'OK. Well, this is what will happen. This'll be allocated to a Neighbourhood Response Team and they'll go and take a look, talk to the neighbour, see what they can find out.'

'Is that it?'

The woman was still yelling in the background and Amy could feel herself growing increasingly irritated. Why couldn't anyone else see how serious this was? Why wouldn't that stupid woman shut up? She closed her eyes in a long blink, breathing out to dispel the anger.

'That's all we can do for the moment,' the constable said. 'If we believe the level of concern is sufficiently high, we'll pursue it further.'

'And what about Becky?'

He looked at his notes. 'That's your sister?'

'Er – *yes.*' *Idiot*, she fumed silently. She'd only mentioned Becky's name about six times already.

He sighed. 'I'll have a word with the MISPER coordinator. The missing persons coordinator.'

'Can I have his or her name and number?'

'I'll ask her to contact you.'

The woman whose son's bike had been stolen was huffing and puffing very close to Amy's ear. She wasn't going to get any further here – she had been well and truly stone-walled – so Amy said a quiet, 'OK, thank you,' and turned around, exiting the building.

But the second she got outside, she thought, No. That wasn't good enough. That wasn't fucking *acceptable*.

She swung round, shouldered open the door to the station and burst back into the front office. She barged past the woman who was still shouting about the bike, jerking her hand upwards to shush her as she opened her mouth to protest. The PC stared at her from behind the desk.

'I am not . . .' Amy began, and it all came rushing out, the scenario she most feared pushing its way to the front of her mind. 'I am not going to be fobbed off like this. My sister has gone missing and so has her best friend and I think . . . I think somebody's got them. Or has killed them. Murdered them. Because Becky would never have written that email, and what about the messages on Twitter, and why has Katherine been acting so weird, and Becky would never, ever go off like that, she wouldn't, she just, oh, God, somebody's hurt her, something awful has happened to her, you have to *do* something . . .'

The bike woman and her son were gawping at her, the drunk by the door had stirred and lifted her eyes to stare, and several other police officers had appeared behind the desk.

A policewoman with curly black hair took her gently by the elbow and handed her a tissue.

'Why don't you come with me, madam,' she said, and she steered Amy into the recesses of the police station. Amy's heart was banging so hard and fast that she thought it might escape from her chest.

The policewoman told Amy her name was DC Amristy and sat her down in a small room that Amy assumed was an interrogation room.

'Why don't you tell me all about it?' DC Amristy said kindly.

Amy began to tell her, the whole story, and when she got to the end, Amristy stood up. 'Let me just go and talk to our MISPER, see what she says.'

'OK.'

As soon as the policewoman had left the room, Amy's phone chirruped. She opened it to find a Facebook status update on her screen.

Becky Coltman has added a new photo.

16

Declan

Wednesday, 17 July

'Glorious day.'

'Hmm?' DI Declan Adams looked up from the screen of his PC and rubbed his eyes. Bob Clewley stood in the doorway of Declan's office, a sweating Starbucks Frappuccino in his hand. He sucked some down and crossed to the window.

'You can't see from here, what with the view being of a multi-storey car park, but it's beautiful outside. I'm going to take the kids down to the beach after my shift.'

'That's nice.'

'Yeah, thought we might go down to Hastings, visit the nudist beach at Fairlight. I love to feel the evening sun on my knob.'

'Right.'

'You're not actually listening to me, are you?' Bob smiled.

Declan sighed. 'I'm waiting for the forensic anthropologist to call.'

Bob turned away from the window and crossed to

Declan's desk, standing annoyingly close. It irritated him that Bob was able to concentrate on anything else when they were working on a case. Although, as Bob would point out, it was barely even a case yet. 'Melinda Moore, this time, is it?'

'Yes.' Neither of them had dealt directly with Moore before, but she had been involved in a case they were familiar with, when a body had been found buried beneath the pier.

After Declan had emerged from the cesspit, he had hung around while the Home Office pathologist came to take the body. The nearest morgue was in Tunbridge Wells but that was in Kent, and they were Sussex Police. That meant the remains were taken to Eastbourne morgue, just a couple of miles from the Major Incident Suite.

Watching while the remains were removed from the hole in the ground, Declan had examined the scene more closely, trying to absorb the atmosphere of the place. There was nothing for miles but farmland, just like the lifeless place where he'd grown up. But this was an affluent area, the countryside all around dotted with million-pound properties, and he wondered why this farm had been left deserted for so long.

The project manager, Fiona Phillips, had told him that the grass above the cesspit was lush and overgrown, unmown for years, the whole place returned to nature. The construction team had had to cut the grass in order to gain access to the cesspit entrance.

'It was sealed?' Declan asked.

Fiona had nodded. 'That was the first thing I wondered too. Did she fall or was she pushed? But the lid was on, firmly in place.'

'Why did you say *she*?'

Fiona looked towards the hole. 'They're always women, aren't they?'

Now, Bob crossed back to the window. Declan knew that he cared, that he took his work seriously, but he also knew the job didn't consume Bob as it did him. Bob didn't spend his nights with the faces of the victims of crime flickering inside his head, with murder victims talking to him, with dead children crying in his dreams. Declan appreciated that Bob was the normal one, the healthy one, and it wasn't just because he'd seen more than the younger man. It was in his nature. The therapist he'd seen after he'd left the Met had told Declan he suffered from exaggerated empathy. He felt too much of other people's pain. It was both a blessing and curse for a policeman.

With the body they'd found in the cesspit – and Declan felt sure that Fiona was right, that it was a woman – it was pure imagination. But last night, as he tried to sleep in a bedroom that was as hot and airless as . . . well, as a cesspit, Declan had been visited by a ghost. Not literally – he didn't believe in that hokum – but in his mind. The dead girl had talked to him, pleaded with him to seek justice on his behalf.

But when Declan's dream-self said, 'Who *are* you?' the girl faded from view.

'So what do we know about the farmhouse?' Bob asked now.

Declan stabbed at a couple of keys on the keyboard and brought up his notes: 'Robertson Farm. The farmhouse was built in around 1830 . . . Not much of this is very useful. Between the Second World War and the 1980s, a lot of the land around the farm was sold off to surrounding farms. Seems like Robertson Farm wasn't very successful. By 1990, there was just one guy living there, a farmer called Derek Jenkins. Right before he died he sold the farm to a property-development company called JWF, which wanted to build a hotel on the site.'

'In the middle of nowhere?' Bob said.

'Maybe a spa. Or one of those places where rich Londoners take their kids to commune with nature. Anyway, the project got bogged down in the usual planning-permission hell until it was eventually put on hold, and JWF went bust at the end of 1998, leaving all of its projects in limbo, including Robertson Farm.'

'It was left to rot.'

'Exactly. For over twenty years, including the time when they were planning to turn it into a hotel . . . so we know that the earliest our woman could have entered the cesspit would be 1990. But I called a local drainage company that specializes in septic tanks and the like, and they said that all of the urine would have evaporated and the excrement would have solidified within a few years of disuse. The skeleton wasn't submerged at all so she must have gone in there at least three to four years after 1990. But hopefully, Melinda will be able to tell us more.'

'The early nineties,' Bob sighed wistfully. 'Good times.'

'Yeah. I didn't even know you existed.' Declan went on: 'JWF's staff would know about the farm and, presumably, the cesspit. We should check out their staff from back then. See if anything sticks out. But right now, the priority is finding out who she is.'

'Cessna.'

'What?'

He looked suitably sheepish. 'That's what everyone's calling her.'

Declan rolled his eyes. 'Have a bit of respect, Clewley.'

'It could be an awful lot worse. Mike Jarvis suggested calling her Latrina.'

The phone rang and Declan snatched it up. 'DI Adams. Ah, hi, Melinda. I've been looking forward to your call. Yes, yes . . . of course, I'll come over right away.'

When he put down the phone his heart was beating faster and he had that tingle in his belly, the one that kept him in this job, the fix he lived for.

He looked up at Bob. 'Sounds like Melinda has got some interesting info for us. Want to come? Or are you going to go and bronze your bollocks on Fairlight Beach?'

The woman's remains were laid out on a bench, the bones looking even sadder in the bright fluorescent light of the lab. In the cesspit, they had appeared muddy brown, but he could see now that the discolouration was more subtle. The bones looked as though they'd been dragged through dirt, the colour of a lifelong cigar-smoker's teeth.

Bob had come along, too, Declan was pleased to note, extending his shift despite the lack of overtime and – doubt-lessly – absorbing the complaints of his wife like a man well-used to disappointing those he loved. Bob's flippant manner had changed now they were in the presence of the bones – he was no longer calling her Cessna. Or perhaps it wasn't the remains that were making him serious and quiet. Maybe it was Melinda Moore.

Melinda, who was in her mid-thirties, had very long red hair that she wore loose, was so pale she was almost translucent and had blue eyes with heavily hooded lids, like a Pre-Raphaelite muse. She spoke with a soft, melodic voice tinged with irony. And she was tactile, too, laying a warm hand on people as she spoke to them. Declan was sure that if she invited Bob into that storage cupboard over there for fifteen minutes of fun, he would forget the family

146

he adored in an instant. Declan would have been strongly tempted, too.

'She was beautifully preserved,' Melinda said, addressing Declan as they both looked down at the skeleton laid out like a woman sunbathing in her back garden, her limbs rearranged now.

'She?'

'Oh, yes, definitely a woman. I didn't need DNA to tell me that. The shape of the pelvis alone tells me this person was female.' She lightly touched Declan's shoulder and he observed how Bob swallowed, watching Melinda reverently.

'She's five foot eight and weighed around nine stone . . . nine stone two. But from her DNA, I can tell a few other things. She was in her early twenties – I would guess twenty-three – and was Caucasian. She had blue eyes and blonde hair. What else? Yes – there must have been a good amount of moisture down there. The body requires moisture in order to decompose. Some of that moisture would come from the body itself – the flesh – but in a dry atmosphere, you would expect to see some mummification. The cesspit was empty?'

'Yes,' Declan said. 'Completely dry. What else can you tell?'

'Well . . . she was naked. But you knew that. Her left hip and left arm are damaged – I would guess from the drop into the pit, where they struck the ground.'

'So she was dropped into the pit.'

'Or fell,' said Bob.

Melinda touched his arm, making him jolt, and said, 'I really don't think she fell in. And not just because the cesspit cover was closed behind her.'

Declan waited for her to continue.

147

'There were puncture wounds in the thorax area – the ribcage.'

'She was stabbed?' Bob was horrified. He had clearly been assuming it had been some kind of unfortunate accident.

Melinda nodded. 'With great force. It looks like they stabbed her in the heart, with the knife driving down, like this.' She mimed somebody thrusting downwards with a knife.

They were all silent for a moment.

'I've submitted the DNA to the national database, to see if there's a match. If we're very lucky, she was once arrested for shoplifting or something. But it will take a couple of days to get the results.'

'Anything else you can tell us right now?' Declan asked.

'Yes, actually. She was suffering from mild scoliosis.'

'What's that?' Bob asked, his cheeks turning a pale shade of pink as Melinda's lips curled in his direction.

'Curvature of the spine,' she replied. Using both hands, she picked up the dead woman's spine and turned it over, tracing a curved line along it with her forefinger. 'As you can see, it's very mild, but it forms a shallow C shape. When she was a young teenager she might have worn a back brace to help correct it. It probably wouldn't have been noticeable once she was an adult though.'

Declan felt little bubbles of excitement in his belly. This, surely, would help them identify this person they now knew was a murder victim.

'How common is it?' he asked.

Melinda tilted her head from side to side. 'It's not my area of expertise . . .'

'It affects three to four children out of every thousand,' Bob said.

Declan and Melinda looked at him with surprise. Bob held up his phone. 'I just Googled it, didn't I?'

'OK,' Declan said. 'And the NHS will have records of girls who have undergone treatment. We know her rough age, too, and we can assume she comes from around here – so it shouldn't be too hard to identify her, even if nothing comes back from the DNA database.' He smiled. 'Thanks for being so helpful, Melinda.'

'Yeah, cheers, Melinda,' added Bob.

Melinda cast a look down at the bones on the bench. 'I hope you find out who she is. And who did this to her. I'll let you know if we've got a DNA match as soon as I hear.'

As they were leaving, Melinda called after them. 'Oh, one more thing I almost forgot to mention.'

Declan turned back.

'The position she was found in, with one hand positioned on her chest . . .' Melinda put her hand on her heart.

'Yes?'

'It's unlikely she landed in that position. I would say she was clutching her wound.'

Declan felt the cold of the cesspit crawl through his veins. 'So she wasn't dead when she hit the ground, despite having been stabbed.'

Melinda nodded. 'Yes. She died down there. In the pit.'

17

Him

I was getting bored of waiting. I knew it was sensible to wait while I set everything up but my desire to be with The One was threatening to overwhelm me. I could take her immediately, but there was something thrilling about waiting just a few more days, getting to know her from a distance, finding out all about her. It was good for me to practise patience, to make it all the sweeter when I got what I craved. But I needed a little snack, something to tide me over, while I waited for my main course. I hadn't had the pleasure of dispatching the Slut personally, and I felt as though I had missed out.

I logged on to Craiglist and browsed through the W4M – women for men – casual-encounters ads, surely one of the best things about being alive in the early twenty-first century. All those desperate women making it so easy for people like me, women who wanted to make their boyfriends mad, who craved a big dick, who didn't want a boyfriend, just someone to make their pussy wet. Reading their words on the screen made me hard.

I read through some of the ads until I found one that looked promising. She wanted to give and get head and she only lived a few miles away. The ad had only been posted fifteen minutes before so the chances were she hadn't been snatched up yet. Using a fake profile, set up with a brand new Gmail account, I sent her a photo, as she asked. The photo was of a guy from a modelling site. I also sent a picture of a fat eight-inch cock from a porn site. She replied almost straight away with her own photo. She was pretty. Not stunning, but good enough. After I'd found out where she lived, using Google Street View to get a good idea of what it was like in her neighbourhood, we arranged to meet at hers.

I drove over. I was wearing leather trousers and a leather jacket; in a holdall, I had handcuffs, my knives and the black corset I like slutty girls to wear. In my pocket, a can of Mace.

She lived on a run-down estate, the kind of place where Neighbourhood Watch means watching out for when your neighbours have gone away so you can rob them. I had driven my cheapest car, and I parked as close to her building as I could, sitting in the car for a good long time to scope out the area and find the right time to approach her flat without being noticed. There wasn't a single passer-by in the hour that I waited, so eventually I deemed it safe to proceed.

As soon as she opened the door, before she could register that I looked nothing like the model in the photo – I am better looking – I sprayed Mace in her face, barged in and dragged her by her hair into her living room. As she recovered from the chemical blast, she opened her mouth to start screaming, so I gagged her quickly then handcuffed her wrists together and showed her my sharpest, most expensive knife. Her eyes rolled like a cow in an abattoir. She was wearing a micro-skirt that exposed a pair of fat legs. Her toenails were painted pink and she had a tattoo of a dragon on her thigh and two no-doubt-nonsensical Chinese characters on her ankle. She was in her late twenties, I guessed, but was ageing quickly.

'You wanted some fun,' I said. 'Now we're going to have some.'

I looked around. Everything was cheap, shabby, in need of repair. The kitchen was so like the one in the place where I grew up that it gave me goosebumps.

There were photos of two young children stuck with magnets to the fridge door. A boy and a girl.

'Nod or shake your head,' I ordered. 'The kids. Are they yours?'

She nodded, tears trickling down the sides of her nose.

'Where are they? With their dad?'

She shook her head.

'Your mum?'

Yes.

'And are they coming back tonight?'

She nodded her head vigorously. I didn't believe her but said, 'We'd better hurry up then, hadn't we? You don't want me still to be here when they get back. Your mum, your kids. I'll kill them too. If you put up a fight, if you scream or try to hurt me, I'll wait for them. However long it takes. But if you make this easy for me, I'll be gone before they get back. As will you.'

She sobbed silently into her gag.

'Let's get started, shall we?'

I turned on the gas hob and pressed the ignition until flames whooshed into life. As the woman on the floor shook with terror, I heated the blade of a knife until it glowed red, and thought about what part of her I might like to take home.

18

Amy

Wednesday, 24 July

Amy couldn't sleep. Her head felt as if it were full of crazed bluebottles, suicide-bombing the insides of her skull. She turned from side to side, alternately wrapping the quilt around herself and throwing it off again. It was too hot, stupidly hot, the fan in the corner doing little more than push warm air from one part of the bedroom to another. She pulled off her long T-shirt and flung it across the room.

She was about to give up and put the light on, maybe catch up with some emails or read a book, when Boris, who was lying on the floor by the window, barked.

She pushed herself up on one elbow and squinted at him through the half-light. Boris never usually barked in the night.

'What's up?' she said, picking up her phone at the same time to look at the clock: 3:17 in the morning.

The dog barked again, hoisting himself up on his long legs and running back and forth between the window and the bedroom door.

Feeling vulnerable, Amy retrieved her damp T-shirt from the floor and put it on, then peeked out through the curtains. Her bedroom looked out on the side of the house and across the street. There was a lamppost a few metres from the window that meant it was never fully dark in her room. The street was empty.

'It's OK,' she said, patting Boris's head. 'There's no one there.'

But she didn't go back to sleep. Instead, she went into the living room and put the TV on, staring blearily at reruns of game shows until dawn, a knife beside her on the sofa and Boris lying at her feet.

'Won't be long,' Amy called out to Gary from the tiny cubbyhole next to the lounge that she used as an office. She had napped during the day and felt a lot better. 'Make yourself at home.'

She had left Gary sitting awkwardly on the edge of her sofa with his shins pressed up against her new footstool. Ordered at cost price from one of the designers who sold stuff on her own website, it was a huge custard cream and she adored it. He was looking around with something akin to astonishment at her flat with its quirky décor – well, *she* thought of it as quirky. The expression on Gary's face indicated that he might have a different word for it. He was patting Boris's head and stroking his ears so intently that Boris keeled over at his feet, looking up adoringly at him.

'What do you think about those photographs?' she added, even though she had already asked him this at least twice. The four photos 'Becky' had posted on her profile were of a typical palm-fringed white sandy beach from different angles. She heard Gary's tut from the next room.

154

'Sorry, sorry. It's really playing on my—'

'Mind,' said Gary. 'It's OK, I understand. But I just don't know. I guess we could try and find out where that beach is, when the photo was taken, that sort of thing. I've got a friend at work, Pete, who should know. He's, like, really into digital photos. Want me to ask him to take a look? He wasn't in today, off sick, but hopefully, he'll be back tomorrow.'

'Yes. Please.'

Amy chewed her thumbnail. There was part of her that didn't want to know – because if there was a way of confirming that the photos really had been taken in the past week and that the beach was in Asia rather than Australia or the Caribbean, then it seemed likely Becky really had gone to Asia. And that therefore, Katherine was probably just on a bender somewhere.

She looked through the doorway at Gary. Did he think she was insane, obsessed? He didn't seem as convinced as her that Becky hadn't posted the pictures – or sent the email, or the mysterious tweets, come to that. Was he just going along with all of this to humour her?

No, she told herself firmly. You're not wrong. It's all been fake. All of it. And Gary *does* believe me. Why would Becky bother to post photos on Facebook without any captions or comments, or without replying to the surprised and envious comments of her friends? 'Wow – lucky you, didn't know you were going on a fab holiday!' 'Send us a postcard, Becks, you jammy cow!' 'Where's that lush beach, babes?'

All unanswered questions – and Becky loved a Facebook chat. Somebody else must have posted the photos, just as they had sent the email and tweeted using Becky's account. But, maddeningly, there was no proof, nothing she could show the police. In fact, the photo on Facebook would make the police even less inclined to believe her.

The printer churned out sixty sheets of A4, each of whose top half featured a drunken, beaming photo of Becky, taken at her last birthday party, which Amy had scanned in, and, in the bottom half, Katherine's Facebook-profile photo. She was stroking a giraffe's nose from some Kenyan safari trip she and Clive had been on at some point. Over the top of the photos, Amy had printed:

MISSING
BECKY COLTMAN AND KATHERINE DEVINE
PLEASE CALL IF YOU HAVE ANY INFORMATION
ON EITHER OF THEM

Her email address was underneath, and the number of Camberwell police station.

When they finished printing, Amy shuffled them together and put them into a Manila envelope. She saw that her printer was flashing a warning to tell her that the ink was low, and she tutted. Then she remembered why the ink was low, the grim task at hand, and thought she'd spend her life savings on printer cartridges if it would only get Becky back.

'I'm going to have to tell Mum and Dad soon,' she said abruptly, going back into the lounge, holding the envelope. 'They're going to kill me already, knowing I've told the police and not them – but what can they do? I'll just say I was hoping that she'd come back, and I wouldn't need to worry them.'

Gary looked up from scrutinizing the old empty dolls' house that Amy was now using to store all her knitting wool inside. 'Silly question, probably, but she couldn't be with them, could she?'

Amy shook her head. 'No, she's not. I didn't think she

156

would be, but I rang them yesterday morning to check. Well, they were out playing golf, so I spoke to their house-keeper. Becky definitely isn't there. Right, I'm ready – shall we go?'

Gary stood up, shuffling slightly to adjust his jeans. He looked smart – his shirt was crisply ironed, he was wearing shoes instead of his usual flip-flops or trainers, and he was very clean-shaven. 'Seeya, Boris, mate, be good,' he said, and Boris narrowed his eyes at them both before flopping down on the tulip-shaped rug in the centre of the room.

'Where do we start?' Gary asked as they emerged from Leicester Square Tube station into the bedlam of a hot summer evening in the city, the air redolent of fried vegetables and exhaust fumes.

'Let's head for Greek Street and Old Compton Street, that area. Whatever that road is closest to Shaftesbury Avenue; then we can work up and down and back. Hope you've got comfy shoes on.'

Amy had always loved these sorts of evenings. Throngs of people on foot, spilling out on the pavements, annoying cab drivers, or smug in rickshaws. Tipsy and besuited, straight from work, or all dressed up for the theatre or a dinner date. Teenagers showing far too much flesh, tourists with their cameras and bumbags strapped to them like bondage, people thrusting leaflets at them for cheap pizza and comedy. Someone in a gorilla suit sauntered past on big, fake, furry claws. Amy wouldn't have been surprised to see people in wetsuits or wedding dresses, or naked. Anything went.

But it was what was under the surface that she really wanted to discover.

They started in Dean Street, and by the tenth pub and

bar they had honed their interrogation down to a set of basic questions:

'Hi – have you got a minute? Were you working on Sunday night?'

'Is there anyone here tonight who was?'

'Did you happen to see this woman?' Pointing at the picture of Katherine and the giraffe. 'She had a date in Soho last Sunday.'

'If you see either of them, please can you call that number? They're both missing.'

'Yeah. She's my sister.'

It got harder and harder as the number of streets they covered crept up. The looks of sympathy were worse than the frustration of those bar staff who just turned away, or pubs where none of the staff would admit to being there on Sunday. As the spiel became more and more automatic, Amy kept imagining she saw Becky burst in through the door of one of the pubs, laughing and talking loudly with her hands as much as her voice . . .

In Old Compton Street, Amy was haunted by the memory of the Admiral Duncan bombing in 1999, imagining the horror of a huge deadly shower of nails, like thousands of bullets raining down on people drinking and relaxing after work . . . Was that guy regretting doing it, almost a quarter of a century on, as he languished forgotten in jail, serving out his six life sentences?

Did someone somewhere have regrets about killing Becky? Suddenly the street noises, the car horns and shouts, the music blaring from open windows all blended into a cacophonous sheet of white noise that made her want to curl up into a ball.

She stopped on the pavement and stared up at Gary.

'I can't do this any more. I'm starting to feel like I'm

hallucinating, and every bar person who says they haven't seen her is like a stab in the heart . . . Sorry, that sounds really melodramatic, but . . .'

She tailed off and turned away, her lip trembling like a toddler's. Gary gave her a hug. 'It's OK. It's hot and packed, and stressful. Let's stop and have a drink. This place looks a bit quieter, come on.'

He took her hand and led her into a bar whose dark interior and lack of blaring music implied that it was the sort of place that didn't come to life till a lot later. It was almost empty inside, just two Japanese girls at the bar in knee socks and kilts, sipping fruity cocktails and giggling.

'Can I help you?' The barman was polishing highball glasses. Amy and Gary sat down on stools at the opposite end of the bar to the girls. 'Gin and tonic, please,' said Amy, and Gary ordered a pint, at least half of which he drank in three gulps. Amy slid a Xerox of the photos of Katherine and Becky across the top of the bar.

'I don't suppose you recognize either of these girls, do you? This one might have been in here on Sunday.'

The barman scratched his facial hair, squinted through the gloom at it and then shook his head. 'Nah, sorry. I'll ask Geoff when he comes in, he was here on Sunday, too.'

'Thanks. Please can you keep it and show it to the other staff as well?'

'Sure.'

He put the Xerox under the bar, walked away and started cutting up lemons. Gary saw the expression on Amy's face and squeezed her knee.

'Did you try and talk to that Clive guy again?'

She nodded. 'He doesn't want to know. I've sent him messages on LinkedIn and Facebook, but he's ignoring them. I don't know his mobile number, and the venue wouldn't tell me – I think he told them not to because they sounded shifty when I asked for it. I gave the promoter my number and asked him to pass it on – nothing. I don't know what Becky did to Clive, but he's not going to forgive her for it.' She stared into her drink. 'I've rarely seen such a look of hatred as the one on Clive's face when I mentioned her.'

'Hmm. Weird, isn't it? Well, we're doing all we can.'

'Unlike the police.'

'We've just got to keep on at them, Amy.'

She smiled faintly at the way he said 'we'. 'By the way,' he added.

'What?'

'I like your skirt. Where did you get it – is it vintage? You look so cute.'

Her smile broadened a little more. There was something so ingenuous about Gary. She wondered fleetingly if he was gay – that wasn't the sort of thing a macho guy would ask – but then she realized that he had just been trying to find something to say that might cheer her up. The skirt was black and full, with a pattern of cherries and daisies scattered across it, and she wore it with a thick red patent-leather belt, and a black vest top.

'Thank you. I made it from some curtains I bought at a vintage fair.'

'Cool,' he said, showing his dimples, and Amy felt very slightly better.

'Right, come on then,' she said, draining her G&T through the straw. 'I feel sufficiently revived. Let's do Berwick Street next.'

'Sure you can face it?' he asked, tilting his head back to finish his pint. Amy watched his Adam's apple bobbing up and down. She nodded and gathered up the envelope and her handbag from the stool next to her. Just as they were

160

walking out, a slim black man walked in, wearing the same uniform as the hirsute barman who'd served them. She stopped him.

'Excuse me, do you work here?'

When he said yes, she handed him a Xerox of the photos. 'I don't suppose you saw that girl with the giraffe on Sunday? I mean – not actually with the giraffe . . .'

He laughed, and then his smile faded and he tilted his head to one side to get a better look.

'Her!' He jabbed angrily at the paper with his forefinger, and Amy and Gary stared at each other with anticipation and dread.

'She *was* in here, and yeah, it was last Sunday, quite late. She was off her face, they both were.'

'Both?'

'She was with this absolute . . .' The guy stopped, presumably worried that they might be offended.

'No, it's fine, tell us, um, Olly,' Amy urged, spotting his name badge. All her fatigue had vanished and adrenaline streamed around her system.

'Twat,' he concluded. 'Loud, obnoxious, offensive. Big guy in an expensive suit, ordered Cristal.'

'Age? Appearance? Did you catch his name?'

Olly thought. 'In his thirties. White. Quite fat – I mean, not fat-fat, but bit of a gut on him. Broad shoulders. Losing his hair. I had to kick him out, he was off his tits – I mean, he was clearly high on drugs. I'm sure she was, too. You can just tell. And one of the customers had seen them go into the toilets together. No, I didn't get his name. I threatened to call the police and have them arrested for doing drugs, and he started shouting the odds. Luckily, they left before anything else happened. I got worried he was going to deck me.'

161

Amy didn't think it was lucky they'd left before the police could be involved. It would have made life a lot easier had there been an incident report on record.

'Wow. Thanks, Olly, you have no idea how helpful that is. But you've never seen this woman, have you?' She pointed at Becky, but Olly shook his head. He read the sheet and looked concerned.

'How long have they been missing?'

'Only a few days. But the police aren't taking it seriously because someone – at least, I think – has been posting on her – Becky's – Twitter account. And putting photos on her Facebook page, too.'

Olly looked slightly embarrassed, as if he wished he hadn't asked.

'Sorry,' Amy said. 'Listen, if you think of anything else, will you call me? That's my number. My name's Amy. That one's my sister; the one you saw is her best friend, Katherine. If she comes in again, please will you let me know?'

'Sure,' Olly said awkwardly. 'Anyway, I'd better get going . . .' He gestured towards the bar, and Amy put her hand on his arm.

'Thank you,' she said. 'Thank you so much.'

19

Declan

Thursday, 18 July

Declan stood on the beach, the pier to his left, bandstand to the right. There were noisy people all around him: families, tourists and EFL students, eating ice cream and candyfloss, rubbing suntan lotion onto pink skin, playing too-loud music out of too-small speakers or phones. A large woman sat reading a paperback, batting away a wasp that repeatedly made a beeline for her ice lolly. Can wasps make beelines, Declan wondered? He'd have to remember to tell Bob that one.

He had driven down to the seafront because he'd needed to get out of the office. More importantly, he'd needed to be surrounded by the living. His pallid colleagues didn't count – they were as starved of sunlight as Declan. But down here, in the first week of the school holidays, it was hard to imagine a more lively display of humanity.

Declan crunched across the pebbles and walked up the steps to the promenade, leaning on the railings and looking out to sea. Eastbourne was known as a place where people

163

came to die, a haven for octogenarians. Compared to London, it was a sleepy town, especially in winter, when the whole place went into a kind of suspended animation, the sands of time frozen on the beach. But, right now, with the sun shining on his upturned face and the smell of the burger van that was parked just behind wafting into his nostrils, it seemed a better place than the city he had loved and left.

Declan's days in the Met had ended two years ago, while he was still a DC, working out of Camberwell nick.

It had been a day similar to this – scorching hot, but sticky and oppressive. It was only a week after the riots had turned the city into a battleground, days when it felt as if the thin veneer of civilization that Londoners lived behind had been ripped away, exposing the true, ugly heart of the city, an ugliness that Declan saw every day. Now, the police had been instructed to arrest looters, the papers full of stories about teens being shopped by their mums and jailed for thieving a bottle of water. Grim days.

One such looter had been identified as a young woman called Jade Hucknall, who lived with her two kids in Marie Curie House, a tower block on the Sceaux Gardens estate, not far from the station, the kind of place where hope goes to die. Jade had been caught on camera thieving a pair of Adidas from JD Sports. An utterly typical case.

On that sticky August afternoon two years ago, Declan had gone along with a PC, Sam Collins, to arrest Jade.

As the two of them had walked across the estate, aware of hostile eyes watching them from every direction, Sam had said, 'Do you know anything about this Jade Hucknall?'

'Yeah, a little. Been done for soliciting once or twice. The father of her youngest kid put her on the game for a while.'

'Nice. Who's the father?'

'Terry Munson.'

'Terry Munster himself?'

'The very same.'

The Munsons – known to the police and the very few people who weren't terrified of them as the Munsters – were one of *those* families. The dad, Pat – or Herman, as he was known – had spent half his adult life inside, but every time he got out he spawned a new kid or two, all of whom were grown up now, all of them following in their father's size-eleven footsteps.

'He's not going to be there, is he?' Sam asked, the apprehension clear in his voice.

'No one has seen Terry for months. Rumour has it he's fucked off up north after getting on the wrong side of someone even bigger and scarier than him.'

'I'm sure he's paying his child support like a good boy, though.'

'Oh, yeah. I'm sure.'

The lift was out of order, they were always out of order in places like this, so they tramped up the stairs, fourteen flights, Declan's heart rapping against his ribcage in protest. Sam, who did 10k runs in his spare time, wasn't even sweating when they got to Jade Hucknall's door.

'You all right?' he asked, as Declan knocked.

He didn't get a chance to answer. The door was flung open and Jade was there, screaming at them, her words barely audible but Declan made out the name Terry as he exhorted Jade to calm down. A toddler was yelling in the background and Declan could hear the CBeebies music pumping out at the kind of volume usually only heard in nightclubs. Declan was trying to get Jade to be quiet, his blood pressure rising so he could feel the blood thrumming in his ears, when a man appeared before them in the flat's hallway. Terry Munster.

Declan didn't even see the gun. All he remembered was a searing pain in his shoulder, a flash of white as he hit the ground and smacked his head against the doorframe, Jade still yelling, the toddler still screeching, and footsteps running over and past him. That, he discovered later in hospital, was Terry legging it. PC Collins was rooted to the spot, wanting to look after Declan, he said, but more likely not wanting to face down an armed psycho with his baton. Terry was found a day later, drinking in a pub close to the estate, boasting about the filth he'd offed.

The bullet had shattered Declan's rotator cuff. Surgery had been quick and successful. Doctors kept telling him how lucky he was. But the real injury had not been to his shoulder – the shot had affected his psyche far more. For the past year or so, he had been slowly falling out of love with the job – the constant hostility, the same sad faces and cases all the time, his growing belief that there was a cancer eating away at society, and the new government's response was to cut police funding and salaries. He was sick of it. Getting shot by a piece of shit like Terry Munster – a shot that, had it been a few inches to the left would have struck him in the neck or face – sent Declan into a spiral of depression. He went to see two therapists, a physio and a counsellor, but, while the former helped him to feel better, the latter made him assess his life and what he wanted from it.

He had given everything to the job. He'd never married, had no children, few friends. He was tired. When he'd joined the police he'd thought he would be working interesting cases, solving crimes, making a difference. But the truth was, he hadn't made any difference at all. The people round here despised the police. The riots had brought that into full view. The underclass saw them as the enemy, the middle class thought they were useless and blamed them for the fear they'd experienced this summer for probably the first time.

But he didn't know what else he could do. When he tried to think of something else, he drew a blank. So he took a sidestep instead. He asked for, and got, a transfer. Shortly after that, he was promoted.

Declan breathed in a lungful of sea air. No, when he remembered that awful summer, and stood on this beach, he didn't miss London at all.

He'd only been a DI for a few months now, and the body in the cesspit was his first really interesting case. But since the apparent early breakthrough that Melinda Moore, the forensic anthropologist, had given them, he and Bob had made very little progress.

Bob had been looking into former employees of JWF, the property-development company that owned the farmhouse where the body had been found. But as JWF had been defunct for almost two decades, tracking down its staff was proving to be a painful business. The former MD of the company had died a couple of years back and his partner had retired to Spain. The guv, DCI Anthony Fremantle, who was SIO on the case, didn't think this route of enquiry was worth pursuing and had instructed them to stop, though Bob had already sent a message to the partner in Spain, to which there had been no reply as yet.

'Wait and see what comes back on the DNA,' Fremantle had said.

But that could be days. As DCI Fremantle had made clear, 'This case is ice cold. We've missed the chance to be hot on the perpetrator's tail by about fifteen years. A few days' wait isn't going to make much difference.'

But Declan was impatient, and persuaded Fremantle that pursuing the scoliosis angle had to be worthwhile.

'All right,' he'd said. 'But don't spend too much time on it. Let's see what the DNA tells us.'

Despite his annoyance at Fremantle's reliance on the great god DNA, Declan was now beginning to think he might be right. Trying to get information out of the NHS was like trying to get through to his mobile-phone company – an exercise in diversion and frustration that had him muttering darkly about red tape and fucking bureaucrats. And after his experiences following getting shot, he was normally the first to praise the NHS.

The main problem was that there was no easy way to get the information, and the clerical staff he encountered didn't know the answers, so they kept passing him to someone else. As he hung on the phone while he was transferred to yet another department, he squeezed the stress putty his niece had bought him for Christmas. It was supposed to have therapeutic properties. Declan found it helpful as a tool for imagining he was squeezing a bureaucrat's throat.

The Spine, which was the central database that held records of all of the patients in the system – pretty much everyone in the UK – had only come into being a few years ago. It was controversial, with everyone from civil-liberties campaigners to conspiracy nuts speaking out against it. But if this system had existed in the late eighties, when the victim would have been receiving treatment, and if the police had had access to it, Declan probably would have found her by now. He could have got a list of all the girls with scoliosis and cross-referenced that against COMPACT, the missing-persons database.

But he had hit a dead end. After speaking to a few of the larger hospitals in the area and trying to get information out of them, he had heard the same refrain several times: it was too long ago, and even if he was looking for a current patient, there was confidentiality to think of and court orders to obtain. He had also done more research into scoliosis while he was waiting on the phone. According to NHS Direct, if the curve was less than 20 degrees, and Melinda had said it was a mild curve, treatment was rarely necessary.

Declan turned away from the railing and started walking back to his car. He cursed when he reached it. A seagull – a giant one by the look of it – had crapped over the windscreen. He sat in the car and watched the wipers sweep back and forth, smearing the guano over the glass. It stank of fish, even though he'd only ever seen the gulls round here eating chips and doughnuts.

By the time he got back to the station his good mood had evaporated. His shoulder was throbbing and he just wanted to go home, watch a film and open a bottle of red.

But as he walked towards his office, Bob came bounding out, looking very much like a puppy that had been given a new ball.

'Please tell me you've had some good news,' Declan said.

He grinned. 'Yep. Melinda Moore just called.' He paused for a moment, perhaps picturing Melinda's lovely bouncy hair. 'She got a hit on the DNA.'

20

Amy

Wednesday, 24 July

Amy had sunk into an introspective gloom on the bus back from Soho. They hadn't discussed the fact that Gary seemed to be accompanying her home, but she didn't care either way. She hadn't thought it through enough to wonder if he would want to stay over, or what repercussions this would bring, but she knew that she did not want to be alone.

Gary nudged her. 'Say something,' he said.

Amy looked out of the window of the bus, then focused in on her own reflection. Even in the dim glass, she could see the dark shadows under her eyes, and the worried pinch of her mouth. She felt as though she'd aged ten years in the last week. She turned back to Gary.

'I don't want to,' she replied abruptly. 'I can't. If I start talking about her again, I'm going to panic, lose it, and there's no point in that, not for either of us.'

He nodded soberly. 'Fair enough.'

Neither of them spoke again until after they had alighted at the bus stop at the end of Amy's road.

'Will you come with me to take Boris out? He only needs to go round the block.'

'Block. Sure, no problem.'

They fetched Boris from the flat and walked in silence along the dark, quiet, suburban pavements, the only sound the jangle of the brass connector of his lead. Amy kept opening her mouth to speak but her tongue was too dry. At some point, Gary reached out and took Amy's hand, and she let him. His hand felt hot and dry in hers. It felt good.

When they returned home, Amy went to the kitchen. 'Wine, or coffee?'

'Wine, please,' said Gary. He took off his shoes and left them neatly by the front door. Amy unstoppered half a bottle of red and was just sniffing it suspiciously in case it had turned into vinegar when Gary padded up behind her and slid his arms around her waist, making her jump.

'Gary! I nearly dropped it!' she said, more loudly than she'd intended, and Gary backed away, looking hurt.

She took down two glasses and poured them one each. When she handed him his, she leaned in close to him. 'Cheers,' she said, giving him a small, apologetic smile.

'Cheers, darling,' he said, looking unsure. She was still face to face with him, and when he'd had a gulp of the wine, she moved even closer until their foreheads were touching.

'Thank you for being such a good friend,' she said, so quietly that her voice was barely audible. 'I couldn't do this without you.'

'You're welcome,' he replied. His breath smelled nice, of beer and wine and mint. He reached to one side, put his glass down on the kitchen counter, and placed his arm back around her waist. 'I'd like to be more than just your friend, you know.'

Amy froze, even though the admission wasn't entirely unexpected. 'Really?'

He nodded, making Amy's own head nod in tandem where it was still pressed against his. His aftershave wafted up into her nostrils, and she felt a rush of tenderness for him.

She pressed her body closer to his. Suddenly she knew that the proximity of warm male flesh was the only thing that could make her stop worrying about Becky. Amy slid her fingers through the gaps between the buttons on his shirt, and stroked his hot, flat belly. It elicited a stab of lust in her so tangible that she gasped. It had been so long since she had touched a man's body.

'Amy,' said Gary in a strangled voice, taking her wineglass out of her hand and putting it down next to his. She immediately wrapped both her arms around his waist, and in one fluid movement they were kissing, neither of them sure who had initiated it, and the kiss was effortless and so erotic that Amy wondered if her legs would even hold her up.

She kicked off her shiny black shoes, and suddenly she was three inches shorter than Gary, which made them both laugh. She stood on tiptoe so that she could carry on kissing him, and he pushed her against the kitchen counter so that she could feel his hard penis press against her. She moaned, and rubbed her fingers through his hair, and he reciprocated by sliding his hand up her top and into her bra, grasping her breast, kneading gently at her nipple with his thumb.

'Oh, God,' she said. 'Gary . . .'

He pulled away momentarily. 'Do you want me to stop?'

'No! No . . . please keep going . . .'

172

He grinned, but didn't replace his hand on her breast. Instead, he pulled up her full skirt, his hand vanishing inside a mass of poppies and daisies on black cotton, and then Amy felt his fingers on the fabric of her silk knickers. It was like an electric shock, and instinctively she reached her own hand out to touch his erection. They stroked one another, kissing continuously, until time slowed down and Amy finally forgot about Becky, a momentary reprieve. Gary lifted her up bodily and sat her on the kitchen counter, and she yanked his jeans down so that she could wrap her legs around his waist and feel him even closer to her.

'I want you, I want you,' he whispered into her hair. Her knickers had come off but she couldn't remember who'd removed them, or when. She reached into his jockey shorts and liberated his cock, almost climaxing just at the feel of his girth in her hand.

'I want you, too,' she said, pushing him away just for a minute to rip off her top and bra. Now she was only wearing the skirt, and the air felt good on her bare breasts as they bounced free. Gary peeled off his shirt and stepped out of his jeans, his eyes wide at the sight of her.

'Condom?' he murmured, and she shook her head, looking stricken. 'Wait – there might be one in my wallet. Don't move.'

She laughed. 'Shouldn't we go to bed?'

'No. I want you right here in the kitchen. Don't you dare move – I'll be right back.'

He ran so fast over to his jacket that he almost tripped over Boris, which made her laugh again. While he extracted his wallet and searched frantically through it, she lifted her bottom so that she could pull the skirt away, too, and she was completely naked, next to her toaster and coffee machine.

173

'Have you got one?' she called, but then saw him bend over himself, and heard the crackle of the foil wrapper and the snap of latex.

I'm really going to do it, she thought, with mingled wonder, excitement and horror. With Gary! Good grief.

But she felt as though she had never wanted anyone so badly. He returned within seconds, his condom-clad penis sticking out in front of him, as naked as she was. His body was taut and muscled, just hairy enough, with tan lines above his knees, on his biceps, and around his neck.

'You're so gorgeous,' he said, kissing her again. Very slowly and deliberately, he spread her legs as he moved his tongue in languorous circles inside her mouth, then down to take her nipple gently between his teeth. His finger traced matching circles around her clitoris.

'You're so *good*,' she panted, and the compliment seemed to make him even harder. She could feel the tip of him rubbing against the sensitive opening of her vagina, but as she moved forward, desperate to feel him inside her, he backed away very slightly, teasing her. She couldn't move any closer to him without risking falling off the counter, so she groaned, and tried to pull him to her. He did it again and again, always stopping at the point of entry, or just millimetres inside of her. She admired his self-restraint – she thought she would explode if he didn't penetrate her fully soon.

'Please,' she begged, and he chuckled. He put his thumb into her mouth for her to wet it, then massaged her clit again. She closed her eyes and could already feel the first shudders of orgasm approaching in the distance. After all this time, she was amazed she'd lasted as long as she had.

'I'm going to—'

'*Come!*' he yelled suddenly, and thrust his entire length

174

deep inside of her with one smooth movement, filling her up. She shouted, too, incoherent cries as he pounded into her, lifting her off the counter entirely, smashing one of the glasses of wine to the floor where it exploded in a river of ruby red that made Boris yelp and hide in the bedroom.

Gary carried her like that across to the wall next to the fridge, still thrusting wildly. She clasped her hands behind his neck and leaned back, allowing herself to sail away on the waves of an orgasm so strong that everything went black, and her world shrank down until all it consisted of was his cock inside her, fucking her so hard that she saw stars light up the blackness.

Afterwards, they slid down the wall together to the floor, incapable of moving anywhere else. The wine and broken glass crept in a slow puddle towards them, and they watched it for several minutes, panting and wordless, Amy cradled in Gary's arms. She noticed that one of the cups of her ivory bra was now stained with Merlot, and that some of the broken glass had gone dangerously close to Boris's bowl.

'Better get this lot cleared up,' she said eventually, and staggered back to her feet. Gary just smiled up at her, all goofy and smug and satiated, but with a hint of his previous uncertainly back again. *What next?* It was a question she wasn't ready for, not yet.

Her mobile phone rang from her bag in the other room, and Amy instinctively looked at the clock on the kitchen wall. It was 1.24 a.m.

'Oh, my God,' she said, and ran for it, not caring how she looked naked. Scrabbling in her handbag, she reached it just before it went to voicemail. 'Hello? Amy speaking?'

She listened for a moment, her hand over her mouth.

'Really? Right. OK. I'll be there in half an hour. Thank you. Thank you very much.'

'Who was it?' Gary had thrown a tea towel down over the glass and spilled wine, and was already gathering up his clothes.

'It was that barman, Olly. The guy that Katherine was with on Monday is back in there again, with another girl. I'm calling a cab.' She paused. 'Please don't feel that you have to come with me.'

Gary looked her in the face. He was still flushed and his hair was on end.

'Let's go,' he said.

21

Amy

Thursday, 25 July

Miraculously, the minicab arrived within seven minutes. Gary and Amy barely had time to try to make themselves look a little less as though they'd just had rampant sex, and to clear up the spilled wine and broken glass in the kitchen. Amy checked that the envelope containing the Xeroxed photos was still in her bag, and they set off, leaving behind a very doleful Boris.

The cab smelled strongly of body odour, and the driver was uncommunicative, which suited Amy fine. She was relieved that he didn't question why they might be going out to a bar in Soho at 1.30 a.m. They hadn't gone more than half a mile before Gary put his arm around her in the back of the car. She tried not to flinch visibly, but forced herself to relax into his embrace.

'Hey,' he said, kissing her hair, 'did you know that Ben Folds Five are touring over here again this year? I think it's in early December – shall we go together? I was going to go with a bunch of people from work, but I'd rather

177

go with you. Not that my workmates aren't cool, or anything – they totally are – in fact, you'll meet them all at our summer party, it's in a few weeks . . .'

Amy made a noncommittal sort of noise. She felt a prickle of irritation, even though she knew he was just trying to take her mind off Becky and their mission.

Less than an hour ago, they had been naked together, he had been inside her – but what made him assume that they were suddenly an item? Next, he'd be inviting her to meet his parents . . .

'We'll see,' she said, and moved slightly away from him. He shot her a hurt look, but although she felt bad, she knew that she didn't currently have the emotional resources necessary to start a 'let's not be too hasty here' conversation with him. She decided she'd do it tomorrow; tell him that she just wanted to be friends. Hadn't she already said that she didn't 'do' relationships? Wasn't that a bit arrogant of him to assume that because they'd had sex, all that would instantly change? Amy's lip curled. Men were so obtuse sometimes.

The cab carried them round the South Circular, almost deserted at this time of night; just a few other taxis and night buses on the road, and the occasional urban fox streaking in and out of alleyways. Gary's hand was warm on her upper arm, and for a moment she relaxed into his embrace. What was wrong with her? Why *shouldn't* he start talking about the future?

But then didn't men always start out being sweet and sexy and kind and loving? Look at bloody Nathan, she thought. He could do no wrong in her eyes, not for months.

'What do we say to this guy, assuming he's even still there?' Gary asked abruptly.

Amy was relieved at the change of subject. 'I reckon we

178

just give him the spiel, show him the photo of Katherine without letting on we're already aware he was with her in there on Sunday. If he denies it, then we can say we know. But let's see what his reaction is. I hope he's not going to be too drunk. That barman, Olly, said he's pretty out of it.'

Gary looked at his watch. 'It's ten to two. He's got to be a pretty dedicated boozer to still be out at this time. Or he's high.'

'Oh, yeah. That's more likely, by the sound of him.'

By the time they got back to Old Compton Street, Amy had convinced herself that the man would no longer be there.

'Can you wait, please?' she asked the cabbie. 'We won't be longer than ten minutes or so – and we might be straight out again if the person we're meeting has already gone.'

The bar was as empty as it had been the previous evening, but the feel of it was entirely different – instead of the happy-hour chilliness of a newly vacuumed pristine place where the chairs were neatly lined up at the tables, it felt exhausted, hot with the drunken exhalations of a night's worth of punters, the floor sticky with spilled drinks and the tables and chairs every which way. Olly, the barman, had vast grey bags under his eyes, and was leaning wearily on the bar. He straightened up in surprise when Amy and Gary came in.

'Didn't really think you'd make it down. He's still here – look.'

He jerked his thumb towards the recesses of the bar, where a row of square seating blocks upholstered in leopard-print fabric formed a kind of sofa. The man sitting there had two girls in short skirts on either side of him; he had an arm round each of them. There was an empty bottle of champagne upended in an ice bucket next to them, plus champagne flutes and shot glasses scattered across their table.

'I ought to go and clear up their empties,' he said wearily. 'But he's such an arsehole that I can't be bothered. At this time of night, I really don't need the sort of abuse he's been dishing out all evening. I told him he was barred, and he just fucking laughed at me. Our bouncer's not in tonight, otherwise he'd have been out on his ear.'

Amy gave him a sympathetic smile. 'Thanks again. It was really good of you to call me.'

Olly shrugged. 'I hope you find your sister and her friend. Can't help thinking that the little twat might well have something to do with it. Watch out for him, OK, he's a piece of work. Do you want a drink?'

Gary and Amy shook their heads.

'Thanks, but we'll just get this over with,' Gary said.

They walked over to the group of three and Amy took out one of her A4 appeal sheets. She folded it in half so that the only photo visible was of Katherine and the giraffe.

'Excuse me,' she said, standing right in front of them. 'Can I bother you for a second?'

The man looked her up and down. His pupils were vast and black, his face looked purplish, and his foot jiggled compulsively. *Coke*, thought Amy. No question. He was mean-looking, with a scar bisecting one eyebrow and thin lips, belly bursting out of an expensive-looking suit for which he had grown too fat. He had the appearance of a gone-to-seed boxer, even though he probably wasn't yet forty.

'You can bother me for as long as you like, sweetheart,' he said. 'As long as you sit on my face while you do it.' He barked with laughter.

Amy blinked, and felt Gary tense next to her. She put a reassuring hand on his arm. The man slapped the thighs of the two girls with him and they laughed, too, but Amy could tell that at least one of them thought he was a prat. She put the sheet right in front of his face, as he seemed to be having problems focusing anywhere but her breasts.

'This woman was apparently seen in here recently. Do you know her?'

Without even looking at the photo, his face changed, and he clamped his hand on his leg to stop the jiggling. 'Are you plainclothes cops or what?'

Amy was tempted to say yes, just to freak him out. 'No, we aren't. She's my sister's friend and we're trying to find her.'

He relaxed again. 'Didn't think so. You don't look like cops.'

'Could you just look at the picture please, Mr . . . um?' Amy kept her voice low and calm.

The man took it from her hand and squinted at it. It was immediately apparent that he recognized Katherine, and Amy held her breath, wondering what he'd say.

'Call me Fraser. Well, well. If it isn't Little Miss Pricktease? Yeah, as it happens, I have made her acquaintance.'

A cockroach skittered past on the wall. One of the girls spotted it and screamed and jumped up, batting at her hair as if it had somehow flown into it. 'Ugh! Fucking cockroach! This place is a *dive*.'

'Can we sit down and talk to you about her, please, Fraser?' Amy asked, smiling as flirtatiously as she could. He narrowed his eyes in the girls' direction.

'Oi, treacles, could you two bugger off for a few minutes while I talk to these nice people? Then we can get back to the part-ay-ing pronto, eh?' He grabbed at the bottom of the one who'd stood up, and she giggled, her cockroach panic forgotten.

'If we don't get out of here soon, I'm going home,' said the other one, swaying as she stood up. She was the one who looked as if she wasn't having much fun 'par-tay-ing' with Fraser.

'Come to the bogs with me, Charlotte, I'm bustin', and I need to talk to you.' Cockroach Girl grabbed her friend's hand and they tottered off to the Ladies' together. Fraser patted the seat next to him, and Amy reluctantly sat down. It was warm with the imprint from Cockroach Girl's buttocks. Gary sat at the table.

'Let me get you good folks a drink,' Fraser said expansively. 'I've been waiting for this useless barman to get his sorry arse over here for hours now and get me some more fizz. The service in this place is utter shite.'

Amy and Gary's eyes met, both of them without words, saying, *Then why do you drink in here, twat?* Probably, Amy thought, because it was one of the few places that didn't currently have a bouncer on the door, and from which Fraser hadn't already been banned.

'So, how do you know Katherine?'

'"Katherine", is it? She told me her name was Kaye. I met her about a month ago . . . Internet dating.'

'Internet dating? Which site?' Gary asked, leaning forward in his chair.

Fraser regarded him like something he'd picked up on his shoe. He pointed at him. 'Listen, pal, I don't like your tone. You might think that you're too good for Internet dating, but I tell you what, it's THE best way to meet birds. Birds who are up for it, anyway . . .'

Gary held up his hands. 'Hey, chill out, I don't have

182

a *tone*. I just want to know where Katherine is. She's gone AWOL.'

Fraser's mood seemed to have plummeted into instant aggression and defensiveness. 'What – now you're accusing me of having something to do with it? Who the fuck do you think you are, coming in here and making insinuations, telling me to *chill out*? You need to—'

Amy glared at Gary, and turned to Fraser. 'Please. Gary didn't mean anything. We're just really worried about her. Anything you can tell us about her would be massively helpful. How did she seem when you last saw her, on . . .'

She was about to say, 'Sunday,' when she remembered he didn't know that she knew.

Fraser slumped back in his seat, leaning his head against the wall and glaring at them both. Amy hoped the cockroach would return and scuttle across him. Horrible man, she thought. What the hell was Katherine doing with a psycho like him? *Could* he have something to do with her disappearance? With a chill, Amy thought that she agreed with Olly – at face value, he absolutely could.

'Um, when did you last see her?' she asked instead.

He shrugged. 'She can't have been missing for long – I went out for a drink with her, just a few days ago. Last Saturday? No – Sunday. We was in here, actually.'

Amy pretended to look surprised. 'Really? Well, that's a stroke of luck, meeting you. You're being so helpful, honestly. Did she say anything about having any more dates lined up? If you could tell me the site, then we can check out who else she'd met on it.'

He frowned again. 'Have you got the police involved yet?'

'Not yet,' Amy said. 'Would you be willing to talk to them, if she doesn't turn up?'

Fraser suddenly felt the inside of his top jacket pocket and then sniffed, running his finger under his nose. It was late, and he was probably very drunk as well as high, but his actions couldn't have screamed *I have cocaine* more clearly than if he'd been playing charades.

'Look,' she said. 'If they do get involved, all they'll want to know is about you and Katherine – how you met, what you did. They won't care about anything else.' She stared meaningfully at his jacket pocket. 'So – which site was it?'

He drummed his fingers on the table. Amy and Gary exchanged looks again. Why wouldn't he tell them? At that moment, the other two girls came back from the toilets and stood awkwardly a little way away. The door swung shut behind them, causing Amy's appeal photo sheet to fly off the table in the sudden draught. It fell onto Fraser's foot, and he bent to pick it up. He was just handing it back to Amy when he stopped, puzzled and momentarily shocked. Amy and Gary froze. Fraser was staring at the other photo, the one of Becky that had been folded out of sight underneath before.

'What?' Amy's voice came out strangled and high. 'Do you know her, too?'

Fraser regained his composure, and smirked. 'As it goes, I do. I've had 'em both. Small world, eh?' He turned to them both. 'Yeah, what I was about to say was, that site, it's called Casexual.com. That's how I know them. They're mates, aren't they? Well, I would hope so, since both of their profiles say that they're into threesomes . . . I'm not into relationships, but I like sex. No crime in that, is there? And from what little I know of these two, so do they. Gagging for it . . .' He stood up.

'And on that note, ladies and gents, it's time for me to take my leave – the next part of my evening's entertainment

184

awaits.' He gestured to the two girls. 'Here's my card, I have nothing to hide, so please feel free to give my details to the police if needs be. There are some very nasty characters out there. I hope they both turn up very soon. Nice girls, they were.' He handed Amy a business card, and actually bowed, before taking an arm of each of the girls and weaving out, throwing a twenty-pound note on the bar as he went. Olly's lip curled, but he picked up the note and put it in his pocket.

Amy couldn't speak, not until Gary had thanked Olly and helped her back into the minicab that had, mercifully, waited outside for them.

'Casexual.com,' she managed as the driver pulled away, her voice shaking with rising hysteria. Gary squeezed her arm. 'You know what that means, don't you, Gary? Do you know what that is, Gary? I know what that is, I've heard of that . . .'

He didn't reply, but tried to put his arms around her. She shook him violently off, speaking louder and faster and higher. 'It's a hook-up site! Gary – Becky was using a *hook-up site!* Oh, my God. She was advertising herself for sex, like some kind of whore, and so was Katherine! What the fuck were they *thinking*? And she slept with – they probably both slept with – that . . . that . . . that—'

'Arsehole,' said Gary, in a flat monotone that somehow tipped Amy's hysteria over into howls of panic and agony so primal that the cab driver pulled over and stared in horror at her, until Gary told him to drive on, to please just get them home.

When they got back to Amy's flat again, Amy went straight to bed, without bothering to take off her make-up or most of her clothes. Gary made her a cup of tea that went stone cold on her bedside table, and she didn't speak or move when he took off his own clothes and slid in beside her. She lay like a stone on her back, allowing him to hold her hand but pushing him away when he came closer, until he turned on his side and started gently snoring.

She lay wide awake for hours, her heart pounding with fear and anxiety. Not even listening to Boris's soft, regular breaths from the floor next to her, or the dawn chorus outside, could relax her. All she could think about was Becky, having sex with that horrible man, and how many others? The sort of people that hook-up sites would inevitably attract. Control freaks like Nathan, sex addicts and perverts.

Murderers?

She was still awake, in a sort of trance of tiredness and stress, when her landline rang at 7 a.m. She leaned across and picked up the receiver.

'Hello?'

'Miss Coltman? It's DC Amristy from Camberwell CID here. We have some news about Katherine Devine. Could you come to the station as soon as possible, please?'

22

Becky

Friday, 14 June

Worst day *ever* at school today. Poor little Simon Pinto has committed suicide. I cried my eyes out in the head's office when she told me – so unprofessional of me but I just couldn't help it. She was almost crying, too, though. We tried so hard to help him but it was too late. In his suicide note he said that his tormentors weren't from this school but from another one, so no wonder we could never get to the bottom of who was bullying him, and he was too scared to tell us. When the head said that his mum and stepdad wanted to invite her and me to his funeral because they knew 'we were the ones who took such care of him', I thought my heart was going to shatter into a thousand pieces.

I almost crawl up the stairs to my flat at five, so tired and upset that I can't do anything for a full half-hour other than lie on my sofa staring at daytime telly, Simon's anxious white face constantly on my mind, and his nervous habit of rubbing his palms on his knees if I ever asked him to read in class or translate anything.

I feel grimy and sweaty but I'm too exhausted to turn on the shower taps for ages, because it would involve moving. Eventually, I manage to drag myself into the shower, and the tepid water streaming off my head makes me feel a little better. I wash my hair, even though it doesn't really need it, and walk naked and dripping into my room. I spread the towel on the bed and lie down, enjoying the cool air on my wet skin. Then I put on knickers and my little black sundress and consider my options for the evening ahead. I could ring Katherine but I think she's out on another date. She didn't teach Simon and, although of course she was shocked, she wasn't as upset at the news as I was.

I pour myself a large glass of cold Pinot Grigio and sit down on the sofa with the laptop, logging straight into Casexual.com. It's becoming a bit of an addiction; so many gorgeous men all lined up for me – skimming over the mediocre/square/overweight ones obviously. It's like Internet grocery shopping – browse, click, add to basket, proceed to checkout . . . And today of all days, I feel so strongly that life is just too short not to seize it with both hands, take new experiences when you want them, experiment to find out what you don't like as much as what – or who – you do. Take risks, be bold . . .

I think I've been hanging out with Katherine too much! She's always saying things like that. She keeps hinting that she wants a Casexual threesome – her, me and a guy of our choice. The thought both thrills and appals me. She says she's over CupidsWeb.com – 'far too vanilla'. I thought it was OK, a few decent men – but she's right: Casexual's a whole other kettle of fish. I feel myself getting turned on just logging in; a naughty pleasure that I keep secret from everyone except Katherine. The adrenaline rush from a regular date gets magnified about a thousand times by a Casexual date, and in some ways I think they are more honest. I mean, all Internet dating is basically about sex, isn't it? So many men dress it all up with flowery stories about their quest for 'the one', and really they just want to get laid. Casexual cuts through all that crap. *Look at me – you fancy me? You like me? Let's do it.*

It's scary, but so liberating. I'm being very choosy, though – I've only had one Casexual date so far, with Milo (possibly not his real name), and it was amazing. Such a revelation. He seemed to enjoy it as much as I did, but when I tried to contact him again for another go, he'd vanished off the site, and his mobile was dead. I hope I find another Milo.

I spend a good hour browsing, replying to messages, sending more out. I feel different when I'm on Casexual, in control and powerful. I'm not offering myself to just anybody, I'm choosing the source of my pleasure. Perhaps the risk element inherent in arranging to sleep with a stranger enhances the thrill of it. Although I would never take any risks myself. I am always totally careful. And if they are crude, or terrible spellers, I discount them immediately. It makes me smile that I could have sex with a stranger, but not one who misuses apostrophes.

Just as I'm perusing the Casexual profile of a guy who calls himself TooledUp, there's a knock at my door. I hastily close my laptop lid and check my appearance in the mirror over the fireplace – I hope it's not that Damian from downstairs, he's always hassling me about the sodding recycling, or dropping round to 'talk about my security', or whatever. He's all right, I suppose. Means well.

It's not Damian, it's Gary from next door. I'm so relieved I invite him in, opening the door wide and smiling at him. He's leaning on the side of the doorframe with a goofy grin on his face. He's pretty cute, actually. Shame I don't fancy him.

'Good evening, Miss Coltman,' he says, inclining his head. 'And how are we tonight?'

I fan my face with my hand. 'We are rather warm, thank you, and knackered after a truly awful day at school, but a glass of cold vino and a shower have gone a long way to putting things—'

'Right,' he finishes. 'Any more of that cold vino? Cheeky of me to ask, I know, since I only came round to see if I could get my *Breaking Bad* box set back again – I've still got a couple of episodes to go.'

'Sure thing, I've watched it all.' I usher him in and go to the fridge to pour him a glass of wine. Having company is helping snap me out of my funk, and also pushing back down my increasingly persistent fantasies about threesomes and anonymous sex . . .

'How was your day?'

As I hand him the wine, he scowls slightly. 'Also pretty shit,' he says. 'I have to get a new job. My boss is such a twat.'

'Oh, dear,' I sympathize, and he spends the next five minutes bitching about her. I find my thoughts drifting back to TooledUp. He looked a bit rough, but Kath would like that. Big muscles, nice smile, lots of tats. A good speller, too, unless he got someone to check his profile for him. And – I find myself growing even hotter – he's after a three-some. I imagine Kath's reaction if I set it all up. She'd be like a kid in a sweet shop! What would it be like? Six legs entwined, being kissed by a woman whilst being fucked by a man . . . four hands running over my body instead of two . . . Kath's smooth creamy skin and red hair in my face, watching TooledUp pounding into her right next to me . . . I'm not gay, but I can't deny it's a huge turn-on. I could definitely kiss Kath, if it was a one-off and there was a man there as well . . .

'Are you all right, Becky?' asks Gary, and my eyes open wide.

'Oh, yes – sorry, Gary, I'm just a bit . . . tired and emotional. One of my Year Nines topped himself today.'

I feel bad at using Simon as an excuse for being distracted, but Gary is mortified. 'Becky, I'm so sorry! That's terrible! Can I do anything to help cheer you up?'

Is it my imagination or did a lustful expression flash across his face? For a moment, I'm tempted, feeling as I am already turned on. But this is Gary-from-next-door. It would be a very bad idea.

'We could go out for a drink, if you like?' he suggests shyly.

I smile at him and drain my wineglass. 'Thanks, Gary, it's really kind of you, but I think I just need an early night.'

He takes the hint and stands up, awkwardly running his hand through his hair and not making eye contact. 'OK then. I'm really sorry about your, um, pupil.'

'Thanks. Sorry I'm being a bit antisocial.'

'No, don't worry, that's fine, sorry for disturbing you.'

Bless him. We seem to have run out of things to apologize to one another for, so I show him back to the door and he leaves. It's only when I sit back down at the laptop, I notice that the *Breaking Bad* box set is still sitting under my TV. I think about taking it across the hall to Gary's, then decide against it. Not tonight. Instead, I write TooledUp a little email: 'Hi! My friend and I think you look great. Fancy meeting up with us?' My heart in my mouth, I hit Send before I change my mind.

23

Him

How did I feel when I heard that that slut, Katherine, was indeed dead; that my perfectly executed – if you'll excuse the pun – plan had worked? Oh, I wasn't surprised. I rarely make mistakes. I've only ever made one, a long time ago, and I got away with that. I knew she wouldn't be able to resist that delicious bag of drugs. I was pleased, though, satisfied that she was out of the way. Another problem dealt with satisfactorily. It's one of the things I'm brilliant at, problem-solving.

I was in a good mood that day anyway, so waking up and seeing on the BBC website that the body of a young woman had been found in a house in Herne Hill, apparently from a drugs overdose, was merely the sugary icing on the freshly baked cake.

It was funny, because within a couple of days there was a tribute page to her on Facebook, one of those ghastly displays of fake emotion, all these cretins posting photos of her and leaving 'heartfelt' messages about what an amazing person she was and how much she'll be missed. There were loads of her pupils on there, kids from her school, gushing away about what a wonderful teacher she was, so cool and not like the other boring teachers. Some of the girls who left posts on the page were cute, all these fifteen- and sixteen-year-old girls who wouldn't know a privacy setting if it bit them on their pert little bottoms. I passed an enjoyable hour looking through their photos. I have an app that searches through Facebook pages looking for pictures of girls in bikinis. It's very clever – it searches for flesh. It's amazing how many young girls post provocative pictures of themselves on social networks. They don't realize that half of them end up on porn sites, or being used as fake profile pictures by phone-sex operators and mail-order brides in Eastern Europe.

Of course, masturbation is only one way of letting off steam online. If I'm in a foul mood, or looking for some light fun, if I want a laugh, I like going onto the pages of cancer kids and leaving comments. You see those pages all the time: 'My 10-year-old daughter is dying of cancer and her wish is to trend on Twitter. Please RT.' They all have links to Facebook and Just Giving pages, or sometimes they have blogs on which they record their fight against sickness. I enjoy going on those pages and leaving comments about how ugly they are, or saying things like, 'Jesus hates you,' or, 'You must have sinned in a past life and now you're paying for it.' I use one of my many fake profiles to do this. I like going onto forums and starting fights too. Poking liberals and goading them into fury.

Looking through the Facebook photos of young girls in bikinis got me thinking about The One again. Those teens were too young for me. I'm not a Jimmy Savile. I like more mature women. The perfect woman is aged somewhere between 28 and 32. That's when a woman reaches her sexual peak, when she knows what she's doing and has the strongest desire. It's all to do with her oestrogen levels. There's a myth that men reach their peak at 18, but let me tell you, I am at my best now.

Peaking and primed for The One.

Anyway, news of Katherine's demise put me into a great mood. I went into the room I needed to prepare for my beloved and got to work. I had moved an iPod dock into the room and I slipped my iPhone into it and put my favourite song on. I sat on the bed and closed my eyes, letting the words and melody envelop me. Do you know that song? Sad Café. *Every day I'm without you hurts a little bit more.* Yes, beautiful, isn't it? It was Her favourite record; she used to play it all the time. Now, whenever I hear it, it's like a million tiny baby spiders crawling up my spine.

The room had no windows, so there was no sunlight to spoil the mood, no drapes to close. I set the lights low to create a crepuscular mood, then set about making the bed. I had ordered new linen: lilac silk sheets and an oyster-pink ruffled quilt cover, plump pillows and expensive cushions. Most men have no idea how to put a duvet cover on and it can be like watching someone attempt to stuff a flaccid cock into a condom. But I was well trained and am excellent at it.

I had bought some art for the walls, some tasteful nudes by Helmut Newton and I stopped to admire them. My favourite, *The Legend of Virginity*, was a fabulous shot of a woman being swallowed by a crocodile, her naked legs protruding from the beast's mouth. Often, that's what I like to imagine myself doing: swallowing a woman whole, taking her all the way inside me, absorbing her. Two becoming one. It's a beautiful image.

Dire Straits' 'Romeo and Juliet' came on and I sang along

softly as I continued to prepare the room. To make sure the room would look right when the time came, I set up a trestle table in the corner (it took me ages to find the perfect position), then covered it with a red-and-white-checked tablecloth. I set out a pair of wineglasses, then went off to fetch a vase and fill it with water. Into the vase went a single red rose. I pressed my fingertips against a thorn, just enough to draw blood, which I licked from my fingers.

Yes, it was perfect.

Next, I laid some lingerie on the bed – Myla, this time. A white bodysuit, complete with stockings and suspenders. I had a feeling my love would want to dress up for me, would want to be naughty. I had toyed with the idea of buying her a vibrator, but decided I would be enough. I *had* bought a crystal butt plug, however, and had spent hours online searching for the perfect plug, one that would thrill my love and fit her perfectly. This one had cost £250, but it was worth every penny.

I took some handcuffs out of my bag and attached them to the bedstead, one pair on each corner. These were designer items too. Only the best for The One, you know.

Finally, I laid plastic sheeting on the floor.

I stepped back and looked at my handiwork. Perfect. I couldn't wait to bring her back to my place. We could, I was certain, be so happy together, have such a good time. As long as she showed herself to be the woman I thought she was . . .

I was tingling all over, sweating with excitement. I was sure that she was going to pass with flying colours. I could feel it beneath my skin, deep in my bones. More than any other before. After all these years of searching, of rejecting and eliminating, I was finally so close to the woman of my dreams.

I went to the computer and sat down. I had bookmarked her website, the one she runs. It's impressive. A decent little site. How clever she is. Not a tenth as clever as me, but not many people are. And I wasn't after her for her mind, after all.

What kind of site was it? Oh, a little shopping site for people who are into crafts and all that shit.

It was called Upcycle.com.

24

Amy

Thursday, 25 July

Amy took off her helmet as she came through the front door, feeling a crackle of static electricity from her hair. She went straight into the living room, trying and failing to keep the tremor of shock out of her voice as she told Gary:

'Katherine's dead. Clive found her lying on the bathroom floor inside their cottage. Massive drugs overdose, they think.'

She knew she had to stay calm, or she would be lost entirely. 'I'm going to go and try and talk to him, see if I can persuade him to let me look at Katherine's computer. I just need to sit down and gather my thoughts for a bit first. I'll make us some coffee.'

Gary looked shocked too: queasy, and white as a sheet. He was sitting on Amy's sofa in his boxer shorts and nothing else, his hands dangling uselessly between his legs. On her ride back from the police station, Amy had almost forgotten he was still here. Boris sat on the floor at his feet, a doleful expression on his sweet face.

'This is terrible,' Gary said in a bemused voice. '*Terrible.* Do you think Becky was doing drugs too?'

Amy took a deep breath. 'No, not for a moment. She hated drugs. But I think what you're really saying is, do I think Becky's dead somewhere too?' She took another breath, gathering her courage. 'Well, yes, maybe I do. I told the police about Fraser and they're going to talk to him. In fact, they knew about him already. They wouldn't tell me explicitly but it seems clear they think it was him who gave or sold Katherine the drugs that killed her.'

Strangely, after her panic attack in the cab the previous night and even in her current state of shock, there was a part of Amy that felt stronger than before. The news of Katherine's death had horrified her, but perhaps it might yet help find Becky.

Amy paced the room. 'I can't believe that Fraser, obnoxious though he is, had anything to do with Becky's disappearance. His reaction when he saw Becky's photo and talked about her – either it was an incredibly sophisticated double-bluff, the kind he didn't seem capable of, or his only contact with her was, well, the contact he told us about.'

'I don't know,' Gary said. 'He seemed like a nasty piece of work to me.'

Amy shook her head emphatically. 'No. I just can't see it. I'm sure whoever faked Becky's disappearance is still out there.'

An image came to her: Becky, aged five, playing hide-and-seek so thoroughly that nobody found her for almost two hours. Their mum had eventually discovered her, sobbing quietly at the back of the cobwebby greenhouse, thinking that she wasn't allowed to come back unless she was found. Amy's heart clenched.

'I feel like it's got to be someone else Becky met through

that hook-up site – probably someone Kath met too. That's why I need to talk to Clive.'

'I'll come with you to see him,' Gary said, gnawing his thumbnail down to the quick. 'I've taken the day off already. I had some time in lieu owed, and—'

'No, it's fine, thanks, Gary,' Amy said, more forcefully than she'd intended. 'It's really kind of you, but—'

'*It's really kind of you, but*—' he mimicked bitterly.

Amy blinked at him. 'What?' There was so much other stuff whirling around inside her head that she barely registered his tone.

'You keep saying that, like I'm some sort of elderly uncle you're humouring, instead of—'

'Instead of what?' Amy's heart sank, although she knew that this conversation was already overdue. She was vaguely curious to know how he *did* see his role in her life – just not at that minute.

'Well, I don't know, Amy. What are we? Friends, or lovers; both or neither? I'm not stupid enough to think we're girlfriend and boyfriend.'

She sat down next to him and picked up the baby bootee she was knitting, desperate for something to do with her hands. Knitting was safer than smoking. Or self-harming. She was on her fourth bootee and had yet to make two that were near enough the same size to be considered a matching pair. For a moment, she pretended to be counting stitches. Gary's words had hurt her feelings, and simultaneously irritated her – surely, Gary couldn't have expected her to give serious thought to their 'relationship', whatever it was, under these circumstances?

'Friends, without a doubt, at the very least,' she eventually said, putting down the knitting again and turning to him, placing her hand on his bare knee. 'I know that I couldn't have got through all this so far without you. But, forgive me, Gary, honestly, with Becky gone and now Katherine dead, I just can't think about anything else . . . I'm really not ready for a relationship just yet – but please don't give up on me? It's not easy for me to say it . . . but I really need you. I'm sorry if I led you on last night. Please don't think I make a habit of it. It was lovely though, wasn't it?' She smiled tentatively up at him but he didn't smile back.

'It was amazing,' he said, scratching his stomach. 'That's why I'm gutted you don't want to do it again.'

'I do!' she protested, forcing herself to look at his knee and not in the direction of his boxers. 'I mean – you're hot, Gary, you really are. But I mean, this just isn't the right time . . . You do understand, don't you?'

Gary removed her hand, stood up and walked towards the bedroom. 'Loud and clear. Probably for the best. I'm going to get dressed now. Are you sure you don't want me to come to Clive's?'

She jumped up and gave him a hug, which he held on to for far too long. 'No, I think I can get him to talk better if I go on my own. But thanks. Make sure you close the door properly when you leave, won't you?'

The police told Amy that Clive had discovered Katherine's body at the cottage, even though the couple had split up some weeks earlier and Clive had officially moved out, so she decided the best way to track him down would be to start there. She had no idea where he'd moved to after the split, but perhaps the old man next door would have a forwarding address for him.

But when she arrived and kicked down the bike stand by the kerb outside the cottage, she saw straightaway that she wouldn't need to involve the neighbour. There was a uniformed policeman outside the partly open front door, and crime-scene tape strung from the hedge on either side of the front gate. A small group of onlookers had gathered a few doors down, gossiping and gaping at the house and at the black private ambulance parked next to two squad cars. With a shiver of horror, Amy realized that Katherine's body was likely still inside.

'Excuse me,' she said to the PC, taking off her helmet and feeling the glaring sun on her face. 'The police told me this morning about . . . what's happened in here. I need to talk to Clive, Katherine's ex. Do you know where he is?'

The PC was a young Asian man with a fluffy moustache and traces of acne on his cheeks.

'He's not here, madam. This is a protected area – the coroner is still inside.' He took out a notepad, flicked it open and hovered a pencil over the top. 'Could I have your name please?'

'Amy Coltman,' she said, trying to look over his shoulder into the house. 'Katherine Devine was a friend of my sister's, and my sister has been missing for a week. I need to talk to Katherine's ex. The police at Camberwell station told me that he discovered the body here last night.'

He laboriously wrote down everything she said, all the while glancing up at her as if worried she was going to shoulder-barge past him.

'So he must have been here earlier,' she pleaded. 'I don't have his number – if you can't tell me where he is, please could you ring him and ask him if he'll talk to me?'

'I'm sorry, Miss Coltman, but we're not allowed to give out witness information.'

'I'm not asking you to give out witness information, I'm asking you to contact him on my behalf.' The glimpse of a white-suited forensics person moving down the hallway carrying a camera – Amy couldn't tell if it was male or female – made her feel nauseous. Would these people be doing the same thing soon, in another house, with Becky's body lying on a floor somewhere?

'Are you all right, Miss?'

Amy took a deep breath and concentrated on an ant carrying a fragment of tortilla chip four times its size across the flagstone by her feet. She nodded, unable to speak, wishing that Gary was with her after all. The PC took pity on her.

'I can tell you, if it's any help, that Mr Clive Dick was met here by a member of the band he plays in. They mentioned they were going straight to the pub to have a drink, for the shock. If you know which pub they mean, you might find him there.'

Amy hadn't known that Clive's surname was Dick. Poor guy. As if things weren't bad enough for him. So – one of his mates from the band had collected him. Which pub would they go to? The only one she could think of was the one she and Gary had been to, where his band had been playing. It was local, and they played there regularly, so it could be the one.

'Thanks – I think I know where he might be. I'll try there.'

'I'll just take your address and phone number, if I may, Miss Coltman,' said the PC, pencil hovering again. Amy gave him the details, put on her helmet, and got back on her bike, wishing that she could accelerate to eighty miles an hour to get as far away as she could from the knowledge of Katherine's dead body – not to mention the knowledge of having to confront a grief-stricken man who already hated her sister and, by default, her.

* * *

'Clive?' she said tentatively, approaching the dark corner of a back room of the Crown where, even at eleven thirty, several empties were accumulating on a small table in front of him. He was there alone, his head buried in his arms, shoulders shaking. Amy's heart sank even further.

She touched his arm and he jumped, staring up at her with wild, streaming eyes. 'You again. I suppose you've heard.'

She sat down next to him. 'I'm so, so sorry, Clive. I really am. I just can't believe it.' Tears filled her own eyes.

'What do you want? I doubt you've come over here to give me your condolences.' He sounded flat and resigned.

Amy sniffed hard. 'Well, I have – but not only that.'

'So your sister hasn't showed up yet.'

She shook her head. 'Clive . . . I know you hate Becky – and for whatever reason you blame her for what happened between you and Katherine, and if she did split you two up, then I don't blame you – but this isn't about Becky.'

Clive lifted up his pint with shaking hands, closing his eyes as he drank deeply, as though the act of swallowing would take away his pain. He was such a funny little man, thought Amy, trying to imagine him and the larger-than-life Katherine together, when they were happy. He looked like Katherine would have eaten him for dinner, although maybe he was one of those men who changed behind closed doors: meek in public, strong in private.

'Isn't it?'

'Not just about Becky,' Amy corrected herself. She bit her lip – this part was going to be hard. 'It's about me, going insane, because I'm convinced something bad has happened to her. It's about my mum and dad and grandparents, who'll all be devastated if it has. It's about everyone who loves her – some of them will be mourning Katherine soon, when they find out. All their work colleagues, and all the boys at school . . . All their friends, who'll have to cope with one death, wondering if it's two . . . Whatever your own personal feelings about her are, Clive, please don't put us all through what you're going through over Katherine. Please?'

Amy had to stop talking because suddenly she was crying too much, and they sat in silence for a few minutes, punctuated only by her suppressed sobs. She delved in her bag for a tissue. She didn't dare look at Clive – in fact, she was worried that he would simply walk out and never speak to her, ever.

Clive's friend reappeared, having been outside for a cigarette. He reeked of smoke and was slightly unsteady on his feet. Amy briefly wondered why they hadn't just sat outside in the garden if he was smoking, but when she did pluck up strength to look at Clive, she knew: he couldn't be out in the sunshine, not when everything in his world was so unrelentingly dark.

'All right, mate?' Clive's friend clapped him on the back, slightly too hard, making Clive's pint glass clink against his front teeth. 'I'm Jerry,' he said to Amy. 'Were you a good friend of Katherine's?' He sounded embarrassed. 'Awful business. Drinking's the only answer. It's my round – what can I get you?'

It wasn't even noon, but they were both well on the way to complete inebriation.

'I'm on my bike, thanks, but a Coke would be lovely,' said Amy, gesturing to the helmet by her feet. Jerry weaved off into the saloon bar. 'Same again for you, sir,' he called back over his shoulder – a comment, not a question.

'He never liked Kath,' Clive said to Amy, wiping his eyes. 'Good mate, though. You didn't like her either, did you?'

At least he was talking to her. It was a start.

'I hardly knew her. Honestly, I only met her once or twice with my sister. I thought she was an amazing artist. I was going to ask her to write something for my website. I've got this crafts website, you see, called Upcycle.com, it's—'

'So what do you want to know?' Clive interrupted. For the first time, he looked properly at her, through bloodshot, heavily lidded eyes. He could pass for a 60-year-old man, thought Amy, bowed by grief and fury.

She took a deep breath. 'You know about the Internet dating, that they were both doing it?'

Clive's mouth twisted with something: disgust, or pain, or both.

'I've already told the police all about that. It's why we split up. Spent hours with them this morning, going over and over it. She would've settled down with me, I know she would. She just wanted to sow some wild oats first.'

'Did they tell you about this guy, Fraser?'

Clive hesitated, as though teetering on the edge of a waterfall.

'They told me there was someone she and Becky both went on a date with. They didn't tell me his name. They think he might have given her the drugs she had on her. God knows, she couldn't have afforded to buy them, the amount they found.'

'Fraser. He's a nasty piece of work.'

'How do you know him? Going out with your – your – *sister*, was he?'

He had clearly been about to insert a choice adjective – all the venom was back in his voice. Amy made a colossal effort to keep calm.

'No, he wasn't. They came across him on the same dating website – they were both members. What I want to ask you is: do you know what Katherine's password is . . . I mean, was?' She blushed. 'For her email. And the website, if you know it, but obviously, I wouldn't expect you to . . .'

Jerry came back with a Coke for Amy and another pint for Clive. 'I'll be in the garden,' he said, with clear relief that someone else was taking a shift at babysitting Clive. 'Need to call in sick to work before I get fired.' He slid his phone out of the back pocket of his jeans and headed back to the garden, ignoring Amy's thanks.

'The police have her laptop,' Clive said coldly. 'Why don't you ask them?'

Amy felt crushed. Of course the police would have taken away Katherine's computer for analysis. Had she really thought it would be that easy? What an idiot. She bit the tip of her tongue hard, feeling saliva flood into her mouth, to try to stop herself crying again.

'I will ask them, of course, but they won't tell me, will they? . . . I found out last night that Becky and Katherine were using a hook-up site to meet men . . . for sex. They both met Fraser through it and maybe there were other men they both went on . . . dates with.' Clive blanched but she had to press on. 'At first, I tried to track down the men Becky had met on the other site, CupidsWeb, but that was a dead end.'

She took a sip of her Coke. 'But maybe Becky met someone on this hook-up site who can help me find her, and if they had both been with Fraser, chances are that there are other men they both met up with too. So, if I can see Kath's emails . . .'

Clive shrugged, and rubbed his hand across his face. 'Listen, no offence, Annie . . .'

'Amy.'

'Amy. No offence, but I don't really understand why

you're talking to me. That's what the police are there for. They have her MacBook. They have all the information. It's been less than twenty-four hours since I found the body of my girlfriend – the woman I thought I was going to marry – on the floor of our house. I get that you're upset about your sister, but you need to go away now, and leave me to get quietly wankered until I pass out and Jerry will take me home so that I can go to sleep without dreaming of my fiancée.'

Fiancée? That was a new one, thought Amy. She noticed he'd dropped the 'ex' as well. Still, she couldn't blame him. She sighed. Another dead end. Back to Camberwell nick, she supposed.

'OK. I'll go . . . and thanks for talking to me, I really appreciate it. Just one thing before I go: what was Kath's email address?'

'It was katherinedevine2@gmail.com.'

'Gmail. So her emails can be accessed from any computer?'

'Yeah. Of course.' Clive made eye contact with her for the first time and Amy saw that, underneath the red veins, he had good eyes – clear, hazel pupils fringed with black.

She held her breath. 'Clive . . . what was her Gmail password? Did you know it?'

He just stared at her.

'Please, Clive?'

'I don't know.'

Everything in her deflated again, and she turned to go. 'Oh. Oh, well. Worth a shot, I guess. Thanks.'

Amy picked up her helmet and put on her leather biker gloves, determined not to cry again. Just as she was turning to go, Clive's hand shot out and grabbed her glove.

'I don't know it for sure,' he said. 'But going on past experience, it's probably some combination of Alice Barrow – her mum's maiden name; Harcourt – the first street she lived on; or 20 April 1986 – her birthday. She always used those.'

Amy put her arms around him and hugged him. His own arms twitched, as though he was going to reciprocate but then thought better of it.

Leaving the pub, she felt a desperate urge to get to a computer straight away. Becky's flat was closer and she had the keys in her jacket pocket. She would go there, use the iMac. She felt an electrical charge inside her, a blend of excitement and terror. This was her final and only lead. If this led nowhere, what would she do? She pictured Becky lying in the dark, lost for ever.

She got on her bike and headed towards Becky's flat.

25

Declan

Friday, 19th July

DI Declan Adams and DC Bob Clewley pulled into a parking space at the end of the cul-de-sac and got out of the car. Declan stretched his legs – his knee had seized up this time – and gently rotated his bad shoulder, while Bob smirked at him.

'Getting old,' Bob said.

'Speak for yourself.'

'Still, at least we are growing old. Unlike these poor bastards' daughter.'

Declan put a hand on his colleague's shoulder to stop him striding straight up to the house. 'Remember, we don't know that for certain. Not yet. We need to talk to them first. Or rather, I do. Let me do the talking, all right? Don't want you going in with your size tens and upsetting everybody.'

The cul-de-sac was in a suburb of Chichester, West Sussex, a pretty place that Declan had visited once before, back in the mists of time, on a school trip to the cathedral. All he remembered about that trip was how he had spent the whole day trying not to stare at Sally Oaks, with whom he was madly in love that week. He wondered where she was now. He hoped she or her loved ones never received a visit from someone like him.

It was every parent's greatest fear: a knock from the police. Declan wondered whether, after fifteen years, these parents were still waiting, still hoping. Still dreading that knock.

But despite the news he was going to have to deliver, assuming the information in the DNA database was correct, Declan felt that tingle of excitement, had felt it all the way up from Eastbourne, wanting Bob to ignore the speed limits and put his foot down.

Declan pressed the doorbell and waited. A dog barked inside and he heard a woman's admonishing voice, ordering it to be quiet. But it was a man who opened the door. He was, according to the information they had, sixty-one, but he looked older, well past retirement age. The remains of his hair were bone white and he was thin, all sharp angles and hollows beneath the cardigan that he was wearing despite the humid weather.

'Mr Corrigan?' Declan said. 'I'm Detective Inspector Declan Adams. This is Detective Constable Bob Clewley. May we come in?'

A minute later, they sat on a salmon-pink sofa, holding cups of tea that Mrs Corrigan had produced with record speed. Whilst her husband was emaciated, Sheila Corrigan was a large woman, just the right side of morbidly obese. Along with the tea, she put down a large biscuit barrel, full of custard creams and chocolate digestives. At Sheila's insistence, Bob took a Jammie Dodger.

Derek Corrigan settled into an armchair, an ancient

Labrador at his feet, his wife in the armchair beside him. On the mantelpiece opposite the sofa were half a dozen framed photos of a girl, her age increasing from left to right along the mantel. A 6-month-old baby, grinning toothlessly, then a little girl with plaits, a pubescent girl with a gappy smile wearing a Brighton and Hove Albion shirt, a skinny teenager clad in black with big silver earrings, a young woman on her graduation day, flanked by her proud parents, and finally a woman in her early twenties, standing in front of a Christmas tree. Blue eyes and blonde hair. She was beautiful.

Sheila saw Declan staring at the photos. 'That's Amber,' she said brightly.

'Our daughter,' Derek added. There was no brightness in his voice, but, beneath the sadness, Declan detected a touch of wonder – disbelief, still – that he could have fathered such an attractive woman.

Declan put his tea down on the table in front of him. 'You didn't ask us why we're here,' he said.

The Corrigans exchanged a look that almost broke Declan's heart.

'We thought that maybe you have some news . . .' Sheila said, the sentence trailing off as if she'd run out of oxygen.

Declan cleared his throat. 'I want to ask you about your daughter. Amber. When did you last see her?'

Derek sent an enquiring look in his wife's direction and she nodded. He said, 'Fifteen years ago. Fifteen years this month, in fact: 31 July 1998. That's when she went to the conference.'

Declan was aware of Bob scribbling in his notepad, and trusted that he would take down everything important. 'Conference?'

'Yes. It was something to do with the Internet. I think . . .

211

well, yes, this was just when everyone was starting to go online. We didn't get it until a few years later – I still can't use it properly, it takes me half an hour to type "Dear Sir", but Sheila here is on it a lot these days, aren't you, love?'

Sheila nodded. 'I use this forum. For women like me.'

Declan waited for her to continue. 'Mothers whose children have run away. Not that Amber was a child when she went.' She swallowed hard and her chin trembled.

Run away. That's what they thought had happened. Declan turned back to Derek, keen to concentrate on the facts, not only because it was his job, but because facts were easier to cope with than emotions. Even the facts he was going to have to reveal during this conversation. 'Do you know where the conference was, or what it was called?'

'I can't remember the name off the top of my head but we'll have the details somewhere. Do you want me to . . .?' He moved to stand up.

'No, it's fine. If you could look it up for me later, that would be great.'

'All right. The conference was about starting a business on the Internet. Amber had done Business Studies at university—'

'She got a 2:1,' Sheila chipped in.

'—and was excited about the thought of making lots of money on the web.'

Bob looked up from his notepad. 'That would have been when the Internet gold rush started. Before the bubble burst.'

'That's right.' Derek nodded. 'Amber was so excited about this conference. She said there were going to be investors there and people from America who'd set up successful websites and were making piles of cash.'

'But you don't remember where it was?' Declan prompted him.

'Not the name of the conference – but it was in Tunbridge Wells.'

That was just a short drive from Robertson Farm, just across the Sussex–Kent border. It was time, Declan realized, to explain exactly why he and Bob were here.

'Mr Corrigan, Mrs Corrigan – it's not going to be easy to tell you this . . .'

He watched Sheila reach out her hand. Derek grasped it.

'A few days ago, the body of a young woman was discovered on farmland in Sussex.' He decided to spare them the detail of the cesspit for now. This was going to be hard enough as it was. 'The farm is close to Tunbridge Wells.'

The couple were staring at him, tears already appearing in Sheila's eyes. Derek looked as if he was about to throw up; Declan wouldn't have thought it possible for him to grow any paler, but he had.

'We took a DNA sample from the . . . young woman. Her DNA was not on the system, but . . . I'm not sure if you know how DNA works, but children have a 50-per-cent DNA match with their parents. Mr Corrigan, your DNA is on the national database.'

He let go of his wife's hand. 'I know.'

Declan paused and looked at Sheila, who had rubbed away her tears with her fist and now looked angry and embarrassed. She obviously knew too.

'I realize the charges were dropped,' Declan said.

'Yes, when that little bastard admitted he'd been making it all up.'

Derek had a tiny flare of colour in his cheeks now; the rosy tinge of anger. 'They took a sample from me way back then. One of the Scouts accused me of doing disgusting things to him. The whole thing was a prank, a stupid so-called joke between boys. But I can't believe my DNA

213

is still in your system, even though the whole thing was dismissed. It didn't even go to trial.'

'It happens,' Declan said. 'And in a way it's a good thing . . . because it led us here. To you.'

Derek lifted his chin defensively. 'It lost me my Scout leader's job, but it didn't ruin my life. Amber leaving us without a word and not coming back – *that* was what ruined my life.'

Declan guessed that Derek's outburst was, although genuine, also a way of postponing what he knew Declan was about to say.

'Do you have any other children?'

'No,' Sheila replied.

Declan braced himself. This was it – the very worst part of being a cop. He had only had to do it twice before, in the company of an FLO, a family liaison officer, and never with a case like this – where the parents had been holding onto a thread of hope for so many years. Now, he was going to snap that thread.

'The DNA of the young woman we found on the farm has a 50-per-cent match with yours, Mr Corrigan. Knowing that Amber went missing fifteen years ago, and that she was your only child, means it is almost certain that the body we found is hers. I'm so sorry.'

From talking to other friends in the force, Declan knew that parents reacted to news like this in a multitude of ways: denial, instant waterworks, fury, calm acceptance.

'But it can't be her,' Sheila said.

So it was denial.

'She left the country. She met a man and left the country. She went to live in Brazil.'

'No, I'm afraid . . .'

Sheila hauled herself to her feet. 'Look, let me show you.'

She left the room and, through a set of double doors, Declan could see her rifling through a sideboard. She came back with a small wooden box, from which she produced a sheet of paper.

Declan took the piece of paper, making sure he held it by the edges. It was a letter from Amber, dated 3 August 1998, typed on a sheet of A4 paper that had lost much of its colour. The letter was short, and, in it, Amber told her parents that she had met a man at the conference and had fallen in love. They were moving to Brazil to start a new life together.

Declan's pulse accelerated. The body in the cesspit had to be Amber, unless the DNA match was wrong. They could double-check that. But the match and the location, together with the timing and the fact that the description Melinda Moore had given them matched Amber's physical features, meant he had no doubt in his mind. The dead girl was Amber Corrigan.

Which meant there were two possibilities:

One – the letter really was from Amber, but she had been murdered after she wrote it, by her Brazilian lover or someone else; or

Two – the letter had been written by the person who killed her.

'Did Amber always *type* letters to you?' Bob asked, reading over it himself. 'It seems pretty impersonal.'

Sheila said, 'Yes, she did. Even at uni. She loved her computers and her handwriting was terrible. She had been pestering us to get on email for ages so she didn't have to bother with stamps.'

'So, all these years, you thought Amber was living in Brazil, without ever emailing or visiting you?'

'Yes. She was. We reckoned she just decided she wanted

215

a new life, and had to shut everything out of the old one to be able to cope with it. She was always single-minded . . . When you turned up today, we thought you were going to say that something had happened to her out there.'

'Look at these,' Derek said, leaning forward and taking something else out of the box. He handed it to Declan.

It was a photograph of a house on a beach. White walls, a terracotta roof, palm trees either side. Declan turned it over. There was no writing on the back.

'That's her house,' Derek said. 'Lovely, isn't it?'

'When did you get this?' Declan asked.

'A year after she went away.'

'And was there anything with it? A note?'

'No. Just that. It's a beautiful place. Beats rainy Chichester, doesn't it?'

'What about the envelope, Mr Corrigan?' Bob asked. 'Do you still have it? And the envelope that the first letter came in?'

Derek looked at his wife, who shook her head. 'I'm sorry. I threw them away. I never keep envelopes.'

'We've often thought about going out there to try to find her,' Derek said. 'But we wouldn't know where to start looking.'

Declan suddenly wanted to shake the pair of them, knock their heads together. 'Didn't this seem out of character to you? For Amber to run off with a guy she'd just met, send a mysterious photo with no note and not contact you again?'

The couple exchanged another look. Sheila spoke this time. 'It *was* out of character, I suppose. She was always very close to me, used to call me nearly every day when she was at university. But we'd had a row, you see . . .'

'It was that bloody boy,' Derek said. 'The one who accused me of those things.'

'Amber didn't know he was lying. The whole thing happened just before she went to that conference, you see. She didn't want to talk to her dad at all . . . And I stood by him, knew the boy must be lying. Amber was upset with both of us.'

'It's the worst thing,' Derek said. 'She probably still thinks I did it.'

Sheila shook her head, her gaze fixed on the photo of the whitewashed house on a Brazilian beach. 'That's not the worst thing. She probably has children of her own by now. We're most likely grandparents.'

Derek reached over and patted his wife's hand as she sobbed. He was staring into space now.

All of a sudden, Declan needed to get out of this room, this house – but he would take the letter and photo with him, along with the picture of Amber when she was in her early twenties, standing in front of the Christmas tree, smiling.

Run away to Brazil? This girl was on a mortuary slab, and somebody was going to have to persuade her parents of the truth of that. So they could bury her.

26

Amy

Thursday, 25 July

Amy trudged up the stairs to Becky's flat, suddenly feeling limp with exhaustion. It was only lunchtime, but she felt as though the day had already lasted hundreds of hours. Inside her leathers, sweat trickled down her spine, and she had an unpleasantly damp feeling in her crotch, as though she'd wet herself. Leathers were fine in winter, but horrible in summer.

Unlocking the bottom lock made her think back to the other day, and how weird it was that Becky hadn't double-locked before she went out – she *always* double-locked. *Could* someone else have been in there? Who? She shivered at the thought, and remembered, too, the other strange incident when someone had tried the door and she'd chased them into the street, but then tantalizingly seen nobody. It had been like chasing a ghost . . .

'Hello?' she called out hopefully, once she was inside, peeling off the sticky leathers and leaving them in a pile on the floor, like a huge insect husk. At that moment, she felt she'd have given a major organ to see Becky emerge bleary and hungover from her bedroom. 'What's all the fuss about?' she would say. 'Didn't you get my email? I decided to come back early.'

But the flat was still eerily silent. Amy switched on the radio – it was tuned to Capital FM, which she hated, but anything was better than the stillness – and sat down at Becky's iMac in her pants and T-shirt.

First, she checked Becky's emails again – nothing new. She typed Googlemail into the Search box, and clicked on it, inputting katherinedevine2@gmail.com when requested, her fingers hesitating over the keyboard when she came to the password box. Her first few suggestions were rejected:

HARCOURT1986

Alicebarrow

Alicebarrow20041986

With a sinking heart, she realized that, even though there weren't many likely words, there was still a huge potential number of combinations of them.

Harcourt20486

HarcourtAlice

HarcourtBarrow86

Still nothing.

A sudden knock at the door made her jump so hard that she bit her tongue. She ran into Becky's bedroom and grabbed a denim skirt out of her chest of drawers, yanking it with difficulty over her hips – Becky was a size smaller. She managed to do it up, still fiddling with the zip as she pressed her ear against the door. She could taste blood.

She couldn't hear anything, so she called out: 'Who is it?'

'It's me, Gary.'

She flung open the door and let him in. 'Hi. I thought it

was the police – I don't know why. And I forgot to put anything on under my leathers.'

'Leathers,' agreed Gary, although without smiling. He still looked wan and stressed.

'Why aren't you at work?'

His reply sounded slightly snappy: 'I told you, I took the day off. Just came back here to change and shower, and heard the radio through the walls. I thought for a moment that it might be Becky . . .'

'Sorry. It's only me. I'm trying to get into Katherine's Gmail account – Clive gave me a few suggestions about what the password might be, but nothing's worked yet.'

Gary moved over to the computer and sat down. 'Let's have a go. What have you tried?'

Amy told him, and he scribbled the options down on a Post-it note, then tried ALICEHARCOURT. To Amy's amazement it worked first time – they were in.

'Beginner's luck,' she said, her heart pounding in her chest. She barged him off the office chair with her hip. 'Let's see what Ms Devine was up to, shall we? God rest her soul,' she added hastily. In the euphoria of Gary guessing the password, she had actually momentarily forgotten that Katherine was dead. Gary didn't seem at all excited, though. Perhaps all this is really starting to get to him, Amy thought. Perhaps I shouldn't have allowed him to get involved.

He got up and stood behind her as she scrolled through dozens and dozens of emails, many of them identical ones from Casexual.com: *Dear Katherine, you have a new private message from . . . Click here to see it.*

'Popular, wasn't she?' commented Gary. 'Put Casexual into the Search box. She might have kept her login confirmation email from Casexual, with her password on it.'

220

Amy shot him an admiring look. She might have thought of that herself, but it would have taken a lot longer.

'You're a star.'

But still he didn't smile. 'Um, Amy,' he said. 'There's something I need to tell you.'

'Hang on a second,' Amy said. 'Just let me do this first.'

He was right – after searching, she found an admin email from Casexual, headed, 'Your login details'.

'Bingo,' she said, and clicked it open. When she saw what it said, she laughed ruefully: Katherine's login details were exactly the same as her Gmail ones – her email address, with ALICEHARCOURT as password.

'I bet she used the same password for everything,' Gary said, almost angrily. 'I hope you don't do that, Amy. It's crazy. Someone could easily have found out everything about her.'

'Maybe they did,' Amy replied soberly, logging on to Casexual.com as Katherine. All the messages loaded. 'I don't, no. I hope Becky didn't . . . Can you turn on the printer, please? I'll print all these out.'

Gary hesitated, but obliged.

'What?'

'Come and sit over here for a second. That thing I need to tell you – it's really important.'

Amy set the printer going with the first email, then reluctantly allowed Gary to lead her over to the sofa.

'It's not about "us" then?'

He tutted, crouching down in front of her, his knees cracking like twigs. 'No, it's not. It's something else. I'm sorry, Amy, but Pete rang me back this morning about those Facebook photos that Becky supposedly posted.'

'And?' Amy's heart sank. It was pretty obvious where this was going. She felt like putting her hands over her ears and singing *lalalala*. In the background, an ad on Capital FM extolled the virtues of nought-per-cent finance on the new season's sofas.

'There's nothing he can do. He can't tell how old the photos are or identify the beach. He used Google Goggles to see if those pictures appear anywhere else on the web – you know, to check if someone had simply copied them from another site – but it came back with no matches.'

'So the photos are originals?'

Gary shrugged helplessly. 'It's impossible to tell. It just means that those pictures haven't been indexed by Google. But they could have been taken from another Facebook account, where the privacy settings are switched on, or scanned from a magazine . . .'

'They could be from bloody anywhere.'

'Or maybe Becky actually took them herself,' he suggested in a soft voice.

'No! It's totally out of character. There's no way she would post pictures like that with no captions, nor respond to any comments. Not unless she's had a major personality transplant. I'm shocked you don't believe me.'

He held his palms towards her. 'I do believe you. I was just saying—'

'What? That I'm making all of this up? Paranoid Amy, who won't believe the evidence in front of her eyes? Becky is *not* in fucking Asia – I would bet my life on it.'

'OK, OK . . .'

She was in full flow now: 'Why have you been going along with it, eh? Have you been pretending to help me just so you could get a shag?'

'For fuck's sake, Amy – you know it's not like that.'

'I bet you—'

'Just shut up. Please!'

She stared at him, but he crossed to the window, rolling his shoulders to relieve some of the tension in them. Her heart was beating hard and her head felt like a bomb that was about to detonate. There was no way she was going to apologize to him. If he didn't 100 per cent believe that something awful had happened to Becky, that she wasn't swanning about on beaches in Asia, then she didn't want him helping her any more. She would just have to do it on her own.

She went back to the computer and doggedly printed out the other thirty-four Casexual overtures one by one. All from strangers who wanted to have sex with Katherine – and Becky, too, probably, although she had been through Becky's emails going back months and there had been nothing from any hook-up sites, only from the much tamer and more conventional dating site, CupidsWeb. She must have deleted the Welcome email, just in case. She knew from Fraser that Becky had been using Casexual too.

She glanced at a few of the messages as they churned out.

You're one hot mama, can I come on your tits?

Wow, lady, you float my boat! Let's be naughty together!

I'm so hard right now just looking at your profile pic. What size panties do you wear?

My wife won't go down on me any more. You would, I can tell . . .

'Ugh,' she said to herself. 'This is disgusting. What the hell was wrong with Katherine? There's nothing exciting about this.'

Another email printed, one word jumping out at her that made her catch her breath. She snatched the paper out of the printer. 'Oh, my God, no.'

'What?' Gary came and looked over her shoulder, his

223

voice still cold. She stabbed at it with her finger and read out loud:

'*So excited about your friend Becky, I looked at her profile and she sounds as hot as you are. When will we three meet? Don't worry, I have enough loving for both of you! I promise you a night you'll NEVER forget. Can't wait to hear from you!*'

It was from someone with the username TooledUp, and he'd attached a photo in the body of the email. Taken in a mirror with a camera phone, he looked buff and oiled, with mean little eyes and far too many tattoos. His pecs bulged like rocks under his skin. He was horrible. Amy had seen enough.

'I'm going to be sick,' she said in a strangled voice, and dashed for the bathroom.

When she returned, Gary had opened the front door. He was holding her bag, which he handed her, the emails, and the keys to Becky's flat.

They were a couple of steps down the hallway when Amy suddenly stopped. 'Hang on – we didn't Chubb the door.'

Gary tutted and turned back. 'The door. Oh, I always bloody forget to do that . . .' He tailed off, and looked so guilty that if Amy had been in any doubt as to what it meant, she wasn't after she saw that look. Her eyes opened wide and they faced each other, held in the toxic spotlight of Gary's revelation.

'*You always forget to do that?*' she whispered. 'You forgot to do it the day she went missing, didn't you? The door wasn't double-locked then, either.'

She backed away from him, and he held out his free hand to her.

'No, of course not, Amy. What do you think . . .?'

'I don't know what to think. Why didn't you tell me you'd been in her flat? Why didn't you tell the police?' Her voice was increasingly shrill, and she realized she was flattening herself against the wall of the stairwell.

'I wasn't in her flat!' he shouted, and made a move towards her, his hand in a fist, his face twisted into an expression she'd never seen on him before. The sheaf of emails spilled from his other hand and scattered across the floor, cascading down the stairs.

'I don't believe you!' she screamed back and, for the second time in less than a week, ran down the stairs, swinging round the corners and ricocheting off the walls. The difference this time was that instead of running after someone, someone was running after her.

Gary was chasing her, full pelt, and when she glanced over her shoulder, he was almost upon her. She grappled with the door handle, but her hands were sweating, her body wasn't working properly. As she finally pushed the door open, Gary bellowed, 'Amy!' in her ear.

He grabbed her, his hands like pincers on her shoulders.

27

Amy

Five years ago

A year had passed since that first row in Kingston. Nathan had begged and pleaded and apologized and said it would *never* happen again and finally Amy had forgiven him.

Of course it happened again.

Not for a long time – long enough that Amy was able to write off that first meltdown as an aberration – but other disturbing ripples began to fan out in its wake, rocking then steadying Amy's conviction that Nathan was the one. Rocking and steadying, until she almost got used to feeling permanently seasick.

Part of her even loved him more for being so jealous – as he said, he'd never feel so possessive of her if he didn't love her so much. She was pretty sure he checked all her texts and emails, and deliberately left her phone around so that he could do so, in the knowledge that there was nothing incriminating on it. She wanted him to feel secure.

That was all OK, she didn't mind that. It was the criticism she found hard, the gradual erosion of her self-confidence and self-belief, crumbling away in a landslide of, 'Are you really going out wearing *that*?' and, 'Oh, babe, I think you'd better only have half that bacon sandwich,' and, 'Leave your phone at home. Don't want you getting texts from other blokes!'

Then they would have sex, powerful enough to bring them both to tears, and the slate would be wiped clean again – until the next time.

They took a holiday together, out to Spain to visit Amy's parents, who immediately loved Nathan. Amy kept catching her mother looking sidelong at him with an expression of quiet awe. Nathan was happier than she had ever seen him, his smooth skin burnished bronze in the hot sunshine, laughing and drinking sangria and complimenting Amy's mum on the paella, and he hardly criticized Amy at all.

And yet he refused to speak a word to her on the plane all the way home, because he claimed she had flirted with the check-in clerk at the airport.

Nobody had ever been so jealous, or worried about losing her. If she was honest with herself, Amy acknowledged that – when she could rise above the constant, low-level harassment – reassuring him made her feel powerful, sexy, desired.

Until the afternoon, five months later, when Nathan shoved her almost casually into the smallest of the built-in wardrobes in their bedroom and locked the door behind her. It all happened so fast that Amy didn't have time to process what was going on, not until she heard the heavy clunk of a padlock hasp engaging. A padlock that she didn't know existed. They hadn't even had an argument, although he had seemed particularly intense all day.

'This is for your own protection, you know, sweetheart. I won't be long, I'm only going to the gym.'

'What? Nathan! No, please, don't, I can't—'

All she heard were his footsteps retreating, and she was left in the pitch-darkness with all his suits still in their dry-cleaning wrappers. The soft clingy plastic attached itself to her head, suffocating her, and she batted it away in panic, her breath coming in harsh gulps of terror.

Amy remembered in a flash the first dinner she and Becky had had with him, when he'd asked about their worst fears.

She rattled at the wardrobe door, pounding on it with her fists and kicking with her heels, but it was more solid than it looked. Surely, he hadn't actually gone? She hadn't heard the front door close, but then she had been making a racket. The silence outside felt as though it was pressing in, seeping into the wardrobe like a poisonous gas. She was choking, fighting the darkness, all her senses on red alert. What if he'd lost the plot entirely, and was waiting outside with a sharp curved knife? What did she really know about him? He had sprung, fully formed, into her life, and rarely talked about his past. She was an idiot to have trusted him. Now she would have to move out, and see the pitying 'I told you so' expression in Becky's eyes.

No. Becky must not know. This could not be the end of her beautiful relationship. Nathan only criticized her because he loved her! She would make it right, somehow. Force him to come to therapy with her. Change him.

She would change him.

She cried and wailed and screamed so much that her throat was raw and she had to make herself stop, in case she used up all the oxygen in the wardrobe.

When he eventually returned, he was actually whistling: 'Father and Son' by Cat Stevens. Amy heard him pottering around in the hallway, hanging up his keys, going to the kitchen and pouring himself a glass of water out of the jug.

'Nathan!' she screamed. 'Let me out!'

He took his time, sauntering into the bedroom. She heard the key engage in the padlock, and her fingers were curling around the edge of the sliding door the moment she saw a chink of daylight, dragging it open. She fell out, gasping, exhausted from sobbing and hyperventilation, lying like a comma on the bedroom floor. Her nails were broken and bleeding from scratching at the door.

'Oh, sweetheart!' he said when he saw her, concern furrowing his brow. 'What's the matter? I wasn't long!'

He reached over to try to pick her up to embrace her, but she rolled away from him. She caught a glimpse of herself in the mirrored wardrobe door – tears and snot smeared all over her deathly white face, her hair standing in crazed spikes.

'Get away from me!'

She staggered to her feet, and he looked hurt.

'What's wrong?' he repeated.

'What's fucking *wrong*? Are you insane? You lock me in the fucking wardrobe when you know I'm claustrophobic, and then you ask what's wrong?'

He sighed and ran a hand through his sweaty hair. 'Amy, baby, I'm sorry – I didn't know it would be so hard for you.'

Amy stared at him, uncomprehending.

'Why did you do it? Are you punishing me for something? What did I do to upset you?'

He reached out for her again, and she flinched away.

'Don't be like that, Amy. It's no big deal, honestly. I just thought you'd be safer in there while I was out. There have been all these dodgy guys getting into the building and trying to sell chamois leathers and shit door-to-door – didn't you see the warning notice in the lobby? And then there's the caretaker, I don't trust him at all. Have you seen the way he looks at you? I just couldn't bear it if anything happened to you, darling, I love you so much.'

He's a psycho, she thought. He's completely bonkers and I'm going to have to leave him. Her heart sank, and next time she looked at him, she saw only concern in his eyes, and the love that up until then she hadn't seriously ever doubted.

Yes, he was sometimes moody and distant and jealous – but nothing like this had happened before.

She walked slowly forwards into his arms, inhaling his damp skin. Even after a workout, he smelled good. His arms tightened around her and gradually she lifted hers to wrap around his waist. Her hands were still shaking.

'I don't know what that was about, Nathan,' she said slowly and distinctly, over his shoulder. 'But it was too much. If you ever, *ever* do that to me again, we're over. Do you understand?'

She felt him nod. He pressed himself closer to her and his cock stiffened against her belly.

'Promise me.'

'I promise,' he said. 'I'm sorry, Amy, I don't know what came over me. I know it was wrong. It's because I love you so much, I suddenly got in a panic about someone coming to the door and raping you, and me not being there. I couldn't bear it if anything happened to you.'

'That's not a normal reaction, you know that.'

He shrugged. 'We're not a normal couple,' he said. He released his grip and took her hand. 'Come on, I need a bath. Can we have one together?'

As the bath ran, they undressed one another. Panicked images of her captivity kept flashing through her head, but Amy forced herself to concentrate on the man she loved, the texture of his skin, the flecks of gold in his sorrowful eyes. Once they were completely naked and the bath was full, he climbed in first and lay down, his erection sticking comically out of the bubbles. Amy got in too and lowered herself down on top of him, the adrenaline in her system transferring itself into sheer animal lust. She closed her eyes and forced herself to forget the past two hours.

At some stage, they rolled over and Amy found herself underneath, the hot water tickling the sides of her face and occasionally sloshing over her as Nathan pounded into her.

'*Slut*,' he hissed into her ear, but her ear had water in it and she wasn't sure she had heard correctly.

She started, and tried to push him off her, but all his weight was on her, pressing her down. 'What did you say?'

'I said, you're a slut, Amy Coltman. A stupid slut. I lock you in a cupboard all afternoon and you still want to shag me? What's wrong with you?'

Amy put her hands against his shoulders to try to push him harder, tears springing back to her eyes. 'Five minutes ago, you said you'd never do it again. Five minutes! Don't you want to be with me? Is this your way of saying we're finished? Well, that's fine with me. I'm leaving. I never want to see you again!'

Nathan climbed out of the bath and stood over her, dripping and furious, an expression of pure hatred on his face. A clump of bubbles slid slowly down his right arm – then flew off and dissipated in the air as he raised his hand and slapped her face, hard.

'You,' he said, almost calmly, 'are going *nowhere*. You're mine, and I'm going to make sure you never fucking forget it.'

He took one of the towels off the rail and wrapped it around his waist. Then he flicked the other one over his shoulder, switched off the light in the windowless room, took the key out of the door and left the room. The sudden silence of the extractor fan meant that Amy, her cheek stinging and aching, clearly heard the sound of the key being turned in the lock.

'Oh, no. Not again. No no no no no,' she muttered, staggering to her feet and climbing out of the bath into the damp darkness. Instinctively, she felt around for a towel, then remembered he'd taken both of them. No towel. No light. Her heart began to pound, and she rattled the door handle. The door didn't budge.

'Nathan!' she wailed, unsure if the darkness she saw in front of her eyes was because she was blacking out. She hit the light switch – but nothing happened. The bastard must have turned the lights off at the fuse box. 'Let me out!'

Silence. She knew there was no point in banging and shouting – and, anyway, all the strength to do so had vanished from her, dripping off her like the cooling water on her body. Gooseflesh broke out all over her wet skin.

Wearily, she climbed back into the bath and lay down so the warmth enveloped her. But how long would it stay warm for?

Another twenty minutes, was the answer.

When the water chilled to tepid, Amy sat up and twisted the hot tap – but only cold water came out. The hot-water tank was empty.

This couldn't be happening.

She lay down again, shivering uncontrollably, but by now the water was cold enough to be of no further comfort. They had no plans for that night, so nobody would miss her. She wished fervently that she'd taken Becky up on her invitation to the movies, but she'd declined. She'd have to go straight to Becky's when he finally let her out . . . Amy made a brief inventory of what she needed to take with her: a few changes of clothes in that overnight bag on top of the wardrobe; toiletries – well, most of them were in here with her, so she could at least pack her contraceptive pills and cosmetics. That might pass a bit of time, especially trying to do so in the dark. Then she made another, longer, inventory, of what she was losing: the three kids they'd planned – kids with Nathan's black hair and lithe bodies – Olly, Molly and Polly. The fourth, if they had one, was going to be Solly – the Jewish one. Their little joke. No more little jokes. No more home, no more leisurely Sunday walks and pub lunches, no more holidays – oh, no, the holiday! They had already made half the down payment on a holiday to Sardinia next summer.

Fuck the holiday. He'd probably have drowned her in the swimming pool if they had taken that villa.

Do not panic, she urged herself. It's not like the wardrobe, it's not a small space. Look – plenty of room to move around. She forced herself to climb out of the bath again, but she was shivering so much that she slipped and fell, banging her knee hard on the lino.

The only thing in the room that could possibly keep her warm was the bathmat, which she put around her shoulders, and a dry flannel she found on the floor, which she draped over the tops of her feet and tucked in.

She sat in that position on the cold, wet lino for hours, all her muscles and sinews and bones cramping into lockdown until it felt as though even the blood in her veins was slowly freezing from the edges in, like a fast-moving stream stilled into winter immobility. Her thoughts kept drifting to Nathan's razor on the basin . . . would it hurt, to slash her wrists? She could do it then get back into the cold bath. No, sod it, she'd bleed all over the lino, let him deal with *that*. Why should she make it easy for him?

Whenever something like this had happened before, she'd forced herself to think positive, think of all Nathan's good points, the beauty of his eyes, the good, kind side of him; thought becoming reality, forcing him to be his higher self, not the lower, baser, jealous one.

Not any more.

Eventually, the blood must have drained from her head because a huge dizziness overcame her, and the darkness was briefly punctuated with tiny dancing stars. Like a fallen statue, she toppled slowly over onto her side, her blue skin taut and marbled over her aching frame.

She had no idea what time it was when Nathan finally opened the door, but light streamed in, so it must have been the next day. He came over to her and wordlessly tried to help her up. She was so cold and stiff that she couldn't object as he carried her into the bedroom and laid her under the duvet with a hot-water bottle.

When she thawed out enough to move, she waited until Nathan left the room to go to the bathroom and then to make tea, slipped out of bed, hastily dressed and shoved a few things into a bag, her muscles creaking and straining under protest, and pins and needles stabbing her hands and feet. Then she hid behind the open bedroom door, her heart rate accelerating until she was sure he'd hear her breathing. He walked down the hallway carrying two steaming cups of tea – she could see him through the thin gap between the door and the frame – and, as his foot crossed the threshold into the bedroom, she slammed the door in his face as hard as she could. He screamed and collapsed to his knees, swearing at her, as boiling tea erupted over him, like lava, and blood spewed from his nose.

Amy looked down at him writhing at her feet, picked up her bag, stepped over him swiftly before he could grab her ankle, and left the flat for the last time.

Underneath the feelings of hollow chill and terror, another burgeoning emotion emerged, growing with every new step away from him:

Relief.

28

Amy

Thursday, 25 July

Gary pulled Amy back into the building, the heavy door thudding shut behind her. She twisted in his grip, pressing herself against the door, her breath misting the glass as she panted with terror. Where was everybody? Where was that bloody nosy neighbour when she needed him? She banged on the door anyway, shouted, 'Help!' Gary was saying her name over and over, gripping the tops of her arms, trying to turn her around to face him. Her bag was at her feet, half its contents spilling out, not a single thing she could use as a weapon . . . she almost always had knitting needles in her bag but, sod's law, not today.

'Amy . . .'

He made another effort to spin her around, but she gripped the door handle and kicked backwards, the steel toecap of her motorcycle boot connecting with his knee.

'Fuck!' He let go and she turned to find him bent over, clutching his kneecap. She shoved him with every ounce of strength she possessed and, off balance, he toppled over, landing on his side.

She grabbed her phone and fumbled with it, pressing 'Emergency call' and managing '9' before Gary jumped up. She held the phone up but he pulled her arm down sharply, pulling a muscle in her shoulder. She yelled with pain, trying to hit him with the phone.

'Get away from me!' she screamed, and the volume made him back away, holding his palms up, breathing as heavily as she was.

'You've got it . . . all wrong,' he said.

'What have you done with Becky? Where is she?'

He moved towards her and she backed away, grabbing the door handle again, holding the phone out with her thumb hovering over the '9'.

'You've killed her, haven't you?'

'Amy, this is insane. Of course I haven't killed her! I haven't done anything with her. Come on, you must know this is crazy.'

'Then what were you doing in her flat that weekend she went missing?'

'Getting a box set.'

'*What?*'

'I lent Becky my *Breaking Bad* box set before I'd seen it all, and she'd had it for ages. I'd gone round before to ask for it back but ended up leaving without it . . . I really wanted to watch it but she wasn't in . . . so I let myself in. I just grabbed it and came straight out again. I forgot to double-lock the door on the way out.'

She didn't know whether to believe him or not. But it was such a mundane excuse, so straightforward, that she felt her conviction wavering, her fear beginning to drain away.

'But . . . why didn't you just tell me that in the first place?'

His face coloured. 'I was embarrassed, wasn't I? I hardly knew you and I didn't want you thinking I'd been creeping around your sister's flat while she wasn't there.'

'Which is exactly what you had been doing.'

'I wasn't creeping. I went straight into the front room, found the DVDs, grabbed them and left.'

'What day was this?'

His eyes flicked upwards, like he was trying to look at his brain. 'Last Sunday – the day you turned up looking for Becky.'

Her breathing had almost returned to normal now. 'I don't know whether to believe you.'

Gary took a small step towards her, but she said, 'Uh-uh. Don't come any closer.'

'Amy, I'm not going to hurt you, I promise. I would never hurt you. I . . .' He trailed off, looking pained.

'What?'

'I'm in love with you, Amy.'

'Oh, hell.'

'I know you don't feel the same way. I get that. I can deal with it. But I swear on my mother's life I would never hurt you. Or Becky. I don't know what's happened to her either – and no, I don't think she's buggered off to Asia, either. I'm just as worried about her as you are.'

'I doubt that.'

He shrugged. Then he stared at the ground and chewed his lip.

'What is it?' she demanded.

'There's something else I need to tell you.'

She backed away again. She could hear music coming from one of the flats upstairs. If she screamed as loud as she could, surely someone would hear her and come running? Why hadn't they heard her before?

'Go on then, tell me,' she said.

'Let's go upstairs. I don't want to talk about it in a public stairwell.'

'No way.' She looked through the door. 'Let's go outside. Where there are people.'

They left the building and crossed the road to the park, Gary limping quite badly. Suddenly surrounded by life, playing children, sunbathers, joggers and dogs running around, Amy felt a lot safer. The sun was warm on her face and her pulse slowed. They sat either end of a bench, half turning towards each other.

'So?' Amy said.

He hesitated. 'You know that night you were in Becky's flat and someone tried the door?'

'Yes . . .'

He couldn't meet her eye. 'That was me.'

Her jaw fell open. 'You *what*?'

'I'd been to the pub and then when I got back I thought you'd be gone. I didn't notice your bike outside. I just wanted to check, see if Becky had come back. But then when you called out, sounding scared, I panicked. I thought that if you knew it was me trying to let myself into the flat, you might think I was weird or that I had something to do with Becky's disappearance. I was quite drunk. Anyway, I ran off and then I had to lie and tell you I was in the pub and go along with the whole thing with the police . . . I'm really sorry.'

She stared at him, incredulous. 'I don't believe you, Gary.'

'It's true, I swear.' He stretched his leg out and rubbed his kicked knee, still not looking at her.

'No, I mean, I can't believe you would do that. I was

239

terrified. And you are clearly a very good actor – you had me completely fooled.'

'I know. I'm sorry. It was stupid – but it was also totally innocent. I hated that I'd scared you.'

She folded her arms. 'Or maybe you thought if you scared me, I'd be more likely to come to you looking for comfort.'

'No, Amy, it wasn't like that. It was just one of those things where you panic and then find yourself trapped and having to lie. I feel shitty about it. That's why I'm telling you now.'

'Hm,' Amy said.

He squirmed, his face turning pink. Amy scrutinized him. She did like him, and felt confident that he was a good guy. But she couldn't allow it to go any further than that. She wasn't ready.

'Listen, Gary, I like you too. And the other night was fantastic, it really was. But I told you – I don't do relationships. I'm not ready, not after everything that happened with Nathan. I'm pissed off that you lied to me, but I suppose I get it, under the circumstances.'

The only word she could think of to describe Gary's expression was 'crestfallen'. But he nodded. 'I'm really sorry. If I ever meet this fucking Nathan bloke, I'm going to punch him in the head.'

She smiled faintly. 'As long as you promise to video it and upload it to YouTube.'

'Deal.'

Amy watched a squirrel descend from a nearby tree, grab a discarded crisp and shoot back up the trunk. It made her think of Boris, who had been badly neglected the last couple of days. She would take him on the longest walk ever later.

'So, if there's really nothing else you need to tell me,' she said, 'I'm going to go home now and walk Boris. I don't think we should see each other for a while.'

'Oh, Amy, I said I'm sorry I lied to you.'

She stood up and he stayed seated, staring up at her like a little boy.

'It's not just that. It's all of it, Gary. I just think we need some distance from each other. It doesn't mean I don't ever want to see you again – as a friend, I mean – but not right now. And – I'm sorry about your knee, I hope it's OK.'

He opened his mouth to protest but then shut it. He looked like a beaten man.

'So,' Amy said, 'I'm going to go now. I don't want you to contact me unless you hear anything that can help me find Becky, OK?'

He nodded and she walked away, her insides aching.

Back at home, Amy gave Boris a cuddle, then went upstairs and ran herself a bath. These days, she always took a bath with the door open, and she could hear Boris padding around downstairs. She didn't want to think about any of it, needed to let her brain rest for an hour, so she leafed through a crafting magazine, looking at a complicated pattern for an Aran dog sweater, trying to work out if it was within her capabilities and, if it was, whether Boris would deign to be seen dead in it. He got so cold in winter.

Unfortunately, the magazine reminded her of how little work she'd done since Becky had disappeared. Never mind knitting dog jackets, her business was going to crumble from beneath her if she didn't spend some time on the site.

Though how could she when all she could think about was finding Becky? How could she do anything? A mammoth To Do list began to populate itself inside her head and before she knew it she was out of the bath, wrapped in a towel, sitting at the kitchen table with her notepad and computer.

She spent almost an hour checking her site stats and making a list of things she needed to do urgently, and another list of things that could wait. The site seemed to be ticking along without her. There were no crises to deal with. The customer-service company she'd employed was answering emails, the community members were chatting among themselves, orders were coming in and being automatically forwarded to the vendors, traffic and registrations were steady. She felt relieved.

Next, she turned her attention back to Becky. So much had happened in the last few days. She felt the need to write another list, to break down what she knew so she could work out what to do next.

She had started by contacting the men from CupidsWeb. She had met Ross, the owner of Wiggins the spaniel, and decided he had nothing to do with it, and had ruled out Shaun because he had been in Canada. There was the third man, though, Daniel, the one who appeared to have no visible presence online. He hadn't replied to her message. She quickly logged in to CupidsWeb and checked. Still no message. Interesting that all his profile photos were set to 'private', she noted. Did that mean that he had something to hide? She typed out another message, asking him to get in touch, and pressed Send. She made a note to follow it up if he still didn't reply.

Then there was everything with poor Katherine. Amy could hardly believe that she was dead, and of a drugs overdose. It wasn't the kind of thing that happened to schoolteachers. The police had told her that Kath had died from an overdose of cocaine mixed with something called china white, a synthetic form of heroin that was far stronger than heroin itself.

'If she had no tolerance to it, and took a large hit, her system wouldn't have been able to handle it,' DC Amristy had told Amy on the phone. She also told Amy that they had indeed arrested Fraser on suspicion of supplying the drug. 'We found a text on Miss Devine's phone that she had sent to Mr Fraser Elliot thanking him for a gift which we assume to be the bag of narcotics.'

'I need you to ask Fraser what he knows about my sister,' Amy said. 'Anything that will help me find her.'

'Do you think he was supplying your sister with drugs too?' Amristy had asked.

'No. But I know he slept with her . . .'

DC Amristy had seemed confused. 'I don't understand what this has to do with Katherine Devine.'

Exasperated, Amy had explained the whole story once more, and Amristy had taken it down, promising to pass the information to the missing-person's coordinator. *Again*, Amy had almost said.

I'm on my own, she thought.

The question was, *did* Becky's disappearance have anything to do with Katherine? All she knew for certain was that they had both been using CupidsWeb, had both slept with Fraser and now, she knew, they had both been using this awful Casexual site. But while Katherine had been found dead in her flat, Becky was missing. No one had sent an email from Kath saying she was going away. The circumstances were entirely different. But then again, it seemed too coincidental that something awful could happen to both of them within a week of each other. While she didn't believe Fraser had done anything to Becky, there had to be some connection.

She patted Boris's bony head. Could Becky have been into drugs too? Had she got involved with drug dealers?

Did Fraser know anything about that? Maybe she should talk to the police again about Fraser, see if they would let her talk to him.

She had insisted to everyone that Becky was not into drugs, but she had never thought that her sister would use casual hook-up sites either.

'I sound like a real puritanical prude, don't I, Boris?' she said to the dog.

She tried to gather her thoughts, stop them from wheeling around the inside of her skull. The only thing Amy could do was stick to the few facts she had, and her suspicion that one of the men Becky had met online must know something that could help her find her sister. And Fraser, she was sure, was a dead end. Yes, he had slept with Becky, and through him she had found out about the hook-up sites. But Fraser giving lethal drugs to Katherine didn't mean he had anything to do with Becky's disappearance.

She picked up the sheaf of printouts from Casexual.com, and picked out the one that had disturbed her most: the message from the guy who called himself TooledUp.

She stared at the photo he had provided with the email, which she had also printed out, in colour. He scared her. Perhaps her view of psychopaths was stereotypical, but that's what he looked like. She couldn't understand how Becky could ever be attracted to someone like him. But maybe she was lying to herself: most women had at some point felt the lure of dangerous men, bad boys who just wanted to fuck you and didn't want to talk about their emotions afterwards. She smiled to herself, thinking about Gary. Then her frown slipped as she examined TooledUp's picture.

She had been thinking that, even though she was afraid, she was going to have to contact him through Casexual.

But, looking closely at the photo, she thought there might be another way, though it was a long shot.

He was looking into a mirror, and in the reflection she could see, behind him, a window with no curtains or nets, and a view out onto the street. On the other side of the street she could make out a shop of some kind. But she couldn't quite make out its name.

She logged back into Katherine's Casexual account and found the original message and the photo. She opened the photo file and blew it up to full size on her screen, zooming in on the shop. It was blurry, but luckily the file was large, so she didn't lose too much definition. Squinting, she could make out the name of the establishment: JEANS LAUNDRETTE.

Noting the misspelling of 'launderette', she Googled it, but nothing came up. It wasn't the kind of place that would advertise itself online. But if she could find it, she would be able to find out where TooledUp lived, and she had an idea.

29

Him

I parked opposite Amy's flat and waited. I was in the black Focus, the cheap car I use when I want to be inconspicuous.

I could see her moving about inside the flat, could detect steam on the window of the bathroom. I licked my lips, thinking about going in. I drowned a girl in a bath once, simply held her under the water until she stopped thrashing, one hand on her throat, holding her under, the other hand between her legs, a finger inside her. I could have done the same to Amy – if I didn't have plans for her.

The dog was a problem. Greyhounds are, according to *Wikipedia* and the numerous doggy forums I checked out, gentle and docile – unless you're a small fluffy creature. But it was risky, and I don't take chances. Especially now, when I'm so close to getting what I've always dreamed of. The last thing I want is a dog bite making me sore on my special day.

So I waited, and watched.

Amy was frustratingly careful with her privacy settings online. Her Facebook page was locked down unless you were her friend, and she barely tweeted. She hadn't been on Twitter since putting out the appeal about Becky. Her website, Upcycle.com, was remarkably impersonal – she barely even got a mention on the About Us page.

She only had one public Facebook status: an appeal about Becky, the same as she'd put on Twitter. But she had a public Pinterest account, though she had only pinned numerous dull pictures of cushion covers and crocheted dishcloths on there.

I thought it would be fun to create a Pinterest board with all the items I'd like to use to torture her: knitting needles, pins and scissors, pliers and mount cutters. I could sew up her mouth, replace her eyes with buttons, shave her head and replace it with wool. Break her spine and turn her into a living replica of the rag dolls she liked so much. Have the dog stuffed and displayed beside her.

That would be fun. If she turned out not to be The One after all.

Sitting in the car, thinking about dolls and pain, made me think about my mum. Denise. She was beautiful, so beautiful. She looked like a doll – like a Barbie, with long blonde hair, a narrow waist, perky tits and big blue eyes. No, I didn't have a dad. Of course, genetically, I did. Someone donated his sperm to help make me, but that was where his contribution to fatherhood ended. Mum never talked about him, not ever. There were no photos of him on the wall between the paintings of the clown and the crying boy. And I liked that. I was the only man in her life.

When I was growing up, she called me her 'little man'. Then, when I hit puberty when I was thirteen and shot up, suddenly I was taller than her and she dropped the 'little'.

She would lie in bed beside me on cold nights – our flat was always freezing in winter – and we would spoon. I loved the warmth of her breasts against my shoulder blades, her breath on the back of my neck. She would be wearing her white corset and sometimes, when the room was quiet and the night was still, she would reach over and take my erection in her hand and just hold it. I would wriggle and squirm all night, my heart hammering in my chest, my penis aching. Eventually, I would fall asleep and when I woke up she would be gone. Usually, I would find her in the kitchen, one of her Duran Duran CDs playing, and she would make me scrambled eggs and kiss me on the cheek before settling down in front of the TV with a packet of cigarettes, rewatching one of her videos: *The Breakfast Club* or *Dirty Dancing*.

She used to talk about girls all the time. 'One day, you'll meet a girl and leave me. What is it they say? A son is a son until he takes a wife.'

She would look up at me with tears in her eyes and I would promise her, 'Mum, I'll never leave you. I swear.'

But then she would brighten and say, 'You're a good boy. A good man.'

Within the walls of that flat, we had our own kingdom. Our world. I would go to school every day, filled with loathing for the other kids with their ugly mothers, desperate to get home to Denise. By the time I was fourteen, that's what she made me call her. She wouldn't let me call her Mum any more, except in public. The only lesson I was interested in was computer science, and Denise bought me a PC from her catalogue, paying it off week by week with the money from her cleaning job.

Sometimes she would lock herself in her bedroom for

days, the door locked, refusing to come out. I could hear her crying inside, occasionally throwing stuff around the room. She had an old ceramic pot in the room, which she would piss in, and the room always smelled terrible when she eventually reappeared, her hair standing on end, eyes bloodshot, skin translucent with grief. I don't really mean her smell was terrible, because it was her – her sweat, her piss, her tears . . . It was perfume to me.

After one of these episodes, she would come into my bed and she would make me strip so she could examine me, exclaiming over my blossoming body, the hairs that sprouted on my chest and groin, my growing muscles, which she loved to squeeze. She taught me how to masturbate and would clap with delight as I came, sending semen shooting across the bed in a glistening arc.

Friday nights were my favourite. That was date night. I would get home from school and watch some TV before going to my room to get changed. Denise had bought me a suit from Oxfam, which had a faint smell of mothballs and had shiny patches on the knees, but which fitted me perfectly. I would put on the aftershave she'd given me and would sit on my bed, shaking with anticipation, waiting for her to call me.

She had the dinner table laid out with a red-and-white-check cloth, a candle burning, two wineglasses gleaming in the candlelight. Denise would be wearing her black velvet dress with her hair pinned back, fully made up, and she always cooked our favourites: prawn cocktail for starters, shepherd's pie for our main and Angel Delight for pudding. Butterscotch flavour. She put her Sad Café album on, followed by Sade or Dire Straits. We didn't talk very much. Mostly, she would tell me how much she loved me, how I was the only man who had never let her down, how she was so happy that she was the woman in my life.

She told me that we would die together, because that is what true lovers do.

'When you're old enough,' she said. 'And before the world tries to take you away from me.'

Then, after dessert and while I smoked a cigarette, she would disappear into her bedroom and come back out wearing her white corset with white knickers, suspenders and stockings. We slow-danced for a while before she led me by the hand into her bedroom, where she would undress me while whispering that we were going to be together for ever . . .

Except we weren't.

She lied to me.

Mid-afternoon, Amy came out of her flat. She had the dog with her, which looked even bigger in real life. They walked off down the road. I waited till she'd vanished from sight then got out of the car and strolled over to her flat. I wasn't planning to do anything. I just wanted to take a closer look at the place. I peered through the window. All very neat and clean inside. Her perfect, ordered life.

I was going to enjoy getting to know her intimately. Finding out exactly what made her tick.

I got back into my car and thought about my options. I decided to take a drive to my childhood home, on the other side of London, thinking that the mnemonic power of the place might help me think. I was amazed by how tiny it was, a box inside another box. I parked outside and watched some kids playing football in the courtyard out front.

I took out my phone and looked at Amy's photo again. I was sick of waiting. Tired of following her around.

Tomorrow, I decided, will be the big day. And it was obvious how I should do it.

At last. After all the false starts, the dashed hopes and broken promises, I will finally get what I deserve.

And so will Amy.

30

Amy

Thursday, 25 July

The café was at the end of the street, a cheerful, independent place that gave free coffee refills and where dogs were welcomed. Amy slid on to a floral padded bench at a window table and opened her laptop, as Boris took a long drink from the bowl of water that Cliff the proprietor had immediately plonked on the floor under his nose.

'Afternoon, Amy. How's things?' he asked, as he patted Boris. 'Haven't seen you two for a while.'

Cliff was a short kindly man in his late forties, swamped in his tightly tied apron, under which he wore a uniform of brogues and bright red cords, the latter matching his cheeks. Amy always thought he should be organizing Hunt Balls or selling antiques rather than running a small tea shop in southeast London.

Amy made a face. 'Boris and I were going a bit stir-crazy at home – needed a change of scenery. Things aren't good, actually. My sister's gone missing and the police aren't taking it seriously.'

She had taken a decision some time earlier that day that she was going to tell whoever would listen, whenever she could. Surely, the wider out in the world the message went, the better chance there was that someone would know something.

Cliff's eyebrows shot up into his hairline and settled back down again into an expression of sympathy and slight panic. 'Good heavens, that's absolutely appalling! When did you last see her?'

Amy swallowed. Perhaps coming out hadn't been such a good idea, although it was true that she hadn't wanted to be in the flat. It had felt as though the walls were pressing in on her, the air fraught with her own recycled anxiety. 'I haven't seen her for weeks, but she went missing a week ago.'

Cliff patted her awkwardly on the shoulder, then wiped his hand on his apron as though Amy's shoulder had been sticky. 'I'm so sorry to hear it. What a terrible worry for you – and for your poor parents. Please let me know if there's anything I can do.'

'Thanks, Cliff. Could I just have a latte, please? And, you still have Wi-Fi here, don't you?'

'We certainly do. Coffee's on the house, my dear,' Cliff said.

Amy smiled at him, and Boris settled down at her feet. She logged herself into the Admin page of Upcycle.com and went straight to 'Create a new post', although not without noticing that since her last visit, forty-three comments had been added to recent articles (an article on growing tomatoes upside-down in planters recycled from laundry bags proving surprisingly chat-worthy).

Her fingers hovered over the keyboard for a few moments as she tried to think how best to word what she wanted to say, typing and deleting the first sentence several times before settling on:

Dear Upcyclers, this is Amy Coltman. Upcycle.com is my brainchild and my baby, and I am the author of many of the articles on here, although I don't usually put my name to them. Please forgive the unrelated content, because this post is something personal to me, and of extreme importance. I really need your help.

My 29-year-old sister Becky has gone missing. Nobody's heard from her for over a week [she decided not to mention the tweet and the Facebook photos] and it is very out of character. I am by now certain that she has come to some harm. You will probably hear about her in the national press before too long, unless she miraculously turns up – but in the meantime, there is one tiny lead I'm [she deleted 'I'm'; no point in letting people know that the police weren't taking it seriously] we're following. Please look closely at the attached photos. The first is of Becky – obviously, if anyone recognizes her, or has seen her recently, PLEASE let me know, or tell the police. (I tweeted and Facebooked this on Monday – thanks to all of you who have already shared it.) The second photo is of a launderette called JEANS LAUNDRETTE (sic). I have no idea where it is other than that it's probably in London. Does anybody recognize it? Please, folks, spread the word. Share this appeal on Facebook, Twitter, LinkedIn, Google Plus – whatever your choice of social networking site. Email it to all your friends and beg them to pass it on to everyone they know. I really need your help.

Thank you,

Amy x

Amy read through it several times, noting that she had repeated 'I really need your help', but deciding to leave the second one in for emphasis. Would it lose her some of her subscribers, who might only be interested in how to decoupage an old lampshade, and not give a stuff about Becky, or would the human-interest angle pique their interest? It could go either way, she supposed – but she didn't care if she lost subscribers. She was fortunate enough to have a built-in audience of over fifty thousand members, most of them UK-based, and she'd be mad not to use them.

With her fingers crossed, she hit 'Upload' and watched as it appeared on the Home page of her site, Becky's pixellated face beaming out at her. Sadness threatened to choke her, but she blinked away the pain of the moment – she had also decided that she was done with feeling sad. Not until she knew for a fact that she had something to be sad about. Becky was missing, but no news was often good news. Until the moment that Becky's body was discovered (God forbid), she refused to be over-whelmed by this any more. It was a problem that needed solving, that was all.

Her appeal would also go out in the monthly Upcycle.com newsletter to all her subscribers, due to be sent that afternoon by the online marketing company – the email included whatever was featured on the site's Home page. So Becky's picture would land in every single mailbox on every single subscriber's computer. And if even a quarter of them shared it on Twitter or Facebook, the number of people seeing it would increase exponentially.

Amy felt better. Better enough to face something she knew she ought to have done days ago but hadn't been able to deal with, and about which Cliff's comment earlier had given her a nudge of guilty conscience: she took out her phone and rang her parents' number. Last time she'd rung she had only asked Carmella, the housekeeper, if Becky was there, she hadn't said why she was asking. She couldn't keep it from them any more.

The long European ringtone abbreviated into a staccato crackle of answer. 'Hello – Mum?'

'No. Is Carmella. Miz Coltman away.'

'Oh. Hi, Carmella, it's Amy again. Is Dad there? When will Mum be back?'

'No. Away. On holidays.'

It seemed as though she wasn't the only one not very good at communicating with her family members. Her parents definitely hadn't mentioned anything about any holiday.

'Where?'

'I doan know. They are in . . . hmmm . . . many places, on the sea.'

'On a *cruise*?'

There was a brief commotion as an obese woman in a wheelchair, pushed by her tiny husband and both talking loudly about lemon cake, came through the door with some difficulty, and Amy had to put her finger in her free ear to hear Carmella's reply.

'*Si*. A crew-se.'

'Where – the Caribbean? The Fjords?'

'Hmmm . . . he go to Miami firsts.'

So, probably the Caribbean then. 'Oh. I don't suppose you know if they got around to getting a mobile phone before they left, do you?'

Her parents never had a mobile because, as they said, they didn't need one in their village in Spain, and it was far too expensive a way to communicate with their family and friends in the UK. They were also complete Luddites when it came to computers and were not on email. Consequently, they never fully understood – or even tried to – what Upcycle.com was all about, nor had any idea how successful a business Amy had made of it.

'No. No phone. Is problem?'

'*Sí* – um, yes. I need to give them an urgent message, if they call you. Urgent! My sister Becky has, er, disappeared. You understand?'

Amy wished she wasn't making this call in a busy café. The woman in the wheelchair had stopped wittering about lemon cake and was listening with shameless interest.

'Sí, I understand. Becky, she is missing. I am sorry for you, Amy. Is bad?'

Carmella's voice softened, and Amy's new tough resolve wavered for a moment.

'Yeah, is bad. It's really bad.'

'Police, he know?'

'Yes, they know. Please could you look for any details of their holiday, Carmella, any information on what ship they're on, or the travel agent they booked it through? And please get them to ring me urgently if you speak to them. When are they back?'

There was a pause while Carmella digested and translated. 'Yes. I look. I have your telephone number, I call you, OK? They home, two weeks? But I tell them call you urgent.'

'Thanks, Carmella.'

Amy terminated the call, half relieved that she'd done all she could to keep her folks in the loop, and half anxious that they would be in for a hell of a shock when they found out – if Becky wasn't safely home by then. She glared at the woman in the wheelchair, transferring onto her some of the anger she felt towards her parents. How could they do something as major as going on a Caribbean cruise without having the courtesy to let her and Becky know? It was as if they had discharged their parental obligation towards their daughters the moment she and Becky left the family home and went to university.

She turned her attention back to her laptop. To her surprise, there was already one comment on her post, from someone she didn't know but who was a regular contributor to the discussion boards: Knittyfreak – *hi Amy, so sorry to hear this. What a nightmare. Tweeted, shared, posted. Praying that your sister comes home soon. Sorry I don't recognize Jeans but I'm in Scotland* ☹

Amy suspected all the comments would be along these lines. She was about to close her laptop when another one popped up: SusieB – *I do!!!! Jeans Laundrette's up the road from me in Epsom (Surrey)! It always catches my eye because of the missing apostrophe! It's near the Londis, which has a post office in it – that might help you get the exact address. I can't remember the name of the road. Good luck – really hope she's OK and turns up soon. SusieX*

Exhilarated, Amy typed a reply: *Wow!!! Susie, thank you so much, that's incredible – talk about an instant response. You Upcyclers are awesome, what a community! I will check it out ASAP – but, in the meantime, please keep sharing Becky's photo? I will keep you all posted. Amy.*

It was the work of moments to search online for post offices in Epsom, which handily yielded a link to the Street

View of the exterior on Google Maps. Sure enough, when Amy clicked on it, the '-rette' of the Jeans Laundrette sign was visible in the left corner of the picture.

'I can't believe it!' she crowed to Boris, who was asleep under the table. 'How easy was that?' Another thought struck her, and she scrolled the cursor around in the Street View. There was the window of the room in which TooledUp had taken his photo – no question. Same nasty UPVC window frame, same small panes of glass.

She nudged him awake with her foot. 'Right, come on, you. We've got to get you home so I can go to Epsom.'

She found Jeans Laundrette with no difficulty at all, other than stopping to consult the Maps app on her iPhone once or twice. There was so much adrenaline flooding through her system that she didn't even pause to remember her initial impression of TooledUp, that he looked like a psychopath. As she walked up to the dirty front door that appeared to give access to the flats opposite the launderette, her breath caught for a moment. Nobody knew she was here. Was she insane? Was she about to find out what fate had befallen her sister? Hastily, she took several photos with her camera phone, clearly showing the street sign and house number, and the view of Jeans, and emailed them to herself with a note that read: 'Last seen here looking for Becky. A man known as TooledUp from Casexual.com lives here and I'm going to talk to him.'

She had no idea which bell corresponded to TooledUp's flat, so she tried a few, but there was no answer from any of them. Unsure of what to do next, she hung around for a few minutes. A Middle Eastern man with a thick beard approached the door, a key in his outstretched hand.

'Excuse me – I'm looking for someone who lives up

there,' she said. He looked at her as if he was about to ignore her, so she moved in front of the door, barring his way. 'It's important.' She took the printout of TooledUp's profile picture out of her pocket and unfolded it. 'Him. Do you recognize him?'

The man's blank expression changed and he scowled. 'Yeah,' he said. 'He's called Halsall. Don't know his first name, but it says P. Halsall on his mailbox. He's a hard man. Watch yourself.'

Amy was momentarily surprised that the man sounded so English when he looked so Turkish, then she berated herself for making racial judgements. He could easily be more English than she was. 'Thanks,' she said. 'Can you let me in to wait for him?'

The man shrugged. 'If you want,' he said, looking suspiciously at her. He opened his mouth as though about to quiz her – and then closed it again, evidently deciding he didn't care either way what she wanted with his neighbour. He stomped away up the stairs, leaving her in the lobby. When he got to the first turning, he looked back. 'He's usually back around now,' he said brusquely, and carried on without waiting for her to reply.

Amy followed him up the first flight and found herself in a smelly, dark hall with doors to two flats facing each other. Free newspapers and pizza leaflets littered the floor, even though the mailboxes were downstairs. It was as though someone had carried them as far up as the first floor and then lost interest in taking them inside. Amy slid down the wall, placed her helmet down beside her and sat on one of the newspapers, which was far preferable to the prospect of sitting directly on the cold, dirty, tiled floor, despite the headline about an old woman who had been beaten to death just down the road from here. From somewhere in the building, she could hear a woman sobbing.

She waited about twenty-five minutes, increasingly aware of her need for a pee. She was just wondering if she dared ask the bearded man if she could use his loo, when the front door opened and closed again, and heavy footsteps came banging up the stairs towards her.

A thick head appeared first, shaved at the sides, with thinning, slicked-back hair on top, and then one of those obscenely muscled bodies that screamed steroids. It was TooledUp, without a doubt, and he looked even more menacing in the flesh that he had in his picture. He stopped short when he saw her sitting outside his door, and she scrambled up.

'Hi,' she said, doing everything she could to stop her voice trembling. 'My name is Amy Coltman, and I need your help.'

He looked at her as though she was something he'd found on the bottom of his shoe. He let the holdall he was carrying fall to the floor with a dull thud that echoed through the hallway. 'Me?'

'Yes. It's about my sister. She's called Becky, and you were talking to her on a dating – well, a hook-up site. Casexual.com. This is a bit delicate . . . you were going to, um, have a threesome with her and her friend Katherine.'

P. Halsall's face turned a thunderous puce colour, and he shook his head as if in disbelief, coming a few steps closer to Amy. It was a narrow corridor, and his bulk was blocking her access to the stairs. He smelled of cheap hair gel and, Amy imagined, those huge tubs of protein powder. She held her nerve.

'It's just that Becky's gone missing, and I'm desperately trying to see if I can find out when she was last seen . . .'

The man put his key in the lock, frowning as though he was thinking about it. Then he opened the door, and Amy instinctively backed away slightly in case he grabbed her. He turned as he walked into his flat and flicked on the lights.

He stabbed a stubby finger in her direction. 'Listen, I don't know who you are, but you have some *fucking* nerve, coming here and mouthing off about my private life. I don't know your sister, so you can just piss off, all right?' He paused, as a thought crawled into his brain, and he gave her the filthiest look she'd ever suffered. 'Unless you're here looking to get some action yourself.'

He stepped closer to her. A vein pulsed in his forehead. 'You look like the type who likes it rough.'

Amy took a deep breath and gathered all the courage she'd never had when she was with Nathan. 'You're disgusting. But I need to know—'

He turned away and slammed the door, and when she closed her eyes, all Amy could see was Nathan's face.

31

Amy

Thinking about the last time she'd seen Nathan always gave Amy a little thrill inside – part guilt, part catharsis, but mostly triumph. It had only been six months ago. Chris had been treating her to a farewell dinner in a big posh restaurant in the West End. How fitting, Amy thought, that she had been with Chris that evening, the same Chris to whom Nathan had objected so strongly all those years ago, giving her the first warning signs that all might not be well with her beloved after all.

'I'll miss you so much!' she had wailed at him over the starters.

Chris had made a face both sympathetic and empathetic, and clinked his wineglass against hers. 'It's only Edinburgh, sweetie, not Sydney. You can pop up on the train for a weekend to stay with us. We have a very comfy sofa bed.'

'I promise I won't spend the whole night moaning,' she said, 'but you're my best friends – pretty much my only friends – and I can't believe you're going. I mean,' she added hastily, 'I'm made up for you both, really, and it's so great that Vince is coming with you and that you've both found such good jobs, but . . .'

Chris made a mock-stern face at her. He had recently cultivated a very pointy bleached quiff that now seemed to jab accusingly at her like a self-important finger. 'What do you mean, your only friends? What about Hannah, and Liz, and those girls you used to hang about with a few years back?'

Amy put her elbows on the table and ticked off her fingers: 'Hannah – took Nathan's side in the split and hasn't spoken to me since, not that I'd want her to. Liz just had her second baby, never goes out, and no phone conversation with her ever lasts more than ninety seconds before she has to go and change a nappy or mop something up. Jo moved to France to restore a chateau with that weird man of hers . . . Honestly, I'm not being self-pitying but, apart from my sister, you and Vince *are* my social life.'

'Move up to Edinburgh then! Boris wouldn't mind a change of scene. You can do Upcycle anywhere – it's not like you're tied to an office.'

Amy smiled, then sighed. 'Nice idea, but I wouldn't want to be so far away from Becky. I'll come and visit, though.'

The waiter came and removed their empty starter plates. 'You'd better, sweetie,' said Chris.

'I'm really glad you tracked me down,' Amy said, feeling slightly overemotional. Chris had found her about a year after their accidental meeting in the bar in Kingston, and after Amy had hastily deleted the text containing his number, terrified that Nathan would go beserk if he spotted it on her phone.

'Well, that's what Facebook's for, isn't it? And I was worried about you after . . . you know . . .'

Amy made a face. 'I know.'

'Do you ever hear from Mr Prince Not Very Charming?'

She shook her head. 'No, thank God. He got an official police caution, which would have mortified him. I haven't heard a thing, thankfully.'

Chris could tell she didn't want to talk about Nathan, so he changed the subject. Their main courses came, and the conversation turned to other things: Becky, Upcycle, Chris's new job as a corporate lawyer for a major Scottish blue-chip company, Vince's new job as a wine waiter for a five-star hotel in Edinburgh, the number of calories in steak with blue-cheese sauce . . . chitchat between old friends. An hour or so passed, and the restaurant dimmed the lights and turned up the music. Their table was quite near the door, and large numbers of people came and went, squeezing past the back of Chris's chair.

Amy was in mid-sentence, telling Chris about the Tuscan holiday she and Becky had been on the previous summer, when she looked up and saw a face across the restaurant that she hadn't seen for almost four years. She froze, and felt the blood drain from her face.

'What's the matter?' Chris asked, swivelling round in his seat to follow her gaze.

'It can't be. We were just talking about him!' she stuttered.

'Not fucking Nathan!'

Amy dropped her head and nodded, utterly panicked. She didn't dare look up but she knew he'd seen her at the same moment she spotted him. Her heart was pounding out of her chest and she felt sick. He was with a group of men, four or five of them, probably work colleagues – they all had 'the look' – urban, trendy, casual, the right shirts and jeans and haircuts.

'He's coming over!' she said in a strangulated voice.

'I'll deal with him,' said Chris, squaring his shoulders.

But it was at that moment that something clicked inside Amy, and she too put her head up and her shoulders back. She did not need to be afraid of Nathan any more – and better still, she didn't love him any more, not an iota.

He approached their table and she gazed coolly at him, taking in the fact that he had filled out quite a lot, and his cheekbones had vanished. He smiled at her, that old, warm, sexy Nathan smile, but Amy was completely unmoved – if somewhat surprised. She had assumed that the police caution had infuriated him so much that he would never speak to her again, and yet here he was, behaving like they were old friends. He walked right up to her and leaned down to give her a kiss on the cheek, but she ducked her head away. Not in panic, just as though she was completely mystified.

'Can I help you?' she asked politely. Firmly.

'Amy! It's so great to see you, darling! How have you been?'

Chris was looking worriedly at her, so she flashed him a small reassuring smile, then frowned at Nathan. 'I'm really sorry – um – have we met?'

He threw back his head and laughed, but it was tinged with uncertainty. 'Amy! It's me, Nathan! You look great. I like the new piercings – that one really suits you.' He pointed at her nose stud. 'And your hair's really grown. Nice.'

Furrowing her brow, she scrutinized him, allowing her gaze to linger for a particularly long time at the stomach straining the buttons of his designer checked shirt, and the layer of podge under his chin. Then she shook her head.

'I'm so sorry. My memory's terrible. Nathan who?'

He rolled his eyes, still pretending to find it amusing. 'Come on, babe, it's *me*!'

The *nerve* of him, Amy thought, acting as though nothing had happened. She knew she was being childish, but she felt alive, exhilarated. Safe. Across the table, Chris was discreetly flexing his pecs and biceps – he was the biggest gym-bunny Amy knew, but even if she'd been there on her own, she knew she would have played the same game. Nothing to lose any more.

He put his hands on his hips, mock-offended. 'All right, Amy, I get it. You don't want to talk to me.'

She shrugged. 'I don't know you,' she said mildly.

'Of course you bloody well know me,' he retorted, his gossamer patience already threadbare, as Amy knew from bitter experience. He couldn't help his voice beginning to rise, and having control over him sent a jolt of pure adrenaline through her body. 'We lived together for four sodding years!'

She smiled. 'I think you've mistaken me for someone else. Sorry – don't mean to be rude, but my friend and I were in the middle of a conversation . . .'

Nathan's face darkened, but Amy felt no fear.

'If you wouldn't mind,' she said, making a small shooing gesture with her hand. Across the table, Chris was smothering giggles. Nathan's eyes narrowed. If there was one thing he absolutely couldn't stand, it was being made fun of.

'I am NOT leaving until you acknowledge me,' he insisted.

At that moment, the head waiter passed, and Amy summoned him over. 'Excuse me – this man is bothering us. Please could you ask him to go away? He seems to think he knows me, but he doesn't.'

All the other diners turned to see the commotion as

Nathan shook the waiter's hand off his arm, purple with fury, and strode off in the direction of the Gents'.

'Go, *Amy*!' Chris said. 'That was utterly awesome. I'm so proud of you!'

Amy smiled at him, noticing that her hands weren't even shaking. 'Thanks. I'm pretty proud of myself, too.'

32

Amy

Thursday, 25 July

Amy stared at the door that the man she had known previously as TooledUp had slammed in her face. Shit. She hadn't thought for a moment that he was likely to be the cooperative type, but he was an even bigger prick than she'd feared. Amy picked her helmet off the floor and turned to go, thinking at least she was unharmed, and *could* go. She headed for the stairs, then stopped.

It wasn't good enough. How could she get back on her bike and ride home, when there was any chance at all that this arsehole knew something that could lead her to Becky?

I've got this far, she thought. She took a deep breath, and walked back up to the grimy front door, hammering on it with her fist.

'I need to talk to you!' she yelled through the thin wooden panels, welcoming the anger, because anger would keep her strong.

She paused to press her ear against the door, and heard the sound of a toilet flushing. She banged again, welcoming the pressure from her own bladder because the discomfort was making her even crosser.

'Fuck OFF,' roared the man from inside.

'Open the door!' she shouted back, matching his volume. 'I'm not going away until you do!'

She paused in her banging, noticing a piece of junk mail lying in a corner of the hall, an offer from Virgin Media addressed to Mr Paul Halsall.

'Paul! I'm serious – I'm not going anywhere except straight to the police unless you talk to me!' She pounded her helmet against the door until she was worried she heard a splintering sound – no need to go as far as criminal damage. Perhaps he'd heard it too, because the door suddenly flew open again and he towered over her, looking angrier than anybody she'd seen since she lived with Nathan.

He's not Nathan, she reminded herself, squaring up to him. He might be twice Nathan's size, but he'd never be able to do half the damage Nathan had to her.

'How the hell do you know my name?' he demanded.

'I know your name, your address, your Casexual profile details, and I have copies of all the emails you and my sister exchanged.' No need for him to know she didn't, in fact, have any such thing. All she had were the messages he had exchanged with Kath. 'Oh, and I have the ones that you and my sister's friend Katherine sent each other too. And guess what – Katherine's just been found dead, under suspicious circumstances. What do you think the police would make of the fact that you were with her recently? I just need a few words with you, then I'll get out of your hair.' She intentionally stared at his thinning hair as she said that. His forehead creased with confusion and – as she had intended – worry.

'Dead – that posh Katherine bird? The art teacher?' He

shook his head, and Amy relaxed a tiny bit, partly because it had clearly come as a shock to him, and partly because it was his first foray into conversation with her.

'You don't want the police to think you're a suspect,' she said, softening her own voice.

His lips tightened into a thin white line. 'Yeah, and I don't need you telling me what I want to think.'

One step forward, two steps back.

'Please. It won't take long. It's just a couple of questions. Katherine's dead and Becky's missing. I think someone's got her.'

'What, and you reckon it's me?'

'No, of course not,' lied Amy. She actually didn't think that he would be holding Becky somewhere, nor that he had the intelligence to be tweeting from her account and posting photos on her Facebook page – but she thought it was entirely plausible that some harm could have befallen her if Becky had been mad enough to meet him for a repeat performance. Squashed under the weight of his muscles, perhaps. She shook away the mental picture of him hauling off her dead sister, hidden in a roll of lino – in her imagination it was the same as the grey, squashed-fly lino in his flat – to some deserted woodland burial place . . . but she just couldn't picture this guy sending that email, pretending to be Becky.

'I don't give a shit about the police, because I didn't have nothing to do with either of them, apart from that one night. And what we did ain't illegal between consenting adults. If you've read our emails, you'll know that they most definitely consented.'

'What happened that night?'

He bared his teeth in a fake smile. 'Gave 'em both exactly what they wanted, didn't I?'

271

'I don't know,' said Amy, keeping her voice level. 'Did you? Why don't you let me in so we can talk about it?'

He folded his arms, his forearm flexors popping menacingly towards her. 'Why should I do anything for you? You're harassing me.'

Amy sighed. 'I'm sorry. I don't mean to harass you. My sister is missing, and I need to find her. Can't you just agree to help me, because you're a decent human being?'

He laughed meanly. 'That ain't how my ex-wife would describe me. So what do you want to know?'

Amy took a deep breath. 'I need to know if Becky was doing drugs. I'm guessing Katherine was, because she OD'd. I need to know if either of them talked to you about other men they'd met, or were going to meet. Do you know a man called Fraser? Did they mention him?'

'That's a shitload of questions,' he said, contemplatively stroking one side of his jaw. 'You willing to pay me?'

'Depends – do you have any information worth paying for?'

They were locked in each other's gaze like two cowboys in a showdown on the High Chaparral.

'As it goes, reckon I do,' he said. 'I'll let you have it, for five K.'

Amy laughed out loud. 'Five grand? You're out of your mind!'

Paul Halsall shrugged and started to close the door. Amy stuck her foot in the gap. 'Wait!'

'You're persistent, I'll give you that. So, what are you prepared to pay? I want cash – there's a cashpoint over the road.'

'I can't get more than two fifty out of the cashpoint in one day.' Amy couldn't believe she was bartering for information like this.

It was his turn to laugh. 'No way. I ain't telling you nothing for less than a grand.'

Amy felt like banging her head against the wall. 'I don't have a grand – and anyway, now that I think about it, I don't even *have* my cashpoint card with me.'

A crafty expression crossed his face as he gazed at her bike helmet. There was something very transparent about him – Amy bet that he counted on his fingers, and silently mouthed the words whenever he read anything. 'What bike you got?'

Oh, no. *Not her bike*. 'Forget it.'

'You forget it, then.' He closed the door again.

She thought about it for several minutes, then knocked again. When he opened the door, she was dangling the bike key from her forefinger, tears in her eyes.

'If I do this, you're not going to screw me over? You definitely have something important to tell me?'

He smiled, a greedy smile but a genuine one, and, for the first time, Amy saw what Becky and Katherine must have liked about him.

'Come in,' he said. He was a big, muscly hard man, but she bet that if he wanted something, he could do a fairly convincing seduction routine. She also bet that he hadn't staged that routine in this poxy little flat, though, with its curling lino in the kitchen and damp circles mushrooming across the Artexed living-room ceiling. Amy knew her sister well enough to know that she'd never willingly have got her kit off in this bleak, tawdry accommodation, and she doubted that Katherine would have done either. Not unless slumming it had been part of the turn-on.

'It's a 1969 Triumph Daytona. Burgundy, 500 cc,' she said miserably, holding out the keys. 'Worth at least five grand.' *And my pride and joy*, she thought, feeling the wind whipping the bits of hair sticking out of her helmet as she rode across Roman roads and down motorways, recalling that sensation of total freedom and happiness. At the back of her mind was the germ of a plan about telling the insurance company it had been stolen, although deep down she knew she was too honest – or too scared – to make a false claim on it. Besides, it wasn't the money. It was her bike, her baby . . .

But Becky was far, far more important.

'Are you serious?' he asked, and she nodded. 'Only if you have something to tell me,' she repeated.

He walked across to the table, took a pad of lined paper and tore off a sheet. Then – his tongue indeed sticking out of one corner of his mouth – he wrote in slanting capitals: 'TRANSFER OF OWNERSHIP.'

'What's your name again?'

'Amy Coltman.'

'I, AMY COLTMAN, CONFIRM THAT I HAVE GIVEN MY TRIUMPH DAYTONA TO PAUL HALSALL NO RETURNS OR COMEBACKS THIS IS A LEGALLY BINDING DOCUMENT.'

Amy, looking over his shoulder, somehow doubted that.

'Sign and date, please,' he said briskly, and Amy took the biro.

'This is crazy,' she said.

'Do you want to find your sister or what?'

It's only a bike. A heap of metal and rubber and chrome and leather. A motorbike. Becky, however, is your sister and you love her.

Amy signed and dated it, then pushed the paper back towards Paul. 'So – what do you know?'

He examined her signature as if it was a forgery. 'She didn't do drugs. At least, she didn't that night, even though her mate was. She said she never touched them.'

It was a huge relief to hear it, but not enough. 'And?'
'That's it.'

She put her hands on her hips. All her fear of him had gone – he was a pathetic, acquisitive creep and she felt prepared to torture the information out of him if it wasn't forthcoming. Why couldn't she have felt like this when she was with Nathan?

'That's *it*? I've given you my bike, for that? It's not good enough. What else?'

He grinned again, like a kid who'd unwrapped a giant Christmas present. At one point he even rushed over to the window to admire his new toy.

'I told you. Your sister was drinking loads but didn't do any drugs when I was there, and I don't think did at all, because she was a bit, you know, arsey about her mate whenever she snorted another line of charlie. We all, er, got it on – I'm assuming you don't need a blow-by-blow description of that?' His face changed. 'Though you can have one, if you like,' he said slyly, and Amy glared at him.

'No, thanks. Then what?'

He pretended to think. 'Hmmm. We was at her place, I think it must've been, 'cos she wasn't happy with the coke being there. That's right . . . after we'd finished, her mate – Katherine? – started banging on about this party they were going to the next day. I goes, "Can I come?" just joking, you know? I remember getting pissed off 'cos Katherine laughs. She goes, "They wouldn't let you in, it's an *Orchid Blue* party. We paid a fortune for it." Snotty cow. Like I knew what a fuckin' Orchid Blue party is. I remember the name though, because I looked it up afterwards.'

'What kind of party is an Orchid Blue party?' Amy asked, although she had a horrible feeling she could guess.

Paul Halsall, a.k.a. TooledUp, hooked the key of Amy's motorbike off her finger.

'I want the ownership document too, you know, the V5C. Proper deal, this. You've got my address. You can post it to me.'

'What kind of party?' she repeated, and TooledUp laughed.

33

Becky

Saturday, 29 June

'Damn, we look good. Smile, babe!'

Kath puts her arm around me, and holds out her camera phone in front of her to capture us both in our finery. She's not wrong – we look great. I snatch the phone off her to examine the photograph, and it's lovely. We're pouty and glossy and look nothing at all like teachers and everything like the sort of women we're presenting ourselves as – beautiful and sophisticated. To be honest, I'd been worried that we wouldn't fit in, that we'd look somehow dowdy or frumpy next to the *real* classy birds. But now that I see us in our slinky cocktail dresses and killer heels, our hair freshly coloured and blow-dried, gel nails in place, our tender skin still smarting from the Brazilian waxes we had earlier, I can relax. We'll fit in perfectly.

With a final squirt of perfume, much giggling and the addition of a few last-minute accessories from her wardrobe (a black feather boa for Katherine, and one of her glittery evening bags for me as it's smarter than my black satin one), we're ready, ten minutes before the cab is due to arrive. Suddenly we hear the sound of a key in the front door.

'Shit!' Kath hisses. 'Clive said he was out at band practice till late! Where do I tell him we're going?'

'Charity ball,' I hiss back. 'Be vague about where.'

Kath calls down over the banisters: 'That you, darling? Becky and I are just off out.'

I hear Clive's feet on the stairs, and his exclamation of surprise when he sees Katherine's outfit. 'Bloody hell! Where are you going? You look—'

'Gorgeous?' preens Katherine, giving him a twirl. The soft chiffon folds of her short dress lift up in a puff, showing her stocking tops and a flash of lace knicker.

He appears on the landing and gives me the evils, as the kids at school would say, before turning his attention back to her. 'Tarty,' he says, wrinkling his nose, and I see Katherine's face fall. She's being massively, hideously, disloyal to him by going to this party – it was her idea, she registered us on the website and booked the tickets; but even so, I still feel a bit sorry for her. Perhaps if she had a boyfriend who told her she was beautiful instead of tarty, she wouldn't feel the need to get her kicks among strangers. I'm not sure why they decided to give their relationship another go, since neither of them seems at all happy. Secretly, I think that Clive's a sap for taking her back when he knows she's been on dating websites.

'Charity ball, sweetie, remember? I told you about it a few weeks ago. Becky's friend is on the organizing committee. It'll probably be really boring – you know, charity auction, we'll probably be on a table with a load of deaf old buffers trying to feel our knees under the table; but hey, it's good to have an excuse to dress up and have a night out, eh?'

278

Clive looks suspicious. 'You'll give the deaf old buffers heart attacks dressed like that,' he says.

'What are you doing home, anyway?' Katherine licks her finger and rubs a tiny mark off the front of her patent-leather stilettos.

'Forgot that I'd told Jerry he could borrow my bass amp. I'm going straight back.'

Clive vanishes into their spare room/office and comes out with his arms full of a black box trailing cables.

'I'll stay at Becky's tonight, so don't wait up,' Katherine says, blowing him a kiss as he stomps back downstairs, the amp's plug banging on the steps behind him. There is a pause at the bottom of the stairs.

'Kath? Can I have a quick word?'

Katherine makes a face at me. She kicks off her shoes and runs down the stairs. I hear frantic whispering, mostly from Clive, and I go for a final pee so that I'm not tempted to eavesdrop. I know that Katherine will tell me anyway.

'What did he say?' I emerge from the bathroom to hear the front door shut, and Katherine is back in the room, spraying hairspray vigorously all over her curls.

'It was a close one!' she crows. 'He's been so bloody clingy since that big row. For a minute there, I thought he was going to insist on coming with us, can you imagine? He made me promise that we're not "up to anything". Honestly, it's quite pathetic.' She gives me a hug. 'I'm so excited, Becks! Just think of all the sexy rich guys we're about to meet. That reminds me – have you got condoms?'

She is completely shameless. At the thought of what we're potentially about to do, my stomach gives a nervous flip. I quash down the thought of what the other teachers at school would say if they knew. Worse – what *Amy* would say.

I wonder, too, what Amy would say about some of the

other stuff I've been doing . . . Like the encounter with that guy Paul, the one who called himself TooledUp. He's so not my type . . . not the type the old Becky would have gone anywhere near. But since all this started, just a few months ago, it's as if this new Becky has been born – a kind of dark twin, a part of me I never knew existed. There is something seductive and addictive about losing yourself, about going far beyond what you would normally do, casting off the shackles, going wild . . . In those moments, in the bedroom with Paul and Kath, I became another person, sexy and crazy and free.

But afterwards, I felt dirty, ill at ease in my skin. I'm not like Kath, who has embraced this side of herself as if it's the true her, what with the drugs and the cheating and all the stuff she gets up to with these men. I know she had quite a repressed upbringing and it sounds as if her sexual relationship with Clive has been far too vanilla. Now she's like a girl who wants to gorge herself on every flavour in the ice-cream parlour.

Maybe I'm becoming addicted to it like her. Because a couple of days after an encounter that leaves me feeling tawdry, I get the itch again. That's why I'm going to this party with her. It's not just because I promised and I know I'll never hear the end of it if I don't go.

It's new. It's different. It's exciting. And God knows, my life lacked excitement until recently.

'At the price we're being charged for this evening, I can't believe that they won't have a few condoms lying around. I bet they're everywhere, in bowls on tables like sweets,' I say, draining my second glass of Dutch courage Prosecco. There's a tremor in my voice, like when I have to speak in public. 'I hope you're right, I hope they are sexy. Imagine if we walk in and there's creepy Greg Stainsbury playing pocket billiards and drooling.'

Kath laughs at the idea that the dishevelled, square chemistry teacher with a comb-over would ever think of attending an upmarket swingers' party. 'In his lab coat with those awful scuffed Cornish-pasty shoes of his,' she agrees. 'We'd demand our money back. Instantly.'

The doorbell rings and we both jump. 'Cab's here!' Katherine says, looking out of the window.

34
Amy

Friday, 26 July

When Amy woke up, after a journey home from Epsom the night before that had encompassed buses, trams, trains and several frustrating directional blunders, the first thing she saw was her helmet lying upturned like a beetle on its back in the corner of the room. She burst into tears, the full impact of what she had done finally sinking in. It felt like a bereavement – whenever she closed her eyes, all she could see were her Triumph's chrome curves and the warmth of its leather saddle, like her own second skin.

She sat in bed with her arms around her knees, sobbing and bereft, for a full ten minutes. It was as if Becky and the bike had merged into one huge loss and, at that moment, Amy felt like giving up. When the tears finally stopped she took a shuddering breath, and got up.

Giving up now just wasn't an option.

Right at the back of her wardrobe she found a suit with a short skirt she hadn't worn for five years, not since she last worked in an office. It was a little tight around the waist and hips, but not embarrassingly so. She paired it with sheer stockings, heels, and more make-up than her face had seen since she went to speak at that conference about digital start-ups two years before. Looking in the mirror as she put her hair up, she didn't recognize the woman gazing back at her.

'Too corporate, Boris? I don't want to look like a legal secretary.'

Amy added a quirky silver-and-beaded Aztec necklace and switched the medium-height heels for her absolute killer heels, the black patent six-inchers. She'd have to take a pair of flat pumps for the journey, though.

'That's better,' she said, putting on far more lip gloss than she would usually contemplate. 'More tarty, but still professional.'

An hour later, she was on the Tube, clutching an A4 printout with directions on it, the sharp points of her stilettos digging into her ribs like daggers through the sides of her bag. She got out at Regent's Park and headed south, glad at every step for her ballet pumps. It was another cloudless summer's day, and sweat prickled at her armpits. It had taken her fifty-five minutes by public transport, for a journey that would have taken her twenty on the bike.

Outside a tall, imposing, Georgian terraced house in Devonshire Place, she switched her pumps for the stilettos, powdered her nose, then rang the bell below a brass plaque bearing the name ORCHID BLUE EVENTS. Her heart was racing, mostly because she still didn't know exactly what she was going to say. *Excuse me, I'm enquiring about one of the sex parties you threw.* She noted the company didn't advertise what it did on the plaque. Orgy organizers. Once again, she felt stunned by her discovery of what Becky had been doing before she vanished.

The door buzzed, and somehow that made Amy feel more nervous than if someone had quizzed her through the intercom. She stepped inside, her heels clicking briskly on the tiled floor, and walked up to the first floor.

When she reached the office, Amy was relieved to see a lone young girl sitting behind a reception desk. Rather than the bored insouciance of the confident PA, this girl, although stunningly beautiful, appeared more rabbit-in-headlights terrified than Amy herself felt. She only looked about seventeen, and might as well have had WORK EXPERIENCE tattooed on her flawless forehead.

'Can I help you?' she squeaked, her nerves immediately putting Amy at ease.

'I'm a prospective client, and I'd like some information please,' she said, smiling at the girl, who didn't smile back, but immediately started ferreting in her desk drawer. She pulled out a large glossy cardboard folder and handed it to Amy, gabbling in a stream of consciousness at her:

'Take a seat please our MD is out at the moment but she'll be back soon and she approves all the applications there's a form inside for you to fill in if you want to but we'll also need some photos although since you're here we could take them here if you want and we need some proof of ID and a deposit on membership and the next party is on Thursday if you're based in London or there's one in Cheltenham—'

Amy held up a hand to stop her. It sounded as though she was parroting every bit of information imparted to her when she'd started that morning – because surely she had only started that morning. It made her want to smile, that the girl wouldn't meet her eyes. Perhaps she was imagining her, Amy, naked in a mask at one of the parties, writhing around. 'Thanks! I'll just read this lot, if that's OK, and yes, I'd like to wait for your MD. What's her name?'

'Mariel Freestone. She won't be long. Um, would you like a coffee?'

Amy accepted the offer of coffee and studied the cover of the glossy file. It was midnight blue, with an artful shaded orchid, photographed to look like genitalia, the way Georgia O'Keeffe used to do in her paintings, and the slogan ELITE CASUAL DATING under the company name. Inside the file were pages of glowing testimonials, arty photos from the parties, an application form and a direct-debit mandate.

Amy started filling in the application form, and had just paused at the 'Occupation' box when the door opened and an intimidating-looking woman in her early fifties – or mid-sixties with a lot of work done – walked in and dropped her big green Marc Jacobs bag on the reception desk.

'Hello, Auntie Mariel,' said the girl. 'Someone to see you.'

'*Miss Freestone* while we're at work, darling,' she replied, her tones clipped and businesslike. She came over to Amy and held out a hand weighed down with large, odd-sized gemstones set in gold. 'Mariel Freestone. How may I help you?'

Amy got up and shook her hand. 'I wondered if we could have a little chat, about membership?'

Mariel Freestone looked at her watch with a flourish. 'I'm afraid I have another meeting in twenty minutes – I just popped in here to pick something up – but if it's quick . . .'

'I'll be quick,' Amy said. 'Thank you.'

'Coffees, please, Gemma,' instructed Mariel, leading Amy into a room off the side of the office.

'Kettle's already on,' Gemma said sulkily.

It was a beautiful high-ceilinged room, stuffed with antique office furniture and a huge Gabbeh rug on the floor. Orchid Blue Events must be doing very well, thought Amy, taking a seat in a shiny leather wingback armchair opposite Mariel's desk.

'So, you're hoping to join?' Mariel scrutinized her so thoroughly that Amy blushed. She paused, still teetering on the verge of lying. But when she opened her mouth, she thought it would just be so much simpler to tell the truth.

'Actually – no. But my sister recently has.'

'Oh?' This came out very frostily, as if Mariel was bracing herself for some sort of complaint.

'I believe she attended an Orchid Blue party in London with her friend Katherine, not long ago – a month, perhaps?'

Mariel tipped her head to one side and made a moue of displeasure with her coral-painted lips. 'I'm sorry – I don't understand why you're here.'

Amy took a deep breath. 'She went missing, a week ago. It's really important that I find out who else was at that party.' She had decided not to mention Katherine's death, sure it would make Mariel slam the door on their conversation quicker than you could say 'PR disaster'.

Mariel shook her head. 'I'm sorry to hear that. But of course, you must understand that I cannot possibly divulge our client lists – they are strictly confidential! We have a duty to our clientele. Why on earth are you here and not the police? Surely, this is a police matter?'

Amy followed Mariel's gaze over to a filing cabinet in the corner. Interesting, she thought. Bet the lists are in there. How old-fashioned. Maybe they didn't keep them on a computer for fear of being hacked.

'The police aren't taking Becky's disappearance seriously because she sent an email saying she was going away. It's fake, but they haven't yet accepted that. They will, of course – but I'm aware that every single day counts, if someone has Becky. I have to find her. Please help me!'

286

Amy's voice was rising, and she actually reached forward across the desk as if to grasp Mariel's skinny freckled wrist. The woman snatched her arm away, with an expression of disgust on her face.

Shit, Amy thought. She's going to think I'm a nutter. 'Sorry,' she said, sinking back down again. 'I'm desperate.'

Mariel stood up. 'Please, no need to apologize. I'm sure this must be an unbelievably stressful time for you. I do hope your sister is found safely as soon as possible.'

She was like a politician with a nonstick coating, issuing bland platitudes.

'I've got a far better chance of doing that if you would help me,' Amy said bleakly.

'I will be happy to help you, Miss . . . *Coltman* –' Mariel looked at her name on the application form to remind herself – 'but you will have to go through the proper channels. I would be obliged to divulge my client lists to the police, but not to anybody else. So I'm afraid that you will have to insist on their help, and the request will have to come from them. If you're not actually intending to join –' she looked again at the half-filled-in application – 'then please excuse me. I need to leave now for my next appointment.'

Amy wondered what the appointment was for – nails, hair or Botox would have been her first guesses. She gritted her teeth. 'I understand,' she said, standing up to leave just as Gemma came in with a tray of coffee and biscuits. 'Thank you for your time. I might just drink my coffee in the reception area, if you don't mind?'

Mariel pursed her lips at her, but nodded, and Amy took a mug off the tray. The coffee was tepid and bitter, with the grounds still floating on the surface, but Amy sat in reception and sipped at it, trying to work out what to do next. Mariel picked up her cavernous handbag again and breezed out with a little wave at Amy, as though they had just enjoyed a girly lunch today.

Gemma stared shamelessly at Amy. 'So, did she say you could join then, or what?'

'She said I could, sure,' Amy replied nonchalantly. 'I just need to finish filling in the form.' She put down her coffee and spent the next few minutes completing the form, all bar the direct-debit mandate. Her mind was whizzing through all the ways she could think of to get Gemma to let her look in that filing cabinet: bribery, violence, appealing to her better nature? Then she had a better idea.

'I'll post it back to you,' she said. 'I haven't got my bank card with me, and I don't know my account number and sort code off by heart for this direct-debit thingy, so I'll have to look it up when I get home. Is there a loo up here I could use?'

Gemma's face lit up – at last, some information she felt confident in giving. 'Out of this door, turn right, up the four stairs to the mini-landing, it's on there,' she said.

Amy stuffed the form in her bag and left, with the taste of the unpleasant Nescafé coating her teeth and her heart banging in her chest. She found the toilet and checked that it was unoccupied. Then she went back to the landing and found what she was looking for, mounted on the wall near the lift.

A 'break glass in case of fire' alarm.

She paused, looking for cameras, listening for footsteps, but could see and hear none. With one brisk jab of her thumb she broke the glass, and an alarm immediately started screaming. She dashed straight back into the toilet and locked the door. Over the din of the alarm, she heard anxious voices and doors opening, feet pounding past her from the offices on the floors above.

'Is it a drill? It's not Wednesday!'

'Can you smell smoke? I'm sure I can.'

'Don't run!'

'Where's the assembly point again?'

'Across the road – come on, hurry!'

The first batch of voices faded, replaced by another batch, presumably workers from the floor above. Amy hoped against hope that Gemma wasn't so thick as to have stayed put. She had to time this right – if she left it too long, the fire brigade would be here. If she came out too soon she might bump into someone. She forced herself to count to twenty slowly, put her pumps back on and her bag across her shoulders, then opened the toilet door and ran back into the Orchid Blue suite. The door was wide open – good old Gemma.

Amy dived into Mariel's office and straight across to the filing cabinet, which, thankfully, was also unlocked. The contents were in hanging files in date order, with the party venue also helpfully annotated. Amy silently thanked whoever Gemma's predecessor had been for being so organized. She snatched JUNE 2013 HOLLAND PARK out of the cabinet and frantically flicked through it – it seemed to be the most recent event, and the most local to Becky. Much of its contents was paperwork relating to the hiring of waiters, payment of florists, providers of finger food. For a moment, she thought there wasn't anything in there about attendees, and then she found it: a heavily annotated printed list of names, mostly ticked off in black pen, some crossed through. In her haste she had to read the list three times before she spotted either Becky's or Katherine's name – but then she did. There they were, ticks next to them both.

It was the only concrete evidence she had of Becky's movements in the past few weeks; with the sight of those few typed symbols on a sheet of paper, something fresh and hopeful leaped in Amy's throat. Becky had been there, on that date, just four weeks earlier. Someone else on this list might well be the cause of her disappearance.

'What the HELL are you doing in here, get out, now!'

Amy leaped up, clutching the sheet. Over the din of the alarm she hadn't even heard the arrival of the burly fireman in full breathing apparatus.

'I'm sorry,' she gabbled, 'I got locked in the loo and then when I finally managed to get out, everyone had gone, and I was just about to when I remembered I had to get this file that I've been working on, the boss would kill me if there was a fire and it got destroyed . . .'

The fireman wagged his heavily gloved finger at her. 'Don't you know any of the basic fire-safety rules? Never stop to collect anything, leave the building immediately.'

'Sorry,' Amy repeated. 'It's my first day here. Is there a real fire, or is it just a drill?'

But the fireman was impatiently waving her out, and she decided it was better not to draw any more attention to herself. As she ran down the stairs, she took out the list to fold it up and put it safely in the pocket of her handbag. Just as she rounded the bend in the stairs to the ground floor, glancing again at the list, she saw something that gave her such a surprise she almost missed her footing and fell the rest of the way – a name she hadn't spotted before in her haste to find Becky's and Katherine's.

'Oh, my God,' she breathed.

35

Becky

Saturday, 29 June

We fall silent as the black taxi creeps closer to our destination through rush-hour traffic. It takes ages to get there. The venue is a massive private house in Holland Park, cake-icing exterior, wrought-iron railings and black front door with huge brass knocker – it's a private house, or members' club, I'm not sure which. I feel utterly intimidated as we climb out of the cab and survey the two large bouncers lurking in the entrance. I smooth my tight skirt down over my thighs and swallow hard. My hand is sweaty from clutching the shiny invitation.

A beautiful hostess with a clipboard, gimlet eyes and wide fake smile meets us inside the front door, and we proffer our invites. 'Welcome!' she chirps, already looking over our heads to see if there is anyone more interesting arriving. We give her our names, and she ticks us off. Then she holds out two velvet-covered boxes. 'Phones, cameras, iPads – all gadgets in this one, ladies, please. Strictly no photography.' She taps a sign on the wall above

291

her head with a lacquered talon: ANYONE TAKING PHOTO-GRAPHS WILL IMMEDIATELY BE EJECTED. NO EXCEPTIONS. 'And take a mask,' she orders, holding out the second, bigger box.

'No photography – that's a relief then.' I am sounding slightly hysterical as we drop our phones into the box and select masks. Mine is feathery, and Kath's white and sequinned. We giggle as we put them on. The hostess rolls her eyes, very slightly.

'Hope they don't sell our phones on eBay as soon as we've gone upstairs,' Kath mutters as we tip-tap on our stiletto heels up the wide staircase. I'm so nervous that I think I might throw up, and I grab a glass of champagne from the tray of a passing waiter. Katherine takes one too. 'Sip it, don't gulp,' she instructs me under her breath. 'Don't look so bloody nervous.'

Easy for her to say. The buzz of voices and music gets louder, and I'm reassured that there is the unmistakeable sound of party conversation. I was half expecting it to be all orgy and no chat.

We are shown into a huge room on the first floor, and I look around, trying to take it all in. Everyone is young and beautiful under their masks, and I remember Katherine telling me that you had to send proof of age with the ticket-purchase money, as over-forties were as forbidden as camera phones.

'No grey chest hair or moobs here,' Katherine says approvingly. It's pretty dark in the room, the lighting artfully flattering and subtle. Small groups of people are dotted about, chatting and laughing and looking far more at ease than I feel; a whole variety of expensive perfumes and aftershaves clash in a fragrant cloud in the air above our heads. The only sign that this might not be a normal cocktail party, apart from the masks, is a couple standing by the window kissing; the man has one hand right down inside the girl's short skirt, and the other is kneading her breast. One of the waiters goes up to them and has a discreet word in the guy's ear, pointing towards a room off the main area. There is a plaque next to its door reading PLAYROOM, and the couple heads towards it, not looking remotely sheepish. I can see the man's erection making a tent of the front of his trousers that he isn't even trying to disguise.

'Can't wait to get in there!' says Katherine, her face flushed in the peachy-red light and her eyes sparkling with lust, enhanced by the sequins on her mask.

'I know, right!' I agree. I do feel turned on too, but somehow my heart is sinking, and for a moment I really wish I was at home in my onesie and fluffy slippers, watching a DVD. The idea of having sex – in public, with strangers – suddenly seems anathema to me.

'Why did we think this was a good idea?' I mutter, trying to sound jokey, but Katherine's face falls.

'Oh, come on, Becky, stop being such a bloody prudish killjoy,' she hisses, and to my surprise she turns and walks away from me, over to where two men and a woman are already mentally undressing one another.

'Cheers, Kath,' I say to her retreating back. I lean against the nearest wall, feeling even more self-conscious. A lone man catches my eye and smiles at me. I raise my glass, and he's over like a shot.

'Hi,'

'Hi.'

I'm tongue-tied. He's very nice-looking but not in the way I usually like – too bland. I like my men to have something quirky about their appearance, and all his features are perfectly proportioned and unremarkable.

'What do you do?' he asks, actually leaning one hand against the wall, making a ladder over my head in that ridiculously predatory way men sometimes do. I can't imagine why they think that endears them to women.

'I'm a teacher!' I say, in the same way that I would've said, 'I'm a clown!' or, 'I'm an Elvis impersonator!' 'What about you?'

'Male model,' he says, so smugly that I almost laugh.

There's a long silence as he scans the room for someone other than me to have sex with. I'm starting to feel actively physically repulsed by all this. Katherine is laughing and gesticulating with her new friends and, as I watch, one of the women leans across and kisses her cheek flirtatiously. My heart sinks. It's only a matter of time before she vanishes into the Playroom, I can tell. I feel irrationally furious with her. Never again, I think, wondering wistfully if there would be any chance of a partial refund of the hefty amount that's just been debited from my credit card for annual membership of this exclusive club. Internet dating – fine. Casexual.com – also fine, for when I want a bit of no-strings sex. At least you can choose in advance who you want to get naked with. Those first few hook-up dates were fantastic – really good, naughty fun. I think wistfully back to Jake and his smooth black skin and infectious giggle. Shame he didn't fancy a repeat performance, it was lovely. Fraser was fun too, even if he was a drug-dealing twat. It was even exciting with Paul, though that was mainly because Kath was there to hold my hand – among other things.

But this? I don't like this. Despite the posh house, the designer dresses, buff champagne waiters and young, beautiful, well-groomed people, this is still somehow just plain sleazy. I didn't think I'd feel like this, but I do.

'Sorry, I'm actually going to go home – headache,' I say

to the male model, to his obvious relief. Ducking under his arm, I head over to Katherine.

'Can I have a word?' I whisper in her ear.

'Is this your friend?' asks one of the men in the group. He's short and hirsute, Turkish perhaps, with a big diamond stud in his ear. 'Come join us, beautiful.' He reaches out and strokes my hair, but I move my head away impatiently, and Katherine frowns. I take her arm and drag her away.

'What is your *problem*?' she snaps. I've only seen this side of her once or twice, when she's tired and high, or perhaps after a particularly hideous day with her Year Elevens. 'We've made all this effort, paid all this money, looked forward to it for weeks, you were really excited – then we get here, and you've got a face like a slapped arse.'

As if on cue, we both hear a brisk slapping noise coming from the Playroom, and some muted giggling. I'm torn between wanting to go and take a look – as several people are – and doing a runner.

Katherine's face lightens, and she twines an arm around my neck. 'Sorry, Becks, I didn't mean to bite your head off. Please stay for a little bit longer? Come on, let's go and check out the naughtiness – everyone else is.'

I allow her to take my hand, and she starts leading me towards the Playroom, along with the Turkish guy and his friend – but then I freeze.

'Oh, no!'

'What?' Katherine stops too, and tries to follow my horrified gaze.

I cup my hand on the side of my cheek in a vain and instinctive attempt to disguise myself. 'I've seen someone I *know*,' I wail, quietly.

'Not someone from school?' Katherine looks equally distressed.

I risk a glance in the direction of the face I recognized. He is also drifting towards the Playroom with a girl; they are laughing at something behind their black masks. I'm sure it's him. 'What the hell is he doing here?'

Katherine stares after him. 'Who is it? Someone you met online?'

'Oh, it doesn't matter . . . listen, I just want to get out of here. I'm sorry.' Seeing someone I know was one of my worst nightmares about the whole thing, and now it's happened, my skin is itching with the desire to run away.

I know what's going to happen next if I don't go now. The Turkish guy is going to suggest that we all adjourn to the Playroom together, a cosy little foursome.

I grab her elbow and pull her aside, out of the earshot of the two men, though I can feel them watching us.

'I'm sorry, Kath, but I really am going to leave now,' I said, finding it hard to get my breath. 'I think you should come with me.'

Anger flashes in her eyes. 'No fucking way. I'm staying. I paid nearly a week's wages to come here. And I like it. I'm not going to pussy out like you.'

I take a deep breath. 'All right. Just promise you text me when you get home safely, OK?' I try to lighten the mood. 'Tell me what you got up to tomorrow – I'll come over for a debrief.'

Katherine shrugs. 'Judas,' she mutters. The diamond-studded Turk beckons us over, which I take as my cue to leave. I kiss her on the cheek, and push her gently in his direction, but like a kid in a sweet shop, I see her attention caught by another man, and she executes a sharp ninety-degree turn towards him. This one is a superior, rich-looking type in a suit that cost more than a family car, looking as if he'd spent all afternoon in a salon getting exfoliated before he came here. Yuck. Even through his mask, I could see that he had squinty eyes, though, and I bet it galled him that he couldn't throw money at that, get them fixed.

The feathers of my own mask are itching my forehead like mad, and as I walk out of the room I can't bear it any more and tear it off, enjoying the feel of the cool air on my skin again, shaking my hair down and looking around to make sure *he* is not around. For some reason, I think about Amy. Right now all I want to do is go to her flat, hug her, apologize for our row and get far away from this world I've found myself in.

36

Amy

Friday, 26 July

Amy had to stop in the street and lean against a railing because she had black dots jumping around in her vision and her head felt like lead, partly from the speed at which she had hurried away from Orchid Blue's offices to avoid being spotted by Gemma, and partly from the shock of recognizing the name on the list of people who'd been at the party. She noticed with a sense of irony that the building she'd stopped outside was a Harley Street psychotherapy practice, just a few doors down from the one her parents had booked her an appointment at, after her 'breakdown', as they referred to her split with Nathan.

She could do with a psychotherapist now. Someone to talk to. Anyone. The long list of things that Nathan had taken from her – self-respect, dignity, confidence, peace – included something else, something that had never been replaced: close friends. He'd gradually alienated all her own friends, and replaced them with new ones of his own – choosing mostly his male buddies, so that when she finally walked out on him, she never saw any of them again. Most of their colleagues had also taken his side after he'd poisoned them against her, spreading lies around the office that she had cheated on him so he'd thrown her out, broken-hearted – another reason why she'd left that place to set up on her own.

She had to talk to Gary. She pulled out her phone and started to gabble the moment he answered.

'It's me. I know I said I wanted a bit of space – but I need to talk to you. This is getting weirder by the minute, I'm finding out all this stuff, please can we meet?' She told him, in a rush, about the sex party, but at the last minute decided not to mention the name she'd spotted until she could tell Gary in person. 'I've got this list of the people who were there—'

'A *sex* party?' he said. 'Becky?'

'Yes. Her and Katherine. I'm in town. Do you get a lunch break? Can I come to your work? I'm really sorry to bother you but you're the only one I can talk to . . .' Her voice cracked, but Gary's voice soothed her, pouring into her head over the sounds of cabs and panic and distant sirens.

She listened as he dictated the street address of his company, Digistar. It wasn't too far away: the purple dustiness of the Metropolitan Line from Baker Street straight to Liverpool Street, turn right, walk five minutes towards Shoreditch, small side street . . .

'Thanks, Gary, I'll be about half an hour,' she said gratefully.

All the way over to Liverpool Street on the Tube, Amy kept thinking about how to approach speaking to Gary. She hoped that he wouldn't be difficult after the way they had parted. By the time she emerged out into the sunshine again she had decided that getting Gary's work address and going there to see him remained the best option: neutral territory, with other people around. Much better than meeting up at one of their flats.

She was so distracted that she bumped into a *Big Issue* seller. He swore at her, then immediately regained his composure, looking anxiously around to check that nobody had overheard. Amy bought a copy of the magazine by way of apology, and checked that she was heading in the right direction.

Gary's office was in a warehouse building down a small one-way street, a typical New Media trendy open-plan 'space', all on one floor, bare brick walls covered with enormous silkscreen prints of classic American movie posters. Amy took a seat in reception to wait for him, wondering if she should discreetly slip her high shoes back on again, then deciding she couldn't be bothered. Instead, she took out the list again and had another look, making sure she hadn't hallucinated the name.

Her phone vibrated, and the screen announced an email from CupidsWeb. Amy opened it just as Gary appeared out of a room off the far side of the office. She looked up and waved at him before reading the message, but he didn't see her straight away. One of his colleagues had called over to him from another glass-fronted room off the main office floor.

When she looked back down at the screen, she saw the email's sign-off first: *Daniel*.

One of Becky's dates – the one she hadn't been able to find any trace of. He hadn't responded to either of the messages she had sent him. Until now.

She leaped up from the reception sofa as if she'd been scalded and, even though she couldn't possibly have smelled it, the long-forgotten scent of Nathan's aftershave flooded her senses, as though she had been drenched with a bucketful of it. Dropping the phone into her bag without properly reading the rest of the email, she ran straight back out of the door of the Digistar offices. She ran at full tilt back to the station, questions piling up one on top of the other until she thought she was going to vomit them all out right there on the street.

She stopped, her breath coming in harsh, hot waves, her feet in the pumps slippery with sweat. As she pulled her phone out of her bag, she realized that she had left the list of party attendees lying on the sofa in reception. She swore, and looked at the screen.

She opened and read the message more thoroughly. The shock of its contents made her knees buckle, and she had to sit down on the edge of the kerb to stop herself falling. As she read it over and over again, her hands shook so hard that she could barely hold the phone.

37

Becky

Monday, 15 July

Last night's date with the most gorgeous man alive is all I can think about during the Year Nine parents' evening. Through the blur of grubby school jumpers and the collage of mums' and dads' faces in varying degrees of smugness, concern or belligerence at their offspring's progress – or lack of – as they shuffle up to my table in the hall and away again three minutes later, like some hellish parody of speed dating, the thought keeps rising to the surface: *Call off the search*.

I think Daniel could be the one. I do, really. I can't believe my luck. I've found someone who seems to be absolutely perfect for me. I can't stop grinning, and feel so benevolent towards humankind that I even tell Jayden Connor's mum that he's 'a good boy really'. Her astonishment is hilarious.

It was one of those dates that just went on and on for hours. The waiters in the restaurant – yes, drinks turned into a lengthy dinner, at his suggestion and expense, at

Retro, the fabulous French place that Kath and I planned to go to when we won the Lottery – were practically putting chairs up on tables around us as we moved closer and closer to each other until our legs were pressed together and our fingers entwined . . .

I wanted to give Kath the low-down at break time. He is a surgeon at a private hospital in Wiltshire. Two brothers, both married. Flat in town, big house near Salisbury, pony in the back field for his niece to play with when she comes to stay. Has been single for two years since his fiancée developed an eating disorder and ran away to 'find herself' in Australia. He never heard from her again but assured me that he's over it now, and from the way he was gazing at me, I believe him. He's funny, considerate, wealthy, independent. Said that I am his 'ideal woman'. Loves his mum. Loves animals.

In the end, though, I didn't tell her anything about him because she made puking noises over the Nescafé when I told her that I was in love, and pretended to block her ears. She's such a cynic. We were going to go to the pub for a post-parents' evening unwinder, so I thought I'd do it then – but she had another last-minute Casexual date.

Since we weren't going out, I decided to stay even later to finish marking my Year Eights' Provence trip write-ups, and it's almost completely dark now that I've finally got out of there. The playground is dusky with shadow and looks oddly still without a seething mass of boys milling around and punching one another. Why do they still call it a 'playground' in secondary schools? A fight-ground would be closer to the truth. Nobody's around – all my colleagues jumped in their cars the second the last parent left, screeching off out of the school gates on two wheels in their haste to escape. Wish *I* had a car.

I walk to the bus stop but the red electronic board flashes at me that the next bus going my way isn't deigning to arrive for thirty-seven minutes – I could bloody well be home by then. So, even though I'm wearing heels, and my bag is heavy, I decide to walk.

I am just wondering whether it would look a bit over-keen if I call him – we've been texting all day but haven't spoken since last night – when my phone vibrates. It's him! Joy soars through me. I change my mind about walking and sit down on the bus stop's hard slatted bench. Although I wouldn't have cared if it had been wreathed in barbed wire; I feel so euphoric that I don't think I'd have noticed.

'Hello!'

'Hello, gorgeous. How's your day been? I've been thinking about you constantly.'

'Really? Me too – about you, I mean. My day's been pretty long. Parents' evening. I couldn't concentrate at all! I just kept thinking about how brilliant last night was.'

He laughs, and it does something funny to the pit of my stomach. 'I wanted to ask you something. What are you doing this weekend?'

'Going on a date with you, hopefully,' I simper.

'Correct! And not just any date, but . . .' He pauses.

'What?'

'Well. I hope you don't think I'm being too forward, since we've only just met and all, but last night was so mind-blowing, just talking for as long as we did, and I feel like you've put some kind of spell on me, honestly, I do . . .'

I laugh delightedly. So this is what love feels like! It's ace.

'Spit it out,' I tease.

I hear him take a deep breath, as if gathering up courage. 'I wondered if – and please say no if you don't think it's appropriate – you might be up for a long weekend away? Surprise European destination. Two rooms, of course – although, ahem, you'd be welcome to visit me whenever you wished; then we'd really have time to get to know one another.'

I'm so thrilled that I'm momentarily speechless, and he mistakes my silence for concern.

'Oh, sorry, Becky, am I moving too fast? It's fine, really – we could just go out to dinner again instead. I swear I wouldn't normally suggest something so full-on so quickly, but I really think we've got something special here, don't you?'

'Yes, I do,' I whisper. *I do.* In my head, I'm standing at an altar in a Vera Wang gown, saying those same words to him. 'And I'd love to go away with you, honestly. I was just a bit overwhelmed. We break up on Wednesday so that would be perfect timing. God knows, I could do with a little holiday!'

He laughs with relief. 'Great! This weekend it is, then. I'll pick you up on Thursday at five, text me your address. Pack a bag, and don't forget your passport!'

38

Declan

Thursday, 25 July

Declan Adams sat at his desk, his eyes sore from staring at the computer screen for hours on end, his stomach emitting a series of growls and gurgles as it tried in vain to get his attention. All he'd eaten all day was an egg-and-cress sandwich from the Tesco Express down the road. He was living on instant coffee and adrenaline and had been since they got back from Chichester, even though that was almost a week ago. This case was completely consuming him like no other.

He had the photo of Amber Corrigan pinned up on the wall, staring down at him with those beautiful blue eyes. With her blonde hair and startling looks, she had the kind of face that people would notice and remember. But after fifteen years?

Declan and Bob had spent a day going around Tunbridge Wells, in the immediate vicinity of the Internet Futures Conference, and Stonegate, the closest village to the farm where Amber's body had been found, asking if anyone remembered her. As Declan had feared, it was too long ago. Nobody remembered faces they'd seen a decade and a half ago, no matter how pretty they were.

The staff at the Pantiles Hotel, where the conference had taken place, had almost entirely changed, and nobody remembered the event, let alone Amber. Of course, everyone tried – everyone wished they could remember – but it was hopeless. What was Declan expecting? Someone to say, 'Oh, yes, I remember her leaving with a really creepy-looking guy. I was so concerned that I took a note of his registration number – in fact, I still have it.'

Yeah, right.

In Declan's experience, getting anyone to remember events from the day before was enough of a struggle, let alone any further back. He and Bob had driven back from Tunbridge Wells in silence, a gloom settling over them. The case had hit a dead end, and their SIO had given them twenty-four hours to make significant process before he moved them onto fresher investigations. Declan looked up at the photo of Amber. It killed him that someone was out there, walking free, after snuffing out this young life.

Bob came into the room, holding a carrier bag. 'All right?' he said, cheerily. 'I brought you some dinner.'

He produced a Ginsters chicken pasty, a yoghurt, an apple and a slice of carrot cake from his bag, along with a bottle of Lucozade Sport.

'Aw, thanks, Bob. You're a legend.'

He ripped open the pasty packet and took a bite. Cold, greasy and saltier than Eastbourne beach – his belly gurgled with appreciation.

'I wish Isobel agreed with you.'

'In the doghouse again?'

'Oh, you know . . .' He shrugged. It was such a common

phenomenon in police stations and offices around the country – probably the world. The police officer whose other half hadn't believed how long their spouse's hours would *really* be when they embarked on a relationship. 'I got the list of the delegates who went to that conference. Bit of a struggle – the company who put it together went bust years ago. Another victim of the dotcom boom.'

'So how did you do it?'

'Ah. There's this website called the Wayback Machine. It's basically a massive archive of old web pages. Like taking a tour of a museum. It's amazing how old-fashioned websites from the late nineties look now.'

Declan took a swig of the Lucozade.

'So I had a stroke of luck. I found a couple of web pages with details of the conference. One page contained a list of speakers and the timetable – all these talks about how Internet dating was going to be the next big thing, how to start an auction site, why Yahoo! was the future of business . . . Then there was another page with a list of delegates. Amber's name was on it.'

'That's amazing. Where's the list?'

'I emailed it to you, of course.'

Declan turned to his computer and logged on to his emails, bringing up the two lists.

The conference had taken place over two days and there were twelve speakers on each day, including a few people who had made up panel discussions. The delegate list was a lot longer. It had clearly been a popular event, with over 200 people attending. The opposite of what Declan had hoped for. Not only did it mean more names to check, but it meant the likelihood of anyone noticing anything that would stick in their memory reduced from unlikely to you-must-be-joking.

'Right,' he said. 'The first thing we need to do is to check this lot, see if any of them have criminal records for violent offences.'

'Already on it.'

Of course he was. 'Maybe we'll strike it lucky and find someone on the list who's currently doing time for murder, and he'll confess the moment we show him Amber's picture.'

'Then we can all go home for tea and live happily ever after.'

'Are you telling me you don't believe in fairy tales, Bob?'

'Only the ones in which little girls get eaten by wolves.' His expression darkened. 'I'd better get home. Might just catch Jessica before Isobel puts her to bed.'

'Good idea. Oh, and good work.'

'Cheers. You should get home too, get some rest.'

'Yeah, I will. Just going to finish this delicious feast first.' He belched. 'Oops.'

'Charmed, I'm sure.'

After Bob had left, Declan snuck outside for a cigarette. He quit once or twice every year, but always went back to it, blaming the pressures of the job. He was thinking of trying those electronic cigarettes. Standing in the car park, he contemplated taking Bob's advice. Go home, have a shower, watch one of the DVDs he'd got for Christmas and still hadn't got round to watching, seven months later.

But the list of names from the conference was calling to him, like a bottle of whisky calling to an alcoholic, and he hurried back upstairs to his desk, popping a chewing gum into his mouth as he went. His head was full of missing girls. He had been looking through MISPER reports all day, wondering how many more there were out there. There was something about the way the murderer had tried to cover up what had happened, by making those closest to her believe she wasn't missing at all, that struck him as well-planned – certainly better-planned than her 'burial' in the cesspit. Whoever put her in there must have known she would be found eventually.

The letter to Amber's parents and the photograph of the house on the beach had gone to the lab to be analysed as soon as Declan and Bob had got back to Sussex. Fingerprints remain on paper for a long time and could be revealed using a chemical called ninhydrin. The results from the lab had come back that morning – the letter had, along with her parents' prints, a good set of prints from Amber, but no one else. The photographs had no fingerprints on them at all. Declan wondered if the killer had gone to the trouble of visiting Brazil, or some other exotic-looking location – the picture could be of a villa in Torquay! – but doubted it. After all, it was easy enough to grab a picture off the Internet and print it out. The Corrigans had thrown away the envelope but, assuming it contained a Brazilian postmark, it wasn't too hard to arrange to have an envelope posted from any country in the world without actually visiting it.

Declan had a copy of the letter on his desk and, returning from his cigarette break, picked it up and read it over for the hundredth time. The fingerprints were a clever touch, because if Amber's parents had suspected that something awful had happened to their daughter, and the police took them seriously, it would have been easy to check the letter for prints at the time. The presence of prints would have made the letter appear authentic, had there not been any evidence – as there was now – that something awful had indeed happened.

It wouldn't have been difficult to do, either – simply get Amber to handle a blank sheet of printer paper, or press her hand against it. Then her murderer could have handled it wearing gloves, written the letter at his leisure and used the piece of paper to print the letter on. Declan smiled darkly. If I were the murderer and it were my printer, he thought, it would most likely have chewed the paper up, wrecking my plans.

So if the killer had been clever enough to do that, why had he dumped the body in such an unsafe location? Had something panicked him and compelled him to get rid of the body suddenly? Did he foolishly believe that the cesspit would never be opened, that it would remain a sealed tomb for ever? Or was there some other reason?

Taking another swig of Lucozade, Declan started to Google the names on the speakers' list from the conference. There were a number of Americans, over from Silicon Valley to teach the Brits a thing or two, but most of the speakers were from the UK. Nearly all of them were still around, still working on the web, and there were a few names he vaguely recognized. There was Maria Lake-Ford, who had started that big travel website, and Marvin Taylor, the guy who had got rich from a site telling other people how to save money. It was interesting how people who worked online rarely seemed to change careers.

He spent an hour on Google, writing down a few notes on each of the speakers. If nothing came back from the Home Office's central record system, HOLMES, one of the next steps would be to talk to each of the speakers to see if they remembered Amber. Then they would have to do the same with the much longer delegate list. He inwardly groaned at the thought.

'Time to go home,' he said aloud.

He stood up, stretching to try to erase some of the aches

and pains from his body. Now he really was looking forward to that shower.

As he made his way out, he saw that a few of his colleagues were still hard at work, including a detective constable with whom Declan got on well, Jessie Redmayne, sitting with her back to the walkway. The DC was a young black woman with big ambitions. Declan had a feeling she wouldn't rest until she was at least a detective superintendent. He headed over to her desk. As he got closer he noticed that Jessie was looking at Facebook – perhaps not so hard at work after all. Declan wasn't a big Facebook user. He had an account, and had been addicted to Farmville during his recuperation period, but these days he barely looked at it.

'Caught you,' Declan said.

Jessie spun round and Declan smiled to show he was joking.

'What are you looking at?' he asked.

'Oh . . . this. It's spreading around Facebook like wildfire. A woman in London has gone missing and her sister posted an appeal, asking if anyone has seen her or knows anything. It's been shared, like, five thousand times in the last couple of hours!'

'That's amazing.'

'The power of social networking, eh? Though no one seems to know anything useful.'

Jessie clicked on the small picture on her screen to show the full post, complete with a large picture of the missing woman.

Declan caught his breath. Suddenly he was no longer fed up about still being at his desk, starving hungry, at 7 p.m. 'Oh, my god.'

'What is it? Do you know her?'

Declan shook his head. 'No. What's her name?'

Jessie pointed. 'Becky Coltman.'

'Wait there.'

Declan jogged over to his desk, grabbed the picture of Amber Corrigan from the pinboard, then hurried back to Jessie. He held the picture of Amber against the screen and the photo of Becky Coltman.

'Fuck,' Jessie said.

'Uncanny, isn't it? They could be twins.'

39

Amy

Friday, 26 July

Dear Amy, I know who you are, and why you really contacted me. I know where Becky is and can take you to her – but you must promise not to tell the police or anyone else or they'll kill her, and you. Meet me at 1 p.m. today in Old Deer Park car park in Richmond. The part of it nearest the community college. I'll pick you up there. I'll be in a black Range Rover. Daniel.

'Are you all right, love?'

It was the same *Big Issue* seller who had sworn at her earlier. Amy gazed up at him, her mind reeling. She nodded blankly and he held out an arm.

'Don't sit in the gutter then. That never did nobody no good.'

She allowed him to help her up and he peered into her face. 'You sure you're OK? You're white as a sheet. I'm sorry about earlier, you know, I hope I didn't upset you.'

She managed a smile. 'No, don't worry – least of my problems. I've got to go. Thanks again.'

Back on the Circle Line, Amy sat as if in a trance. People were giving her odd looks, and one or two kindly souls asked if she was OK, but she brushed them off. She changed onto the District Line at Earl's Court, waiting on the platform for the arrow on the old-fashioned overhead sign to click down, to indicate that the next train was destined for Richmond. She focused on the arrow, finding it hard to gather her thoughts into any sort of coherent order.

Who was Daniel, apart from a guy Becky had been on a date with? How did he know she was Becky's sister – unless he had Becky, and *she* had told him? This at least meant that Becky was probably still alive. Her heart gave a momentary flip of joy that she might shortly see her.

But she would be insane to get into Daniel's car without telling anyone where she was going. Now it really did sound as if Becky had been kidnapped. Was she just walking straight into a trap?

Who could she tell, if not the police?

She thought about her life. No partner, no relationship with her parents, no close friends apart from Chris and Vince, now settled far away in Edinburgh. She didn't even have her *bike* any more. OK, she had a good business, but who cared about that?

At that moment, she didn't. She realized with something like shock that she actually didn't care what happened to her. If Becky was dead, she would want to die too. And if Becky was still alive, then Amy had a chance of saving her.

Nobody had come to rescue her, Amy, from Nathan. There was no way she would abandon Becky to the same fate. She had to go and try to save her, even if it was the last thing she ever did.

315

Apart from Becky, Boris was the only real tie she had. But what sort of a rubbish owner had she been to him, particularly in the last couple of weeks? He had spent so much time cooped up in her flat, with just a brief leg-stretch morning and night. He deserved better. She thought of him with a pang of guilt, imagined him pricking up his ears every time he heard a step outside.

Gary could have been a tie, perhaps. Although he had lied to her.

But he could do one more thing for her. She tapped out a quick text to him: *Sorry I rushed off. Going to meet Daniel from CupidsWeb. Got a lead on Becky. Tell no one. But if you haven't heard from me again by . . .* She hesitated. How much time should she allow? *. . . 6 p.m., then call the police.* After thinking about it for a second, she forwarded the message from Daniel too. Then she had another idea. She sent him a second text with her iCloud login, which would give him access to her Find My iPhone app, which was provided by Apple to make it easy to find a lost or stolen iPhone. All you had to do was log in to your Apple iCloud account and you were shown a map that pinpointed the exact location of your iPhone. She'd had to use it once before when she'd lost her phone, and had been able to locate it at a café she'd been in an hour earlier.

For a moment, she considered calling the police, but Daniel's message expressly forbade it. It wasn't worth the risk.

The train pulled into Richmond Station and Amy checked the map on her phone to see which way she needed to walk to get to the car park behind the college.

The time was 12.47.

Walking across the zebra crossing outside the station, it

all felt like a dream to Amy, as if the past week had stretched out into at least a year, people and events moving in and out of focus as if underwater. The only person in sharp focus now was Becky. Amy kept her mind's eye firmly fixed on her.

Her legs began to shake as she could see the car park ahead, but she made sure she walked with just as much purpose. It took a few moments to find the bit of it that backed onto the college – it was round a corner and in a quieter annexe of the car park. She looked around her, but all the stationary cars were empty and silent. There was nobody around. She sat down on a verge, her heart pounding like a jackhammer in her chest. It was 12.54. Gary hadn't replied to her messages yet. She felt sick. If she'd been the praying type, she would have prayed.

At 12.59 a black Range Rover with tinted windows drove slowly into the car park. Amy stood up uncertainly, and gritted her teeth to stop the fear showing on her face. *Think of Becky*, she repeated to herself. She wondered if Daniel would look like his CupidsWeb photographs and she thought again that it was a bit suspicious that he had only had 'private' photos on the site. She had seen them when she logged in as Becky, but not when she first contacted him under her own made-up name, which meant that he had given Becky specific permission to view them. It was a classic ploy by anyone worried about being seen on Internet dating sites, and it usually indicated that they were already spoken for, or nefarious in some other way.

She couldn't see through the tinted windows. She scrunched up her toes in an effort to stop her legs shaking. All her instincts told her to turn and run, but she had to do this, for Becky.

The car pulled up next to her and sat idle for a few

moments, the engine falling silent. The passenger door popped open an inch.

Trembling, she approached it, and pulled the door fully open.

A man – Daniel – sat in the driver's seat, his face turned away so she couldn't see it. All she could tell was that he had brown hair and was about six feet tall.

'Jump in, Amy,' said the man mildly, and she climbed in, pulling the door shut behind her.

'Where's Becky?' she said.

There was an odd, chemical smell in the car, like air freshener mixed with cleaning fluid.

He still had his face turned away from her, though his voice sounded familiar. She wanted to grab him, make him look at her.

But she didn't need to – he swung round and faced her.

'You!' she said, recognizing him but still not being able to place him. 'Where's Daniel?'

He smiled, the cruellest smile she had ever seen, and she instinctively went for the door handle. But he was quicker – the locks clunked shut. The smell intensified and, like a cobra, he struck suddenly and silently, lunging for her face with something white and toxic. Chloroform.

The last thing Amy realized – as the planes circling in a holding stack in the sky above her contracted into tiny, shiny dots, then vanished – was Daniel's true identity. But by then it was far too late.

40

Declan

Friday, 26 July

Declan hurried towards the SIO's office with the photo of Amber Corrigan in one hand and a picture of Becky Coltman in the other. He'd hardly slept, despite his exhaustion, imaginary conversations playing out in his head all night. The first conversation he needed to have was with the SIO, DCI Anthony Fremantle – and here he was, not in his office, but walking purposefully towards the exit.

'Sir,' Declan called.

Fremantle turned his head but kept walking, and Declan hurried to catch up, wishing this fucking sweltering summer would end so he could stop sweating whenever he exerted the slightest bit of energy.

'I need to run something by you, sir,' he said.

'Is this about your cesspit woman?' the SIO replied, still walking.

Declan fell into step beside him. 'Yes. Amber Corrigan. Look at these photos – the picture on the left is a woman called Becky Coltman who was reported missing by her

319

sister last week. The resemblance is startling, don't you think?'

'Hmm. They do seem a little like each other.'

He hadn't stopped to look at the photos properly, and Declan felt like grabbing his elbow and making him stop, telling him that this was more important than whatever meeting he was heading to.

'I think they look like sisters,' he insisted.

'Is that possible?' They turned a corner, the exit only a few metres away now. He needed to be quick.

'No, the Corrigans only had one child. But that's not the point. I don't think they are sisters – but what if the person who murdered Amber is doing the same now? What if he goes after women who look alike – and his latest victim is Becky Coltman?'

'That's quite a leap,' the DCI said. They were at the exit. Declan put his body between Fremantle and the double doors, causing Fremantle to raise a perfectly shaped eyebrow. Perhaps he's off to a male grooming parlour, Declan's brain chirped. He managed to stop himself imagining Fremantle getting a back, sack and crack.

'Maybe. But I want to check it out.'

'Is this other woman one of ours?'

'No. She's from London.'

'And have you spoken to your former colleagues in the Met?'

An officer barged through the double doors as if they weren't even there, almost knocking Declan to one side, allowing the DCI to shuffle past him and grasp the door handle, ready to get away.

'Not yet. I wanted to run it past you first, sir. I want to go up to London, talk to the MISPER coordinator in Camberwell, where Ms Coltman was reported missing.'

He exhaled through his nose. 'Your old station? It seems like a waste of time to me. Give them a call instead. I want you here, not running off to your former stomping ground. OK?'

Declan sighed. 'OK. Sir.'

As soon as he got back to his desk, feeling deflated and faintly embarrassed by the encounter, he called Camberwell, surprised to find that he still knew the number by heart. The phone was answered by an officer he knew from the old days, Simon Fletcher, and they spent a couple of minutes catching up, even though Declan was itching to get past the small talk.

'Who's the MISPER coordinator these days?' he asked, when Simon had finished telling him about how the whole borough – no, world – was going to hell in a handcart.

'Jane Reeves,' he replied.

Declan didn't recognize the name. 'Can you put me through to her?'

'Sure, hang on.' But a short while later, he came back on the line. 'She's away from her desk. I'll get her to call you back.'

Declan hung up, then sat and drummed his fingers gently on his keyboard. Bob was off duty today but he thought about calling him, dragging him away from his family so he could run it all past him, see whether Bob thought he was going insane. Declan trusted his judgement.

Jane Reeves was either having the longest fag break in history or was suffering from a bad case of the squits. Declan called Camberwell station again and was told Reeves was still absent. 'You mean the MISPER coordinator is a MISPER?' Declan asked.

He couldn't bear the tension, so went to grab himself a coffee from the vending machine in the corridor. As he returned to his desk, his phone started ringing and he rushed to snatch it up, spilling a searing hot splash of liquid onto the back of his hand.

'DI Adams.' He was a little out of breath.

It was Jane Reeves.

'Thanks for getting back to me. I'm calling about a MISPER, name of Becky – or Rebecca – Coltman.'

Jane Reeves said, 'Hang on, let me check the system . . . Yes, reported missing by her sister, an Amy Coltman, on 21 July.'

'And can you tell me what progress has been made trying to find her?'

'Hmm. Well, none as far as I can see.'

Declan wanted to reach through the phone and shake the rather bored-sounding Jane Reeves out of her torpor.

'None?'

'No . . . Well, it's been marked as low risk.'

Declan waited in vain for the woman to elaborate then gave up and said, 'Why's that?' It was like dragging information out of a five-year-old. He sucked the back of his stinging hand.

'Because . . . she sent an email to her sister saying that she was going on holiday.' There was a pause while Jane Reeves read the notes on screen. 'But, apparently, the sister was very insistent that it was out of character.'

Declan felt his heart speed up. 'Have you got a transcript of the email there?'

'Yes . . . hold on.'

She read out the email.

Declan doubted if he would ever have another moment like this in his entire police career, this certainty that he had stumbled upon something big; the ordinary man in him going cold inside, but the police officer growing hot with excitement. He felt as if the whole week's events, all his work, had been leading up to this one revelation.

'Wait there,' he ordered. 'Don't hang up.'

He scrabbled on his desk for the Amber Corrigan file, opened it and pulled out the letter Amber had supposedly sent to her parents. He stared at it and said, 'OK, read it to me again.'

Jane Reeves intoned: '*Dear Amy, I'm going away, and I'm not coming back. Don't try to find me. I'm going to Asia, probably. I've always wanted to visit Vietnam and Cambodia. Sorry about our row. It's not your fault. Tell Mum and Dad not to worry. Look after yourself. Love B.*'

Declan read the Amber Corrigan letter to himself.

Dear Mum and Dad, I'm going away, and I'm not coming back. Don't try to find me. I'm going to Brazil . . .

Then she talked about meeting a man who she'd fallen in love with. It ended:

Don't worry. Look after yourselves. Love Amber.

Apart from the middle lines, the wording was identical to the Becky Coltman email.

'Holy shit,' he said.

'Excuse me?' said Jane Reeves.

'I need the name, phone number and address of the sister.'

As soon as he'd disconnected the call, he tried to ring Amy Coltman, but it went immediately to voicemail. Unable to stay seated at his desk, he dashed off to DCI Fremantle's office but he wasn't back yet. He tried Amy's number again. Same result.

'Sod this,' he said, and walked as quickly as he could out of the building and to his car.

It was a two-hour drive from Eastbourne to Amy Coltman's flat in south London. The traffic on the A22 heading up to town was refreshingly light, the woman on the sat nav stayed quiet for most of the journey and Declan turned her off as soon as he hit the South Circular. He knew these roads. Coincidentally, Amy lived just a few streets away from Declan's old flat, which he had sold when he left London. But the similarity between the Corrigan letter and the Coltman email had to be more than a coincidence, especially when you factored in the physical similarity between the two women.

All the way up, Declan couldn't help but wonder: how many more women were there who had vanished in the same way?

How many more victims?

As he reached Camberwell, his shoulder started to throb. It had to be psychosomatic. This was his first visit to the area since he'd cleared out his flat and fled to Sussex, and it wasn't just the weaving, beeping traffic that was making his blood pressure rise. Sitting at a red light, he could have sworn he saw Terry Munson, the toe-rag who had shot him, waiting to cross. But it couldn't be him. He was locked up, hopefully being gang-banged in the showers every day, although knowing him he'd be running his own gang in there, enjoying as good a time as it was possible to have at Her Majesty's pleasure.

By the time Declan reversed into a parking spot outside Amy Coltman's place, waiting a minute for a silver Honda to vacate the space, he had managed to get a grip on himself and his imagination. He rang Amy's bell and heard a dog bark inside, but there was no answer. Brilliant. He tried to call her again, but the phone was still going straight to voicemail.

As he stood on the doorstep, he wondered what his next move should be – go and see his old colleagues at the local station; start following proper procedure? That would be the sensible thing. The proper thing to do. But Declan felt like a man on a mission, reluctant to hand over this case to anyone who would care about it less than him. As well as his desperate urge to find Amber's killer, he now felt a duty towards Becky Coltman too. She was the only person right now who knew the connection between the two women. And there was something else too. When Terry Munson had shot him and he had spent all that time recuperating, fleeing London like a quitter, he had felt useless, a failure. He had lost his self-respect.

This was his chance to put that right. Not just for the women involved, but for himself.

He rang the doorbell again and waited for the dog to stop barking. Amy Coltman clearly wasn't at home. Declan went back to his car and rummaged through his bag until he found a notebook and pen, intending to leave a note for Amy asking her to call him urgently. But as he was writing it, his phone rang.

It was Bob.

'Isn't it your day off?' Declan asked.

Bob grunted. 'Yeah. Isobel is sending daggers through the wall right now. But I've got something that's pretty interesting.'

He stood up straight. 'Go on.'

'So, you know the property-development company that owned the land where Amber was found?'

'JWF.'

'That's the one. Well, I left a message with one of the former owners, the guy who retired to Spain. Jonathan Pye. He just got back to me.'

Declan's pulse accelerated. 'Come on, stop teasing me.'

Bob laughed. 'I'm getting there. Patience is a virtue, you know.'

'And rage is a sin.'

'All right, all right. Keep your hair on. Where was I? Oh, yeah – Pye is one of those old guys with the memory of an elephant. I got the feeling he could have regaled me for hours with tales of all his exciting property developments over the years. Robertson Farm was, according to him, a right pain in the arse. They could never get planning permission from the local council. Red tape, something about NIMBYs in the village not wanting all the extra traffic the hotel would bring. Then, in 1998 – autumn, he thought—'

'Just after Amber's murder.'

'Yes, someone approached them wanting to buy the land. Made a good offer too, according to Pye. But Pye's partner didn't want to sell, was sure they could still get the hotel project off the ground. It had become something of a mission for him, apparently. Anyway, the deal fell through and they were stuck with the farm and then they went bust a few months later – for which Pye blames his partner.'

'OK. And what was the name of the company that wanted to buy the land?' Declan fished a cigarette from its packet and lit up. The air was so still that a cloud of smoke hovered around his head before drifting away slowly.

'Denison Limited.'

'Right.'

'After I got off the phone to Pye, I checked the Companies House website. Because it seemed like quite a coincidence – somebody trying to buy the farm so soon after Amber's murder. I mean, if I was a murderer and had dumped a victim on a piece of land that didn't belong to me, I'd want to try to buy that land too – remove the risk of someone else finding the body. Denison Limited was registered in 1998, just before the application to buy the farm. It never traded – looks like it was a shell company. And there was one director listed.' He paused. 'Name of Lewis Vine.'

Declan threw his cigarette to the pavement. 'Why do I know that name?'

'Because he was at the conference.'

41

Amy

Friday, 26 July

When Amy came round she was lying on her back on a king-size bed, candlelight casting flickering shadows against a wall that seemed to be undulating – or was it just her head spinning? She felt so nauseous that she couldn't tell. The candles were scented, a rich, cloying smell that she could not place. The room was hot, which was fortunate because all she had on was an unfamiliar and very horrible white corset. She had no idea where the rest of her clothes were, or her handbag and phone.

The man who had drugged her was Lewis Vine, Gary's friend, the social-networking expert. Lewis Vine, whose name was on the Orchid Blue party list.

So it was Lewis Vine who had Becky. She shivered. She had sat with him in a restaurant, listened to him give her advice about how to find Becky. But where was she? What had Lewis done with Daniel? Nothing made sense.

The bed was covered with a satin quilt that felt slippery under her cold skin. There were pillows behind her to prop

328

her up. Her arms were outstretched and handcuffed to the corners of the metal headboard, and they ached like hell. There were no windows in the room so she had no idea whether it was night or day. Was this what Becky was enduring too? For one confused moment, Amy thought she *was* Becky.

A movement made her jump – the sound of a key being turned in the lock and the door opening. Lewis walked in. Amy sat up as far as she could, trying to conceal her terror with belligerence.

'What's going on? Where's Becky? Why have you tied me up? Where's Daniel? I was supposed to be meeting Daniel, not you. What do you want?'

'That's a lot of questions, Amy. I'm the one who's going to be asking the questions, so just shut up, all right? There's a good girl.'

He sounded jokey, but his eyes were like flint as they roved up and down her body, critically but approvingly, examining her as though she was a carcass hanging from a meat hook. Perhaps she soon would be. His manner was completely different to when she had met him at Waterloo, when she had thought he was a marketing-obsessed businessman. He had been wearing a wedding ring then, she remembered. He wasn't wearing it now.

'Please tell me where Becky is,' she persisted. 'Please.'

A look of boredom flashed across his features, and he shrugged. 'How would I know?'

'I don't believe you. You've got her too, haven't you? You sent the email to me. But you fucked up . . . You didn't know she'd been to Cambodia before. You won't get away with it, you know that, don't you?' She rattled the handcuffs with her wrists in frustration. 'You made out that you didn't know her – you pretended to help me. But you knew her all along. Did you know she was Gary's neighbour?'

Lewis smirked. 'That was a surprise, I have to say.'

'And then he asked you to help me find her.'

'Yes. When I found out Becky had a sister . . . well, I had to meet you. And you are even more beautiful than her.'

Sweet Jesus, Amy thought. Gary had unwittingly sent her into the path of the man who had already taken her sister.

Lewis changed the subject. 'I thought you might want to use the bathroom – here, let me.' He approached her and Amy shrank away from him as he bent over her with a key, undoing the set of handcuffs that tethered her left hand. Amy's mind went into overdrive – should she try to gouge his eyes out? Punch him in the throat? Then she saw what was in his other hand: a pistol-shaped object in black and yellow, with a large square muzzle, like a big ugly toy.

'It's a Taser gun,' he said casually, aiming it at her. 'And I will use it on you if you do anything stupid.' As if in response, the gun crackled, like a massive, menacing wasp. When her arms were freed she let them drop meekly to her sides.

'Over there,' he said, helping her off the bed and towards a different door. 'Do a bit of exercise while you're up, too – you know, get the blood flowing again.'

She glared at him and went into the bathroom on unsteady legs, closing the door behind her, looking wildly around her. No lock, of course. No mirror that she could smash. No window, no towels. For a moment, she was taken back to the night she had spent locked in the bathroom by Nathan, and bile rose in her throat. She gritted her teeth. Either all men really were bastards, or she and Becky were the unluckiest women alive.

If Becky even *was* still alive.

Amy did need to pee, badly. She went over to the toilet but could not work out how the corset undid. With her still-numb fingers, she fiddled with the poppers on the crotch, feeling even more nauseous to think that Lewis must have put her into it when she was unconscious. His fingers would have brushed against her pubic hair. Her breasts didn't properly fit into the cups of the corset either, implying that he had stuffed her into it. She managed to sit and pee, but then had to turn straight round and vomit into the bowl, unable to shake the thought of Lewis undressing her. Was he going to rape her? What was wrong with her, that men seemed to think they could do exactly what they wanted with her? The only man who had helped her recently was Gary, and she had rejected him.

Amy did up the corset again, rinsed out her mouth under the tap and took a long drink of water. It went against every instinct she had, to open the door and walk back out there to Lewis and his Taser, but she knew she had to.

'Good girl,' he said appraisingly when she returned, and gestured to the bed. 'Up you get.'

He was treating her like a puppy, she thought, allowing him to handcuff her again. She decided that all she could do was to go along with it.

For now.

Oh, please God, she thought, let Gary have got her text.

'Why did you help me with the social-networking stuff when it could have helped me find her?' she asked.

He raised an eyebrow and she answered her own question. 'Because you knew it wouldn't do any good. That no one would have seen her or would know what had happened to her. Please, tell me where Becky is. You promised – in the message you sent me.'

He stepped back from the bed, appraising her. 'The message Daniel sent you.'

'But you *are* Daniel.'

His lips twitched. 'I was Daniel, yes. And Becky loved Daniel.' He leaned closer to Amy until his nose was just two inches from hers. His breath smelled of cloves. 'But that's the thing, Amy. You have to be very careful about people you meet online. They're not always what they seem.'

42

Becky

Sunday, 21 July

My first reaction is utter confusion. I feel like a baby who goes to sleep in his pushchair at home and wakes up at the cheese counter in the metal seat of a supermarket trolley, blinking at the bright lights.

How can I be here? My packed suitcase is sitting across the concrete floor of the garage looking reproachfully at me. So . . . that meant I *had* gone away for that weekend, or at least had tried to. I'm sure we were meant to be going away together . . . As my woolly head slowly clears, I try to think through the options. Some kind of delay? Was I in danger, and he brought me here to get me out of the way . . . of what? A terrorist attack? The dirty bomb I've had nightmares about for years? Are we safe here? Where is he? I try to stand up but I can't, and I don't immediately understand why until I realize I can't move my arms or my legs – they are tied to the chair I'm sitting on. The corners of my lips feel strange and stretchy, and that's when I clock that I've been gagged, too.

It's dark in here apart from one small standard lamp, and cold even though there are chinks of sunlight coming in under the up-and-over metal door. I am wearing an unfamiliar thick jumper – a Guernsey, I think. That sort of heavy, oily wool. I don't know whose it is but I'm grateful for it. I can't feel my feet.

I can't begin to think about the implications of being tied to a chair and gagged. I've been *kidnapped*!

It's got to be a bad dream. Panic starts to ferment inside me and I begin to thrash about, moaning through the gag. The chair starts rocking, harder and harder – then I fall, sideways, and my head must have cracked on the concrete floor because the lights go out again.

Next time I wake up, I'm not alone any more. He's here! Someone has come for me! He's standing over me and the sharp smell of antiseptic fills my nostrils. This time my head isn't just woolly, it's pounding, and I think I'm going to vomit. But he's here! *Oh, thank God*, I try to say, *thank God it's you, get me out of here!* But it comes out as *Mmmnh mmmnh mmmmnh*. He dabs at a very sore lump on my forehead with some extremely cold sodden cotton wool, but he doesn't attempt to remove my gag or untie me. I entreat him with my eyes, then frown and shake my head – the pain nearly makes me throw up. He's refusing to meet my eyes! Why isn't he untying me? Why?

When he speaks, his voice seems to come from a very long way away, streaming into my ear like the sun's rays under the door, oozing out of the cement between its breezeblock walls. 'I'm sorry, Becky,' he says. He still won't look at me. 'Try not to panic. You won't be here for ever. It's for your own good. Trust me.'

334

43

Declan

Friday, 26 July

'Have you got an address for Lewis Vine?' Declan asked.

'Yes, hang on . . . He lives in a place called Claygate, in Surrey. He's actually a well-known businessman. I Googled him – he's a millionaire several times over. We should go up tomorrow, pay him a visit.' Because Sussex and Surrey shared a major-crime investigation team, there would be no problem with worrying about whose jurisdiction it fell under.

'I can go and see him now,' Declan said. 'I'm in London. It shouldn't take me long to get there – only about half an hour. I think it's near Esher.'

'Sir, I really don't think you should go on your own.'

He thought about it. The murder was fifteen years ago, and although there was no statute of limitations on murder, if Vine was Amber's killer, he would probably think that he'd got away with it. He wouldn't be sitting at home waiting for the police to call. Declan tried to imagine how he would feel in his situation: the attempt to buy the property was a logical move. If he owned the farm, he could move the body, or fill the cesspit with cement, make sure the remains were never found. He would probably have panicked when the sale fell through, especially as his name was now linked with the property. But as time had gone by and nothing had happened, he must have felt increasingly safer.

If Declan turned up now, Vine wouldn't immediately think it was in connection with Amber and his guard would not be up. He ought to go back to Eastbourne, talk to the SIO and the rest of the team. But the moment Vine was alerted to the investigation, he would hire a lawyer. As a millionaire, he would be able to afford a top defence lawyer – who would no doubt argue that all they had was circumstantial evidence. There was no forensic evidence against him, no witnesses. There was a strong possibility he would get away with it.

And Declan had made a promise to Amber that he didn't intend to break.

If he surprised Vine, caught him unawares, he would be able to see how he acted when a police detective came to his door. He would be able to get some measure of him, maybe get him to say or do something incriminating.

'I'm going to go and talk to him now,' he said, explaining his reasons to Bob.

'Let me drive up,' he said. 'Come with you.'

'No. That would take ages. I want to go there now.'

He sighed. 'Just be careful.'

'I will. Listen, I'll call you back in a minute. Can you go online, get some more information about Vine? Thanks.'

If he had been lucky on the way up, with clear roads and a lack of roadworks, he was now paying the price. It was gridlock all the way out of town, but at least the slow-moving traffic gave him a chance to get his thoughts together and prepare for his encounter with Vine.

Ten minutes into the journey, he called Bob using the hands-free kit on his phone.

'I'm really sorry to do this to you on your day off. Can you talk me through what you found out?'

'It's OK. Although we could have picked a better day for it. Isobel wants to try for another baby and today's the day. She's in bed reading *Fifty Shades of Grey* and getting in the mood. I hope she doesn't want to try anything too scary.'

Declan couldn't help but smile.

'OK,' Bob continued. 'Here's Lewis Vine's *Wikipedia* page. Hmmm . . . Dotcom millionaire, born 12 February 1974. Grew up in north London, raised by a single mother. He didn't go to university – apparently, he caused some minor controversy by saying that uni is a waste of time. He set up his first dotcom business in 1997, a games site called SilverJoystick.com. Then he expanded into gambling – had one of the first British poker sites. Wow.'

'What is it?'

'He sold them both in January 2000 for six million quid. Just before the bubble burst. Clever bastard – cashed in just in time. Then he seemed to disappear for a little while before setting up BulletProofClub.com in 2003. He sold that a few years later after it became the UK's biggest life-style site for men. He hasn't given any interviews for years, apparently, but he now works as a consultant.'

OK, so he was a good businessman. Declan knew that already.

'What about his personal life?'

He watched the cars rush past on the opposite side of the road, every one of them well over the 50-mph limit.

'Hold on. Nothing about him being married or having any kids. He seems to keep a pretty low profile. Hmm, we need to check if he's got a record.'

'Can you do that urgently?'

'As soon as I've put the phone down. Isobel's going to be looking for someone else to fertilize her . . . Right, there's a link here to an interview with him on *Forbes*, from 2002. Let's see if there's anything interesting on there.'

Declan waited while Bob clicked and skim-read the article. 'This is quite interesting. Apparently, his mother died when he was fifteen, a few days before his sixteenth birthday. She committed suicide. He says he looked after himself from that point – I guess he must have turned sixteen and avoided the care system – and in this interview, he says that he's been independent and driven from that point on. The interviewer asks him if he's got a special woman in his life now and he refuses to answer. Doesn't seem to be anything else interesting about him.'

'Thanks, Bob. I'll let you get back to Isobel now. After you've checked if Vine has a record.'

'Yeah, all this stuff about dotcom millionaires and suicidal mothers has, like, really got me in the mood.'

'Take care, Bob. I'll talk to you later.' He hung up.

So Vine was a loner with no family, driven to succeed after his mum killed herself. Declan had learned that a lot of successful businessmen had psychopathic tendencies because it made them ruthless, able to make hard decisions that other people might balk at. Was Lewis Vine one of those people? Of course, only a fraction of psychopaths actually murder people. But so far, nothing he had learned about him had made him think he was anything less than his prime suspect.

He passed the sign for Claygate, turned off the A3 and

soon found himself on a quiet country road. After five minutes, he pulled up outside a huge house in a secluded spot on a quiet lane. Mock-Tudor, Declan decided, and enormous, with gables and surely too many chimneys. It must have easily been worth four million. The house was set a long way back from the road, which had no pedestrian traffic. A secluded spot, far from prying eyes.

He got out of the car and walked up to the stable gate that blocked the entrance of the circular drive.

He could hear banging and someone shouting so he pushed open the gate and hurried up the drive. As the front of the house came into view, he saw a man standing by the front door, banging on it and shouting, '*Lewis!*'

Declan walked as quickly as he could, his shoes crunching on the path, making the man turn round. He was tall and annoyingly good-looking, though his eyes were wide with anxiety.

Declan wished he'd got Bob to text him a photo of Vine, but this obviously wasn't him, unless he was calling his own name.

'What's going on?' he asked.

The man looked him up and down. 'Who are you? Neighbourhood Watch?'

Declan flashed his warrant card. 'Police. Can I take your name?'

'It's Gary Davidson. I was just about to call your lot when—'

He was interrupted by a noise from inside the house. A scream.

339

44

Amy

Friday, 26 July

As Lewis went to fasten her to the bed again, Amy said, 'I need to go to the bathroom again.'

'What? You've just been.'

'I know. But I couldn't go. I was too scared.'

He stroked her cheek. 'You don't need to be afraid, Amy. I'm going to take care of you.'

She shuddered at his touch but was relieved when he gestured towards the bathroom door. She scurried through. She didn't really need to pee. She wanted to delay the moment when he put the cuffs on her as long as possible. She needed space to think.

How the hell was she going to get out of here?

Once again, he looked around the bathroom, taking in everything, looking for a crumbling brick, something she could use as a weapon. There was nothing. Just the toilet and the sink – both sturdy and solid. She rattled the loo seat, wondering if she could get it off so she could attempt to hit Lewis with it, but it was firmly attached. Could she try to scald him with hot water from the tap? No, she had nothing to transport it in.

Then she noticed, set high in the wall, a small vent. Looking over her shoulder, nervous that Lewis would open the door at any moment, she lowered the toilet lid and stood on it, reaching up. But the vent was still six inches beyond her reach, and it didn't look as if it would open anyway, even if she could somehow get to it.

As she stood on the toilet, a wave of fresh fear crashed over her. She was stuck here with a madman. There was no way out. Her only hope was that Gary had got her message and had managed to use the Find My iPhone app, or that some other passer-by might come miraculously to her aid.

She screamed as loudly as she could, aiming the blast in the direction of the vent.

Lewis rushed into the room, swearing, and grabbed her, pulling her roughly off the toilet and through the door. He pushed her onto the bed.

'There's no one around,' he said, a little out of breath. 'No neighbours. No one ever walks past this house. But if you do that again, I'll be forced to hurt you.' He grabbed her left wrist and cuffed it to the bedpost, then her right.

'OK?'

She turned her face away.

Lewis returned later, unlocking the door and backing in, carrying a small card table that he set down on the floor at the foot of the bed. He smiled coldly at her then went out and fetched two ladderback chairs, which he set up on either side of the table. On his next trip, he came in carrying a red-and-white-checked tablecloth, which he lay across the table, and a tray on which were two small stainless-steel plate covers, crystal wineglasses and a bottle of wine. He set these on top of the cloth. Finally, he moved one of the candles from beside the bed onto the table.

Then he walked back across the room towards Amy.

'Let me go, Lewis,' she said, trying to stop her voice wobbling. 'This has gone on long enough.'

The room was so dim that Amy could hardly see his face, but she heard him breathing: quick, shallow breaths. He said something, so quietly that she couldn't make it out.

'I can't understand you.'

He took a step closer to the bed and Amy saw that he was wearing a cheap suit that looked two sizes too small for him. Weird, she thought. When she met him before he had been dressed sharply.

'I said, "You're beautiful."'

He came closer still and Amy had to remind herself to breathe, as though his fast breaths were using up her own allowance of air.

'So beautiful.'

She tried to smile at him, to make some connection. 'Why . . .?' Her mouth was so dry, her tongue felt like a slug that had been drenched in salt. Must be the aftereffects of the chloroform, she thought. 'Why don't you unfasten the cuffs? My arms really hurt.'

He sat down on the corner of the bed, reeking of aftershave, as if he had tipped a bottle over himself. 'That's exactly what I plan to do, Amy.'

He reached out and touched the inside of her thigh. His palm was rough and dry and she pulled up her legs, trying to squirm away from him, but the quilt was so smooth she couldn't get any purchase on it and she slipped, the cuffs pulling her arms, tugging at the sockets.

Shaking his head slightly, he took the key from his pocket again and unfastened the handcuffs from her wrists, left then right. Amy immediately crossed her arms over her chest, rubbing her upper arms, trying to massage away the cramps. He reached across her and she shrank away, but he grabbed hold of her hand and tugged her.

Amy looked over at the door, wondering if she could hit him this time, push him over, make a break for it. But her arms were so sore and weak, and he had locked the door again, the key in his pocket.

He sat her down at the table and pulled up the opposite chair. He smiled at her, that same sick, queasy smile that was as cold as the Arctic. There was a CD player in the room and he picked up the remote control and pressed Play, filling the room with cheesy eighties music.

He opened the bottle of red wine and poured two glasses. He took a sip from his glass, then lifted the other glass and put it to Amy's lips. She drank. The wine was thick, bloody, probably very expensive, but her taste buds felt shot from the chloroform and the fear. She gulped down a mouthful but it didn't quench her thirst. Maybe it would help numb the pain, she thought.

He suddenly snatched the glass from her and threw it across the room. Amy heard it smash against the wall behind her. Then he grabbed her by the throat.

'You swallowed.'

'What?' She could hardly speak. Hardly breathe. But he wasn't squeezing, didn't appear to be trying to strangle her. Not yet.

'You weren't supposed to swallow.'

'I don't understand.'

He removed his hand from her throat and his voice

changed, became gentle. He stroked her cheek with a finger. 'Let me show you, sweetheart.'

Sweetheart.

He lifted his own glass and took a gulp, keeping the liquid in his mouth. Then he leaned forward and pressed his lips against hers. Amy kept her mouth shut at first, but he jabbed her beneath the table in her churning stomach with his fingers, hard, and her lips opened involuntarily.

The warm wine poured from his mouth into hers.

She wanted to spit it out, to spit it in his face, but she forced herself to swallow. Another cold wave of nausea rolled through her and she had to stop herself from puking.

'That's the way. Delicious?' he said, pulling away.

Amy nodded, her stomach roiling, tears rolling down her cheeks.

He set aside the glass and studied her. 'So like your sister. Beautiful – except for *that*.'

He looked down at her tummy and she pulled it in, as though trying to make it disappear. What was wrong with her stomach? Her skin was covered with goose bumps, even though it was so hot in the room. He moved around the table and crouched beside her chair, thrusting his hand with difficulty down the front of the sheer corset until he grasped between his finger and thumb her gold belly bar, the little star with the tiny diamond that usually made her feel so sexy. So that was what he had seen through the fabric, seen and disapproved of. Glancing down, Amy thought his hand looked like an alien moving under the front of the corset, or a child rummaging in a Christmas stocking. She braced herself for him to move his hand further down, between her legs.

'I don't like this,' he said. He seemed to be talking to himself. 'You shouldn't have this.'

344

With sudden force, he ripped it out.

Amy screamed. The pain was searing, making her vision flash white. Blood poured from the hole he'd made, staining the front of the white corset crimson. She could not prevent herself sobbing.

He stood up. 'Shut up!' he shouted in her face.

She realized she couldn't stop. Not this time.

'Shut the fuck up!'

He stomped away across the room, shouting, 'You're ruining it. Shut up!'

Amy looked down, trying to see the damage, trying to be quiet. She sniffed back snot, the taste of his saliva and the wine in her mouth, a great throbbing pain in her belly. Blood blossoming across the corset as though she had been shot in the stomach.

'Nathan, don't!' she cried, without realizing what she'd said. He stiffened. '*Nathan?* You don't even have the courtesy to call me by my right name?'

He came back across the room again, into the candlelight. His face was twisting with tension, as if he was trying to control his anger. He was breathing quickly, loudly, completely different to the suave, controlled man she had met for coffee.

Eventually, he sat back down. Amy's stomach was throbbing with pain, blood oozing thickly through the silk corset like porridge through a sieve. He noticed and handed her a napkin.

'I forgive you,' he said. Then his face twisted into that strange, cold smile again. There was excitement there, but no warmth. 'I have something for you.'

He went over to the corner of the room, picked up what looked like a suit carrier and unzipped it, producing a dress. Black velvet. He brought it over to Amy, draping it across two hands as if it was the finest fur. It stank, not of mothballs, but of body odour and dust, as though it hadn't been washed for years. In the half-light, Amy was sure she could see some kind of revolting crispy white stain on the hem.

'Put it on,' he ordered.

Despite the stench and the heat in the room, Amy was relieved to put something else on, to cover herself. She moved slowly to try to manage the pain in her gut, wincing when the dress came into contact with the wound.

When he saw her in the dress his pupils dilated and his breathing changed. He was aroused.

Fear spiralled up inside Amy. He hadn't yet done anything to her sexually – but now he was definitely aroused. She wrapped her arms around her breasts.

'Sit down.'

So maybe he wasn't going to rape her. Yet.

He pushed a bowl towards her. Prawn cocktail. It stank even worse than the dress, making her stomach flip over. It took all her self-control not to vomit.

'Tuck in,' he said, and she lifted the spoon, her whole arm shaking.

'I love you,' he said, and her head jerked up with shock. There was something experimental about the way he said it, as though he was trying the words on for size. Was he some inadequate creep who couldn't get a woman? It seemed so odd, from what she remembered of meeting him before. He'd seemed so harmless then, and now it was as though several layers had been stripped away, leaving his ugly psycho self, exposed for her to see. The word *alien* came to her mind again.

He was looking expectantly at her and she thought, *No, surely not* . . . He wanted her to say it back?

Nathan's bullying tactics suddenly faded into insignificance in the face of this pure insanity.

Stalling for time, she took another mouthful of the prawn cocktail, forcing herself to block out the fishy smell and swallow the food, to try to keep some strength in her body.

'I love you,' he repeated insistently, not taking his eyes off her for a second. She dug into the bowl and took another, bigger mouthful. Then she paused, pretending to think, and leaned in towards him as if for a kiss. She made out that she was chewing the prawns and then, with all the force she could muster, spat them out, right into his face.

'You fucking psychopath,' she screamed, jumping up and throwing the table over before she had time to think about the wisdom of what she was doing. 'Let me go! LET ME GO! LET ME GO! LET ME GO!' Her voice raised in pitch and volume until she was screaming the words over and over at the top of her lungs, even though it made blood pump out of her bellybutton and she felt that she was going to explode in a red haze of panic and pain.

45

Declan

Friday, 26 July

Declan took a step back as Gary hammered on the door, yelling Amy's name. The scream had undoubtedly come from within the house – deep in the house, from the volume of the cry. But there was no doubt: it had been a woman's scream.

'Hold on,' he said. 'You think *Amy* Coltman is in there? Not Becky Coltman?'

Gary turned and stared at him as if he wasn't really seeing the other man, his eyes wild with panic. 'Yes, Amy has been trying to find Becky and figured out that she went to this high-class sex party . . .' He broke off, staring up at the windows.

'And?'

'She came to see me at work but rushed off before we could talk. She dropped this list –' he pulled a sheet of crumpled paper from his pocket and waved it in his direction – 'and when I looked at it, I saw what she must have seen: Lewis's name.'

'You know Lewis Vine?'

'Yeah, he's a friend. Amy's met him. But he never . . . he never told me he went to that sex party, even though he knew we were looking for Becky. Amy texted me to say she was meeting up with Daniel, who was one of the men Becky went on a date with, and she also sent me her Find My iPhone details so that I could trace her. It led me here.'

'Hang on, what's Find My iPhone?'

Gary explained. 'I couldn't believe it when the dot on the map showed the iPhone was here, at Lewis's. The only explanation I can think of is that Lewis and Daniel must be the same person.'

Gary banged on the door again while Declan went up to the front window to try to look in, but the curtains were drawn tight despite it being late afternoon. Taking a few steps back, he saw that the upstairs windows were also heavily curtained.

'Oh, God,' Gary was saying. 'Amy. What's he doing to her?'

Before Declan could say anything else, Gary dashed away, heading towards the right-hand corner of the house. Declan had no choice but to follow, jogging after him.

They followed a path along the side of the huge house, both of them scanning the wall for a way in. But there was nothing but a sealed wooden door and more windows, all with their curtains pulled so tightly closed that not a chink of daylight would have penetrated the interior. The screams had ceased, which made Declan even more fearful about the fate of the woman inside. Gary sprinted off ahead of him again, and Declan ran after him until they reached the back of the house.

A vast, neat lawn stretched out ahead of them, and a small cluster of buildings stood nearby – a summerhouse, a little

349

shed, and what looked like a converted stable. In other circumstances, it would have seemed idyllic, peaceful, but now the silence was eerie. He couldn't even hear any birdsong, just the faint sound of cars passing in the distance. Adrenaline had rushed through his body so rapidly that he was dizzy, but the constant throbbing in his shoulder had gone.

Gary stood by some French windows, rattling the handle, but they wouldn't open.

'The key's in the lock,' Declan pointed out.

Gary looked around and, as Declan took out his phone, ran off to the shed. As he kicked at the shed door, Declan called for backup, giving his location and briefly explaining the situation. Claygate was the kind of place with just one full-time police officer plus a couple of PCSOs – police community support officers – with the nearest station two miles away in Esher. As he disconnected the call, Declan watched Gary kick open the shed door then emerge a few moments later holding a spade.

He marched up to the French windows and lifted the spade above his head.

'No,' Declan ordered, trying to grab the shaft of the spade. 'I've called for backup. They'll be here soon.'

Gary shook his head, but lowered the spade. 'Soon is too long. He could be killing her *right now*.'

He pushed past Declan and rammed the head of the spade into the glass pane immediately next to the door handle, reaching through to turn the key. As he pulled his hand out, it caught on a jagged piece of glass that cut deep into his skin. Blood sprang from the wound, trickling over his wrist and up his forearm, but he didn't seem to care. He pushed open the door and they entered the house. Declan hoped Gary hadn't hit a vein, though it would serve the stupid sod right if he had.

Gary moved fast, striding through what Declan believed would be called a summer sitting room, with a strange mixture of antique and IKEA furniture, and cardboard boxes piled in the corners as if the owner had got bored halfway through unpacking. He caught Gary's arm.

'Be careful.' He wasn't sure why he was whispering – all the banging and smashing of glass had probably sent Vine running through the front door, if he had any sense.

Gary slowly pulled open the door, the spade held aloft in his other hand. He peered through into a long hallway. It was dark, but some sunlight had followed them into the house through a fanlight over the front door, illuminating half a dozen erotic photographs on the wall – naked women, all blondes, each with a similar look to Amber and the Coltman sisters.

'Where the fuck is he?' Gary said.

They crept along the hallway, listening at the two doors they passed. No sound. Gary opened one while Declan tried the other. Two completely empty rooms with closed curtains.

The hallway led into an entrance hall, with a staircase that wound up to the first floor.

Declan called up the stairs: 'Police.' But unsurprisingly, there was no response. He opened the front door and left it standing open, so when backup arrived it would be easy for them to get into the house. It would also mean it would be easy for Declan and Gary to get out if they needed to.

Gary went up the stairs and Declan followed, their footsteps silent on the thick plush carpet. He felt foolish, with Gary leading the way everywhere, and deliberately overtook him as they reached the top of the staircase. More drawn curtains. More erotic pictures on the walls. A woman being eaten by a crocodile. But apart from the images, the house had the air of a place that wasn't really lived in. This huge house should be a home to a big family, kids and dogs running about. At the very least, a Hugh Hefner-style mansion. But it felt like an empty, unloved gallery. It seemed hard to believe that a scream had rung out from here earlier. There was no sign of life – or recent life – at all.

Declan and Gary explored the first floor, opening doors and peering into rooms.

'There's no one here,' Gary said.

Declan began to speak but Gary looked over his shoulder and edged round him, jogging back down the stairs. Declan followed him, round the edge of the staircase, until they reached another set of stairs – stairs that led down.

'We should wait for backup,' Declan said again, quietly.

But Gary ignored him and Declan followed; he knew that he would have gone down there himself anyway. Who knew how long backup would take to arrive?

Once at the bottom of the tiled stairs – no plush carpet here – it was as if they had left the house and entered another building entirely, as the space opened out around them. It was much more than a basement, more like a bunker. The acoustics felt completely different, as though the subterranean ions had rearranged themselves into new formations. The corridor stretched ahead of them for thirty or forty metres. Opening the nearest door, Declan found himself looking at a narrow swimming pool. He stepped into the room and stared at the still turquoise water shimmering beneath bright spotlights.

Gary was already striding down the corridor, banging on doors, leaving small blood splashes in his wake.

'Lewis,' he shouted. 'Where the fuck are you, you freak? Where's Amy?'

At the end of the corridor, Declan could see an open door. Gary paused – he must have noticed it too – before walking towards it, the spade raised. There was music coming from the room, something from the eighties that Declan hated. Hurrying after Gary, he glanced at his phone. No signal. Shit. He knew he should turn back, go upstairs and wait for the other officers to arrive, but he was compelled to go on, to look into the room.

Gary stood there, looking around with horror. A small table lay on its side, a half-eaten meal scattered around it, and there was a bed in the corner with handcuffs attached to the metal headboard. Aside from the luxurious-looking satin bedclothes, it looked like a prison cell, or the kind of room you'd find in a nuclear shelter.

'Look,' said Gary, pointing to the floor near the upturned table. Blood. It was dripping off the bed, spreading out in a small but viscous pool around a dirty discarded plate.

From the other end of the long, silent corridor, a door slammed shut.

46

Amy

Friday, 26 July

Amy screamed in Lewis's face, drawing on all the anger and desperation inside her and channelling it into that cry, a cry that contained all the pain she'd felt since Becky had disappeared – no, before that, since the horror-days with Nathan. Years of locking down her emotions, of bottling it all up inside her, of being nice, strong, normal Amy – she hit Lewis with it now, this primal scream that bounced off the walls of her cell and caused something to start banging above their heads, an insistent *thump thump thump* that Amy barely registered as she let Lewis have it, have it all.

He grabbed her by the throat and squeezed hard, trapping the scream inside her.

'Shut up,' he yelled. 'Shut . . .'

He stopped dead, looking up towards the ceiling, noticing the banging from above and letting go of Amy's throat, sending her stumbling backwards until her shoulder blades hit the wall in two painful spikes.

As she coughed and tried to get her breath back, rubbing

at her windpipe and wiping her eyes with the back of her hand, she looked around for a weapon, but before she could focus on anything, he grabbed her wrist and pulled her over to the door, deftly stepping around the small puddle of blood on the floor from where he'd ripped open her bellybutton.

He dragged her down the corridor, hissing at her to stop struggling, his grip on her wrist so strong that she pictured the bones inside snapping. The banging from upstairs had stopped and she wanted to scream again, 'Come back, don't go . . . I'm here,' but before she could gather enough breath, Lewis opened a door at the end of the corridor, close to steps that must lead up to the house, and shoved her inside.

It was a galley kitchen, like one you might find in a small fast-food restaurant, stainless-steel surfaces gleaming dully beneath a fluorescent strip light, the stench of the food he'd served her hanging in the air.

He pushed her up against one of the worktops, grabbed a knife from a block that stood on the surface and pointed it at her face. 'Make a noise and I'll cut your tongue out.'

Over his shoulder, she could see the other knives in the block. If she could distract him, get past him, she could get hold of one and . . .

He noticed her looking and a thin smile appeared on his face.

'Stop looking at those or I'll cut your eyes out too.' He reached behind him and moved the block of knives into a cupboard above his head. She wondered where the Taser gun was and realized, with some relief, that he must have left it in the room he'd just made her leave.

'Want to threaten any more of my body parts?' she asked, her mouth so dry the words came out half formed.

'Don't tempt me, Amy.'

'Why are you doing this?' she said. She was praying that the banging at the door was the police. 'Maybe we can talk, you can make me understand. Maybe we could go out for dinner properly sometime. That would be nice.'

He sneered at her. 'You're not The One.'

'What do you mean?'

'You wouldn't understand. I thought you might, but you don't. You're not who I thought you would be.' He wouldn't meet her eye and, even though he was holding a knife to her throat, he struck her as vulnerable – a pathetic and awkward man with a whine in his voice, a million miles from the wealthy-businessman image he portrayed to the outside world. 'I should never have compromised.'

He looked at her now, his face twisted with contempt. 'You're not all you're cracked up to be.'

She was bewildered. What the hell was he talking about? She opened her mouth to ask him but heard a noise overhead. It sounded, faintly, like something smashing.

'Shit.' Lewis slid open a drawer and took out a miniature remote control, which he pointed at a TV unit mounted above their heads.

The screen flickered to life and Amy realized it was an interior view of the house. Lewis pressed a button a few times, the scene on the screen changing from room to room until it showed what looked like the entrance hall behind the front door. Two people walked into view. A man with black hair, and—

'Gary!' she exclaimed, her delight quickly turning to fear. Gary was walking into danger. Just like she had.

'Your fucking boyfriend. Did you tell him you were coming here? I warned you not to.'

'No, I swear, I—'

'Whatever. Looks like he's brought a friend with him. Who is he?'

On the screen, they watched as Gary and the other man went up the stairs, then came back and disappeared through a door. They're coming down here to the basement, Amy thought. Lewis's reaction told her she was right. He grabbed her arm and turned her round, clamping his hand over her mouth and holding the knife lengthwise against her neck.

He pressed the remote again and they watched as the two men walked along the corridor, right past the room they were in now. Amy longed to scream, but Lewis clamped his hand more firmly over her mouth. What would he do if I bit him? she wondered. She could smell the bitter scent of the skin on his hands, but couldn't open her mouth to get it between her teeth.

As soon as Gary and the other man entered the cell she'd been kept in, Lewis opened the kitchen door and pulled her out, accidentally letting the door slam behind him. He quickly pulled Amy into another room and she found herself staring at a long swimming pool.

Oh, God, he's going to drown me, she thought, pulling against him, but he pulled back harder, dragging her past the pool and behind a screen, then into a changing room where a bank of lockers stood. It was as if he'd had the place done out to look like a school locker room. She didn't have time to speculate further, as he took out a key and opened one of the lockers, from which he produced another key.

He pulled back a plastic curtain to reveal another door. He opened it with the key he'd taken from the locker and pushed her through.

More steps, leading down.

'Move it,' Lewis hissed, locking the door behind them

then forcing her to descend the staircase until she came out into some kind of antechamber.

Entering the room behind her, he switched on the light, and Amy was momentarily thrown by what she saw. Expecting some dark dingy basement full of cobwebs, or a torture chamber, instead, the room looked like a small flat and she was standing in the living room. A tatty brown sofa stood in the corner, next to a dining table with two chairs. The wallpaper was maroon, with a pattern of white flowers and a painting of a crying boy hung on the wall, next to another picture of a clown, on a black velvet background. On a sideboard along one wall stood a silver Aiwa stereo system with a double cassette, just like one Amy had owned when she was a young teenager, with the lid of the turntable standing open. The TV looked ancient, too, and was connected to a VCR. A few videos were scattered in front of it on the threadbare carpet: *Dirty Dancing*, *Fatal Attraction*, *The Breakfast Club*.

Above the sofa hung a huge framed photograph of a blonde woman with a little boy, the kind of portrait Amy and Becky had posed for with their parents when they were kids. The woman had a Princess Diana hairdo and was wearing a velvet dress, and the boy – who was undoubtedly Lewis – was wearing a child's suit, an awkward smile on his face. With shock, Amy realized two things at once: first, the dress was the same one she herself was wearing now; and second, apart from the hairdo, the woman in the photo had a startling resemblance to Becky – and to Amy, too.

Lewis noticed her staring at the photo.

'Beautiful, wasn't she?' he said quietly.

'Your . . . mother?' Amy asked.

He nodded. 'The perfect woman. In every way.' His whole manner had changed, become softer, more relaxed, despite everything that was going on, the fact that – whatever happened – surely, Gary would bring the police here soon. It was as if Lewis didn't care about that now – a realization that chilled Amy to her core.

'What happened to her? Your mum?' she asked.

'She left me all alone,' he said.

'I'm sorry . . .'

'When I was fifteen. A few days before my sixteenth birthday.' He sat down on the sofa, a spring audibly twanging beneath him, leaned back, gesticulating with the knife as he spoke. 'She killed herself. Sat in the bath and slit her wrists. Did it the right way too, up the arms not across.' He traced a line up the inside of his forearm with the knife.

Amy waited for him to continue. 'She promised we'd be together for ever.' His eyes narrowed. 'But she lied.'

He fixed his gaze on Amy. 'Every woman lets me down. Every woman I've ever met. Do you know how long I've been searching for The One, Amy? I thought it was Becky, then you—' She tried to speak but he talked over her. 'So many women over the years.'

He looked at the wall behind her and Amy turned, noticing three shelves that lined the walls. On the shelves stood a collection of large jars. Shivering, she took a step closer. The jars were filled with clear liquid and in each one, sunk to the bottom of the jar, lay what Amy realized with a rush of sickness was a body part.

A finger, a pair of blue eyes, a whole foot in a huge jar. There were other, unrecognizable organs too. A heart, perhaps, in that one. Something worse in the next . . .

'So many women failed me,' Lewis said from behind her.

She turned slowly, her hands crossing her chest. 'Lewis . . . does one of these . . . belong to Becky?' She swallowed.

He smiled enigmatically.

'Please, I need to know.' Her voice broke into a sob, and Lewis stood up.

'Oh, Amy. You are as beautiful as your sister. You're so much more beautiful when you cry. Maybe you *are* The One, after all.' He glanced at the picture of his mother. 'You look so much like her.'

He took a step towards her, holding the knife up. 'Sweet Amy . . .'

Someone banged on the door upstairs and shouted, 'Lewis!'

'Gary,' Amy breathed. He'd found the entrance to the sub-basement.

Lewis's expression transformed to one of fury. 'That fucking arsehole.'

He strode into an adjoining room and came back with another pair of handcuffs. He snapped one cuff around Amy's wrist and the other around his own. Then he pointed the knife at Amy's face. 'Do exactly as I say. Walk up the stairs and don't speak.'

She ascended the stairs, with Lewis one step behind her, wanting to scream and shout, the knife tip against the back of her neck stopping her.

'Gary,' Lewis said in a raised voice. 'I've got Amy here. If you try to do anything to me, I'll kill her, and then I'll kill you and the bastard you're with.'

A man's voice from the other side of the door said, 'Lewis, don't do anything stupid. More police are on their way.'

More police, Amy thought. So the man with Gary must be a cop.

'Step back from the door,' Lewis said. 'I want you both to step back six feet from the door. If you come any closer than that, I'll cut her throat. Ready?'

The policeman said, 'Yes.'

With the knife held against Amy's throat once more, Lewis unlocked the door and pulled it open, pushing Amy ahead of him, back into the locker room. He had the arm that was cuffed to hers wrapped around her waist.

Amy found herself looking at Gary, who was sweating, his eyes wide, a garden spade in his hand and blood trickling down his arm. Beside him, the policeman was holding his palms outwards in a placatory gesture.

'OK,' the cop said. 'We'll let you past. Just let Amy go.'

Lewis didn't speak. Instead, he grinned at Gary. 'Want me to kill her?'

'*Let her go*, Lewis,' Gary said. The two men stared at each other. Amy looked from one to the other. If they got out of this alive, she would have a lot of questions for Gary about his friend.

'Drop the spade,' Lewis ordered, pushing the blade against Amy's skin. Gary obeyed and it fell to the ground with an echoing clatter.

Lewis dragged Amy through the locker room, making sure she was facing Gary as he pulled her towards the pool room. He addressed the policeman. 'You're going to arrange to get me out of this house or Amy dies.'

'OK, OK. Take it easy,' the cop said. 'Let's talk, Lewis. I'm Detective Inspector Declan Adams. I want to help you.'

Lewis must know there's no way he's going to make it far, even if he gets out of the house, Amy thought. Or is he that delusional, that much of an egomaniac?

'I want you to call your police colleagues, tell them to back off.'

The policeman, Declan interrupted him, speaking in a calm, measured voice. 'I can't get a signal down here. Let's go upstairs so I can call.' Beside the cop, Gary was bristling, coiled, looking as though he was ready to spring. The policeman caught Gary's eye and shook his head. All the time they were moving closer to the swimming pool.

Lewis stopped and Amy felt his stance change, as if it had dawned on him at that moment that his desperate attempt to escape was doomed. They were standing just a foot from the edge of the pool, the knife still against Amy's throat, but his grip on her had loosened. Gary still looked poised to spring into action, the policeman slightly behind him.

Lewis started to speak – and Amy bit his wrist, making him cry out and lower the knife for a second. Gary went for him, leaping towards him like a sprinter coming out of the blocks. Lewis raised the knife again, shouted, 'No,' but Gary was on him, and Amy lost her balance as Lewis thudded into her. Gary grabbed Lewis's hand and squeezed his fingers, making him drop the knife. Lewis tried to fight but only had one hand free. Gary grabbed his throat and pushed him towards the pool, dragging Amy with him. She shouted Gary's name repeatedly; Lewis was yelling, too, and Gary was roaring.

The three of them teetered on the edge of the pool and, for a moment, everything froze. Lewis had his back to the water, Amy was on her knees beside him, and Gary held him by the neck, stopping him from falling in. Declan yelled a warning.

Looking up, Amy saw Gary say something to Lewis, a few intense words, but she couldn't hear what they were because Declan was shouting too loudly.

Amy tried to stand up – but as she got to her feet, Gary pulled something out of his back pocket. It was the Taser gun that Lewis had threatened her with earlier; Gary must have found it in the cell. Gary jabbed it onto the side of

Lewis's neck and he yelled out in pain, falling into her. She watched in horror for a split second as he went over the edge into the pool, banging his head on the edge as he went.

Dragging her with him.

Everything was silent in the water. Lewis sank straight to the bottom of the pool, blood pluming from the wound on his head. Amy tried to pull upwards, but her head was half a metre from the surface, Lewis acting as an anchor. She swallowed water, could feel it filling her lungs and she struggled, frantic, trying to hold her breath. Gary and Declan jumped into the pool after her. In the churning water it looked as if they were trying to lift Lewis but he was a heavy, dead weight. They couldn't lift him high enough. Amy pulled and pulled on the cuff, swallowing more water in her panic, and then the policeman was right there, gripping her wrist, his black hair rising from his scalp in front of Amy's eyes, and Amy was sure it was the last face she was ever going to see.

She blacked out.

47

Declan

Declan came out of the house, so pleased to feel the sun on his face after the horrors they'd found in Lewis Vine's weird underground flat, including jars full of body parts, which would need to be taken away for DNA analysis. In a bedroom with bloodstained sheets, they had found a computer that contained dozens of video files, but they were encrypted so wouldn't play. The computer would need to be sent to the Hi-Tech Crime Unit for analysis.

The grounds were swarming with police now, including the local officers who had taken so long to reach the house (though it had, in reality, been less than fifteen minutes), traipsing in and out, calling to one another in clipped, muted voices. Lewis's drowned body had already been carried out and taken away in a private ambulance.

Amy sat in the back of another ambulance, shivering and desperate for news. Gary sat beside her, holding her hand. He kept apologizing, saying he wouldn't have Tasered Lewis so close to the edge of the pool if he'd thought Lewis

364

would fall into the water. Amy rested her head against his shoulder.

Declan stepped into the ambulance.

'Are you OK?' he said.

Amy stared at him. Declan wondered what would have happened if he hadn't managed to find the key to the handcuffs in Lewis's pocket, somehow maintaining enough composure beneath the water to unlock the cuff on Amy's wrist.

At least, Declan thought, I managed to save one life.

He took a phone out of his pocket. It was an iPhone in a purple case with a jewelled effect on the back. He held it up to Amy and said gently, 'Do you recognize this? It was in the outside bin.'

Gary and Amy both spoke at the same time. 'It's Becky's.'

'Oh, god,' Amy said. 'Is there any sign of her?'

Gary squeezed her hand.

'I'm sorry, Amy,' Declan said. 'There's no sign of her at all. We've searched every room, looked everywhere.' He couldn't meet Amy's eye. Instead, he looked out of the ambulance at the grounds, the pretty lawn that stretched for half a mile. They were going to have to dig that lawn up, along with the rest of the gardens. That, he felt sure, was where the bodies were buried.

He forced himself to look into Amy's grief-stricken face.

'Becky's not here.'

48

Becky

Tuesday, 23 July

I open my eyes and for a moment I have no idea where I am, even what my name is . . . My head is pulsating and there's a white mist before my eyes, as if I've developed cataracts while I was asleep. Asleep? Was I sleeping? I try to raise my head but a sharp pain stabs my brain and I screw my eyes up against it. Slowly, I open them again.

I'm not in the garage any more. He moved me into the bedroom of some musty, poorly lit flat a day or two ago – or is it three? Time has melted like those Salvador Dalí clocks since I've been here. When I woke at first, I thought in my blurry, confused state that the man who had me was Daniel – or Lewis, to give him his real name. But then I remembered what had happened.

He says he's going to have to kill me if I scream or make a fuss, but he won't tell me why. He says it almost apologetically.

He talks to me when he comes in with food. It's weird not to hear him finishing my sentences, but I don't have any sentences to finish so he can't. I am refusing to speak to him at all – not that I can, most of the time, because he keeps me tied up and gagged when he's not with me.

When I was first in here, he used to sit by my bed and gaze at me, reminiscing about stuff I don't remember and don't understand. Then he would get himself worked up and the expression in his eyes would change. It's an expression I recognize well, have seen on the faces of other men: that look of lust, of being so turned on that he can't concentrate on anything else. That's when he pulls off the knickers I've been wearing for days and strips off himself, so he's naked, and he climbs on top of me, crushing me with his body. I try to fight, but my hands are cuffed to the bedposts. I squeeze my thighs together but he wrenches them apart, digs his nails into my flesh. So I lie there, as still as I can, my head turned away, eyes squeezed shut, thinking about other things. I replay lessons in my head, picture myself walking on a beach somewhere, imagine myself and Amy taking Boris to the park.

While he's doing it to me, he talks, tells me he loves me, that I'm beautiful, that he knows I love him too. He tells me he's never going to let me go.

Afterwards, he cleans me with a baby wipe and puts his clothes on with his back to me. His face twists with loathing – of me, of himself, I can't tell. I don't care.

I just want it to stop.

One day, he comes in and he's furious, his face pink and sweaty. He screams at me, tells me he hates me, that he's going to kill me. He approaches the bed and puts his hands on my throat and I try to scream through the gag.

He lets go, his eyes wild and unfocused. Then he tells me again that he loves me, that he wants me to forgive him.

'You do this to me,' he says, his voice strangled. 'It's your fault.'

He leaves the room and I try to ignore the hunger pains, the cramping in my belly, the soreness. I close my eyes and replay everything in my mind again – if I ever get out, it will be important that I remember how I got here.

I'm in a car. I can hear voices. A man, and another man.

'I've recorded you,' one of them says. 'Videoed the whole thing. What did you use, chloroform?'

I recognize the voice, but can't place it. I roll my eyes and see the car door is open. If I really concentrate, I can hear every word they say.

The other man says, 'And what are you going to do? Take that to the police? I would just have to tell them about Amber.' His voice is familiar too.

'I didn't kill her,' the first man says. 'You did. It was you who stuck the knife in her.'

'And you held her while I did it.'

'I didn't know you were going to kill her.'

'Yes, I fluffed that one – having someone else with me was a big mistake. But I got better – a lot better. You may not have wielded the knife but you did your bit – and helped me dispose of the body.'

I shudder. And at that moment, I remember. I was in the car with Daniel. We were supposed to be going away for the weekend. I had been so full of anticipation, thinking that finally I'd met a man worth getting excited about. Instead, he had lunged at me, holding something in his hand, something that smelled of chemicals.

I concentrate on what they are saying. The first man,

368

the one who isn't Daniel, says, 'I don't want to have this argument again. There's no proof, no evidence linking me to Amber. But I've got proof that you abducted Becky. I've got it right here. So, what, have you been doing this for years? Got a taste for it after Amber, did you?'

Daniel replies: 'Something like that. Looks like her, doesn't she? Like Amber. That's what attracted me to her when I saw her at that party. And, yes, of course I recognized you, you idiot. Becky is perfect; physically, temperamentally. She's so much like her.'

'Amber?'

'Like my mother. So what do you want?'

The man who isn't Daniel answers Daniel's question: 'Her,' he says. 'I want her.'

'You want to save her? And let her go to the police the second she—'

'No. That's not the plan. I said, "I want her."'

Daniel laughs. 'For yourself?'

A moment of silence in which all I can hear is my heart thumping. Nausea clutches at my throat and I swallow it down.

'I don't know,' Daniel says. 'She's perfect. She could be The One. The woman I've been searching for all these years. Do you know how many women I've had to eliminate in my quest to find the perfect one?'

'I don't want to know. I just want Becky. You might think she's the one. But I do too. I love her.'

I try to raise my head again, this time managing to push myself up, my head howling in protest, so I can see them through the open door. Yes, Daniel, and the other man, with his back to me, standing a few feet apart, squaring up to one another.

'She's got a sister,' says the man I can't see, walking closer to Lewis. His voice is so familiar. 'Her name's Amy. She's just as hot as Becky. A year or so older, but you wouldn't guess it. She's innocent, whereas Becky's been around the block a few times; she's tainted. You always told me you like girls who haven't been with too many men.' He takes out his phone and taps the screen a few times, before showing it to Daniel.

My phone. Where is it? I look for my bag, where I always keep it. I can't see it anywhere.

Daniel says, 'Hmmm. She looks . . . nice.'

'I can help you get to her. If you give me Becky.'

'Been around the block, eh, has Becky?' Daniel says. 'All right. It's a deal. I'll send a letter like last time, or rather, an email, so no one looks for her. I've got Becky's phone – I took it off her when I knocked her out – so I'll have access to her email.'

He'll have access to everything on my phone, I think. My Facebook, my contacts. My whole life.

And then they shake hands, like it's a business deal. My brain may feel as if it's been wrapped in acid-soaked cotton wool but I still understand what has just happened. They have just agreed to trade me and Amy, as if we are football stickers.

Well, that's not going to happen. Not if I have anything to do with it.

Bracing myself against the certain rush of pain in my head, I sit up, half fall out of the car, and try to run. I have no idea which direction to run in. I am stumbling towards a big house. Daniel shouts, 'Hey!' and then footsteps are pounding after me. I look over my shoulder and see them both, running towards me, their faces twisted, like two strangers – not the two

*nice guys I knew before. Because now I know who
the other man is, and the shock of it makes me scream.*

*They catch me and push me to the ground. Gravel
scrapes my knees and palms.*

*Daniel drags me back to the car and tells his friend
to hold me while he gets something. I thrash and try
to spit at them, at the man who I thought I knew but
who, now, has a strange expression on his face, like a
father looking at his newborn child. The last thing I
see before Daniel puts the chemical-smelling pad on
my face again is my next-door neighbour, gazing down
at me with the expression I've sought all my life.*

'I love you,' Gary says, and I black out.

'You know what, Becks?' Gary says when he comes back
into the room where he's been keeping me, the room in
which he's kept me prisoner; raped me, terrified me. 'I used
to watch you through the spyhole in my door. Your hips
looked so slinky and sexy when you walked. It's so unfair.
I loved you so much, I thought you liked me – and you
end up going out with a creep like Lewis? If you knew him
like I know him, you wouldn't want to go out with him.
You've had a lucky escape.'

A lucky escape. That's what he calls it. To be passed from
one madman to another. From my memories of waking up
in the car and from what Gary has told me since he brought
me here, I've been able to piece together the awful truth
about what's happened to me.

Daniel, the man I thought I was in love with, was really
a psychopath called Lewis. He and Gary knew each other
from a long time ago. They murdered a girl called Amber,
although Gary protests his innocence and says it was Lewis
who wielded the knife.

371

According to Gary, Lewis was at the Orchid Blue sex party and spotted me there. I look just like Amber, he says, and both of us look like Lewis's dead mother. Lewis developed an obsession with me which led to him setting up a CupidsWeb profile and contacting me to arrange a date. He knew I was on CupidsWeb from chatting with Kath at the party.

But Lewis wasn't the only one obsessed with me. Gary was watching me; my every move, and when I set out to go on the date with the man I knew as Daniel, Gary followed us. He watched as Lewis began to drag my unconscious body out of his car, then stepped forward – which was when they did their deal. Me for Amy. After that, Gary brought me here – first putting me in a garage then bringing me into this musty, mothball-stinking flat.

Thinking of Amy, I shake my head violently and Gary must be curious because he removes the gag.

'Where is she? You have to tell me. If that bastard hurts her . . .' I pull against the handcuffs but my muscles are weak and I slump back onto the bed. I try to lash out at him with my foot because my arms are still tied to the bedhead, and he feints neatly away to avoid me.

'Calm down, Becky, or I'll have to hurt you,' he says, and the coldness in his voice makes me shudder.

A tear slides down the side of my cheek and I can't wipe it away. Oh, God, Amy. I'm so scared – even more terrified for her than I am for myself. The thought of anything happening to her . . .

I shudder, and Gary sighs and stares towards the curtained window. The curtains are horrible, mauve and green stripes and fat flowers. I can taste my own bad breath in my mouth and it makes me feel sick. I haven't cleaned my teeth since I've been here.

He looks pensive.

'All I wanted – and it's a simple thing; not too much to ask, surely? – was for you to love me the way I loved you. That night when we made love, you kissed me so passionately, remember?'

Gary strokes my bare leg and I try not to recoil.

'I watched you afterwards when you fell asleep. Allowed myself to dream of a future with you. A time when we would be together, for ever, and you'd adore me, worship me, and everyone would be so sick with jealousy because the most beautiful, sexy, clever, funny, sweet, feisty, adorable, fragrant woman in the whole world belongs to me.

'Do you remember the first time we met, when I moved in? I was carrying that box of DVDs up the stairs and you came running down – you almost sent me flying! I was about to yell at you, then I saw your eyes . . . oh, my God, I was smitten. You smiled at me. I got an instant hard-on!'

I try not to glance at his crotch in case the memory produces a similar response.

'I used to watch out for you, learn when you came and went so I could accidentally on purpose bump into you . . . you were always friendly, but I could tell you weren't interested. It did my head in, that you were seeing other men, you and your mate, Katherine.'

He pauses, staring at me with a twisted expression, almost curious.

'She's dead, you know. Katherine. Drugs overdose, apparently, a couple of days ago. But it was Lewis, I bet it was. Getting her out of the way so he could have you.'

A strangled sob slips out of my throat. Katherine, *dead*? I can't believe it – and yet I can. At that moment, I wish I could swap places with her. I'd rather be dead, sailing away into oblivion on a cloud of cocaine, or whatever.

Anything would be better than stuck here in this stinking room with Crazy Gary, whose only defence seems to be that he's less insane than Daniel, or Lewis, or whatever his name actually is.

I can't think about Katherine right now. I'm going to pretend I didn't hear it. It's too much to take in.

'I dreamed about you all the time,' he says.

'We could be together now, Gary,' I plead. 'I didn't know you felt so strongly about me. It won't come out, about Lewis. We could run away together, just you and me . . .'

He ignores me.

'I couldn't stand it when you brought a man back to your gaff. I wanted to break down your fucking door and punch his lights out. I could hear you, you know, through the wall. It *killed* me. That was when I decided I had to try harder to get you to like me. Do you remember that time I came over? I made up some story about some kids trying to break in, and you were scared so you invited me in. We talked for an hour – it was fantastic! I was so happy. You were telling me all about your job, the kids at school . . .'

Gary gets this faraway look on his face. 'I wanted to ask you out, but it was too soon. I didn't want to scare you off. At least we were mates by then, though. But then you started Internet dating.'

He almost spits out the words. 'More men! What was wrong with you, Becky? You changed. You were so sweet and innocent – wholesome. Not any more . . . you turned slutty . . . It was sexy as hell, though – I wanted you so much . . .'

I think back to the horribleness of it all and I agree with him. What the hell *was* wrong with me? How could I have thought it was a good idea, to go on hook-up sites and to sex parties . . .? The threesome with Katherine – I can't believe she's dead. Her throaty giggle, and smooth skin . . . but I'm not gay. I didn't like it, and I would never do it again. That Paul guy was foul, I felt defiled afterwards. So why did I go to that nasty, tawdry sex party too? It occurs to me how persuasive Kath really was. I would never have done any of that stuff on my own.

'I thought I had no chance. But then I did! Do you remember that night when we made love, Becky? It was the best night of my whole life. You were incredible; so beautiful. You tasted like dark bitter chocolate and your skin was burning with a million tiny fires that I tried to put out with my tongue . . .'

'I remember,' I tell him, trying to sound eager. It was a stupid mistake, a moment of weakness on my part. He'd come round late one night asking for his *Breaking Bad* box set, and I was feeling excited and distracted, emailing Paul. After Gary went back to his place, I noticed he'd left the box set behind and, although I originally decided not to, I changed my mind and took it across to his flat. He'd been delighted to see me, and we had a drink together and ended up in bed. It was all right, as I recall. He didn't last very long and . . . I don't want to think about it. Not now. Not ever again.

But if he still loves me then perhaps I have a chance . . .

He looks at me now with accusing eyes. 'You didn't want me, though, not even after that incredible night. You told me you were going out on a date with Katherine. That was when I bought you that new iMac. You were so naïve, thinking you'd really won it in some competition you never even entered! Honestly, Becky. How could you be so daft? All I had to do was install a bit of software that connected your iMac to my computer – any idiot who's ever worked in IT could do it – and, guess what? I could read all your emails, watch your screen in real-time. I just packaged it all back up and left it outside your door with a letter telling you that you won it in a competition that all CupidsWeb users were automatically entered in.

'Every night, I watched you surf the net, instant-message Katherine and your sister Amy – until you had that big row with her – I knew because you told Katherine about it. I saw you update your social networks, browse Casexual.com. I watched you apply for Orchid Blue and arrange to go to a sex party with Katherine. I almost vomited at the thought of you taking part in an orgy. I decided I had to go too. I applied and got accepted, even though it cost a fortune.

'It was a masked party, so I thought I'd be safe. I had my hair cut. Even got a sodding fake tan to match the fake name I gave when I booked. I didn't want you to recognize me. I was so nervous. I really thought I might be able to get to have sex with you again. But then it all went wrong. As soon as I walked in, I saw Lewis. Even with the mask on, I knew it was him. I hadn't seen him for fifteen years, not since . . . that night. I was so shocked. I didn't know what to do. I hoped he wouldn't recognize me – although *you* did, didn't you? I bet you were shocked to see me there.'

I nod. 'Shocked' had been an understatement. That's why I had legged it as soon as I saw him. It just seemed so wrong, on so many levels, that the next-door neighbour with a crush on me had shown up at this expensive sex party.

I don't tell Gary that, though.

'Katherine was chatting me up, remember? Then you came over, saw me, and stormed out.'

Gary's face falls at the memory. 'I knew then I had no

376

chance with you. And it got worse – frigging Lewis saw you rip off your mask on the way out, and decided that you were his next conquest. He comes over to us, asking all about you and I thought, oh, shit, I remember what happened last time he had that expression on his face . . . he was obsessed. So obsessed that he didn't clock it was me at all, with my mask on, fifteen years since he'd last seen me, which was something at least . . . He was banging on about you being like Cinderella, not even leaving a glass slipper . . . twat. I was so scared for you. I left the party after you did, thinking that whatever happened I had to make sure he didn't find out who you were.'

Over the next couple of weeks, Gary says, he continued to spy on me on the iMac he'd given me. I'd emailed Kath saying I didn't want to go to any more Orchid Blue parties or use Casexual any more. I told her about the epiphany I'd had at that party, how disgusted I felt with myself and that I didn't want to do it any more.

Gary was delighted, he says, and thrilled that he hadn't been the only reason for me leaving so hastily. But then, he says, something terrible happened: I got a message through CupidsWeb from a guy called Daniel. Daniel said he loved my profile, told me all this stuff about how he was tired of empty sex and wanted to find a soul mate, and we arranged to meet.

And Gary was reading all this on his own computer! I feel sick at the thought of Gary having read all my lovey-dovey emails with Daniel.

Then I feel even sicker, thinking what Daniel had in store for me all along – if Gary can be believed.

'I watched you check out his profile, Becks, and when I saw his photos and realised Daniel was really Lewis, I freaked. I couldn't work out how he'd found you at first. I panicked. I couldn't tell you about him, obviously.'

'How did he find me?' I ask.

Gary grits his teeth. 'Your stupid friend, I assume. Katherine must have told him at the party about you both using CupidsWeb.'

I nod slowly. I suppose that must have been it. I wish, from the bottom of my heart, that I'd never met Kath. Or Gary. Or Daniel/Lewis.

Gary starts crying. His shoulders heave and quiver and his nose turns red and starts running. 'I had to watch you, Becky, falling in love with fucking *Lewis*! You were messaging Kath, saying how wonderful he was, how different to all the others, how you were falling in love with him! I couldn't bear it!'

Gary's voice rises to a wail and I look at him, astonished and fearful. Does he really expect me to feel sorry for him? 'Anyway, I don't want to talk about it any more.'

He puts a new strip of tape over my mouth, picks up my empty plate and leaves without asking me if I need to use the bathroom.

49

Amy

Monday, 29 July

'There's someone here to see you.'

DS Bob Clewley spoke into the phone, glancing over at Amy, who sat fidgeting on the uncomfortable slippery faux-leather reception seats. Amy hadn't been to Eastbourne since she was a child, though she had a vague memory of her and Becky playing in the amusement arcades on the pier. Becky had put all her money into the grabber machine, squealing with delight when she finally managed to get hold of a Snoopy toy. Becky still had that Snoopy in her bedroom.

Declan Adams came out to reception and gestured with his head for Amy to follow him, leading her to an interview room and instructing Bob to fetch Amy a cup of tea.

'How are you doing?' Declan asked.

Amy knew she looked rough. She hadn't slept at all in the three days since Lewis Vine had abducted her. She had spent much of that time staring at the TV, wrapped in a blanket with Boris beside her. Sky News had rolling coverage of the goings-on at the 'house of horror' in Claygate, as body after body was dug up, an endless gallery of faces of missing women appearing on the screen, their families finally achieving some kind of closure – including the family of Amber Corrigan, whose purse had been found among Lewis's possessions.

There was no closure for Amy. The phone and a bag had been the only trace of Becky, proof that she had encountered Lewis, along with hair containing her DNA in his car. On the phone, a message from Katherine, sent just after Amy had been to see her, asking Becky what she was up to. Then she had sent another text asking her why she hadn't replied.

Have you gone away with Daniel? Katherine asked. *I'm going to have to tell Amy if she keeps pestering me.*

'Lewis must have seen that text and realized Katherine could expose the email about Becky going away as a lie,' Declan said. 'So he had to deal with her – stop her talking to you. Looks like Fraser didn't give her the fatal drugs after all.'

But so far not a single atom of Becky had been found inside the house, let alone a body. Police were scanning CCTV from the areas around Lewis's house and office, trying to trace his movements over the weekend when Becky went missing, but he didn't appear to have done anything except go to work, go home and, Amy discovered to her horror, spend one afternoon lurking outside her own flat.

Gary had been round both days since, making Amy soup that she didn't eat and drinks that she couldn't stomach. She begged him for every detail he knew about Lewis, but he claimed to be as shocked as she was about his friend's secret life. He had met him a couple of years ago, he said, at a networking event, and had thought he seemed like a nice guy, someone who knew their stuff when it came to social networking. He deeply regretted introducing him

380

to Amy. He had no idea how Lewis had encountered Becky, but he assumed he must have seen her once when he came to Gary's flat, and maybe Gary had told him she used CupidsWeb – another thing he regretted. But he had no idea that Lewis was a psychopath – of course he didn't.

'No one ever does, do they?' he said reasonably. 'People always say serial killers seem normal and nice. I saw a programme about it on TV. They're everywhere, living among us.'

She had shivered as he'd trailed off, realizing he'd said the wrong thing.

Last night, she'd asked Gary to stay – not for sex, but just to hold her. He respected her wishes, didn't try anything, just held her in his strong arms. With him beside her, she was able to sleep at last.

Just before she woke she had a dream, a flashback to the fight at the moment that Lewis had fallen into the pool, dragging her with him. She awoke gasping for air. Sitting on the toilet a minute later, a memory from the dream came back to her. Just before Gary had Tasered Lewis, the psychopath had said something to him.

She went back into the bedroom and looked down at Gary, who was sleeping peacefully.

Then she went outside. Her beloved bike was parked by the kerb. Yesterday, she and Gary had gone round to Paul 'TooledUp' Halsall's and told him in no uncertain terms that the bike was hers, that the agreement she'd signed was worthless. Gary had squared up to him until Paul had chucked the keys at Amy, snarling, 'It's a piece of shit anyway.' Fortunately, he'd turned out not to be at all tooled up.

If only it was so easy to get Becky back.

Now here she sat in the interview room opposite Declan and Bob, a steaming mug of tea in front of her.

She took a deep breath. 'When Gary and Lewis were fighting by the swimming pool, Gary said something to Lewis. You were yelling so loud, I couldn't hear what he said.'

Declan shook his head. 'Sorry, I didn't hear either.'

'But there was CCTV in the room, wasn't there? I saw it when he flicked between the rooms, when he had me in the kitchen.'

'Why do you think it's important?' asked Bob.

Amy sighed. 'I don't know. It was just, from the expression on his face, Lewis looked disappointed. And Gary – well, I could swear that he *smirked*. I'm sure he did. It didn't come back to me until I replayed it in my head when I was in bed last night.'

'And are you sure it wasn't just a dream?' Bob asked.

'There's only one way to find out,' Declan said, getting up from the desk.

They sat and stared at the small monitor as Bob forwarded through the recording from Lewis's pool room.

'He had it set up to record twenty-four hours a day and to tape over the previous twenty-four hours every day. I guess he was scared of someone breaking in and finding what he'd been doing,' Declan said. 'Luckily, we found and stopped the system the other day.'

Amy watched Bob forward through the recording, hugging herself when it got to the point where Lewis took her through the pool room and opened the door to his underground flat. Bob fast-forwarded until they saw Declan and Gary appear, then onto the point where Lewis and Amy re-emerged. When they got to the fight beside the pool, he slowed it down. There was the moment when Gary, the camera pointing across the pool at his face, had said something to Lewis, just before Gary Tasered him. Bob stopped and rewound.

'Can you zoom in?' Amy said. 'It's too small.' The camera had been mounted on the wall so it was only just possible to see Lewis's lips move.

'Let me try.' Bob fiddled with the controls, zooming in on Lewis's face.

'It's so pixellated,' Amy said, frustrated. She was both relieved and horrified that she hadn't misremembered the moment.

Declan peered at the screen, his nose just inches from it. 'It's impossible.'

'We might be able to clean this up,' Bob said, 'and make it clearer.'

'We need someone who can lip read,' Declan said.

Bob looked at him across the desk. 'What about that girl who works in analysis? The deaf one.'

'Good idea.'

Bob left the room, leaving Declan and Amy staring at the frozen monochrome screen, Gary and Lewis suspended in the moment before Amy had plunged into the pool.

'What do you know about Gary?' Declan asked. 'He's your friend, isn't he?'

Amy had to turn away from the screen, the memory of what had happened next was too painful. 'I did suspect him of having something to do with Becky's disappearance last week.' She explained about the incident with Gary forgetting to double-lock the door. 'But he convinced me it was an innocent mistake. He seems so nice and . . . normal.'

'They often do,' Declan said.

Nathan's face entered Amy's head and she nodded. 'It's just because he was friends with Lewis . . . I'm sure he is nice and normal. I mean, we know that Lewis is the killer. I just want to know what Gary said to him, and why.'

Bob re-entered the room with a young woman he introduced as Samantha. She sat down at the desk and peered at the screen, Bob zooming in as close as he could, fiddling with the picture to make it as crisp as possible. Amy watched Lewis's lips move again and a cold finger traced its way up her spine. It was his expression, the disappointment in his eyes. Like his old friend had let him down.

'Can you tell what he said?' Declan asked Samantha, and Amy watched the deaf woman as she gestured at Bob to rewind it and play it again.

Amy rode her bike back up to London. DI Adams and DS Clewley needed to speak to their SIO and run a couple of background checks on Gary before driving up to interview him again.

'Go straight home,' Declan said. Amy had already texted Gary to check he wasn't still at her flat. 'Lock the door – just in case. Don't try to talk to him. Don't do anything stupid, OK?'

She promised not to.

But as she weaved through the south London streets, she couldn't help but take a slight detour past Gary and Becky's building and, as she passed, she saw Gary come out, carrying a black holdall. He was looking down, so didn't see her. She watched in her mirror as he got into his car and pulled off.

Fuck it, she thought, and turned the bike round, following him at a discreet distance.

The traffic through south London was thick and bad-tempered as always. Amy felt calm, no sign of an impending panic attack, no sweating palms or booming heart. The likelihood was, Becky was dead. But at least she might finally know.

At some point, she entered Kent, and soon found herself in Bromley, a town Amy had been to a few times on shopping trips. Gary drove through the suburbs, seemingly unaware he was being followed. Then he stopped on a quiet residential road and got out of the car. He looked left and right but didn't see Amy as she parked further up the street behind a van.

Gary got out of the car and trotted up some steps, letting himself in to a big tatty house, clearly converted into flats.

Amy jogged up the road and stood outside the building, her heart thumping hard. She didn't know which flat he'd gone into. She paused, and realized she should call Declan on the mobile number the policeman had given her. It went to voicemail so Amy left a message saying where she was.

She walked up to the door and braced herself, her finger hovering over the panel of buzzers, wondering which one to press.

50

Becky

Monday, 29 July

It is days before I can get Gary to talk any more. I feel
so weak that my lips barely move, and he has to feed me
with a spoon, like a baby. Soup or porridge, gloopy stuff
like that. When he leaves again he doesn't bother to put
the duct tape over my mouth because he knows that I
don't have the energy to scream. He's calmer. He seems
almost . . . happy.

He has just helped me to the toilet and watched me as
I pee. I'm past caring. I catch a glimpse of myself in the
bathroom mirror and literally don't recognize myself.

'Can I have a bath?' I whisper. 'I stink.'

'Yeah, you do,' he says, a look of disgust on his face.
'But I wouldn't worry about that if I were you.'

His whole manner has changed. He doesn't look at me
with those puppy-dog eyes any more. Instead, he looks at
me as if I revolt him.

Like I'm a mess that needs to be cleaned up.

He escorts me back to the stinking bed and pushes me

down onto the sheets, securing the handcuffs. My arms spasm with pain.

There's something I need to know. I'm afraid to ask, but force out the words. 'Please tell me, Gary. Amy, is she . . .?'

'Yeah, Amy's safe. Lewis is dead. You don't need to be worried about Amy . . .'

I'm confused, but so relieved. Amy is safe! 'Oh, thank God. If Lewis is dead, you can let me go! He can't drop you in it with the police any more – and I won't, I swear.'

'No, but you might. And I can't take that chance. Besides . . .'

'What?'

'There's something you should know. I didn't know whether to tell you or not, but I think I should. The thing is . . . Amy and I are in love.'

What?

I gape at him in confusion.

'I'm sorry, Becky. For a while, I thought I loved both of you. I loved you first, so much, but there's only so much rejection a guy can handle, you know. I mean, you don't even seem to enjoy it that much when we make love these days. After you went missing—'

'After you kidnapped me—'

'Well, I was helping Amy look for you. We got close . . .'

I can't help a weak laugh. 'You were helping Amy look for me, even though you had me locked up in your dead mum's flat all the—'

'Time. I told you, to stop Lewis getting to you,' he insisted stubbornly. Then he sat up straighter. 'He really was a psychopath, you know. Two dozen girls, they think. Body parts in jars, torture chamber in his basement. Sick, sick stuff. You had a lucky escape . . . But now – I'm sorry, Becks. It's too risky now for me to keep you here. You've become a loose end. I don't want to break your heart but I think we should end it.'

'Please, let me go! I won't tell anyone, I promise.'

'Don't be stupid. How could you not? That's what exes always do, isn't it? Blab about their past loves.'

He picks up a pillow and studies it. 'I've been trying to think about the best way to do it. Stabbing is so messy. I don't want you to suffer too much, Becks. I mean, I did love you not so long ago. You'll always be special to me. Amy and I will always remember you. And I'll look after her for ever. Don't you worry.'

He comes towards me with the pillow. 'Try not to struggle too much,' he says.

I scream.

51

Declan

Monday, 29 July

'We had a deal.'

Those were the words that Samantha had read on Gary's lips. *A deal.* As Samantha told them what she could see, Amy had clutched her chest and Declan had felt that quickening of his own blood, the addictive jolt like a strong shot of coffee.

Declan had quizzed Amy, asking her for every piece of information she had about Gary Davidson, making her describe her encounter with Gary and Lewis, and how Gary had acted when she had first gone round to see Becky after receiving the email.

Amy looked stricken as she talked, kept rubbing her arms, her eyes wild with horror. After Bob had left the room to look Gary up on their database, Amy had stared at Declan. 'I slept with him,' she whispered.

Declan had sent her home.

Now Bob came back into the office, his face grim. 'He doesn't have a criminal record. In fact, I can't find any record of him at all. No National Insurance number. No passport. Gary Davidson doesn't exist.'

'He exists, all right. That's just not his real name.'

'We should get going,' Bob said.

Declan, though, was deep in thought, remembering the video he had watched the day before. It hadn't taken the Hi-Tech Crime Unit long to decrypt the files; they had found a series of videos that Vine had made in which he described each of the murders he had committed. Watching him talking into the camera, casually describing the torture and murder of two dozen women over fifteen years, was chilling. Some of the recordings featured clips of the women's mutilated bodies, or gruesome stills, and Declan wondered if he would sit and watch them back, reliving his crimes for kicks. Whatever, this was his legacy – and Declan wished he could delete every one. Imagine if the videos leaked onto YouTube . . . every sicko in the world would be attracted to them like flies to shit.

Among the recordings Vine had left behind was a short clip that had been recorded five years ago. In it, Lewis had shorter but thicker hair than he had when he had died, and several days' worth of stubble. He sipped from a mug of tea or coffee as he spoke, peering directly into the camera:

We met her at the reception of this conference I spoke at. I can't even remember what it was called. Lots of losers thinking they could make a quick buck out of this newfangled invention called the Internet, every witless business in the world thinking the web was paved with gold. Very few of them as clever or talented as me.

My talk went brilliantly, and afterwards I was approached by a young woman who wanted to talk

to me about an idea she had for a site. The moment
she started speaking I stopped listening. I was too busy
staring. She looked exactly like her. Denise. My beau-
tiful mother.

At that point, Declan had paused the video and taken
down the photo of Amber, holding it beside a photo of
Denise Vine they had found at Lewis's house. To say that
Amber and Denise looked the same was stretching the truth
to its limits. Yes, they both had blonde hair and blue eyes,
but Amber was far prettier than Lewis's mother, whose hair
came from a bottle, whose eyes were bloodshot and dull,
whose face was puffier and rattier and, let's face it, uglier
than Amber's. The young woman Lewis had encountered
in the hotel was – just like Amy and Becky – a highly ideal-
ized version of Denise Vine, a woman who'd abused her
teenage son before killing herself.

Declan had restarted the video.

I wanted to take Amber – that was her lovely name
– back to my hotel room right away, to impale her on
the sheets. But then I was whisked away by the confer-
ence organizer, and Amber was swallowed up by the
crowd.

I saw her again later that evening, at the drinks
reception. I was sitting with Gavin, and we were
already at the end of our second bottle of champagne.
Plus, Gavin had done some coke and was talking
bollocks as usual. I half listened . . . and then Amber
drifted into view.

She came over and asked if she could sit with us. I
acted as warm and friendly as I could, and nodded
and smiled as she talked about her frankly shit

business idea, her words obscured behind my visions of myself sucking her nipples and rubbing my cock against her cherubic face.

Gavin bought a third bottle of Bollinger and Amber had a few glasses. She got giggly. She started telling us about her oppressive, tedious parents. I made sympathetic noises. I told her that maybe I could help her with her business, give her advice, maybe invest some capital. She got terribly excited. Gavin sat there, staring at her like a dog staring at a chocolate biscuit.

I suggested that we go for a drive, go and get something to eat. I'd heard there was an excellent gastro-pub just out of town. We could talk more about her business idea and maybe work out a start-up plan. Excited, and a little tipsy, Amber agreed.

I drive well when I'm drunk. I was driving a Jeep back then, when I wasn't cruising around in my Porsche. Amber got in the back and Gavin sat next to me. We exchanged a look. This was in the days before roasting became a familiar term, but I could tell he had that kind of scenario in mind.

We drove out into the countryside. It was a warm evening and the air throbbed with the sound of grasshoppers. I saw a 'for sale' sign out front of a farm, with the name of a development company, which told me the property was empty. The dark farm buildings were just visible in the moonlight. I pulled up and indicated for Gavin to get out and open the gate. As we drove through, Amber goes, 'Where are we?' She was really groggy by then.

I got out of the Jeep and opened Amber's door, taking her hand and helping her out. As she leaned forward, I got a good eyeful of her creamy breasts and *it took all my self-control not to reach out and grab them.*

'This isn't a gastro-pub,' she said.

'I thought we could take a little walk,' I said. I felt as if I was in a film, speaking movie dialogue. 'It's a beautiful night for it.'

Maybe it was the way Gavin was staring at her, but suddenly Amber looked frightened. 'I want to go back,' she said.

'Come on, let's go for a walk,' I replied, ignoring her plea.

She said again that she wanted to go back.

Which was when I grabbed her tits, with both hands, giving them a squeeze. She screamed, so I clamped my hand over her mouth and pushed her to the ground. She bit me. The little bitch actually bit me. My vision flashed red and suddenly it was like I was staring down at Denise, and I remembered how she had promised to love me for ever, but had abandoned me, and in that moment a pure hatred enveloped me.

'Hold her,' I said to Gavin, who was panting with drunken lust. He stared at me. 'Fucking hold her.'

As Gavin held down Amber, his hand over her mouth, I ran over to the Jeep and took the knife from the glove compartment. I had been carrying the knife around for months. When I put it in there I told myself it was for self-defence – a lot of people were jealous of me – but maybe, secretly, I had been dreaming of this moment.

I walked slowly over to where Gavin had Amber pinned to the grass and told him to step aside, to let her go.

For a moment, she looked at me with relief and gratitude.

Then she saw the knife.

I heard Gavin say, 'What the fuck?' but all I could think about was how this bitch had pretended to love me, made me so many promises, and deserted me, left me all alone in this cruel, sick world, and with all my strength I plunged the knife into the spot where I knew it would hurt her the most. Her heart.

When my ears stopped rushing and my vision returned to normal, I became aware of Gavin pacing around beside me, going, 'What have you done?' I told him to shut up then held out the knife to him.

'Here, take this a moment.'

Gavin always did what I told him. He took the knife gingerly.

'We did it,' I said, looking up at him.

He froze. 'What?'

'We both drove her out here. We both held her down. We both touched the knife.' He dropped it like it was a turd. 'You and I.'

'Oh, God, oh, shit, what are we going to do, Lewis?' he said, like a big pathetic crybaby.

I looked over my shoulder at the farm buildings. 'Wait here.'

A few minutes later, I came back, looking down at the bloody body stretched out in the moonlight.

At that point I didn't own this place, this house. I had an apartment in the city. Nowhere to dispose of bodies. And this was my first time. I guess I wasn't thinking too far ahead. I didn't have a system like I do now. I thought the cesspit would be a good enough place to dispose of the body. As we dragged her across the grass, and stripped her – I still have her clothes somewhere, in a black bin liner – I told Gavin not to worry, that I would buy this property, unaware that the bastards would refuse to sell it to me.

As Amber's body fell into the pit and we replaced the cover, I felt an intense wave of power rush through me. The sweetest feeling I've ever had. The only comparable feeling was the love I felt for Denise on those nights when she held me. I suppose I knew, right then, that I would continue to seek out that feeling. Love. And power.

We drove back to the hotel. I was splattered with blood so I parked outside, with the lights off, and sent Gavin in to get me a change of clothes and a wet flannel. That was enough for me to get to my room, where I had a shower and got dressed again. After that, we went downstairs and rejoined the reception, talking to as many people as we could so they would think we'd been there all along. No one mentioned Amber, and why should they? She was nobody.

The next morning, driving back to London, Gavin and I agreed never to see each other again. I would give him some money, a redundancy package, which he seemed pleased with. I wonder what the stupid fool is doing now?

Declan turned to Bob. 'Gavin. Gary. That must have been him. Hardly the most imaginative name change.'

'You think that's what Gary was talking about when he said, "We had a deal?" The agreement not to see each other again after Amber's murder?'

'I don't know. Maybe there was something else. More recent.' Fifteen minutes had passed since Amy had left. 'Let's go and find out.'

52

Amy

Monday, 29 July

Amy was about to start pressing buzzers when she heard footsteps from inside. She quickly ran down the steps to the basement flat and crouched, looking up. Gary came out, still carrying the holdall. He looked pale.

He entered the passageway that divided the houses and Amy counted to three, then ran back up the steps and followed.

There were garages at the back of the block, tatty-looking constructions with rusting doors. Amy waited at the end of the passageway and watched as Gary peered around, then opened one of the doors, lifting it just enough to duck under and go inside, shutting it behind him.

Amy took a deep breath, trying to think straight. She had no weapon. She should call Declan again and wait. But she had to know what was in that garage.

She pressed her ear against the garage door, but couldn't hear a thing. What the hell was she supposed to do? She tried to call Declan again but it was still going straight to voicemail. Should she call the local cops? Gary could be murdering Becky right now, if she wasn't already dead. She couldn't wait any longer, not after the slow, suffocating agony of the last ten days, the horror of not knowing.

She reached out and turned the handle, bracing herself as she pulled the door towards her, wincing at the noise it made as she pulled it up and open, taking a step back as she expected Gary to come running out at her.

Nothing happened.

The garage stood open. There was no one there. Just a stack of boxes around the edge, a rusting bike hanging from two fat nails, some bags of rubbish in the corner.

Her breath shuddered out of her as she stepped out of the warm sunshine and into the garage.

She heard a noise, a shuffle, and, as she turned her head, Gary sprang out from behind the stack of boxes.

He grabbed her by the throat, pushing her against the wall, her back slamming against brick, winding her. As she bent double, he ran to the door and slammed it shut. A dim light flickered in the ceiling. Gary stood in front of her, more a shadow than a man.

'Where is she?' Amy panted.

He didn't reply, just threw himself at her. Amy ran towards the door, tried to pull it open, but he was on her, tugging on her shoulders and throwing her to the floor. He tried to jump on her but she rolled, screaming, 'Where's my sister?' at him as she sprang to her feet. She was fitter than him, and faster. But he was stronger.

Gary had his back to the garage door. She had to get past him. If Becky was alive, she must be in one of the flats . . . so what had he come out to the garage for? Then she saw it, lying on the floor beside the boxes he'd sprung out from: Becky's suitcase. It was open, a dress spilling from inside. He must have come out to the garage to collect it, to make sure there was no trace of Becky left in here . . . Oh, God, was she too late? Was Becky already dead?

He saw her looking at the suitcase.

'I loved her,' he said, out of breath and sweating heavily. 'But now I love you, Amy. I had to get rid of Becky so we could be together. Me and you. And Boris, of course.'

'You're fucking insane.'

He looked hurt. 'Insane. That's what Becky said.'

As they spoke they moved in a slow semi-circle around the garage, Gary blocking her from the exit with his body.

'Is she dead?'

'Dead?' he echoed, as if the thought hadn't occurred to him before. 'Don't be sad, Amy. I *saved* her, from Lewis. He was going to kill her. He would have done terrible things to her, like he did with Amber. What he did to her before he finally finished her off . . . I'll never forget it. But I made Becky's last days nice. Loving. At least she was looking into the eyes of someone who once loved her when she—'

Amy screamed and rushed towards him, clawing his face with her nails. He yelled out and tried to grab her wrists, but she kicked him in the balls as hard as she could and he went down hard. She jumped up on top of him and punched him in the side of the head, pummelling him with her fists. But he shook her off, sending her onto her back, standing up and kicking her hard in the ribs.

'I don't want to hurt you, Amy.'

'Fuck off, Gary.'

He came at her again, his bleeding face twisted with panic and almost unrecognizable in the gloom of the garage. He swung a punch at her, connecting with her shoulder and sending her spinning and crashing into the back wall of the garage, colliding with the hanging bike.

She fell to the ground, the bike falling on top of her. Gary came towards her, his face contorted with anger and fear, the same expression she'd seen when he'd chased her out of his building, but even darker, his true self showing through. Right now, standing there with his fists clenching and unclenching, he reminded her of Nathan, and how weak she'd felt back then.

But not now.

If Becky was dead, she didn't care any more. This man had lied to her, cheated her, treated her with utter cruelty, just like Nathan. She had let him fuck her. She had let him fuck *with* her.

No one would ever do that again.

He came towards her, his arms outstretched, and she scooped up the long, thick nail that had fallen from the garage wall as the bike had dropped, and as Gary threw himself onto her, she raised her hand, the head of the nail flat against her palm, and thrust it into his eye.

He screamed so loudly that, within moments, someone banged on the garage door. Amy staggered over to it, pushing it up and open to reveal a bald, muscular man who said, 'What the hell?' when he saw Gary lying on the floor at the back of the garage, clutching his face, blood spurting from between his fingers.

'Call the police,' Amy shouted, as she ran out of the garage towards the flats.

But as she arrived at the front of the building, Declan and Bob screeched up outside and jumped out of a squad car.

'What's going on? Are you OK? I just heard your message, we were on our way to talk to Gary at his flat.' Declan grabbed hold of Amy by the shoulders but Amy broke free.

Her words came out in a rush: 'Gary's round there he's

injured I stabbed him in the eye a guy is guarding him I think Becky is in here in one of these flats . . .'

'OK, calm down. Deep breaths.' Declan tried to restrain her again.

'No!' She ran up the steps to the front door. 'We need to break the door down.'

'Didn't you just say Gary is round the back? Well, let's go and get the keys off him.'

Declan unlocked the door to the flat and pushed it slowly open. The moment he stepped inside, Amy pushed past him and ran into one room, then out and into another. The flat stank of sweat and something sweet and synthetic like cheap scented candles or a plug-in air freshener. It was decorated like an old lady's place, old-fashioned furniture, green wallpaper. It must have been Gary's mum's or grandmother's.

She stopped dead.

'Oh, God.'

Her sister, her beautiful sister, lay on her back on the bed. Both hands were cuffed to the bedstead. She was naked, her eyes closed, a pillow lying half across her face. She looked so skinny, as though she hadn't eaten since she'd vanished, and her skin was grey. The smell of unwashed human flesh rose up from her and Amy realized Gary must have lit the candles to disguise the rank odour.

Tentatively, Amy crept up to the bed. Tears spilled from her eyes, falling onto Becky's skin as she leaned over her, moving away the pillow, brushing her hair back from her face with shaking fingers, touching her blue lips. Declan stood behind her, watching silently. Bob was downstairs with Gary, who had still been sobbing and clutching his eye when they'd found him. An ambulance was on the way.

Amy spotted a pair of small keys lying on the bedside

cabinet and unfastened the handcuffs, gently lowering Becky's arms so they lay by her side. Amy sat on the bed and leaned over, hugging her sister's cool body.

'I love you,' she whispered. 'You're safe now.'

She kissed her cheek and stroked her face.

'I found you.'

Epilogue

Amy stood and watched the removal men carry Becky's furniture and belongings down the stairs and into their van. She looked up at the window of Gary's flat and rubbed the goose bumps on her upper arms. For a moment, she thought she saw him looking out at her, standing there with his shirt off like the first time she had met him. But that was impossible. For one thing, he was in custody awaiting trial for attempted murder, kidnap, false imprisonment and rape, which he admitted; Sussex Police were also planning to charge him for the murder of Amber Corrigan, which he denied. For another, the Gary in the window had two good eyes while the real Gary wore an eyepatch now. Amy had been to his first appearance in court and seen him, the patch making him look sinister and, at the same time, pathetic.

'I was happy here,' Becky said, following Amy's gaze.

Amy turned to her. 'Were you really?'

Becky shrugged, then her eyes glinted. 'A hell of a lot happier than I was at Gary's mum's place, anyway.'

Ever since she'd started talking again, this had been Becky's way of dealing with it: flashes of night-black humour.

She'd been in hospital for days, suffering the aftereffects of shock and semi-suffocation – for a while, the doctors had feared she had sustained brain damage from lack of oxygen from when Gary had put the pillow over her face. Had Amy not arrived when she did, the slender thread attaching Becky to life would certainly have snapped and she would have been lost for ever.

Amy had spent most of that time sitting by her bed, only going home to sleep and walk Boris. But now, Becky was out, and coming to stay at Amy's for a while. Until she felt strong enough to find a new place to live.

Amy looked at her sister, so thin and pale, smudges beneath her haunted eyes. She had tried to persuade her not to come along today but she'd insisted.

'What did you do with the iMac?' Becky asked.

'I was going to take it to the dump. But I couldn't bear to, so I wiped it clean and donated it to the Oxfam shop round the corner.'

'You should have smashed it up.'

Amy pulled her sister into an embrace, wincing at the feel of Becky's ribs pressing into her. At that moment, Damian from next door came out and asked them if they'd like a cup of tea. He stared at Becky, whose forehead was still pressed against Amy's shoulder, with that look people give victims of trauma, a blend of fascination and awkwardness. He was nice, but Amy shook her head and Damian nodded and went back into the building.

Amy was still waiting for her own post-traumatic symptoms to hit. Everyone told her it would come – that, like Becky, she should be seeing a counsellor. But the strange thing was, she felt strong. Far stronger than she'd felt in a long time, as if the events of the past weeks had built up her psychological muscles, given her new powers.

Perhaps it was just that she was concentrating so hard on looking after Becky, but for now she was glad. She walked with new purpose, talked to doctors and lawyers with confidence. She knew now that if she bumped into Nathan on the street, she wouldn't tremble or crumble. She wouldn't spit on him or scream at him either. She would simply ignore him again.

'That's it, love,' said one of the removal men, a tall Polish guy with glasses. 'All done.'

'All right. Our dad is waiting at my place. He'll let you in.'

That was another good thing that had come from this. Their parents had flown over the second they'd heard what had happened. Amy hadn't spent so much time with them since she'd lived at home, although she was now looking forward to their return to Spain. There were only so many times she could watch her mum clean all the glasses in her flat while conducting an awkward conversation with Boris.

The removal men drove off and left Amy and Becky standing on the pavement. It was a beautiful late summer day. School would start again soon, but Becky wouldn't be going back. Not yet.

'Let's go for a walk,' Amy said.

They linked arms and walked in silence along the road, the traffic rushing past them. Couples walked by, hand in hand. The man who walked the streets muttering to himself shuffled by. A kid outside Costcutter dropped his Cornetto on the pavement and started crying.

They crossed the road and walked down the alleyway alongside the train station, past the hairdresser's and the Internet café. Amy glanced inside the café and her gaze fell upon a young woman with light brown skin who was tapping away at a computer. Through the window, Amy could see what site she was looking at: CupidsWeb. There was a picture of a good-looking man on the screen and the young woman smiled to herself as she pecked at the keyboard with her fingers.

Amy had an urge to rush inside, to yell at the woman, tell her to be careful, to get off that site, go out, go to the park, join an evening class, go to a bar, get chatting to that cute guy in the corner shop, arrange a date with a friend of a friend. Meet someone real, in the real world.

But she knew the woman would flinch away, would gawp at her, think she was insane, maybe remind her that 30 per cent of relationships start online these days; that it was perfectly normal.

Perfectly safe.

Amy pulled Becky closer towards her and nodded at the pub just past the station.

'Fancy a pint?' she said, and Becky smiled.

Continue the thrill ride with even more great books from No.1 bestselling author. Voss & Edwards!

Fear is contagious...

CATCH YOUR DEATH

Louise Voss & Mark Edwards

THE NUMBER ONE BESTSELLER

A DEADLY KILLER - A WARNING WRITTEN IN BLOOD...

ALL FALL DOWN

Louise Voss & Mark Edwards

FROM THE BESTSELLING AUTHORS OF CATCH YOUR DEATH

He's Watching Her...

KILLING CUPID

Louise Voss & Mark Edwards

THE RUNAWAY BESTSELLER

Can't get enough of Voss & Edwards?

For exclusive interviews, competitions and the latest on their new releases, just visit:

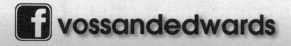 vossandedwards

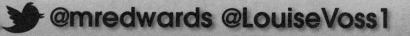 @mredwards @LouiseVoss1

www.vossandedwards.com

Want to hear about the latest crime and thriller releases?

Read interviews with your favourite authors?

Access exclusive content before the books have even hit the shops?

Be part of the action with

Killer Reads

The one-stop shop for the best in crime and thriller fiction.

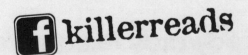 killerreads

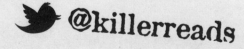 @killerreads

www.killerreads.com